RAHAB'S REDEMPTION

RAHAB'S REDEMPTION

by
Cynthia Davis

FOOTPRINTS FROM THE BIBLE

CROSSINGS BOOK CLUB
Garden City, New York

Published by Crossings Book Club, 501 Franklin Avenue, Garden City, New York 11530

Book design by Christos Peterson

ISBN: 978-1-58288-215-4

Printed in the United States of America

⚜ Prologue ⚜

"MY MOTHER." A STOCKY man stood in the doorway in one of the finest homes in Bethlehem. Auburn hair and beard framed the surprising blue eyes the man inherited from his father.

No longer a youth, the wealthy landowner maintained the home his father created for a bride many decades earlier. That bride, now an elderly woman, looked up from the dish of beans she was slowly sorting. Her hair, once more radiantly red than the color her son sported, was now white where it could be seen peeking from under the veil of a widow. The hands, once smooth, soft and graceful were now painfully gnarled and wrinkled.

"Yes, my son." The smile she gave was tender and held a hint of the beauty that enchanted men a lifetime earlier.

Boaz shifted his weight and seemed uncertain about his errand. He glanced at the maid sitting cross-legged on a mat nearby with a bowl of the beans in her lap.

"You may finish these in the kitchen." Sensing her son's embarrassment, the mother handed the wooden bowl to the servant woman.

"Yes, mistress." Obediently the girl gathered bowls and the burlap sack of unsorted beans before bowing from the room.

Once they were alone the old woman gestured her son toward a cushion. "Come, sit beside me and tell me your heart."

He hesitated at the door a moment longer. Rahab studied the man. The shoulders were as broad as those she long ago admired in her husband. The soldier she married as a young woman was strong from wielding the sword in battle. Boaz gained his strength from a lifetime of work in the many fields he owned.

The woman knew that he was as tall as his father and would loom above her by at least a cubit if she stood up. Taking a deep breath the man crossed the room to squat on the mat abandoned by the servant.

"My son, what troubles you?" A voice made tender by the love she held for this only child urged him to speak.

It was unusual for Boaz bar Salma to be speechless. When a sigh was the only answer, Rahab looked more closely at her child. The normally neatly combed hair was in disarray. The man looked as though he had not slept well for days. The beard his restless square fingers ran through was not oiled or combed.

"Are you ill?" A new concern brought a frown to the woman's face. Had the man been closer she would have felt his face for a fever.

"I do not think so." Finally the silence ended.

Boaz leaned forward almost ready to speak, but then sat back. A flush of red crossed the proud face.

"I have spoken foolishly." The blurted words only made his mother more confused.

"Foolishly?" she repeated with a raised eyebrow.

With face averted the man mumbled an incoherent explanation, "I . . . foreign girl . . . threshing floor . . ."

Rahab tilted her head in concentration. Then her face cleared.

"Is it Ruth of Moab, Naomi's daughter-in-law?" The newcomer to Bethlehem was the only foreigner in the area.

The man groaned and buried his face in his hands. Clutching the already disarranged locks, Boaz nodded.

"My son, tell me." Patiently the woman leaned back on her pillows and waited.

"I am a fool," the man castigated himself.

"Start from the beginning," suggested the mother when her son seemed unable to begin an explanation.

"It is harvest time." With the seemingly irrelevant observation, Boaz finally began.

"Yes," agreed his mother.

"Those who have no means of support may glean after the reapers." In a monotone the law was stated.

"Yes." Again the woman nodded when her son stopped speaking. "All widows and orphans are provided for by the Law of Moses."

"Naomi, widow of Elimelech, cannot bear the burden of gleaning." Still Boaz kept his head bent beneath his hands. "Her daughter-in-law has taken on the task."

"Yes, I heard that," Rahab assented when the man paused.

With red mantling his face, Boaz spoke with a rush. "The girl came to my fields at the start of the barley harvest. Because of her loyalty to Naomi, I urged her to follow my reapers from field to field. It was to spare her the work of finding a new landowner each day." The man spread his hands and shrugged. "It seemed the kind thing to do. I told my workers to let some extra grain fall to the ground for her and to see that she had food and drink. I meant to be compassionate. Does not the word of the Prophet Moses command us to care for those weaker than ourselves?"

"You did well, my son." Rahab smiled at the man who lifted tortured eyes to her.

"Throughout the wheat harvest I kept her close to my own women. I would not let anyone mock her for her accent." With a frown Boaz remembered a confrontation. "Ahaz, the miller, tried to prevent the girl from beating out the grain one day. I quoted the Law to him."

"My son, I heard from Abigail that you did more than quote the Law," Rahab spoke with a smile. "She had to clean the blood from his garments after you smashed his nose."

"He had no right to turn her away because her family is from Moab. When she married Mahlon, she became an Israelite. Ruth left behind her old life to stay with Naomi."

Rahab noted the tender tone when her son spoke the young woman's name. A slight smile remained on her lips. The man seemed lost in thought.

"You still have not told me your trouble."

His mother's voice reminded the man of the reason for his visit.

"I am not a young man," obliquely Boaz approached the topic again.

"You are a handsome man in the prime of his life," argued Rahab proudly.

"Last night I slept at the threshing floor with all the young men. There was dancing and drinking and celebration. We slept where we found a spot." Again the words were spoken in a rush.

"Yes, my son, I have attended a harvest festival or two," the woman wryly reminded the man who now paced the floor. "Many a night your father and I did not return home. I remember one fall when you were just weaned . . ."

Boaz held up a hand when it appeared Rahab would continue her reminscing. He paced restlessly. At the window, the man stared out across the small town. He barely saw the familiar mud plastered homes nestled against and in some cases into the hillsides. Children played in the street with a variety of dogs and lambs. Above the town were tree dotted hills where fat-tailed sheep grazed under the care of shepherd boys. Boaz owned many of the terraced fields lower down where wheat and barley grew. They were barren now that the harvest was gathered in.

A dirt street ran the length of the town. At the northern end stood the cairn marking the burial spot of Rachel, wife of Jacob, the patriarch of all the tribes of Israel. Only a few miles further north stood the city of Jerusalem, best known for the huge threshing floor of the Jebusites. To the south the road stretched toward Hebron. Beyond that was the desert inhabited only by the Nabatean horse- and spice-trading nomads.

The man roamed away from the window.

"Ruth came to me last night." From the far corner of the room the son faced his mother. "I was drunk and did not know it until early this morning. It was not even light when I roused and there she was beside me."

"What did you do?" Rahab almost held her breath for the answer.

Big hands shook as Boaz raked them through the increasingly disheveled hair. Rahab watched her son stalk to the window again. Then he focused on the patiently waiting old woman.

Plunging to his knees beside her, Boaz confessed. "I gave her a generous gift of the newly beaten grain—all her veil could carry—and sent the girl away from the floor before anyone else was awake."

"And?" the woman tilted her head and waited.

"I told her that I would act the kinsman unless the son of Samson does. He is Elimelech's nephew and has a better claim to the property of Elimelech." The curly head fell onto his mother's knee as it had when he confessed some childhood sin.

"I am glad!" Joyfully Rahab clasped gnarled hands together. "Ruth will make you a fine wife."

Low-voiced Boaz spoke his fears, "She is of Moab. How can I bring a foreign woman into this house?"

When the man did not look up, Rahab smoothed the reddish hair with one hand. Many thoughts tumbled through her mind. No one saw the nod of decision before the mother spoke. Only for her beloved son would she break the silence of decades and tell of the past she left behind so long ago.

"My son, it is time you heard my life story. Most have forgotten that I was not born Hebrew either." The old woman patted the mat beside her. "Come, my son, see that God looks beyond nationality and even beyond choices that men can find unforgivable."

Slowly, Boaz rose and seated himself beside his mother. His brow was puckered with confusion. Looking into bygone years, Rahab began her tale.

1

MY FATHER OWNED THE best-known inn between the Tigris and Damascus. Hamash was one of the fortunate of the city. We had enough wealth to live in a comfortable house across the courtyard from the sheds and pens where the animals were housed. Most of the inhabitants of Jericho and the surrounding towns bedded their animals in their homes. The very poor slept in a hovel with the beasts. Some residents were able to provide a second floor of family sleeping quarters. Our dozen servants, mostly slaves from the northern hills or southern desert, slept in the lofts above the animals. I never thought about the men and women who waited on my every need. It was the way my life was. I pitied my friends who did not have someone to comb and braid their hair in the morning.

My three brothers were half-grown by the time I was born. Perez at thirteen was oldest. Jonadab, a year younger, was a constant shadow for his brother. Hamul, the youngest, was ten. There were other children who did not live past the dangerous and tragic infant years. Mother never spoke of the five babies who died so young. My birth when she was twenty-eight was a constant source of joy.

My father loved me. I never really doubted that. With his love came the expectation of great accomplishments. I dreamed of marriage to the son of the *gal*, the chief of Jericho. Hamash of Jericho had even higher aspirations.

"My little princess, you will make me proud." Nearly every day the man crooned his dreams to me. "With your amazing red hair and gentle ways, you are certain to attract the eye of an important man when the time is ripe. Who knows, perhaps the priests will set you aside for service to Astarte."

What my father said was partly true. I did have hair that flamed in the sunlight. The gentle ways and soft words of an obedient woman were harder to learn. I had a way of speaking my mind that my mother and the women of the household deplored. Both Mother and Father were very indulgent of me. My childhood was filled with much greater freedom than most girls of Jericho. Hamash encouraged me to ask questions frowned on by my nurse. I was always intrigued by the multiplicity of the gods worshipped by our guests. It seemed strange that each nation had different gods.

"How can there be so many gods?" My question at five brought a smile to my mother's face although her answer was less than satisfactory.

"Someday you will understand," was all she would say.

I knew that the woman did not find the endless procession of gods and goddesses confusing. To her the pantheon of Astarte, Baal and the rest were not frightening individuals controlling human life with rage and might. Unlike most of the residents of Canaan, my mother trusted the goodness as well as the power of the holy ones. She believed that every god was only a manifestation of some single greater power. To my child's mind each god was another in a succession of somewhat frightening rulers more powerful than even the chief of the city. The *gal* had the power of life and death over the inhabitants but the gods controlled each person's destiny.

Our home was shared with an ever changing and endlessly fascinating stream of visitors to the inn. Eagerly I listened, learned and watched the guests with their news from far away. Stories of other cultures and other gods intrigued me. My mother encouraged my curiosity and finally answered my nagging question.

"How can there be so many gods?" I asked the question again when I was six.

"The gods are all one." In her response was the essence of deep faith. "It is people who make the many forms of the gods.

We try to control and explain our lives. Ascribing the blame or honor to a deity makes the joys and sorrows of life more bearable. Yet there is One above all. The oldest stories tell of Abraham the Wanderer who came from Ur at the command of that One. His grandson left a legacy in the town called Bethel. He believed it was the very entrance to the house of the god he called *El*."

I knew that the woman referred to the rituals her father still maintained at Bethel.

"The town was named Luz until Jacob, called Israel, met his god there. His vision of a ladder to heaven has always been revered by the residents. A yearly sacrifice from a special herd is made to honor that god. My father was the keeper of the flock. I remember each year he chose the finest animal to honor the *El* of Jacob. Your grandfather swore that it was the blessing of that god that gave me the beauty to attract a man of wealth like your father. My family has a long history of being chosen for honor by the rulers of the heavens. You are one of those touched by the gods as well."

The explanation only confused me further. However, it silenced my questions for a time.

Later, I overheard my mother warn her husband, "Your daughter is not a humble servant of the gods. In her blood runs the faith of my father who looked beyond the rituals in Bethel to find true understanding."

Father laughed. "My Rahab will learn what is necessary. Do not trouble yourself, Wife, with this talk of faith. The priests can divine who is to serve the goddess. There is no need for her to practice humility. My daughter is special and marked by Astarte."

Jericho was dedicated to Astarte, goddess of the moon, fertility and war. Her worship dominated every aspect of life. Each home had a representation of at least one of the favored animals of the goddess in some niche. In our house each room had an image of the goddess. My bedroom was no exception. Above the door a proud winged lion guarded me on behalf of his mistress. I feared the figure for the creature seemed to be waiting to pounce should I fail to fulfill the destiny everyone said I was plainly marked for.

"The mark of the blessed lady is on you," old Hulda, my nurse, fondly stated again and again, usually when combing and braiding my heavy red hair. She firmly believed that Astarte had set me apart. "You were born on the date of her Feast. It is well known that such as you are beloved by the gods."

Astarte was known to have a brilliant head of flame-colored hair. Her priestesses dyed their brown or black hair the same color with henna. That I was born with curls of the favored color set me apart. It was an embarrassment to me. Other children teased mercilessly, especially Elon, son of the potter.

"Rahab was dipped in henna."

"Carrot curls from eating too many carrots."

"How can you sleep with flames on your head?"

At first I ran home sobbing from the boy's words. Always Hulda and my mother would comfort me.

"Astarte marks those she has chosen. Some are known by the mark of her kiss on their body like Sarah the wife of Elam, captain of the soldiers of Jericho," the old nurse assured me. "The city was richly blessed when she served as Daughter of Astarte."

The woman had a dramatic red imprint starting under her right eye and disappearing under the neck of her tunic. Although she usually pulled her veil tight around her face in public, I saw her at the well once when the wind whipped her veil away.

"I am glad I'm not marked like that." My horrified whisper was met with a soft chuckle from both women.

"Your hair is your beauty as well as the sign of Astarte's favor." Mother's confident words gave me courage to face my tormentors. I even began to be proud of my looks.

"Astarte has chosen me over you, Elon." Standing boldly in the middle of the street I shouted a childish defiance to my nemesis. "The gods will punish you for your words."

The chubby boy laughed at me.

"The flames have gone to your mind," he jeered.

"You will see." I tossed my head and turned away in pretended disdain. It would never do to let the boy see the stinging tears brimming in my eyes. "Astarte will feed you to the dogs."

I felt a clod of dirt strike my shoulder. I refused to turn around until I reached my gate. Then the shrieking behind me made me look. The boy was beating off a large dog that had him by the arm. All the other children were racing away with cries of terror and screams for help. Terrified at what my words caused, I ran wailing to my father.

"Elon . . . dog . . . help." The gasped and sobbed words along with the cries from the street sent Hamash and two servants on a run from the yard.

I cowered in a corner of the sheep pen sobbing in terror until Perez found me. My brother carried me to my mother. Even there I continued to sob and whimper.

"I did not mean it." Almost hysterical, I wept in her lap. "It is my fault that the goddess struck Elon!"

"Elon has been tormenting that dog for weeks. Today the gate was open and the animal got his revenge." Even my father's explanation did nothing to ease my conscience.

I repeated over and over with tears, "It is my fault. I said Astarte would send dogs to eat him."

Finally Hulda coaxed me to drink some tea. The herbs in the infusion allowed me to sleep. Still in my dreams I saw the great jaws of the dog chasing me and cried out. When I wakened, I was cradled in my mother's arms on her sleeping mat. I had not been held so since I was weaned at three. Lying very still, I stared out the small window that let in a soft spring breeze and the early morning light. In the western sky, just above the hills of Canaan, the fading sliver of Astarte looked like a barely open eye balefully watching me.

With the slightest of whispers I begged forgiveness—"I am sorry Astarte"—and then covered my head with the blanket.

I remained hidden until my mother drew away the covering. "Come, Rahab, it is morning. You cannot sleep all day."

Fearfully I peered toward the window, half expecting the eye to still be staring in condemnation. All I saw was sun lighting the tops of the hills. Astarte had gone to her palace for the day.

Elon did not die, but his arm hung useless. Every time I saw the boy I was reminded of the results of my rage. Neither Hulda nor my parents were able to convince me that the bully brought about his own punishment.

"I cursed Elon," I sadly explained over and over. "I warned him that Astarte would feed him to the dogs. And it happened!"

Nothing anyone said was able to convince me that the goddess had not acted on my behalf.

⌁ 2 ⌁

MONTHS PASSED. I REFUSED to set foot outside our courtyard. Summer came and went. It was tempting to accept the invitation of my friends Adah and Jerusha.

"Rahab, come and see the new doll I have," Jerusha coaxed from the street.

"Would you like to come and have a honey cake from my mother?" Adah knew my weakness but I did not respond to the temptation.

"Go on and have some fun," urged both my mother and Hulda.

My only response was to shake my head and run to my room. I was too fearful to venture beyond the gate because I was sure that Astarte would exact some vengeance on me for Elon's injury. Eventually my friends stopped asking me to join them for games in the street or rambles up the nearby hills.

During the evenings I hid in the corner of the room listening to the talk of the guests. Discussions of battles far to the south of Jericho did not really interest me but they kept my mind from dwelling on the result of calling on the goddess. The harvest and new year feasts were celebrated. Still I refused to attend the ceremonies at the Temple. It was not until the spring Feast of Astarte that I finally left the safety of our home.

"All Jericho attends the yearly feast," Hamash told my mother. "Will your daughter attend?"

I paused in the hall to hear the woman's reply. "My husband, Rahab knows that to remain home would be an affront to the gods."

"It would not help my standing in the counsel either," grumbled Hamash. "If I have to explain her absence, it will be an embarrassment."

My breath caught on a gasp. It was true; I must accompany the family to the groves and Temple. The disapproval of my father was worse than the gods' displeasure. For his approbation I would do anything. I prayed for courage that night. It seemed that the waning shape of the moon smiled at me.

"Mother, may I wear your linen veil to the ceremony next week?" I asked the next morning.

"That veil is so long you would have to wrap it around your shoulders two or three times. It would be much too large for you." The answer did not surprise me.

"I am nearly as tall as you." My arguments were prepared. It was true that as my eighth birthday approached, I had shot up in height until I nearly looked my mother in the eye. "I do not have a veil so lovely. It is just the color of the new gown Hulda has made for my birthday."

The woman looked at me. I could see the indecision on her face.

"Are you certain you want to wear a woman's veil? Until the goddess awakens your cycles, you do not have to cover your head."

"I want to wear something of yours." My final plea was spoken through unfeigned tears. Impulsively I buried my face in the woman's lap as she sat before the loom.

"Very well." Soothing me gently my mother stroked the red cascade of hair. "You may wear the veil if it will make you feel better about attending the Festival."

"Thank you!" Tears gone, I hugged her neck.

Preparation for the Feast of Astarte began at sundown with the rising of the third new moon after the Darkest Night. The two weeks of ceremonies were designed to welcome Astarte back to the sky and beseech her blessing of fertility on the flocks and fields as the warmer weather approached. Everything started in the sacred grove beyond the city walls. Here the priestess and Temple maidens performed the holy dances to entice Astarte,

Queen of the Heavens, to return in blessing. Each family gave their sacred teraphim to the priests for blessing. On the night when the goddess stood high in the sky, full and heavy with promise, the High Priest performed the ritual union with the maiden honored as Astarte for the Festival. Everyone knew that no matter how many times she consummated her union, the goddess remained a virgin. The fortunate girl chosen as consort served as the "Daughter of Astarte" for the next year. The title meant she lived in the Temple and was served by the priestesses. It was a great honor and usually the lucky girl was wed soon after her year of service.

"This year the gods have chosen Esther, daughter of Michabaal," Hulda responded to my question as she braided my hair.

"Jerusha's sister!" I was amazed.

My friend had said nothing about the selection of her sister for this honor. It was true I had not seen my friend or her family recently. For a moment I felt guilty for being so obsessed with my own fears that I abandoned my friends.

"The announcement was made at the festival of the recent full moon," my nurse responded. "You have not attended any ceremonies since the last Feast of Astarte when you celebrated your seventh birthday."

There was more sorrow than reproof in the woman's state-ment. I hung my head and resolved to seek out my playmate after the Festival.

"Esther was fortunate indeed. She will make a lovely Astarte. Many men will flock to the Temple this year with offerings in return for union with the Daughter of Astarte." Hulda spoke to my mother, but I listened intently.

I was not sure what the Temple maidens did. I knew that my brothers visited the women regularly and claimed that their money was well spent. No one would answer my questions, insisting that I was too young to understand. Now with my friend's sister as the chosen one, I was more interested than ever.

"Hulda." Mother glanced at me in warning.

"Oh, yes." Guiltily the older woman stopped talking.

"But why do men visit the Temple?" Again I tried for an answer. "Mother, I know I am old enough."

"Maybe next year." The reply was spoken in a soothing tone, but did nothing to ease my impatience.

"I want to know now!" With a pout and stamp I stood in the center of the room looking from one woman to the other.

"Rahab"—a frown emphasized my mother's words—"we will talk after the Festival."

I knew it was useless to probe for an answer. It was not a subject I wanted to broach with my father. My curiosity was left unsatisfied. Preparations for the feast left me little time to ponder the question before it was time for the ceremony.

We made quite a show on the way to the Holy Day of the Festival. Proudly I wore my new gown and the veil borrowed from Mother. Hamash and my brothers oiled their beards and hair until they shone in the torchlight. Soft leather boots were a yearly extravagance for the Feast, as was a new cloak for each man. The new gown and shawl that Mother wore flowed smoothly to the ground. I was certain that no other woman could be as lovely. Her blush of pleasure when she unfolded the gift from my father still made me smile. Even the servants wore new tunics and every head of hair was carefully combed, braided or oiled.

It seemed as if all of Canaan packed the open pavement before the Temple steps. Nearly everyone was dressed in something new. The Feast celebrated new beginnings. Each year I promised to be a better girl and obey my parents. The resolution rarely lasted the week of the Feast.

"I will not pester my mother about the Daughter of Astarte." This time I promised to forget my fascination with the Temple maidens.

A trumpet blast heralded the arrival of the priests. In grand array the High Priest and Priestess stood in front of their entourage of lesser priests and acolytes. From the top of the ascent, between the Pillars of Astarte, the chief priest spoke.

"Welcome, servants and petitioners to Astarte. May the goddess grant you rich harvests and strong beasts in this year. She will keep in mind your generous gifts. We greet Astarte who comes to be readied for the Day of Union."

At the words, trumpets blared. A cart moved through the crowd, drawn by a year-old ox. In the cart stood Jerusha's sister. I easily recognized her by her lack of height. Esther was a short girl. Both Jerusha and I were already as tall as the older girl when I celebrated my sixth birthday. The elaborate moon-adorned headdress, veil and flowing cloak concealed her body. In the cart Esther looked very small and alone. I was sure that those in the back of the congregation could not even see the arrival. All along the route from the groves to the city citizens watched the progress and joined in the procession. They now merged with the crowd near the Temple.

"Behold the Chosen of Astarte," intoned the priest to the cheers of the assemblage.

When the cart, surrounded by a bevy of maidens, reached the steps, Esther was lifted high. Her feet must not touch the ground until after the rooftop union at the height of the Festival. I thought I saw Jerusha amid the girls surrounding their queen, but it was only a glimpse and I forgot her as the ceremony began.

"Astarte, accept your handmaid." The words were answered, as every year, by the crowd in unison.

"Astarte, bless us."

Esther was carried to the Temple for secret rituals that took place prior to her sacred union. At the foot of the steps, the cart became an altar on which the ox was sacrificed and then burned.

All through the night until the gray dawn began to lighten the east beyond the walls of Jericho, the priests led long prayers. The crowd ebbed and flowed with comings and goings of men into the Temple and women returning to homes with exhausted children.

When I saw Elon and his parents moving down the street, I shrank back into the shadows near the Temple. There was a convenient corner near the steps leading to the roof of the ziggurat where I crouched unseen. I was sure that someone would accuse me of the injury to Elon. Hamash and my mother were nowhere in sight, or I would have run to my parents. A few minutes later my brothers wandered close to my hiding place.

"I am going to visit the Temple," Jonadab told his wife as the group stood together. "Perhaps Astarte will bless you with a son."

"Yes," the young girl nodded.

One hand covered her belly protectively. In the year since her wedding, Penninah had not conceived. It was a source of great sorrow to her and tension in the family, for Perez was already a father although wed only six months. The hasty ceremony made my mother cry although cuddling the baby was now one of her joys.

"Look at how strong little Hamash already is," she crooned to the infant named after my father. "My child, you will grow to be like your grandfather."

Hamul addressed his younger brother in a patronizing way. "Ask for the maiden who last was chosen of Astarte. Cast your gift before her and perhaps you too will be a father."

"Lie with the Temple maidens rather than your wife and you will never have a son. You waste your seed on them." The parting shot from Perez was spoken so low I would not have heard it if I had not been crouched in the shadow.

"At least I did not rush the betrothal bed." A half snarl was the man's response as he brushed past his brother.

"Is that what the men do?" I caught Perez's arm when he turned from his feuding brothers. Half fearful I gasped out the question. "Do men lie with the maidens of Astarte?"

The image of Esther and her attendants, even Jerusha, forced into an intimacy I only partly understood from watching our dogs was horrifying. I knew Esther was four years older than Jerusha, who was two years older than me. However, I could not imagine willingly performing such service.

"Sister, ask your mother." Impatient, the twenty-year-old tried to shake off my hand.

"She will not answer." Tenaciously, I clung to my brother.

Frowning at me the young man put his broad hands on my shoulders. He stared down at me. In the light of the torches lining the Temple steps I could see his indecision.

A little afraid, I still persisted. "I want to know."

"Very well." A sigh of resignation came from Perez as he began a rapid explanation. "The maidens in the temple are servants of the goddess. Anyone seeking a blessing brings a gift to the priestess. A fine goat or heavy weight of silver buys the honor of union with the Daughter of Astarte."

"Esther!" I gasped in horror at the thought.

"She will be known as the Daughter of Astarte this year," the man corrected. "Lesser gifts purchase the services of one of the other girls. Yes, we lie with the Temple maidens. It is not like going to the Street of Whores. These girls represent the goddess and offer blessing in answer to prayers."

The tone was almost harsh and defensive as my brother finished speaking.

"It is an honor to be chosen to serve in the Temple." A little more gently the young man added when I did not speak, "Your friend is greatly blessed to be the Consort at the Feast of Astarte. Perhaps you . . ."

The man suddenly stopped speaking. With a pat on my shoulder he hurried away. I was left with much to consider. For many days I remembered his final words and wondered what he had almost said. Toward the end of the Feast, I heard Hulda whispering to one of the serving girls.

"Penninah would be fertile if she made an offering to Astarte like our mistress did before Rahab was born."

"Really?" The girl encouraged the old woman to continue talking.

"You were not here then," the elderly servant preened as she boasted of her long service. "The lady made a special gift for the goddess. The priestess said that Astarte was pleased. Sure enough in the proper time, our little girl was born. We all knew that she was a gift from the goddess as soon as we saw the red hair."

"Do you think that the goddess would answer a petition from Rahab?" The question stopped me when I started to move down the hall.

"The great lady honors her chosen ones," my old nurse nodded emphatically.

When I saw my brother arguing with his wife, I made my

decision. Although I knew that it was men's work to make offerings to the gods, I took out my most cherished possessions. One
was a doll bought for me from an Egyptian trader. She owned
more gowns than I would ever possess. I thought her too precious for play, but enjoyed dressing the wooden figure. The other
was a necklace of fine shells with a pendant of blue lapis purchased from the merchant from Tyre for my just passed birthday.

I draped the necklace around my neck and sat with the doll
for a long time. One finger softly caressed the wooden face so
smoothly polished it felt almost real. Finally I drew a deep breath
and laid the figure in her teak box. Each little embroidered dress
was folded and placed beside the doll. I allowed myself one last
stroke of the cheek before lifting the necklace over my head. For
a moment I paused, hesitant to give away my newest possession.

"The goddess deserves the best," I consoled myself. "Surely
this pendant of lapis will please Astarte. It is the stone she loves
above all others."

I let the necklace slide through my fingers onto the doll and
her clothes before I could change my mind.

"Rahab." My mother's voice startled me.

"Yes, my mother." I shut the lid quickly and slipped it under
the blanket.

"What are you doing?" The tone was curious but I still felt
guilty.

"Playing with my doll." I comforted myself that it was not
really a lie. I had played with the figure before putting her away.

"That is good." There was a nod of encouragement and the
woman moved on about her tasks.

After she was gone, I hid the box under my cloak and hurried from the room. Now that the decision was made, I did not
dare stop. If I thought about the doll I would be tempted to
forego the sacrifice. I slipped through the gate and raced down
the street. Without a pause, I dodged a cart and ignored the call
of my friends playing in the field.

"Rahab, where are you going?"

"Come and play with us."

My one thought was to reach the Temple and offer my precious gift to Astarte. There were many men standing near the main entrance but I remembered seeing a side door that was often open. Perhaps it was unlocked. No one noticed an eight-year-old girl scurry around the corner. The carved wood door was ajar. I dodged inside after a glance around.

It was dark inside the hall. I stopped for a moment tempted to retreat. Memory of Penninah's tears forced me to keep moving. On tiptoe I crept forward. The great hall where the goddess lived had to be near. I had heard my father and brothers talk about the beauty of the statue and size of the room.

"It is a vast room," Hamash told me once, when I asked where the goddess lived. "There is white marble and limestone with decorations in lapis and other precious stones."

It seemed a long way from the outer door to the center of the Temple. I began to think I was lost. Then I rounded a corner and caught my breath. Indeed the goddess was glorious. The first thing I noticed was the blue of lapis in the torchlight. There were many of the rare and precious stones imbedded in the pillar the statue stood on. Astarte towered over the expanse of floor. In the pavement were all the phases of the moon sparkling with gems and lit by many torches. I noticed images of winged lions and scorpions as well as snakes around the room. They adorned the wall hangings and pillars. The animals appeared to be honoring and guarding the goddess.

In front of the goddess were piled offerings of all kinds. Rich skins of leopard and lion, exotic feathers and gold caskets from which spilled jewels and bangles were some of the items that caught my eye. The room looked deserted. I inched forward slowly, clutching my treasured offering. It now seemed paltry in comparison to the riches I saw. Only the desperate hope that Astarte would be merciful drove me forward.

I finally reached the pillar on which the figure stood. Trembling now, I did not dare look up at the staring eyes of blue.

"Please great goddess, take my gift and give a baby to Penninah so Jonadab will love her." The words were a barely audible whisper.

My hands shook with fear as I added my small box to the

mound of gifts. Now that my mission was complete, I only wanted to escape. Rapidly I backed away from the statue, not daring
to turn my back. When a hand gripped my shoulder, I leapt in
fright and almost screamed.

"Rahab." My name softly spoken caused me to turn. "What
are you doing here?"

It was Esther who held me tight by the hand and dragged me
into a nearby room. My friend's sister looked different with her
hair dyed red in honor of the goddess. It was braided into a
crown that still left many of the long waves free to flow over her
shoulders. Heavy kohl outlined her eyes, and the lips that
frowned with concern were red with some cosmetic. I barely recognized the woman as my friend's sister.

Softly she repeated her question, "Why are you here, Rahab?"

"I brought an offering." Stammering, I made the confession
before bursting into tears. "Jonadab is angry at Penninah for not
giving him a child. Mother asked Astarte for a baby and I was
born. I gave my Egyptian doll and the new shell necklace to
Astarte. Surely the goddess will honor such a sacrifice."

Suddenly I wished I had not come and that my doll was still
safely in her place at the foot of my bed. The thought made me
cry harder.

"Hush." Fearfully, Esther put a hand over my mouth to stifle
the sobs. "You are lucky I am the one who found you. The priestess would be angry to find a child in the sacred hall."

I held my breath to stop the wrenching sobs and futilely
wiped at my flowing eyes with the edge of my tunic.

Esther appeared to be thinking.

"You must leave. How did you get in?"

"The side door was open." I made a vague gesture in the
direction I thought I came.

A smile turned up the corners of the painted lips. "Yes, it
would be."

Although I waited, no explanation followed the cryptic statement.

"Can you find your way out the same door?" The question
was asked after a moment.

"I think so." My reply was a little hesitant.

"Then you must hurry. It is almost time for the evening ritual to awaken the goddess. All the maidens will be gathering."

Esther moved to the curtained doorway.

"Wait here." The girl moved away rapidly. In a moment she returned.

"You cannot leave this here," she explained, pressing the box back into my grateful hands. "It would be too hard to explain how such a gift came to be at the feet of the goddess. Come, you must leave now."

With a finger to her lips she motioned me to follow.

"Will the goddess hear my prayer?" I hung back to grab the soft hand and ask my urgent question.

"Astarte may honor your courage; who can say?" The answer was not what I hoped for.

"Hurry." Impatient now, the older girl led me out of the room and down the hall past curtained doors I had not noticed on my way in. At the corner, Esther pointed the way.

"Straight down this hall, turn right at the wall. The door will be at the end. Be very quiet and stay close to the wall. Go." A shove emphasized the urgency.

The walk to the door seemed even longer than the one coming in. My heart pounded with fear of discovery. Behind one or two of the curtains I heard the rumble of a man's voice. Then the door was ahead of me. It was still slightly open. Without a sound I slipped through the opening. Nothing outside seemed to have changed. Men still talked in the street. Dust from the carts hung in the air. A dog looked up from his bone but did not even bark as I leaned against the outer wall of the Temple. After my fear ebbed, I began to walk home. Dark was creeping across the valley toward the hills when I reached our courtyard.

My brothers and father were busy with an arriving guest who had camels and baggage to be cared for. No one saw me slip up the stairs to put the doll away.

Hulda's shuffling step arrived a moment later. The old woman grumbled, "Rahab, here you are. Hurry, you are needed in the kitchen. The chief of Moab has come with his son."

Obediently I trotted ahead of the old woman to take my place at the kitchen tasks. It was a relief to be busy with the normal daily chores because I doubted that I would be able to sleep. I could still see all the animal guardians from the Temple of Astarte staring at me when I blinked my eyes. It seemed likely that they would haunt my dreams as well.

As I carried trays of fruit to the men I caught snatches of their conversation. It seemed to be an argument about some new god. Immediately I started to listen.

"There is no god but Astarte, Queen of Heaven and patron of Jericho. Is not the city dedicated to her image in the moon? The Great Lady provides protection from all invasions."

"This people claim the ancient god of Abraham the Wanderer has rescued them."

"Bah, Abraham is long dead and buried in the hills at Macpalah. He is only a legend now, along with his god."

"The sons of Israel have defeated powerful warriors all across the Sinai and now turn their eyes toward Moab and Canaan."

They were still disagreeing when I was sent to my bed.

For a week the stranger stayed at the Inn of Hamash. He met with the elders and priests of the city in an attempt to gain their support and arms against the invaders nearing his southern border. The leaders of Jericho refused him the aid he sought. One evening I overheard another conversation between the chief of Moab and my father. Angrily the foreigner paced about the courtyard and recited the reasons he hated the people he called the Children of Israel.

I understood that the invaders he feared followed a different god. It seemed to be the god Mother spoke of as Jacob's El. The repeated tales of miracles in the Land of Kings seemed unbelievable. I recalled that my mother spoke of hearing such stories from her father. The men from Moab, like my grandfather, talked of water turning to blood and burning hail. These were phenomenon beyond my understanding. Still, I shamelessly listened from my hidden perch in the tree near the door.

"The god of this people split the waters of the sea," the man from Moab warned. "They claim Canaan as their homeland. The leader has told them that their god has given the land to them. Do not think Jericho will be spared. Your leaders are blind."

My father spoke soothingly with a forced smile. "The walls and fortifications of the city can withstand any assault by desert rabble."

"The rabble perhaps"—it seemed the chief of Moab sneered—"but what about their god?"

"Astarte and her consort are true gods," Hamash angrily shouted. My father rarely allowed guests to disturb his composure. I cringed in my covert while he sputtered. "This people do not even know what their god looks like. How can such a deity have any power?"

I shuddered with fear of the unknown and wondered if an invisible god might really be more powerful than the cold statues in the Temple. When listening to my mother's stories, I never considered that the god my grandfather sacrificed to might not even be represented by a statue. I resolved to ask how such a thing could be.

"You will see," the chief of Moab warned. "If my people are defeated, your vaunted city will fall, too. This people have learned warfare against the Amalekites and Amorites. They will not fear a walled city."

After the man retired to his room with his son, I heard my father complaining to Jonadab. "Guests must be treated with courtesy, but that Moabite tries my patience. All this talk of defeat at the hand of an invisible god is foolishness. The tales he tells have been recounted for a generation. Your mother sung them as bedtime stories to you and your sister. If their god is so strong, why do the refugees from Egypt still wander homeless in the desert? Their leader is an old man and a fool to think of leading women and children through battle to claim some vague promise."

"Father, I heard that these refugees have a new leader who will take over when Moses dies. Someone called Joshua," my brother recounted. "He is a trained fighter and their new commander."

"It matters not." With a shrug, my father dismissed the subject. "Jericho will stand though all around her fall."

In the morning I sought my mother for an answer to the question that bothered me.

"Mother, is the god of my grandfather and the herds of Bethel the same as the god of the refugees from Egypt?" I interrupted the woman at her weaving.

"Rahab, my daughter, like me you can see that there is holiness in many things. The gods are one . . ."

"Yes, I know you say that," I interrupted, a little impatiently. "But this god of the Hebrew is invisible. How can that be?"

"Are any of the gods really visible?" The response gave me pause. "Is Astarte real?"

"But of course." My reply was confident. "I have seen the statue of Astarte in the Temple."

A guilty gasp ended my comment. Mother did not seem appalled or even notice my claim of having seen the goddess.

"Who made the statue?" The woman seemed busy adjusting the warp on her loom.

"I . . . I . . . I . . ." Finally, I shook my head.

"What is more real? The statue or the entity it represents? Would Astarte be more or less real if you could not see the statue?" My mother's almost blasphemous questions made me gasp.

"I . . . but . . . she . . ." Stammering was all I could do as I struggled to understand the question posed by my mother.

"Men carve a statue in order to give a focus for the religious celebrations. It is hard for people to remain faithful to something unseen. The Children of Israel do seek to follow the same god that their ancestor Jacob dreamed of at Bethel." Finally an answer was given to my question. "We will see if they can continue to worship what they cannot see."

A serving crisis called the woman away and I sat staring at the window for a long time. Many tumbling thoughts struggled in my head.

"If the statue really is not Astarte, then surely the moon is her manifestation. I will pray to the moon herself." Finally the solution came to me.

Secretly I climbed up to the rooftop and conversed with

Astarte each night. There seemed to be no response, for Penninah remained barren. After a year passed, I even ventured to approach the unknown deity of the Hebrew. I stared at the fading sliver of the moon moving toward the western hills. Below me the animals dozed in pen and stall. Nothing stirred as far as I could see along the street. No lamps glowed in windows. All was silent.

With a little shiver of anticipation and guilt, I turned to face the south where the Children of Israel and their god lived. Fear almost kept me silent. I took a deep breath.

"Please, unknown god, if you are invisible, maybe you are here. Mother says there is holiness everywhere," I hesitantly whispered the prayer. "I . . . I beg you to give Penninah and my brother a son. Do you hear me?"

Nothing stirred. The foreign god gave no more response than Astarte. I slipped back inside, only to return to my vigil the next night. It was still several moon turnings before it seemed my prayers were answered. Penninah announced that she was pregnant.

I was sure that my secret was safe until I met Jonadab that night as I climbed back down after thanking the moon for her answered prayer.

"What do you do every night on the roof?" A frown accompanied the question.

Rapidly, I tried to form a reply but the truth slipped out. "I asked Astarte to give Penninah a baby."

"How can this be?" my brother probed. The young man's sneer made me angry.

"I prayed and she heard my petition." I did not mean for the statement to sound arrogant.

"Is that true?" Fingers tightened on my shoulder.

"Why would I make up such a story?" Angry and hurt by the doubt evident in his eyes, I slipped from the man's grasp and ran to my room.

My brother told Hamash. The news that Rahab's prayer brought a child to Penninah's womb began to be whispered around the house. Then the story seeped into the streets.

Pointing fingers and whispers began to follow me.

"That's Rahab, chosen of Astarte."

"I always said she was special."

"You can tell by the red hair. It's a sign from the goddess."

"Her prayer opened the womb of her sister-in-law!"

"Surely the priests will seek her out."

The last statement proved to be prophetic, although I was not told until all the plans were made.

3

PENNINAH WAS SAFELY DELIVERED of a son. Happily I played with my nephew. The months slid by. Adah and I resumed our games. I missed playing with Jerusha, who remained in the service of the goddess even after her sister was wed.

"It is fortunate that the priestess was willing to allow the young daughter of Michabaal to continue her service in the Temple even after the man died." An overheard conversation between Mother and my nurse explained her absence.

"Yes," Hulda agreed. "If the girl had not stayed in the Temple there is no telling what would have happened to the poor fatherless child."

"Perhaps some family would have taken her in," suggested my mother.

"There are no living relatives left," sighed the old servant.

I felt very sad even though the next comment eased some of my concern.

"The priestess will take good care of Jerusha." My mother seemed to be trying to ease her own conscience. "We could not have accepted the responsibility for another little girl."

Briefly I wondered if I could have convinced my father to offer a home to my friend. The subject was never raised in my presence. Somehow I knew that I was not supposed to know about my friend's changed status.

I was kept busy with my own changing life. My birth remembrance came and went; the Feast of Astarte also was celebrated. Days passed in a peaceful rhythm of learning the woman's skills of sewing, weaving and cooking with Hulda, Mother and the other women. I treasured the soft hands of my mother guiding me at the loom.

At the harvest she taught me to make the spiced bread that was a yearly treat. Only Mother held the secret to the tasty and moist dessert.

"Pay close attention to making the bread correctly so it is not spoiled," my father and brothers teased. They were all eager in praise of the anticipated treat. "It has been a year since we tasted it."

From her own trunk my mother brought out an alabaster bottle. The top was sealed over with wax.

"These spices are precious. Your father purchased them especially from the traders as a bridal gift. They remain fresh when sealed in this jar," the woman explained as almost reverently she peeled away the wax and removed the stopper.

We all inhaled the sweet, spicy aroma that filled the kitchen.

"Hold the spoon," Mother ordered.

A carefully measured amount of the mixture of cinnamon, cloves, nutmeg and some other secret ingredient was poured into the spoon and then added to the flour.

"Now we will seal the bottle again or the spices will grow stale. I am pleased that they have remained fresh all this time."

I held my breath, watching the care with which the woman dripped candle wax over the top of the stopper. All the time she turned the bottle so the seal was evenly distributed all around the top.

"Put it away for the next special event," Mother told Hulda.

All the women smiled when the servant suggested, "Perhaps it will be when we celebrate Rahab becoming a woman."

I shook my head, not wanting to remember that too soon my body would force me to leave childhood behind. Already my flat chest was showing signs of the approaching change.

"There is time enough for that." Mother seemed to agree and drew me close to her side.

However, before the Longest Night arrived, I did begin the flow that signaled my womanhood.

Hamash was delighted, "The gods have made their choice! It is as the priests foretold."

I wondered what he meant. My unspoken question was soon answered. No one could miss the booming announcement when my father and brothers returned from visiting the Temple. I thought they went with the appropriate offering that signaled my readiness for marriage. My heart leapt to my throat when I heard his words.

"My daughter is blessed by Astarte. She has been named by the Lady of Victory to become the Daughter of Astarte at the Feast." The man lifted me up in a bear hug, "Rahab, my daughter, you will bring great honor to this house. There will be great blessing for Jericho as well!"

"Yes, my father." It seemed no one noticed or cared about my subdued response.

"Child, it is a great honor to be chosen." Mother tried to console me. She alone seemed to understand my distress.

"I do not want to leave you. I do not want to live in the Temple. I am not holy. I will fail." In the woman's arms I wailed my excuses, finally sobbing out, "I am afraid of Baal!"

"My daughter, every girl fears her marriage bed. Be assured that all will be well. The act is not something to dread." Her attempt at consolation fell short. "Think of the great honor you bring us all. The gods have singled you out for greatness. I have always known that you were one of the chosen. Whether named *El* or Baal or Astarte, I knew you would serve the gods, my dearest child."

The reminder of my election by the gods was not entirely reassuring. As the soothing words continued, I did quit sobbing. Mother began to paint a rosy future for me.

"You will be much sought after when your time in the Temple is complete. The needs of the gods will have been satisfied. Then a husband will be found for my Rahab. A handsome and wealthy man will pay the house of Hamash much for the honor of Rahab as wife. I will hold your children on my knee."

The prospect brought comfort to me although I still dreaded

the fast approaching Feast. All too soon the day came for my introduction into the ways of the Temple. I learned that I would live within the sacred walls for a full moon turning before the Feast of Astarte.

"My daughter, you have brought me great joy." Hamash held me close for a long moment at the side entrance to the Temple.

It was the same door I used nearly four years earlier on my clandestine visit to the goddess. Now the door stood open. A woman appeared. My father bowed. When I stood immobile, the man nudged me forward.

"Priestess, I bring my daughter Rahab as arranged." My father sounded humble.

The woman responded almost absently, "Yes, the goddess is pleased. You will have blessings from her bounty."

A heavily ringed hand took my cold fingers and drew me across the threshold. When I glanced back, Hamash was already many steps down the street. Silently the door closed behind me. The priestess and I were alone in the long hallway, but I sensed the presence of other eyes and ears in the curtained alcoves.

With an effort I swallowed my fear, along with the tears that threatened. Almost gliding, the woman moved forward and I trailed after.

The days that followed were indescribable. My body was bathed daily. Oils were rubbed into the skin until it was as soft as a newborn babe. My red hair was much admired. It too was washed and treated with herbs and oils until it shown.

"We will not need henna for the hair this year." Everyone nodded agreement when the priestess made her announcement.

There were other lessons too. I learned arts for enticing the shy and pleasing the bold. I was terrified by the explanations of my duties.

"How can Astarte demand such acts? What blessing can come out of my union with a man?" More than once I questioned the reason for our sacrifice.

The priestess frowned at my presumption. Kohl-outlined eyes narrowed and reddened lips thinned angrily as the woman leaned toward me. I half expected a slap from the clenching fists.

"You are the Daughter of Astarte, chosen by lot. The goddess has signified that you will represent her in the coming year. What greater honor is there? Your own mother was a maiden in this Temple. Think on what we do as an offering to the Lady. Through our obedience Astarte brings fertility and blessing to those who come to us." The words were a hissed threat. "Do not tempt the Great Astarte with your questions."

I was silenced by the news of my mother's service in the Temple. She had never spoken of it. All night I sat in my tiny room trying to understand why the woman never mentioned her life within the walls when she knew I would be entering the sacred halls myself. For a long time I tossed and turned on my pallet unable to sleep because I was haunted by the images the priestess evoked with her revelation.

"Someday I will ask Mother about her time in service to Astarte." With the promise to myself, I was able to fall asleep at last.

I never again asked any questions even though I still worried about the rapidly approaching ritual.

One day I saw Jerusha. It was not a surprise. I now knew that many of the Temple maidens were orphans without a father to provide for them. Rather than starve in the streets, such girls were taken into the service of the goddess until their death. Younger girls were trained to welcome the men who came for blessings and union with the Temple maidens. The oldest women served the maidens and cleaned the Temple precincts.

My friend was more voluptuous than when I last saw her five years earlier. At first she seemed to hold back. I hurried to hug the girl.

"Jerusha, I am so glad to see you."

It was true. She was the first girl close to my age I had seen. All the priestesses and servants who attended me were mature women long in the service of Astarte.

"Tell me what it is like here," I begged.

With an enigmatic smile and a hint of bitterness my friend replied, "You will learn soon enough. It will be different for you than for me. You are 'chosen,' just as Esther was. Some of us are not so fortunate. When Esther left here and was wed, I had to stay behind. Our father died leaving no dowry for me during the year of my sister's service."

I remembered the conversation overheard years ago. It was easy to see that the girl was not happy to have remained in service to the goddess. For a moment I felt guilty about not talking to Hamash about offering a home to my friend.

"Can you stay with me?" It was an inspiration that I hoped might make up for my imagined neglect.

"As your servant, like I was for Esther?" The bitterness was more pronounced. I thought I caught a hint of tears in the girl's voice.

"I thought . . . as my friend." I was a little hesitant in the face of the rancor.

Stiffly and vehemently the words came, "There are no friends here."

"The priestess said I would need someone . . ." Again my voice trailed off. I felt tears rise to my eyes.

"I doubt that I would be allowed. I have already served the Temple for five seasons. The Daughter of Astarte is supposed to have a virgin . . ." As she spoke the anger seemed to abate. With a hint of the friend who once followed my lead into all sorts of adventures, she added, "You could ask the priestess."

"I will." My promise was swift. "There is no one I would rather have at my side."

I tried to ignore the uncertainty that rose in my mind around Jerusha's hint that she was no longer a virgin and therefore unsuitable to be my companion. Everywhere I turned there seemed to be more questions than answers. Perhaps my friend could help me discern my role in the plan of the gods. I dared not doubt the rites lest I incur the wrath of the Queen of Heaven. Still there were many questions that hovered on my lips as I saw the mechanisms that the priests and servants of Astarte used. The smoke and wheels that initiated the sighing responses of the goddess did not deepen my faith or invoke awe. My mother would understand and not condemn my curiosity, I was sure. Everyone else seemed sure that I was chosen by Astarte.

At first the priestess frowned at my request.

The woman repeated my friend's excuse, "Jerusha has lived here and already served the Daughter of Astarte. Surely you know another young girl you could choose."

Stubbornly I shook my head. "Jerusha is my dearest friend. I do not have another."

It was true. Adah was betrothed to my oldest brother, Hamul. My mother was delighted that the man had finally chosen a wife. My brother was not so very old, but Perez and Jonadab were already well established as fathers.

For a long time the priestess studied me. I could tell by the way she pursed and twisted her lips that she was thinking. At last, just when I was beginning to fidget under her gaze, the answer came.

"Very well, I will speak to Jerusha. If she is willing to serve you, she will be your companion. It could be a good thing." The last musing was to herself. I almost missed the words in my rush of relief.

"Thank you, mighty Lady." With a low bow I hurried to my room.

That evening Jerusha brought my food. From that night, she was always at my side. I was able to relax with my friend and forget the coming ritual. Jerusha had changed, though. A look of wariness and cunning replaced the relaxed and joyful demeanor I remembered.

"Do not ask me about the rites and rituals." The scorn with which the girl responded to my first question cut short any conversation I hoped to have. The apparent trickery by the priests did not concern Jerusha. Almost rudely my friend reminded me of the upcoming union, "As Daughter of Astarte you will have no time to be perplexed about the way the goddess is made to act. You will have other duties as purveyor of the blessings from the goddess."

Too soon Astarte grew dark. The time of the Feast of Astarte was at hand. Each night everyone residing in the Temple accompanied the priestess to the grove. Within the circle of tall trees all the women danced. A fire burned endlessly in the center of the circle. The secret chants and rituals handed down through hundreds of generations were again spoken. Small figures of stone and wood were passed through the fire to be taken to the fields and flocks. Each family owned at least one of the teraphim. Hamash had several, I knew. When the well remembered little figure from my bedroom was brought forward, I felt a rush of homesickness. In the glow of the fire, the lion did not seem as frightening as when he stared at me each night.

Elaborate robes and veils waited in my room one morning when we returned from the evening worship amid the trees. After the night of dancing and wine, I had almost forgotten my upcoming duties. Fear came rushing back and almost choked me when I saw the garments.

"Rahab, see how gorgeous this gown is!" Jerusha nearly danced with excitement while holding up the filmy drapery for my inspection. "You will be lovely. The purity of the white veils will accentuate your lovely hair. All know that yours is the color of Astarte by her whim, not through the use of henna. Without a doubt Jericho will be doubly blessed this year by your union with Baal."

Her words were echoed again and again by the priestess and attendants who arrived to prepare me for the ceremony.

"Astarte will be honored with you as her maiden."

"Blessings will abound in flock and field."

"Baal will be pleased to be consort of such a beautiful Daughter of Astarte."

"Offerings will pour into the coffers of the gods."

The words washed over me while I stood silent under the ministrations of the women. My body was anointed with oils. All the lotions were scented with the lily that was the chosen flower of the goddess. The same white flowers were braided into my hair as a crown. Like a bride, my palms were painted with henna. My lips also were reddened. Kohl widened and shaped my eyes to look as round as the moon at her fullest. The sacred snake symbols of Astarte were painted on my arms.

A tunic of sheer linen was put over my head very carefully in order to not disturb the women's handiwork. In the mirror I blushed to see my body more revealed than concealed by the material. The embroidered gown that covered the tunic was slightly more modest. I was even more grateful when the shimmering cloak was draped over my shoulders. Jewels and gold thread formed the phases of the moon in endless variety all over the material. I was surprised by the weight and forced myself to stand upright and not slouch.

Finally the headdress and veil were brought. It seemed unnecessary to conceal my identity from the worshipers. Everyone in Jericho always knew who the chosen consort was long before the Feast. The semitransparent material allowed me to see the gratified and delighted expression on every woman's face.

Jerusha spoke for all, "You are truly like Astarte, Queen of the Heavens."

Murmurs of awe and agreement came in response.

"Let us go." It was the priestess. The woman stood regal and tall at the entrance to my room. Her own vestments were of shimmering embroidered silk.

I was led by the hand to the waiting cart. On the wood I saw Astarte's winged lion painted. It reminded me of the legends of the goddess riding to victory on such a beast. My thoughts flashed back to seeing Esther in the procession. Was it five years ago that she was Astarte? From Jerusha I knew that the woman was now a widow. My friend worried about her sister and hoped that the priestess would allow her to return to serve in the Temple.

Young girls ran ahead, scattering leaves and flower petals along the road. Jerusha and my other attendants walked behind. The ox moved steadily forward on his circuitous route to the grove. Within the sacred trees I stood before the fire while more invocations were spoken. Then a torch was lit from the holy fire and placed in my hand. Stepping into the cart, I rode back to the city and the steps of the Temple. It took all my concentration to stand straight under the gaze of all Jericho. The torch must not waver in my hand and I gripped it so tightly that my arm ached. I refused to let my mind move past the procession.

Musicians played a rhythm when the cart stopped. The words of the ceremony rolled over me unheard. Blindly I stared through the veil. Apprehensive thoughts receded when I forced myself to focus on a crease in one horn of the bull that would soon be sacrificed.

A shout of acclamation informed me that the priest representing Baal approached. The torch was taken from my hand by an assistant priest. It would be used to light the sacrificial fire. Strong hands grasped my waist and lifted me out of the cart. Cheers of praise and joy followed as I was carried to the top of the Temple steps.

Between Baal and the priestess of Astarte I stood motionless. The sacrifice of the bull seemed remote. I remembered the wine pressed to my lips by the priestess just before the veil dropped over my face. Briefly I wondered if it was drugged, for everything seemed unreal.

The crowd shouted with joy when the blood of the bull spurted upward. Smoke from the fire drifted up the steps.

"It is a good sign," the priestess whispered. She stood erect and unmoving beside me but I noticed her hands relaxed when the sacrifice was completed.

"The gods are pleased," the priest announced over the roar of the crowd. "Let the Feast begin."

Unexpectedly, the concealing cloak was stripped away. Briefly I was exposed to the view of the watching multitude before the priest lifted me in his arms and mounted the steps on the side of the ziggurat. At the top waited the tent prepared for the ritual consummation.

High above the exalting city I found myself standing beside the priest of Baal. The horned headdress loomed high and made the man appear taller than ever. The muscles in the broad chest rippled when in a dramatic movement I was lifted high. Suspended from the two broad hands, I strangely felt no fear. My heart began to thud and I began to tremble when the man who was Baal turned and lowered me under the canopy.

"Are you afraid, Daughter of Astarte?" Baal's first words to me were gentle.

Neither my lips nor my mind could form an answer.

"You are trembling. Are you afraid?" The query was repeated when I made no response.

My head barely moved in a nod.

"Do not fear. The lovely Daughter of Astarte should be bold in honor of the goddess."

I sensed almost reproof in the words and forced myself to breath in and out while my garments fell to the floor. That first time I focused on the tiny sliver of a moon that hung over the western hills.

"When Astarte reaches fullness the Feast will be over," I reminded myself, concentrating on the thought as if I could make the moon expand any faster.

The roar of satisfaction that burst from the priest along with his seed was echoed in the street. Proudly, the man carried the cloth we lay on to the parapet and waved it like a flag as a symbol that the virgin sacrifice had been completed. In the morning there would be a procession through town and out into the fields and vineyards. The cloth bloodied by my virginity would be waved over the land and animals to induce fertility and sprouting. If there were seedlings by the time Astarte was full, the promise of a rich harvest was real.

"Astarte, bless us!"

The shouted petition rolled upward past me to the moon now slipping away behind the hills. It was as though having witnessed the sacrifice, Astarte was satisfied and willing to retreat. Briefly I felt betrayed and bereft that even the goddess would desert me to a destiny I did not desire.

The days that followed began in fear and pain. They ended with regret. I learned to know the contours of the man and to enjoy the experience of a man and woman joined as one. For twelve more days the priest and I lived on the roof of the Temple. Food was brought to us through a hidden door in the roof. At the end of the Feast, when Astarte bulged with promise and the fields were dusted with the faintest of green, I followed Jerusha down those stairs and back into the living area of the Temple. Only the women who served the goddess lived in the Temple precincts.

The priests served monthlong cycles. They returned to their homes and families each night.

At each full moon, when the priests and maidens gathered together to honor Astarte, I hoped for a fuller revelation of what the priest hinted in the intimacy of that fortnight. Many times over the next months I pondered the prophetic words from my consort. They lingered in my heart like some dormant seed in the fall.

"Daughter of Astarte, there is a holy fire in your soul. The gods have something special for your life." With an angry frown the man had refused to elaborate when I begged for more information. "I cannot see the future."

"Please, goddess, help me to know what you have in mind." Every day I pleaded for an answer. "Tell the priest of Baal so he can tell me. I know I am only a girl and unworthy of revelation myself."

No answer ever came and the intimacy of the Feast was never repeated during the monthly coupling of Baal's priest and the Daughter of Astarte. The incense-filled hall induced lassitude and sensuality but not conversation. I became used to the words of the invocation of Astarte.

> "Bigger than the mountains am I,
> The Empress of the gods am I,
> The Queen of heaven am I,
> The earth's mistress am I."

Rich men from Jericho and beyond sought me as an intermediary to the gods. The priestess was pleased for the offerings were rich, especially after Nabu, the wine grower, sought me out.

"Pray to Astarte that my wife can conceive." The plump man approached my couch, almost trembling from his anguished desire and the hope that a successful union with my body would provide him with an heir.

"I will beseech the goddess." It was the standard reply to all petitioners.

My assurance and gentle encouragement must have given the man boldness. He returned at the next moon turning and the next. On the third visit he fell into my lap.

"Daughter of Astarte, my wife is indeed with child. Thank you! Thank you!"

Unlike many of my visitors, Nabu was gentle as well as grateful.

He left a rich purse on that visit, promising, "When my son is born, I will give twice as much to the great goddess."

"May he be a healthy boy." I whispered the prayer after my visitor.

The man must have told all Jericho that my prayer was effective. Word spread. From as far away as the Land of the Two Rivers and the Negev petitioners came. The son of the chief of Moab appeared at my door one day. I recognized him from the time he stayed at the Inn of Hamash while his father sought aid from the leaders of Jericho. It was obvious that the young man did not know me. He fell on his face just inside the curtains over the doorway.

"Daughter of Astarte, have pity on a foreigner."

"What do you seek?" Satisfaction edged into my heart to see the arrogant brought low.

I was surprised to realize that it still stung to remember a comment overheard as I fed the chickens in the early morning light not so long ago. Neither man noticed me.

"Ties with the house of Hamash will improve the chance of aid to Moab." The chief of Moab was apparently attempting to convince his son of the advantage of an alliance.

"The daughter of Hamash has no beauty to enslave a man. Skin and bones with long legs will never gain her a husband, even with the hair of fire." Child though I was, the scornful words hurt.

Now that same young man groveled at my feet. An ironic smile came to my lips when I considered the situation.

"What does the son of Moab seek from the gods of Jericho?" I repeated my question haughtily.

"Daughter of Astarte." Awkwardly fumbling at his belt, the man produced a heavy purse. This he laid at my feet while still kneeling. "I seek rest for my father."

"Your father?" Astonished at the request, I lost a bit of the cool detachment I tried to maintain with every petitioner.

"If the Daughter of Astarte will permit, I can explain." The young man's hands raised in a supplication.

Graciously I inclined my head, curious to hear the explanation.

"It has not been a year since my father, Zippor chief of Moab, came to seek help from the council of Jericho. It was not the first time we came and were refused. 'A horde has come out of Egypt' we said. 'They threaten our borders. If Moab falls, Jericho will be next.' Your leaders laughed at us and with taunts refused to hear our words."

"Taunts?" probing the wound gave me some satisfaction.

A dark frown creased the broad brow and heavy eyebrows drew together at the memory.

"Yes." The remembered words were spat angrily into the air. "'Our walls are the only defense Jericho needs. She will withstand any band of rabble lost in the desert for forty years. Go back to your tents, Moab. Cities such as the Queen of Canaan have no need for an alliance with herders from across the River.' They dismissed us rudely."

Grief replaced the darkness of anger as this man, Balak, continued.

"My father heard the words and his heart cracked. Since we returned to our land he has been as one dead, yet living. I lead the people in his place but would rather have my father restored."

"And the people of Israel?" For some reason I was curious about the nation who claimed only the one, unseen God.

"The people have swept into Moab just as we feared. Their tents fill the land. Shittim is dwarfed by the multitude. I have failed my father. Would that I could die in his place and he would rise up to defeat this people." Grief stricken the young man bowed his head to the floor.

I opened my mouth to say something, unsure how to answer

such a petition. My visitor looked up and continued.

"I sent to the east, to the city of Pethor. The elders of Midian who share my distaste of the rabble accompanied my father's counselors. They sought Balaam son of Beor, a mighty seer. At first he refused to come. His response seemed odd. 'Adonai has refused to let me go.' Eventually he was persuaded to come to Moab. Even then he did not curse the sons of Israel as I demanded." A huge sigh escaped the young man now staring past me into his memory.

"Three times I sacrificed bulls and rams. Three times I asked Baalam for a curse on the Children of Israel. Three times the seer responded by heaping blessing upon blessing on the swarm. In the end, he prophesied destruction on all nations by the refugee horde. I sent him away in disgrace."

Silence reigned as I considered the young man's words. The intriguing Children of Israel had been blessed by Baalam. This was a man famous even in Jericho for his insights into the future. The seer was sought by leaders from the Euphrates to the Great Sea.

"Now I seek Astarte here in her city and her temple. Through you, fair Daughter of the goddess, I beseech the Mighty Lady of Victory to act. She has let these hordes sweep through Moab and Midian. Surely Astarte is stronger than this god of slaves." The voice rose in challenge. "Let her raise Zippor to health so that he can defeat these locusts in her name."

Still I said nothing. My mind was too busy pondering Baalam's words "Adonai has refused to let me go." Why had the seer used the term Adonai rather than Baal or one of the other gods? Adonai means lord. What lord did he mean? Was Baalam implying that the god of this people was lord of other gods?

When I did not respond, Balak lowered his voice. The rage was gone.

"If no one can stop this invasion, then give my father peace with his ancestors lest he see the downfall of Moab."

"May Astarte hear your desires." Absently I spoke the prescribed words and accepted the man's weight.

My mind was elsewhere even as Balak consummated the act

he paid for. Long after the prince of Moab left, I sat staring at the lamp that always lit the figure of Astarte astride her winged lion in the niche beside the door.

"The strange god of the Hebrews has led this multitude from Egypt to the very border of Jericho." I addressed the goddess with a plea. I no longer feared the figure as I had the one guarding my childhood bed. "Rouse yourself and strike these invaders with scorpions. The gods of Midian could not stand before this invisible god, nor it seems can the gods of Moab. Yet Moab also calls on Baal and Astarte. Why do you not defend those tribes? Even Baalam obeys the command of this god of refugees and blesses them. Astarte, this is your city. Surely you will be able to keep out this new and strange foreign god."

The flame flickered as if in answer. I caught my breath and stared as the wavering light disappeared. The lamp of Astarte in each room was carefully tended. Fresh oil and a new wick were added each morning so that the flame would never go out. Could it be that in response to my questioning prayer the lamp had gone out?

Barely daring to breathe I tiptoed across the room. I was only partially relieved to see that the reason the flame extinguished was that the wick had sunk below the oil. Such a thing had never happened before. Carefully I replaced and relit the wick from my bedside lamp. I shook my head to erase an unbidden and frightening thought.

"Perhaps it is not Astarte, but this invisible god who has power." The whisper in my mind lingered and returned at odd times over the next few weeks.

It was late summer when I was surprised to see Balak offering another bag of silver for my intercession.

"Daughter of Astarte, the goddess has acted." The statement surprised me.

I glanced quickly at the lamp beside the statue. The flame burned brightly and mocked my fears.

"There is dissension in the camp of the invaders. Some want to settle, marry girls of Moab and settle within our borders. The leader, Joshua, opposes such action. The goddess has brought division. May she continue to trouble the Hebrew." Satisfaction was in the tone.

Somehow I was prompted to ask about Zippor, "And your father?"

"Sleeps with his fathers in the Great Under." A shade of sorrow crossed the bearded face. "It is best. He might not see the advantage of alliance with members of this people. There are even some in Moab who oppose such a move. I believe that if they become one with us in covenant Moab will be strong. The soldiers of the Hebrews will offer protection to our borders. The sons of Manasseh, Gad and Reuben are seeking to settle within the land."

I heard the desire for dominion and power in the eager words. With sinking heart I let go of the vague idea that the god of the Children of Israel was above such things as quarreling and power grabbing. Suddenly their god seemed weak and more like the gods of Canaan than an all powerful being. The people would become part of Moab and the promise lost. I knew I should feel relief at the assurance of safety for Jericho and Canaan. Instead I felt betrayed. Only then did I realize how much I wanted the God of Israel to be real.

"May Astarte bless your desires." The rote words meant nothing and my mind was far from the union with Balak.

My year of service was almost over before I again heard news of the Children of Israel and their god.

❦ 4 ❧

ONE LATE WINTER MORNING I was summoned by the priestess. She sat in the Chamber of Wisdom between the Hall of Astarte and the Hall of the Gods. The priest of Baal sat beside her. I was surprised. Rarely did the priests enter the sacred precincts of the Lady. Seeing the stern faces, I began to tremble and tried to recall what fault I might have committed.

"Daughter of Astarte." Despite her serious expression, the priestess did not sound angry. "You have served the goddess well. Much profit has been added to the Temple by your service."

I could think of no reply. Nervously my hands twisted the material of my gown.

"Men report that blessing comes from your intercession." The priest leaned forward to stare at me. "Even against the Children of Israel and their god, your prayers have proved effective. Balak of Moab reports that some of the refugees are peacefully settling near Shittim and Beth-Peor. He credits your intercession with the goddess."

Unsure whether to nod or bow, I simply stood dumb, staring back at the pair.

"Your year of service is drawing to a close. Soon a new Daughter will have union with Baal to bring fertility to Jericho and the land."

I did nod in response to the words of the priestess. Already the young woman who would perform the ritual was within the walls of the Temple. Although I had not seen her I knew she was present. The child was as naïve and innocent as I was not quite a year earlier. I hoped Astarte would give her courage.

"You must now decide your path," the woman continued. "Perhaps you dream of a husband and children. There is honor in that."

"However," the man interrupted before I could reply, "greater honor can be found in further service to the goddess."

I felt a shudder ripple through me at the thought of becoming one of the myriad Temple maidens who suffered silently under the usage of the men of Canaan and beyond. For a piece of silver any man could bed one of those women and so obtain a union with the goddess, if not the blessing of lying with the Daughter of Astarte. Jerusha was graphic in her description of what she endured during the half decade after Esther left the Temple.

Seeing my response, the priestess explained, "We see your calling as service outside these walls."

My confusion must have been obvious. I felt my forehead pucker in doubt. It was unheard of for a Temple maiden to leave the precincts except to wed. A smile crossed the woman's lips, and above his beard the priest of Baal bared his teeth in a grin.

"Your favor with Astarte is well known. You, your servant girl and anyone else you choose will have lodging in the city wall. The place will be called the Inn of Astarte. Visitors to the city who do not have time for a visit to the Temple may stay there and so receive a blessing of the goddess. Your inn will be sought out because you are the chosen of Astarte." It seemed simple while the man explained the idea. "Profits from food and drink will be for you and your companions. Offerings to Astarte will be due to the Temple."

The priest spoke confidently. I could see he was sure I would accept the carefully laid-out plan. My mind ran in circles. It seemed too good to be true. I would be as independent as a woman ever had a chance to be. Still, I hesitated, wondering what gain the pair who presented the plan expected.

"You are wondering what the Temple and Jericho will gain from this arrangement." The priestess easily read my thoughts.

Slowly I nodded.

"Simply this." Her response was soft and serious. "Any word

of the refugees from Egypt is to be reported to us. They must not be allowed to cross the Jordan. The god they proclaim is false. Astarte will not allow the advance of this rabble."

I almost asked, "Then why do you need me?"

The priest forestalled me by rising. "Daughter of Astarte, I once told you that I foresaw great things for you. The Mighty Lady has spoken her desires. We will talk again tomorrow. Think on what we offer."

"Yes, think well about your choice." It was almost a threat whispered in my ear by the priestess of Astarte as she brushed past me.

I stood alone for several minutes before wandering back to my alcove.

Jerusha accosted me as I dropped the curtain in place. "What is it? Why were you summoned?"

The room felt cramped. I wished I could walk through the fields to clear my mind and make the most important decision of my life.

"What happened? What is the ruling?" My companion almost stamped in her impatience when I remained silent.

"I must think." My immediate answer was clearly unsatisfactory.

"Rahab"—strong, small hands caught my arm—"you have to tell me."

For the first time in my life, I refused my friend.

"No, this is my decision. I have to think. Leave me alone."

Affronted by my tone, Jerusha dropped her hands. Tilting her head haughtily, the girl started from the room.

"I have to get it clear in my head. Then I will tell you." I was not sure if my half-conciliatory words were heard.

The curtain dropped into place and I was alone. Perversely, I immediately wished Jerusha was beside me. She was not in sight when I peered around the doorframe hoping to call her back.

"Your inn will be sought."

"Report to us."

"Think well about your choice."

"I foresaw great things."

"Service to the goddess."

"Husband and child."

The words spoken by priest and priestess chanted in my mind. I did not feel peace. Fear and confusion reigned.

"What shall I do?" The question was not addressed to the goddess in her niche. Rather it was a cry from my heart to my mother. I longed to be held in her arms and hear her advice.

Hamash promised a fine marriage after my service in the Temple. I wondered if a man had been chosen for me. If I accepted the offer from the priest, would I disappoint my family? Perhaps my father would be proud if I agreed to serve the Temple and Jericho as a sort of spy. I admitted that the idea of running an inn appealed to me. The day to day operations of the inn always interested me more than they did my brothers. A shudder of revulsion rippled through me at the thought that perhaps visitors would expect me to continue to offer my bed on behalf of Astarte.

"I would send such men to the Temple, to you, goddess." It was a promise whispered in the direction of the statue. "My bed will be my own."

I had not reached any decision, even though the day slipped past. It was time for the evening ceremony welcoming Astarte to the sky. Distantly I heard voices chanting the opening chorus of worship. I would be missed. In a panic I grabbed my headdress adorned with the crescent moon. After racing down the corridor I slipped into my place beside the tall statue just in time to raise the silver pitcher and pour water into the basin. The rising moon was reflected in the water through one of the windows carefully placed in the very top of the wall. Our lives were governed by the rising of Astarte. Our day began with her appearance. Each evening, we welcomed worshipers after the ceremony until the sun rose in the morning.

"I will not miss timing my life to Astarte's rising." I realized that I had made my decision when the thought slipped into my head as I watched the water pouring out.

Even as I accepted a pouch of silver from the governor of the city and assured him of Astarte's favor, I felt anticipation at the

coming change. My mind was busy with ideas for the inn. I barely noticed the grunting efforts of my visitor or his groan of grat-
ification.

Jerusha entered as soon as the man left. Her wary expression
caused me to hold out my hand.

"Well?" she asked again.

"I have been offered a chance to serve Astarte and Jericho by
operating a small inn to spy out news of the refugees from Egypt.
The rulers of our city want news of these foreigners who worship
a god so different from our gods. With word of their plans, an
invasion can be forestalled. We will not be overrun like Midian
and Moab." All in one breath I gave her the news.

Wide-eyed, the girl sat back on her heels.

"An inn . . . of your own?" My friend was almost speechless.

I nodded in reply and waited for further response.

"It is too good to be true." Jerusha's warning echoed my fears.

"We must trust the priestess and Astarte that all will work
out," I protested, trying to convince myself and my companion.

"Wouldn't it be wonderful?" A dreamy look appeared to
replace the normal watchful wariness.

"I can choose who is to serve me. You and perhaps Esther
would be my assistants."

The thought of Jerusha's sister, now a destitute young widow,
came as I spoke. Even though the priestess had allowed the
woman to return to the Temple after her loss, I did not envy her
position. Her duties included doing the tasks that even the slaves
disliked. On more than one occasion I saw her cleaning the
refuse pots kept in each room.

"Oh, Rahab." Suddenly the girl was transformed into the
enthusiastic friend from playtime in my father's house. "I have
dreamed of leaving these walls. Perhaps we can find husbands as
well. Esther has been in poverty since her husband died and
would welcome a new husband, I am sure."

The longing sigh of my companion remained in my mind
even as I stood before the priest of Baal and High Priestess. The
summons came soon after the sun rose. With one hand I smoth-

ered a yawn as I followed the servant to the Chamber of Wisdom. The man and woman sat with heads bent together. I could not hear the whispered words. My presence caused the priestess to straighten. Her hands tapped the arms of her chair betraying a slight nervousness about my response.

Without preamble the man spoke, "Have you decided?"

"Yes, my lord," I responded, bowing my head.

"And . . ." Frowning, the priestess prompted when I stared silently at the floor hoping I was making the right decision.

"I will serve Astarte as you want." My throat was suddenly dry. I swallowed desperately trying to drive away the sudden terror that gripped me.

"That is good." Satisfied, the priest leaned back. A smug smile appeared on his lips. "Balak will be pleased."

"Balak?" Startled, I looked up.

"Yes, the chief of Moab came to me with the idea. The governor of Jericho has already agreed. Now you have shown that Astarte approves." A trap seemed to close as the man spoke.

"Balak is to be owner and sponsor of the endeavor," the priestess explained. "You are just a child. No woman could manage such an establishment by herself. Foreign visitors will feel welcome to stop at your inn since it is not run by a resident of Jericho."

"As if they will need such encouragement." A low-voiced interruption from the priest of Baal was accompanied by a look that sent the blood pounding through my body in memory of my initiation a year earlier.

"All is ready." Ignoring his comment, the woman rose. At her gesture, I followed the graceful figure back to my room.

"Tomorrow the Feast will begin." It was a statement of fact. "You with your chosen companions . . ."

"Jerusha and her sister Esther, the widow," I supplied, when the woman paused for a response. A satisfied nod indicated approval.

"You will leave here with Balak at the beginning of the celebration. Reports will be delivered weekly when you come to worship the goddess." The priestess patiently explained the plan. "No one will question the continued devotion of a former Daughter of Astarte."

More instructions followed about the running of the inn and treatment of guests. I barely listened. Even with the weekly reporting and under Balak's unexpected and unwanted supervision, I could feel a breeze bearing freedom beginning to waft toward me.

"Everything you need will be provided by Balak," the woman finally concluded. "Serve him well and you will please Astarte."

"Yes, great lady." For the second time that day I bowed low to the woman who had been my guide and mentor over the past year. Gently she laid one hand on my flame-colored hair.

"Rahab, Daughter of Astarte, you have been singled out for greatness. Do not fail the gods." In a rustle of linen, the woman left me alone to ponder her words.

Jerusha interrupted my musing. The curtain was pulled back to reveal her eager face.

"Rahab, I heard it all! We are really going to have an inn!"

Although I smiled at the awe in my friend's voice, I too felt a thrill at the opportunity. Not even Balak's arrival with a request for a final union with the goddess for blessing on his inn dimmed my anticipation.

❦ 5 ❧

HAVING THE INN WAS both better and worse than I expected. At first I feared that I had made a terrible choice. Balak arrived the morning of the Feast to convey us to the house.

"Come, the city is concerned with the arrival of the new Daughter of Astarte." His blunt words were an order.

The man hurried us through the passage and out the side door. Jerusha, Esther and I each carried a small bundle of possessions. We had very little of our own. All the Temple maidens were allowed were the tunics and gowns we wore, our combs, face creams and cosmetics.

Balak handed each of us a hooded cloak. I was grateful for the concealment and drew the hood tight around my face. The furtiveness of our actions made it almost seem as if we were fleeing. We walked rapidly behind the man, away from the chanting crowds. I was sure no one noticed us. All eyes were fixed on the garlanded cart bearing another young girl to her destiny.

I remembered my own trepidation of a year earlier. It seemed longer and I felt much older than the thirteen-year-old virgin who now entered the Temple. I risked a glance back but was unable to see the chosen of Astarte. Esther caught my hand in a sympathetic squeeze.

"It is hard to be replaced," she whispered, mistaking my curiosity for longing. "This is an undreamed-of opportunity. I am grateful to you, Rahab, my sister's friend. Forgive me for my resentful thoughts at your arrival."

"Of course." The confession surprised me and I patted the hand still holding mine.

"Hurry," Jerusha urged, signaling us forward.

We turned the corner and left the crowd behind. A chariot waited in the deserted street. A boy of about eight held the head of the horse. Balak helped Esther and then Jerusha step up onto the floor of the chariot. I was the last to be lifted into the conveyance. Then he stepped in and took the reins. It was fortunate that we women were slender. The chariot was built for two men, not for twice that number. I found myself pressed between Balak and Jerusha while Esther gripped the railing on the front with both hands. With her short stature, she could barely look over the railing.

Balak moved the reins and the horse started forward. When we began to roll, the boy jumped aside and grabbed a strap at the back of the chariot as we passed. I feared he would fall when the horse trotted faster, but the child braced his feet on the back edge of the chariot and grinned at me.

I recognized the street when we arrived. It led to the main gate. Balak stopped by a tall door. Two narrow steps led up to the entrance. The boy dropped to the ground before we even completely came to a stop. He caught the horse's chin strap as soon as the man drew rein.

Timidly I proceeded through the door that our escort flung wide. My friends followed. The wide hall that greeted our eyes was surprising. Steps led into a sunken cooking area on one side. A large brazier occupied the center of the room just as in the Inn of Hamash. I was familiar with the arrangement of cushions and stools around the low tables as well. Against the far wall was a narrow stairway to the upper area. Our guide led the way. Esther and Jerusha sighed in delight at the large sleeping areas.

"For your guests." The announcement did not dim their excitement. "You will live up here."

Our attention was directed to a ladder. When no one moved, I grasped the rungs and started up.

"Come on. It really is quite airy here." The surprised enthusiasm of my voice encouraged first Jerusha and then Esther to follow me.

We stood in an enclosed rooftop area. Through airy lattice,

the city was visible to the east. A small door led to an open area of roof. Curious, I stepped outside. It appeared that our house-top was a little taller than the city wall. From my newly discovered vantage, I looked westward over the valley between Jericho and the hills of Canaan. By looking straight down I could see the jagged rocks of the defensive works around the city. A little further out a trench and more rocks formed an outer bulwark. It was no wonder that the people of Jericho slept secure in the belief that the city was impregnable. I could see the head of the soldier overlooking the gate. There did not seem to be need for any other guards.

Balak spoke, "You will draw up the ladder at night so none of the guests will bother you."

My face must have betrayed astonishment at such consideration for our comfort and safety.

"You are not prostitutes, although surely some will think that you are. Your role in this house is to obtain information from travelers about the plans and movements of the refugee rabble from Egypt who pollute the land of Moab. I have learned that those who plan to remain in my land only want to take it over as their own possession. With the leaders of Jericho, we will be able to defeat their invasion. I will drive them from Moab." The man's face changed and his voice became harsh as he poured out the hatred he harbored. "My father will be avenged. These cursed Children of Israel caused his death as surely as if they drove a sword into his heart. May the gods so treat me if I do not drive the blasphemers from both Moab and Canaan. Like locusts they eat the produce of the land. They offer nothing but empty words of promised blessings by their god in return. Astarte is witness. May she judge for my cause."

When Balak ended his tirade, both Jerusha and Esther stood with mouths and eyes wide open.

"Surely the gods will hear you." With a placating tone I sought to calm our patron.

"Yes." Some of the tension left the man as he turned to me, "The gods will listen to you. You are blessed of Astarte. I see how your hair proclaims her favor."

It appeared the anger was gone to be replaced by the lust I saw growing on the broad face. One hand reached out to caress my red hair. Gently the man tucked a thick strand behind my ear.

"Your ears will learn the plans of this people. We will crush the invaders and their god. Astarte has set you aside for this. I will gain blessing through you."

"We must make the inn ready for guests." I hoped to distract Balak with practical matters.

"Esther and Jerusha can do that." The reply was thick with passion as one hand smoothed my hair and the other drew me closer. "Go."

My friends scurried down the ladder at the command, leaving me alone.

"What payment do I receive for my patronage?" It was not really a question.

"We will spy for you." I tried to forestall the inevitable. "Astarte will give you victory."

"Yes, and that pleases me almost as much as possessing your body," the man spoke close to my ear.

I did not weep until after Balak left me alone. The room no longer felt like an airy sanctuary. I knew that, from me at least, the man would require satisfaction. When I finally descended, the chief of Moab was gone. Jerusha and Esther already had the fire going and stew bubbling in a pot.

"See what we have." Esther eagerly showed me the baskets with cheeses and jars of wine and oil. There were bins of flour and meal as well. "Soon the market will have fresh fruits and vegetables. We will live like the wealthiest of women!"

"That will be good." I tried to take an interest.

Secretly I wondered why travelers would bother to stop at our inn rather than the fine establishment my father owned. I should not have worried. Balak and the leaders of Jericho must have given instructions to the guards at the gate. Any foreign visitor asking for lodging was directed to our door. The *gal* of the city even provided a stable area near the gate for the animals of such travelers.

It was only the second evening that we were in our home

when a knock sounded. Jerusha looked at Esther who looked at
me. As calmly as I could, I walked across the room and opened
the door.

"Is this the Inn of Astarte?" A very plump visitor stood on the
step. By his turban I guessed he was from the Negev.

"Yes, welcome." With a wave of my hand I gestured our first
guest inside.

Jerusha hurried forward with a cup of wine. Esther took the
cloak that the man discarded. Bemused, our visitor looked from
one to another.

"The guard spoke the truth." The astonished assertion burst
from the man. "I was told this was an inn run by women."

"Yes." Jerusha found her tongue and a dimpled smile. "Let
me show you to your room, or would you prefer to have some
stew first?"

Even before we served the trader his meal a second knock
sounded. This time a haughty merchant from Haran entered. He
too was amazed to find only women in residence. I rather feared
that our guests would assume that something beside food and a
bed were offered, but neither man suggested anything improper.

Over the next days and weeks our fame and clientele grew
until we were forced to hire a girl to help clean and to visit the
well for us. Esther took over visiting the market for bargains. She
did not seem to mind the whispers and innuendo from the merchants and neighbors. I was relieved to let others face the rumors
and gossip about our inn. Everyone in Jericho had something to
say about the arrangement. The kindest remarks labeled us as
eccentric and foolish women who would soon come to their
senses. More often the comments branded us as harlots. When I
ventured to the market I was sure that the murmured words held
contempt directed toward me. Others were loud in their condemnation.

"There goes the harlot."

"Too bad she shamed her family."

"Such an honorable father."

Jerusha presided over the bedroom arrangements. I was left
to welcome, entertain and question our guests about the poten-

tial invaders. Nearly everyone had an opinion about the Children of Israel.

"Rabble and troublemakers, they are the scum of Egypt."

"I think they must have great fortitude to survive the desert."

"What kind of leadership is it to wander for a generation in Sinai?"

"It is the old god of the hill shrines and desert nomads that they claim to follow."

"Only the most unsophisticated even remember the old gods."

"Baal and Astarte are true rulers of the heavens."

I let the debate rage around me and reported the views faithfully to the Temple. Some of the comments gave me something to ponder. Occasionally one of the guests seemed to have real news about the Hebrew people.

"I have seen them on the march. These are not a warring people. Women and children accompany them," a horse merchant from the Negev told us one evening.

Even though he was jeered at by the three other occupants of the room, the man and his son held firm.

"This people believe that the god of their ancestors Abraham and his sons Isaac and Jacob lead them," the older trader insisted.

"Not everyone believes that Baal and Astarte are the true gods," the younger man spoke boldly. "There are those in the desert who remember and still honor the god of Ishmael. He was the true son of Abraham the Blessed and ancestor of the faithful of *El*."

Sneers and even a murmur of "blasphemy" from the Babylonian spice merchant only made the pair more bold.

"Could Astarte or Baal have provided water and food, even meat, for such a crowd over the past forty years?" It was a challenge that had to be answered.

"Astarte would not have left the faithful to wander lost for forty days, much less forty years," argued Boraz, a regular visitor from Tyre.

The old nomad's response kept me awake for several nights seeking to resolve the question he posed. "What if the God of

Abraham was not punishing the people, but teaching them to trust in God alone? The desert is unforgiving to fools, yet Moses and the God of Abraham have brought out of the wilderness more people than the number that left Egypt. Your gods have power only within their walls. The God of Abraham is not tied to a Temple. Who can stand against a God who acts from Egypt to Sinai, Moab and beyond?"

Ignoring the angry murmur that greeted his query, the old man rose from the cushions with a grace unexpected from one of such advanced age. In the desert way, the trader touched forehead, lips and heart in a salaam of farewell.

"My views are but those of a humble nomad. May the gods you follow give you rest, my friends." To me he offered a second bow, "I will seek my bed now. Accept my apologies for burdening your hospitality with such contentions. Come Esau."

Followed by his son, the horse merchant mounted the stairs to the room allotted. The remaining men soon followed to roll in blankets in the neighboring room. Dawn saw the nomads on their way. It was not much later that the other merchants departed for the market.

Jerusha approached me breathlessly after our guests departed, "We must report the words of Ishmael and his father."

"Yes," I nodded absently.

The conversation of the previous night raised new questions in my mind, but I knew our duty to Jericho and to Astarte.

At odd times over the next weeks and months, memory of the intensity of the dark eyes beneath white eyebrows would return. The question "Who can stand against such a god?" became an almost constant whisper in the back of my mind.

Sometimes, after Jerusha and Esther slept, I quietly tiptoed to the corner of our room. The door provided access to my rooftop sanctuary. I loved the quiet of the evenings with only the moon for a companion.

"I do not understand you," Jerusha shook her head at me. "Do you think Astarte will talk to you?"

"The roof is for drying our clothing and the vegetables we will store over the winter," Esther added.

"And of course for Balak's flax," I could not help adding bitterly.

We had barely settled into a routine when Esther opened the door to find our patron waiting in the early summer afternoon.

"I have come to see how my investment prospers." It was an announcement that struck fear in my heart.

"You must come in." My friend appeared flustered by the unexpected arrival.

I stood up and gripped my hands in my clothing to hide the shaking.

"You are welcome." I was relieved that my voice was steady.

The man stood in the center of the room. His eyes took in the new cushions and the addition of a hanging oil lamp.

"I see you have made some changes." There was a sneer in the observation.

"Yes, Jerusha made the pillows for our guests' comfort," I agreed, trying not the show my angry reaction to his tone.

"It is good that you have time to do such things." The half smile made me wary.

I wondered what the man was planning. His next words did not calm my uneasiness.

"Have you a room for me to spend the night?" Balak asked. "In the morning we will discuss business."

"Of course." Jerusha jumped to her feet. "You will have the best room."

For most of the night I sat on the roof wondering what the man from Moab had come for. Only after our other visitors left did we learn.

"There is a cart in the street," Esther reported when she returned from the well.

"Good." Balak stood up with a stretch. "That is the load of flax from my fields near Jericho. Your roof is the perfect area for drying the stalks. I will see that it is beaten out at the proper time so you can spin it into thread. You will then use it for weaving."

I found myself staring open mouthed at the man.

"We do not have time," I started to argue.

"If you have time to make pillows, I am sure you have time

to weave fine material for me to sell." The sneer returned to lips and voice while Balak narrowed his eyes in warning.

Esther spoke up when I said nothing. "We will be happy to do as you ask."

"I thought you would." Without looking at me the man strode to the door.

Two servants carried bundle after bundle of flax through the door and up the stairs to the roof.

"You will turn the flax daily," Balak instructed us carefully. "My servants will take it to be beaten and bring you the fibers for weaving. In the fall I will return to get the cloth."

"Yes, master." Esther lowered her head submissively.

I gritted my teeth and said nothing.

"If you do well and I make a profit, I will give you a portion," the man added as he prepared to leave.

In the fall Balak came to collect our woven goods. He sold the fine cloth and continually promised an accounting that we never saw. Each summer brought new supplies of flax to dry. Even when the roof was full of piles of flax I spent time outside in the darkness.

Alone, I pondered the many gods and sought the truth. In the stillness of the night I could look across Jericho. The moonlight shimmered on the rooftop of the Temple reminding me of my life as servant of the goddess. Three times a new Daughter of Astarte had been chosen for the sacred union with Baal. Still I had no answer to the question that nagged at me. More and more often I asked the moon.

"Astarte, are you truly powerful?" There was never a response.

One day a message arrived from Balak that added to my confusion.

"The Rabble of Israel is gathering strength. They have turned against Midian. Listen closely to find what you can about their plans." A servant from Moab repeated his master's order.

I sought the goddess, "Astarte, will you protect us? Can you defend us?"

The queries became more urgent with each passing night.

Travelers gave us news of the defeat of Midian and of the death of Balaam. It saddened me to hear that the old seer was dead in battle against the Hebrew hosts. I tried to force myself to believe that the statue in the Temple did have power against the invisible god of the coming invaders. The harder I tried to ignore them, the more I heard the rumors of miracles attributed to the one called the God of Abraham, Isaac and Jacob.

Esther and Jerusha hung on the news avidly. Their questions opened the gates of memory. Each visitor had a tale to tell.

"The sea was opened for the refugees but closed over the Egyptian army. Not a man was left alive."

"A cloud of quail descended on the camp to feed all the people."

"Even when poisonous snakes were awakened, the people did not die. Moses set up a bronze serpent as a cure."

"Moses is dead. Joshua is leader now." The news came from the trader bound for Haran. "He has never led such a people."

"I hear that he spoke to a messenger from the god that has no name." Another merchant from the Negev shared news that made me shiver with an unnamed disquiet that was almost a thrill of anticipation.

"Oh, how can that be?" I barely heard Jerusha's gasp or the chuckled response.

"It is just a story among the weavers." With a hand the man pulled my friend into his lap. "Come my pretty, I'm sure we can find more entertaining topics."

Long after my friends slept, I stared through the lattice at the moon moving slowly up the sky. Never had I heard that Astarte sent a messenger to speak to her faithful. I began to wonder if this strange unseen and unknown god was more powerful than Astarte.

"Are you there, Queen of Heaven?" My question went unanswered for many moon turnings. Doubts kept me from praying to Astarte. The moon seemed very distant and silent.

It was my father who asked me to attempt intercession with the goddess. He came to me mid-morning soon after the great

Feast was complete. It had been five years since I saw the man. My last glimpse had been when he left me at the door of the Temple. After a moment of hesitation, Hamash entered my inn. Silently he stared around the comfortable room before turning to me. I waited, unsure why my father had come.

"Your mother is dying." The statement sounded harsh but I heard suppressed emotion. "If you truly have the ear of the goddess, ask for my wife to live."

"Oh," a cry of sorrow slipped out. "I will ask the goddess to visit Mother as the Bestower of Strength."

The man stood silent in the center of the room. He seemed to make a decision.

"We heard stories of your life. I see they were wrong." It was a grudging acknowledgement. "Come to see your mother."

Hastily I grabbed the veil near the door. It belonged to Esther, but I did not care. Beside the man who seemed a stranger, I walked through Jericho. We reached the familiar sights and sounds of the Inn of Hamash. I could understand his doubts about my establishment. We had no stables and only one serving girl. My father kept many men and slaves and animals.

"She is upstairs." With a wave of one hand, Hamash directed me to my mother.

When I saw the frail, gray-haired figure, I could not suppress a sob. Slowly dim eyes opened.

"Rahab?" The whispered question brought me to the woman's side.

"I am here. Astarte will listen to me. You will be well." Through tears I tried to sound encouraging.

"It is enough that you came." A weak hand tried to lift from the blanket to touch me.

I caught the thin fingers in my palm. There was no weight to the fragile bones and no strength to grasp my hand.

My heart cringed in fear. In a desperate whisper I begged, "Astarte, please give life to my mother."

Days passed while I sat beside the pallet. Astarte did not act. Any change was for the worse. My mother was slipping away despite my petitions. I turned in desperation to the God of Israel. If the goddess would not heal my mother, perhaps the god of her childhood memories could come to her aid.

"Can you help, invisible god of miracles? Surely the service of my grandfather at your shrine must count for something." While stroking the transparent hand I challenged the one I could not dare believe in.

It did indeed seem a miracle the next morning. My mother looked at me with clear eyes. Her words, however, caused my own eyes to blur with tears.

"Child, let me go to my ancestors. The sand of life is almost out. Do not hold me back. You must not grieve that I go to join Ereshkigal, Mistress of the Great Under. She is sister to Astarte whom you serve. I will be at peace among the ancients. Remember, I love you, my dearest child, my Rahab. May the Holy One of your grandfather show you a broad path to peace and faith."

Then, slowly, eyelids closed over the gray eyes. When her shallow breath stopped, I fell across my mother in a flood of tears. Only later did I ponder the astonishing gift of her last words.

"Did the God of Israel or Astarte give me that gift?" I questioned the starry sky while looking out the window of my childhood room.

As always, there was no answer in the wind. However, I could not forget that there was no change until I prayed to the unseen and unknown god. Astarte seemed powerless and I stopped offering my prayers to the moon goddess.

The body was prepared for burial, knees folded against her chest and hands carefully placed together under the chin. I was reminded of the way an infant sleeps when I saw the freshly wrapped figure. With great sounds of weeping, the professional mourners led the way through Jericho. I wanted to scream my anguish to the sky. Instead I followed my brothers and father to a place just outside the city where the wealthy laid their dead. The very poor actually dug under their floors to inter a body, but Hamash could afford the proper placement within a small building. My veil was wrapped tightly around my face so that no one would observe my grief. Tears slid down my cheeks to be caught in the material. I felt bereft with the loss of the only person who ever truly understood my longings and doubts about the sacred things. Even the sight of the moon through my window that night did not ease my sorrow.

In the morning I prepared to return to my home.

"Stay here. Leave the life of innkeeper behind," urged Hamash. "My daughter should not be thought of as a harlot. I have seen that the gossip is not true, but you must leave that way of life. I will find you a husband."

For a moment I was tempted. It would be so nice to be the protected child again. Then I remembered the vow to Astarte, made to the priestess just before I left the Temple.

"As long as Astarte, Queen of Heaven, orders my life, I will offer her my service." The words now seemed a chain that bound me to a life I deplored.

"My father, I have promised to serve the goddess." As gently as possible I refused the man who loved me. "I will not intrude upon your life and become a burden. There would be few men who would seek me as wife. I am past the age for marriage."

The stories of my life would also dim any suitor's ardor, but I did not add that. Hamash frowned at my response. He saw in my eyes recognition of what I did not say. A hand reached out to touch my shoulder. With sudden emotion I was drawn against the broad chest. How long I stood clasped within my father's love I do not know.

"My reputation would be a buffer." It was the only argument the man offered.

He thought it would be enough. I knew better. With regret I shook my head. Tears stood in my eyes as I made the decision that I knew I must.

My refusal of his offer was painful. I tried to explain even though the words sounded empty to me as I spoke.

"Father, I cannot ask this of you. I must serve the goddess as I swore in the Temple. The Lady who gives the laws does not forgive betrayal. It would only bring sorrow to this house."

"Then return to your life of harlotry." The sudden anger frightened me. "I see that I was mistaken in thinking that the rumors were lies. My daughter is dead to me."

Hamash turned away. Rapid footsteps carried him from the room.

"My father."

He never heard the tearful whisper nor saw the beseeching hand I held out.

Slowly I let my hand drop. My feet dragged as I crossed the room to gather my cloak. It felt like a leaden weight around my shoulders. The veil I wrapped around my face hid the tears that flowed all the way back to my home. Service to the goddess was no longer an honor or joyful service. Now it was an onerous burden that separated me from my father. My life stretched ahead of me devoid of hope.

↞ 6 ↠

EACH SUMMER BROUGHT NEWS of the threat from across the Jordan. Stories long regarded as the invention of imaginative traders were now shared as fact at the well and in the market. Nearly every visitor to my inn had another incredible incident to relate.

I was reminded of my childhood when my mother shared the tales she heard in Bethel as a child. In a way the memory made me feel closer to the woman who now slept in the family tomb. My heart remembered being held close to her heart while she recited the stories.

"The children of Abraham the Wanderer are a tribe without a country." The story always started in the same way. "Abraham bought land at Mamre for a burial chamber but owned no land himself. His grandson Jacob, the one who came to be called Israel, took his entire family to Egypt over ten generations ago when a famine ravaged the land. He only returned when his sons brought him to Mamre for burial. So many Egyptians came that the place is known as Abel-mizraim to this day. It means 'mourning place of the Egyptians.'"

"Why didn't his sons return after the drought ended?" Invariably, one of my brothers would ask the question.

"Who knows?" With an expressive shrug the woman continued her tale. "They were wealthy in Egypt until Pharaoh felt threatened by their power."

"Then what happened?" I had to insert the eager question every time, even though I knew the answer.

"After many generations, Pharaoh ordered each newborn

baby boy to be killed. He thought that would crush the spirit of the Children of Israel." It was always with a sad shake of dark curls and faraway look that Mother recounted the slaughter.

"But it did not!" Now, years later, I remembered my triumphant claim. "Their god helped them."

"So it seemed." A shrug was always the response. "We know that Astarte is Queen of Heaven and the Lady who gives Victory. Even though this people claim to worship another god, perhaps it is only a manifestation of the goddess. My father always reminded me, 'My daughter, do not be confused by many gods. There is only one True God.' We think there are many when we see the different ways the god acts for we cannot understand the truth."

"But then what happened?" Anxious to move the story to my favorite part, I invariably interrupted the theological explanation.

"A great leader . . ."

"Moses!" I eagerly supplied the name.

"Yes, Moses, who was once a prince in Egypt, returned." A smile from my mother was reward for my enthusiasm. "He demanded freedom for the descendants of Jacob. When Pharaoh refused, the mighty Nile ran red like blood, insects consumed the crops and many people died. Finally, Pharaoh allowed the slaves to leave."

"Even then the wonders didn't stop!" Excitement kept me on the edge of my seat.

"Who is telling the story?" my father would demand with a laugh.

"You are right, the waters of the sea divided to let the refugees pass and return to their place to drown the Egyptian army. Since then the people have wandered the wilderness seeking their homeland." Mother completed the story with a promise. "They say that their god will tell them when it is time to settle."

The tale that entranced me as a child was almost too real now as rumors reached Jericho of the massing of the Children of Israel.

"Yes, the rabble is becoming an army." The priestess confirmed the stories when I shared the reports from various traders. "You must be vigilant. They are certain to send spies into Canaan soon. Moab has become home to some of the families, but most will seek to enter the land they claim that their god has promised them."

"Is it true that the new leader will not allow any soldier to rest until all have a place to inhabit?" I was curious about other rumors that were shared.

"Joshua is a capable general and will keep the army focused on the goal of what they call the Promised Land." A frown marred her smoothly painted face as the woman answered my inquiry. "That is why I am sure he will send spies. Keep your ears open and report anything suspicious."

I walked home with the instructions of the priestess ringing in my ears. The dusty streets passed under my feet without conscious thought. Playful children and dogs did not distract me from my confused thoughts about the approaching menace. It seemed inconceivable that any force would seek to attack the city of Jericho. However, the stories of the wonders done by the strange god for the Children of Israel hinted that this was no ordinary army.

"We are to be vigilant," I reported to my friends in a low tone. Already our guests were gathering for the evening meal.

"If they are led by their god, why do the people need a general?" It was Jerusha who asked the question that night when talk turned inevitably to the people of Israel.

"The god they follow is invisible," an elderly wine merchant responded after a satisfied belch. "Even if such a god exists, men must have a leader to go ahead of them into battle."

"Their god lives in the great gold covered box that goes ahead of the people on the march," inserted a horse trader from the Negev. "I have seen it. The priests and trumpets all in procession are quite a sight, but not such a lovely one as you, my dear."

Alone much later, I sat on the roof staring across Jericho. It was hard to imagine a multitude of men and women gathering for the invasion that many predicted. Everything seemed peaceful as I looked toward the hills not far away. Five miles away to

the east was the mighty Jordan. The floodwaters of the early harvest time in the spring kept even traders from crossing without a
long trek to the north where the Jabok entered the current.

"Surely there will be no attack at this time," I consoled
myself, not sure I believed my own words.

Spring came but no invaders were seen. The Jordan rose
higher every day. In the streets an undercurrent of hysteria was
growing. At daily gatherings in the market and at the well women
asked questions and offered fearful predictions.

"We will be consumed by their swords."

"I will offer extra sacrifices for protection."

"The women and children are part of the army."

"They will burn the city. Not a man will be left alive."

"Our children will be slaughtered."

Each day the servant girl brought a new alarm.

Esther tried to calm the fears of the girl. "The walls of Jericho
are thick and our armies are strong. No army could ever invade
the city. The defenses are too good."

I kept my own doubts to myself. If the god of Abraham, Isaac
and Jacob was as powerful as all the stories claimed, the army of
Israel would not be stopped by a wall or soldiers. Jerusha seemed
to be excited about the possibility of war, while Esther became
more fearful as the days passed.

Summer loomed. Soon the flax would be brought to us.
Neither Jerusha nor Esther enjoyed climbing onto the roof to
turn the bundles of flax so it could dry evenly. It would fall to me
to do that job as it had every harvest for six years. After it dried,
we beat the plants until the fibers separated to be spun into
thread. Esther was more than willing to spin the yarn and Jerusha
enjoyed the weaving, but drying the flax was not a task they willingly did. Even though the rough bundles scratched my arms, I
enjoyed the solitude of the rooftop too much to insist that my
friends do their share of the turning of the flax.

Preferring not to think about a possible invasion, I busied
myself with shaking out blankets, refilling lamps and trimming
wicks in preparation for the evening's guests. The tasks finished,
I wandered up to our room. As I gathered the pillows into neat

piles I allowed my mind to ponder a question raised on a rare evening when we had no guests.

"What kind of man would you marry?" Jerusha had broached the subject a week earlier. Happily she expounded on the handsome, broad-shouldered trader she preferred.

"That sounds like the son of old Ephraim, the wine seller," Esther teased. She was delighted when her sister blushed red.

"You prefer Ephraim himself, I suppose," countered the girl. "He is so rich you would never know hunger again."

"Since you have never been hungry, you do not understand what it is like," the older woman responded, flushing with anger. "If Rahab had not brought me here, I would have long ago starved without a husband to care for me. Only the kindness of the priestess allowed me to serve, even as a slave, in the Temple."

"I am sorry, sister." Abject and apologetic, Jerusha hugged her sister and the subject was forgotten.

I had no answer then and still could not envision a man who might desire me as a wife. In frustration I beat the hapless pillows as tears of self pity slid down my cheeks. I finished my frantic cleaning at the window that faced toward the hills of Canaan. The brown hills usually calmed me but not on this day.

"My mother." From somewhere deep within, I called to her. "Am I never to know what it is like to have a man care for me instead of just lust for my body? Will I never hold a child in my arms? My mother, entreat the gods for me. Astarte has closed her ears to my prayers."

"Why would you need another man?"

I whirled at the sound of an arrogant chuckle. The man tossed aside his turban and outer robe. A beckoning finger summoned me from across the room.

"Come, little Rahab, I will make you forget this foolish repining."

My feet obediently carried me across the room. Balak was a frequent visitor. Although I no longer feared him, I still hated his attention.

"I have brought the first load of flax." After his needs were satisfied, the man lounged against the pillows. "It will need to dry. My servant will bring it tomorrow and carry it to the roof for you. When ready, you will be able to spin it into the fine linen so prized by my customers."

"Yes," I agreed without enthusiasm.

I did not join the guests after Balak left. Instead I drifted into a restless sleep troubled by dreams in which I searched for a child amid armed men who snatched at my clothing.

Heavy-eyed I greeted the day, awakened by the arrival of Balak's servants with our first load of flax. Until the end of the harvest, the man would not seek my bed. I was grateful that he would be busy with his servants in the fields near Jericho. The Moabite leader had acquired much land and wealth through the patronage of the city elders. He would return to Moab with his profits to spend the winter months with his wives. The thought made me smile in relief, even as I stretched my back after carrying the last bundle to the roof and spreading the plants in the sun.

"Let us go to the market," Esther suggested one crisp morning. "The merchants from the eastern desert have new cloth. I want to find material for a harvest dress."

"You go ahead," I yawned. "I did not sleep well and want to take a nap."

"Are you alright?" A slight frown of concern crossed Esther's plump face.

"Fine, just sleepy." I waved my friends away with another yawn.

Jerusha studied me for a moment with a pucker between her eyes.

"If you are sure you'd rather stay here than shop . . ." At last the girl shrugged.

At my nod the sisters each wrapped a shawl around head and shoulders. They hurried out, eager to find some new dress or bangle for the celebration. I knew that they would be gone all day. The servant girl was gone as well, for we decided that she deserved a day with her family before the crowds arrived for the feast. Gladly the girl had hurried off to their home.

Alone, I wandered through the house, adjusting a pillow here and refolding a blanket there. It was a rare gift to be by myself. I savored each moment. The silence was soothing. Outside, Jericho hurried about her business. Officials and merchants, mothers and maidens, rich and poor, all played a part in the busy life of the city. I was happy to be apart from it for a time.

The day passed too rapidly. I paused by the window over-looking the street after arranging the pillows in our private room on the roof. Rarely did we open the shutters that kept out the noise and dust of the crowds. Afternoon shadows darkened the street as I pushed open the lattice. Pebbles and dust showered down on unsuspecting passersby. An officer glared up at me as he brushed the debris off his embroidered coat.

"Rahab, harlot of Jericho, may your house be barren," he roared angrily, causing several heads to turn.

The words stung, and I almost drew back. Some impulse of mischief made me dust off the windowsill instead. A cloud of dirt floated to the street. Most of it landed on the man's upturned face. He sputtered angrily as he spat out dust. Chuckles from the crowd emboldened me.

"Why, Omar of Gilgal, I thought you would have gone home to your wife." Innuendo heavy in my words I smiled. "Your business here, um, in Jericho, was long ago completed."

"I have been meeting with the *gal*," the man sputtered, red in the face, to the delight of listening ears. "We must all stick together against this Hebrew threat."

Immediately Omar was surrounded by eager questioners. He moved off down the street. I was forgotten. Two men lounged in the shadow of the house across the road. Curious, I watched them gesturing. Obviously there was a difference of opinion. Only when Omar was out of sight did they step out and look up at me.

"You are Rahab, and this is the Inn of Astarte?" The younger man spoke in an oddly accented voice.

"I am Rahab and this is the Inn." My nod brought a short consultation between the two strangers.

The elder kept glancing nervously around and shaking his head. He seemed to be urging his companion toward the gate.

"We seek lodging." Again it was the younger man who spoke. "We can pay."

"Very well," I agreed with a sigh. My day of solitude was over. "I will let you in."

I pulled the shutters closed and latched them. Something about the accent of my guests intrigued me. It was not one I had heard before. Walking down the stairs I tried to identify what locale these travelers could be from.

At first I thought the men had left. No one was in sight when I opened the door. Then from the shelter of the shadows below my window appeared the strangers.

"Come in." The invitation was barely needed, the two men were already inside and shutting the door.

"Is anyone else here?" For the first time the older stranger spoke.

My eyes opened wide at his pronunciation. I now recognized the accent. It was Egyptian. When I was a little girl, officials came from the Land of Kings to collect tribute from the leaders of Jericho. Often they stayed with Hamash. I could still remember the way their oddly painted eyes had searched every corner for something to tax. The finest animals were driven to the hill fields when word came of the approach of Pharaoh's agents. Jewels were hidden away and older blankets put on the pallets.

"Great masters, as you can see the year has been but a poor one." My father always begged the same excuse.

It had been years since I heard Semitic spoken with an Egyptian accent. The old Pharaoh died long ago. His successors had been too busy fighting among themselves to worry about the far-flung province of Canaan. We had gained a measure of inde-pendence even as we lost the protection of the Egyptian troops. They were withdrawn to serve in the Black Land. Now my heart beat rapidly even though the men in my house didn't look Egyptian.

"Woman." Irritation was evident in the sharp word when I did not speak.

"Do not frighten her." The warning was low. To me he added,

"We are strangers here and my friend is unsure of the customs."

The younger man laid a hand on his companion's shoulder. I shook my head and returned from my musing. A suspicion began to grow in my mind.

"You are Hebrews from beyond the Jordan." In an awed tone I voiced my thought.

The older man reached for his dagger with an oath. Again the younger stranger stopped the action.

"We are strangers seeking lodging," he repeated as deep blue eyes held mine.

My heart tumbled in fear and excitement as I stared into eyes the color of the lapis Astarte preferred. I had never seen anyone with eyes of such a hue. In their depths I saw not a horrible invader but a compassionate individual. Just a hint of a smile lingered on the lips I glimpsed beneath a brown mustache.

"All Canaan has heard of how your god delivers your enemies into your hand. No one can stand before you." Under the intense stare of my visitor I babbled almost hysterically. "The citizens of this city are afraid. We have heard of the defeat of the princes of Midian and Ammon. Our *gal* knows that Israel is encamped at Shittim, and only the waters of the Jordan keep us safe."

"Woman." A warning growl from the elder foreigner did not stop me.

The truth burst out in a torrent that surprised even me. As I spoke, I realized that I had made a decision without knowing it.

"Yet I know that your god can defeat the gods of Canaan. Surely only a true god can accomplish the mighty deeds I have heard of."

"You see, this woman will not betray us," the younger spy confidently spoke to his friend. The smile was back when the young man faced me. "Can we stay here? Are you alone?"

"For now we are alone. Jerusha and Esther will be home soon," I admitted. "The inn will be busy tonight."

"We should leave the city now." Anxiously the older man turned to the door.

"If I recognized your accent and guessed your mission, others may have as well. You cannot leave by the city gate. The officers will arrest you."

I tapped my finger against my lip in thought. What I dared to think of was treason. Yet it might be a way to save two lives. I never dreamed that it would save mine as well.

"I will hide you." My voice sounded unnaturally breathless and hoarse. I had to stop for a deep breath.

Suspiciously the older man stared at me with narrowed eyes.

"Why?" A furrow between the young man's brows indicated his confusion.

"Your god is *Adonai*. I heard of the God of Abraham, Isaac and Jacob from my mother. Her father kept the shrine of Jacob at Bethel. Even Balaam from the Land of the Two Rivers obeyed your god. Jericho will fall before you." Again my words came from some unrecognized place. "All I ask is that you spare the lives of those I hold dear."

"You have more faith than some in the camp." A brief grin lit the handsome face. "We will do as you ask."

"Come then." Anxious now, I hurried to the stairs. "Up here."

Behind me, I heard remonstrating.

"Jamal, what choice do we have?"

"If you were not entrapped by her looks, we would be out of the city already, Salma bar Nashon."

"The gates will be watched. The woman is right. You saw how that merchant looked at us. It was you who pointed out the boy running from the market toward the gates."

"On your head be our death."

"God will protect us. The woman Rahab believes."

After their discussion, the men followed me up the stairs.

"This house is built into the wall," I pointed out when we reached the upper floor. "Along the parapets the guards of Jericho stand watch."

My hand pointed out the window to a soldier lounging a block away in each direction. It was the only concession to the increased threat of invasion. More men patrolled the wall.

"Here, though, is our roof. It is above the level that the sentries can see. In the heat of the summer I often sleep out here. Now it is in use for drying flax. No one will come out."

With the ease of practice, I scrambled over the flax onto the roof. As always, my eye was drawn to the hills that had been my mother's home. I remembered our discussions about the god of Jacob whose flocks my uncles must still tend. Surely the men who stood behind me followed the same god.

Salma stood trustingly beside me. Jamal peered nervously around and kept close to the wall.

"Wait here. I will bring food and blankets. If anyone comes searching for you, the flax can cover you."

As I spoke, I arranged the stalks to form mounds rather than a flat surface. A body lying flat would be invisible, unless you actually stepped onto the roof. I left the two spies squatting beside the doorway in the deepening shadows.

Rapidly I gathered bread and fruit from the kitchen and two blankets from my own pallet where they would not be missed. I heard Jerusha calling my name as I slipped through the door onto the roof.

"Here are food and blankets." I panted a little from my haste and nervousness. "My friends have returned and soon customers will be arriving. You must remain quiet because the men will eat their evening meal and then bed down near the windows below you."

"May your generosity be blessed."

The man called Salma spoke low. His lips were close to my ear. Briefly a warm hand covered mine. I felt my face redden at the intimacy of the position. Glad of the shadows, I only nodded and slipped back through the door.

"Here I am," I responded to Jerusha who still called my name. Her voice was closer as she climbed the stairs. "I was just straightening the cushions."

We met at the doorway.

"Look what we found for you." The woman's excitement was explained as she unfurled a length of soft green Egyptian cotton.

"For me?" My hand stroked the material as my friend draped it around me. She was almost dancing with joy.

"Isn't it exquisite?" Esther appeared beside her sister. "I got some in red and Jerusha has blue."

"This must have cost many shekels," I said, still fondling the cloth in awe.

"Not so much." Esther proudly explained her bargaining tactics, "The merchant was only too glad to lower the price for a night of lodging here and a glimpse of the well-known Rahab of Jericho, the beloved of Astarte."

For some reason the allusion to my role in the house made me uncomfortable. I was sure that the men secreted on the roof could hear every word. After my confession of faith in their god, I wondered what they were thinking.

"You must wear the embroidered linen," Jerusha was urging. "You will look lovely. Somehow you always look virginal in that."

Over my protests I was hustled into the room. The slim embroidered tunic was dropped over my head after scented oils were applied to my arms and throat. Esther arranged my hair so that it appeared artfully disordered. With a nod she secured her work with a comb.

"Go on downstairs. I hear someone at the door." Jerusha gave me a shove. "We will be down soon."

Sighing slightly, I trotted down the stairs to open the door. Three men stood outside. One was obviously the Egyptian cloth merchant. His black squared-off wig and kohl-rimmed eyes told the nationality before he spoke. Timon from Shechem, a regular visitor, grinned a greeting. The third man was one of Balak's shepherds. I knew he came to collect his master's percentage of the profits for the month.

"Come in, gentlemen." As cordially as six years of practice taught me, I ushered the men inside. "I am Rahab. Welcome to the Inn of Astarte."

"Well did your friends speak of your beauty, Rahab, beloved of the gods." It was the Egyptian who spoke effusively. "Surely not even Isis is so beautiful."

A broad hand reached out and caressed my cheek. With the ease of experience, I moved my head and turned to lead the way to the cushioned alcove across the room. Timon frowned with almost brotherly protectiveness and Balak's man chuckled at my evasion.

"Come, gentlemen." Jerusha crossed the room and beckoned our guests to be seated. "Rahab will bring food and drink."

Grateful for the interruption, I moved to the kitchen where a jar of wine waited. A brief thought of the men hidden on the roof caused me to bite my lip with misgiving.

"God of spies, keep them silent," I breathed, fearful that a stumbling movement or cough would betray my secret.

With the jar of wine on my shoulder and a platter of meat in my hand I crossed the room. Esther took the tray while Jerusha began to pour the wine. Her cheerful chatter kept the men entertained and even diverted my mind from my hidden visitors.

At the sound of heavy pounding, however, I was roughly reminded. When I opened the door my breath caught in fear. A captain and four armed soldiers stood impatiently in the street.

"Where are the men who came to you this afternoon?" The captain spoke in a curt tone, bringing his torch close to the door to illuminate his face and mine.

"This afternoon?" I pretended ignorance. "Our evening guests have just arrived."

"The strangers that came here from the market," the man snarled.

"Oh." I pretended sudden understanding and hoped my wide-eyed act was believable. "They did not linger. When I learned they had no money, I sent them away."

"When was this?" Suspiciously, the soldier peered more closely at me.

"Before the gates were shut." Vaguely, I shrugged as though uninterested in men who had no money. "I suppose they went out and have gone away. Were they thieves?"

"Those two men were spies from the camp of Israel. They came to see our defenses. You have let them escape," he spoke accusingly.

I opened my eyes even wider and in pretended shock gasped, "Spies! How dreadful! You must stop them before they can reach the crossing! We will all be slaughtered in our beds!"

It was an impressive performance gleaned from watching the reaction of many of the other women in town. I even clung to the captain's arm as if in terror.

"You are sure that they are gone?" Some of the sternness was gone from countenance and voice as I pressed close to the man.

"If I had known who they were I would have cajoled them into remaining so you could arrest them." With a pout and a sniff of pretended tears I added, "How can you think that I would hide spies? I serve the Lady of Victory."

"No, no." My interrogator hastily patted my arm. I was not sure if he was more alarmed by my tears or my reminder that I was in the service of the goddess. "It is just that no one saw them leave."

"Would you like to search this house?" I stepped back and gestured regally for the troop to enter.

"I . . . well . . . yes . . . perhaps it would be wise." Decision made, the captain signaled for two soldiers to follow.

The trio accompanied me on a tour of the house. Every room was opened for inspection.

"What is this?" Jerusha was outraged at the interruption.

"The captain believes that we have sheltered some Hebrew spies." My voice was loud with feigned outrage.

As I hoped, an outcry erupted from our guests that would cover any movement on the roof. I prayed that the men had hidden themselves.

"Captain, what do you base this on?"

"Hebrew spies in Jericho!"

"Is no place safe from this scourge?"

"How can you accuse Rahab of such action?"

"Egypt is well rid of such trouble causing rabble."

It took several minutes for order to be restored. Somewhat sheepishly the captain tried to explain.

"The men were heard in the market. Their accent gave them away as spies. A boy followed them here, but no one saw them leave. It is my duty." The man straightened his back as if to intimidate us.

"Are you satisfied that none but our evening guests are

here?" Jerusha questioned in a voice that dripped sarcasm. "Or are you going to search the rooftops too?"

I had to clench my fists to stop the sound of dismay that rose to my lips.

"Yes, yes," the soldier nodded, "just a quick look at the roof."

"We are drying flax there." Esther entered the conversation for the first time. "There would not be room for a man to hide."

"It is my duty." The man stubbornly stood his ground.

"Follow me." With what I hoped was the appearance of willingness I led the way up the stairs and opened the door to the roof.

I did not dare breathe as the captain held his torch out to shed light on the piles of flax. I smiled when he turned back into the room.

"My apologies," the man mumbled on the way back to the downstairs room.

"You were just doing your duty." Filled with relief I could absolve the soldier now.

"Enjoy your evening." His parting words to our guests were almost a leer.

"Perhaps the men are yet within your reach," I suggested somewhat haughtily. "If you hurry you might intercept them before they reach the Jordan. May the goddess speed you on your way."

"Never fear, we will find the spies and if we learn that you did aid them . . ." A hand clenched on sword hilt left little doubt as to the result.

"I serve the Queen of Heaven." My words offered their own threat.

The captain set off at a rapid trot toward the gate. I clung to the doorpost for a moment before turning back to the inn.

"Thanks be to the god of the Hebrew spies. You have acted to save your servants," I whispered, a brief prayer into the night. A cool night breeze brushed my cheeks like a comforting caress.

The room was buzzing with talk of the search and the possibility of invasion by the refugees from Egypt. Jerusha and Esther plied the men with wine as they talked. The merchant from the

Land of Kings was vocal in his condemnation of the nation and scorn of their god.

"I was just a boy when Pharaoh drove the rabble from our borders. The talk of blood in the water and plagues on the land are lies created by this people to cover their own treachery. They claim to have a god who leads them, but what god would abandon the faithful in the Desert of Sinai?"

Eventually our drunken guests staggered to their rooms. The subject of the refugees from Egypt was thoroughly exhausted. Balak's servant lay across the front door. In our room, Jerusha and Esther confronted me.

"Why did the soldiers come here looking for spies? Did they seriously think we would help the enemies of Jericho?" As always my friend was outspoken.

Briefly, I admitted to having spoken to a pair of strangers in the afternoon. What I did not share was the way one handsome young man smiled at me. I knew I would dream of deep blue eyes that sparkled above the broad mouth.

"I had no idea they were spies." My shocked confession was convincing.

There were no more questions. After a few more complaints about the rudeness of the captain, my friends bid me good night.

"It has been an upsetting evening," I stated, opening the door to the roof. "Go on to bed. I want to sit in the moonlight until I am calm."

"I will never understand you." Jerusha shook her head but made no other argument to my stepping out into the night.

I knew my friends believed it was devotion to Astarte that drove me to the solitude of the moonlight. More often it was my search for a real god to believe in.

Before long even breathing told me that my companions slept. Still I sat beside the door watching the moon travel down the arch of the sky until darkness was complete. Finally, I softly closed the door and tiptoed out onto the roof.

"It is safe." The whisper sounded loud in the dark silence.

A rustle of flax and Salma's head emerged from a pile to my

right. The man sat up and nudged a nearby lump. A second figure materialized.

"The soldiers have gone to search for you toward the Jordan."
I felt I owed the men an explanation. "If you go into the hills and
wait until the patrols return, you should have no trouble reaching your camp."

A nod of agreement signified approval to my suggestion.

"You are wise as well as beautiful."

Surprisingly touched by the young man's words, I felt tears in
my eyes.

A terse question came from the other man, "What payment
do you want?"

"Just that you spare my household when your god gives
Jericho into your hand." My request was bold but seemed to meet
with approval.

For the first time, the older spy nodded and I saw a hint of a
smile in the dark.

"You are indeed a wise woman. If you do not tell our business to anyone, we shall truly spare all in this house." I heard the
promise with relief.

"In the Name of the Living God, as you saved our lives, so
will we save you and yours." Salma placed his hand over his
heart as he made the oath.

My breath caught at the solemnity of the moment and tears
tickled the back of my eyes. I refused to acknowledge the sudden
longing to be forever protected by this young man and his god
that rose in my heart. Instead I moved softly to the outer edge of
the roof.

"I will lower you from here. Astarte has gone to her bed.
There is little chance of the sentries seeing you along the wall in
the darkness. Zalmuth lies beside the door so you cannot leave
that way even if there were not eyes in the alleyway."

"As you say." I saw a flash of teeth as the young man smiled.

It was the work of a moment to link the ropes that had tied
the bundles of flax together. Jamal tested the knots and nodded
satisfaction.

Salma issued instructions, "You will go first. I will hold the rope. Rahab, will you be able to bear my weight as I descend?"

"I am stronger than I look," I assured the young man with a smile.

Quickly the older, heavier spy slipped over the edge and disappeared down the wall as Salma played out the rope slowly.

"May the God of Abraham, Isaac and Jacob be with you until we meet again." The brief blessing was followed by a brotherly kiss on the forehead before the young man began his descent.

I had to brace my feet and lean back against the rope wrapped around my body to keep it from slipping through my hands as I felt the full weight of the Hebrew. In a short time the tension went slack. Leaning over the edge I could just see the two men disappear into the underbrush. Reeling in the rope, I rolled it into a coil before allowing my hand to go to the crimson belt Salma draped around my neck as a final gesture.

"Hang this in your window." I remembered the softly issued order. "When the Lord God gives us victory, we will be blameless of your life if this is not hanging from your window. Because you did not betray us, your life and the lives of your family are sacred to God."

7

OCCASIONALLY I PONDERED THE words "sacred to God" in the days that followed. It was a strangely comforting phrase. A disgruntled patrol returned to Jericho after three days of fruitless searching for the spies.

"Onan told Sarah, who told Hannah, who told me that there was no trace, not even a footprint of the men." Jerusha shared the information with us when she returned from the well a week after my clandestine night's work.

"How can that be?" Esther asked in amazement.

"Perhaps they were not men but angels," I suggested slyly.

"Do not be silly," scolded my friend. "They were men. You said yourself that you talked to them."

"Well," I shrugged, "then maybe their god hid them."

Neither of my associates suspected the truth. No one commented on the new decoration hanging in the window of our upper room. Tied to the lattice was the scarlet rope. At night, before sliding between my blankets, I often touched the reminder of Salma's promise.

"God of Salma and the Children of Israel, how can I find you? You really do seem greater than Astarte. You are mighty and freed the captive nation but can you free me from this bondage?"

There was never any answer. The god of Salma was as silent as Astarte who calmly rose and set. Sometimes I wondered if the young man and his companion had safely reached the camp at Shittim. Almost impatiently I listened for news. The Feast of Astarte would soon be celebrated. Already a maiden was selected and secreted in the Temple to learn the ways of Astarte.

It was a renewed sense of dread and increased patrols of soldiers that hinted at an imminent danger. The winter growth of barley was harvested under the watchful eye of armed soldiers.

"The Hebrews are on the march." Balak's servant confirmed my suspicions when he arrived to collect the monthly rent and the linen thread spun by Esther and Jerusha. "This will be bad for business, says my master. Already the chief of Gilgal has secretly allied himself with Joshua. That will give the rabble a foothold not five miles from the walls of this city. I must return swiftly lest I be trapped within Jericho."

"What are we to do?" Esther looked very fearful.

Jerusha moved close to her sister. With a hug, she spoke with reassurance. "We will survive as we always have."

"You are to stay here and keep the inn open." The servant from Moab issued his master's instructions. He offered the suggestion of hope. "I do not think that the Hebrew can breech the walls of this city. They will give up and turn in another direction. You will be safe."

"Do you really think so?" Esther eagerly grasped the assurance.

The man brusquely snarled the response, "Have I not said so?"

"Which is why you hasten to return to Moab?" For the first time I spoke.

Balak's steward looked down in a brief embarrassment. He was aware of the sarcasm in my voice.

"My master bids me hasten." His excuse was hollow, as was the assurance he offered. "The marauders could move west from Gilgal into the hills toward Bethel and Shechem. Those are the holy places for their god. They will not attack a city such as Jericho. The fortifications here are too strong."

I had heard all the boasting before and interrupted, "Go to your master then. Tell Balak that the women will remain to see that his investment does not perish."

"My master will expect an accounting when he comes again." The words were a warning.

"Balak will receive what he is due when he comes." I lifted my chin and stared straight at the servant of the man I despised. My eyes were slits of disgust.

"Of course, I meant nothing." Stammering under my gaze the man hastily wrapped the turban around his head.

Barely taking time to fling on his cloak, Balak's servant hurried away from the house.

"If he comes"—the oath was spoken only to myself—"there may be nothing for his trouble."

I had no time to waste on rage toward the man and his master. My friends needed me. Esther sobbed in terror while sitting on the lowest step. Even Jerusha expressed fear for the first time.

She grabbed my arm and wailed, "We are women, servants of the gods of this city; no mercy will be shown us. Where can we flee to?"

"As servants of the gods, we must trust the gods," I replied. "Astarte will protect her own."

My mind and hope was not on the statue in the Temple, however. I was placing my trust in a young man with deep blue eyes whose smile visited me in the night. The red cord in the upper window reminded me that I had the sworn promise of Salma of Israel. The time was not right to tell my friends, so I sought to comfort them with empty words of faith in Astarte. Each day brought a new alarm. It was hard to watch the increasing terror in Esther's eyes.

With the end of the barley harvest, the annual spring flooding of the Jordan arrived. I could barely believe the report brought by a trader from Zarethan one evening. The town was a day's walk to the north. The man leaned forward and gestured wildly to emphasize his news.

"I saw it myself!" At our skeptical faces the voice cracked as the trader repeated his claim. "From the fords at Adam to the Salt Sea, the waters of the Jordan dried up!"

"How can such a thing be?" Jerusha voiced the question on all our minds.

My heart began to beat rapidly at the explanation the man offered.

"The priests of Israel stepped into the River with the ark of their god. The waters simply stopped flowing. The Children of Israel crossed on dry land! They have set up an altar on this side of the Jordan with twelve stones taken from the riverbed. It took all day for the people to cross. The priests stood still in the channel. Their sandals were not even damp."

"You saw this yourself?" the words breathlessly burst out.

"I saw the dry river and the multitude of people on this side, yes," the man affirmed with a nod.

"Then they are only a few miles from the city," Esther wailed in fear. "We are doomed."

"Pretty lady, do not despair." Our visitor patted the plump hand. "This rabble has turned north, toward Gilgal."

Reassured, the woman allowed our guest to hold her hand. Jerusha refilled the goblet with the strong spiced wine the inn was famous for. Talk turned to more entertaining subjects, such as the Festival a week away.

"I wish I could stay in Jericho. I hear that the ritual union of Astarte will be special this year. The priests want to call down protection for the city."

"So we have been told," Jerusha nodded. The information was widely shared in the marketplace. "Have another cup of wine. Perhaps Astarte will send you a dream."

Later, as I pointed out the pallet in his chamber, the man groped for my hand.

"You were the Daughter of Astarte. Tell me about it." His slurred words and staggering step left little doubt that our visitor would soon be asleep.

"There is time later for such stories." I gently removed my hand and with a slight shove directed the man toward the bed.

He stumbled forward, "Later, pretty lady . . ."

Turban and cloak tumbled to the floor only slightly ahead of their owner who toppled onto the blankets and was snoring before the curtain fell into place. I made my way to the room I shared with Jerusha and Esther. Astarte did not shine but I knew where the scarlet cord hung motionless in the window. Gently I touched the talisman.

"God of Israel, you are mighty," I confessed under my breath to the night sky. "To stop the mighty Jordan's flood so your people might cross on dry land is an event unheard of. None of the gods of Canaan have done such a thing. I know that you have indeed given this land into the hand of Joshua and his armies. Let them remember the promise of the spies so that I too might find freedom."

I fell asleep to dream of Salma and his companion standing on the bank of the Jordan. Morning light through the lattice awakened me. The trader from Zarethan stumbled down the stairs late. Esther was ready to cover the bread and bean curd set out for our meal. Rapidly the man stuffed his mouth and hurried to the market.

I agreed to take the water basket to the well in the absence of our serving girl. She recently married a guest from Ai. Both Esther and Jerusha accompanied me as if afraid of staying in the house alone. All the streets were abuzz with fearful speculation. The man from Zarethan was not the only person to have seen the nation of Israel cross a dry riverbed.

"It was as though there had never been water!"

"The soldiers are without number."

"Our gods will save us."

The last sentiment was uttered by the priest of Baal. He stood in his chariot, surrounded by servants and subordinates. Not a hair of his oiled and curled beard was out of place.

"Bring offerings to Baal and to Astarte. No desert tribe has a god who can stand before the mighty Lady of Victory." Loudly the man intoned promises. "The gods are testing us. If we will remain faithful, we need not fear these nomads. Like a wind they will be gone. Already they turn north from Jericho. Behold, the feast of the great goddess is near. Astarte will rise and trouble this rabble when we bring acceptable tribute to her feet. The Lady will send scorpions and snakes among the rabble."

"Yes, we must make offerings to Astarte."

"I will bring the finest of my flocks."

"The goddess will save us."

"The rising of Astarte will see the defeat of these refugees."

Fear was turned to hope as each person took comfort in the presence and assurance of the priest. Plans were made to placate the goddess.

"What is the meaning of the dry river?" From the edge of the crowd rang out the question. "Their god dried the Jordan so the invaders could cross."

Again the air was filled with fearful exclamations until the priest overrode the noise.

"It was a rock slide that stopped the waters above Adam. The living water is flowing freely today. Astarte has now entrapped these outsiders. She will ride forth on her winged lion. The army of the rabble will be overconfident and fall into disarray against the armies of Canaan."

I admired the man for his confidence. Once again the men and women were reassured.

"Bring your finest offerings to the Temple. Then will we find safety in the wings of protection that spread over Jericho."

With this final reminder, the priest and his retinue solemnly moved on up the street toward the Temple.

"I am going to give Astarte the silk cloth from Egypt," announced Jerusha. "It is my most prized possession. Surely the gods will heed such a gift. Fortunately, I have not yet made it into a gown."

"Of course, it is perfect. Blue is the color of the goddess." Esther eagerly joined the plan. "I too will give my length of cloth. What about you, Rahab?"

I turned from watching the almost desperate eagerness with which many of the people were discussing their offerings.

"You may have my silk also." The statement was made with an offhanded shrug. "If a gift to Astarte makes you feel secure, I will not stop you."

"Do not you believe Astarte will keep the city safe?" Esther was appalled by my disinterest.

"What I believe will have little bearing on the actions of any god." If I sounded slightly cynical my friend did not notice. They did not seem to hear my next comment either. "The priests play on the fears of the people to enrich the Temple. We have seen that for ourselves."

"I will take the cloth to the Temple myself," Esther stated.

She hurried back to our home with Jerusha close behind. I followed more slowly. The words of the priest had not brought any religious fervor into my heart. Instead I was saddened by the greed of the Temple leaders.

Esther became obsessed with placating the gods. Each day she carried our profits to the coffers outside the Temple. Women were not allowed inside the building, even those who had served within the walls. I was angry when I learned that one of the young priests had rudely refused to accept an offering from my friend.

"Astarte has no need for the soiled offerings of harlots. Perhaps the men of Israel will find your favors pleasing and spare you."

With coarse words and even blows the woman was driven from the Temple precincts. Spirit broken, Esther refused to leave her room. She wept endlessly. Even Jerusha was unable to comfort her sister.

Rumors swirled in the city. We heard the armies of Israel camped just north of Gilgal. The chief of that city greeted them as friends. Such news did not ease Esther's fears. More and more soldiers patrolled the streets. Every stranger was scrutinized closely.

"It is a huge encampment." A flax merchant from the hills around Ephron made his report.

The man lounged in our room with a cup of the spiced wine in his long fingers. A plate of roasted lamb was within reach. Our business had diminished with the Israelites so close. The merchant was the first to arrive in a week.

"Have they indeed circumcised every man?" Jerusha curiously asked.

A grunted nod was the man's reply. He chewed the slice of meat before explaining, "It is true. In the middle of hostile territory their god demands mutilation."

Our guest shifted uncomfortably as though feeling the flint knife himself.

"Perhaps their god protects them," I suggested.

"So it would appear," assented the merchant. "The chief of Gilgal has been visited by emissaries from Ai and Bethel but an alliance is slow in forming against this people."

"What will happen?" Jerusha wanted to know.

Our visitor shrugged, "Who can tell? I return to my home tomorrow. The land of my fathers will not fall to invaders without a fight. We will be prepared to defend our homes."

In the morning we heard the tramp of a troop of soldiers marching down the street. It appeared that at last Jericho was arming herself.

"They are preparing for battle," Jerusha spoke in a subdued tone.

"What will we do?" her sister darted panic-stricken looks around the room as if she was a trapped animal.

It was then that I took the women into my confidence.

"We will not die." My confident statement caught the attention of my friends.

"How can you say that?" Jerusha stared at me in disbelief. "I thought you did not trust Astarte."

"When the armies of Israel come against Jericho, it will fall." My reply was not the answer she sought.

Esther sobbed and Jerusha glared at me. I held up my hand when she would have spoken again.

With a nod of reassurance I announced, "We in this house will be spared."

"How can you promise such nonsense?" the younger sister sputtered angrily.

"I have the oath of the spies." The admission was not easy to make.

"You did hide them!" Jerusha was shocked. "I would never have believed such treachery."

Remembering Salma's parting kiss, I shrugged, "They were young men. How could I see them slain?"

"You are not often easily persuaded." Suspicious eyes stared at me.

Leaning forward, I tried to explain my gradually developing

beliefs. "This god of theirs has brought the Children of Israel so far. No one will be able to stand against them. We have heard of the miracles in Egypt. A god who frees slaves and feeds a multitude in the wilderness is a great god. The armies of Ammon and Midian have fallen. Balak himself was powerless against the invasion. If not for the settling of a few of the people within the borders, Moab would be no more. Canaan is a land long promised to these people. My mother told me of the shrine still kept at Bethel for making offerings to this god from generation to generation."

Esther was no longer crying. She stared at me in astonishment.

"You believe this?" The question was incredulous.

"Yes, Jericho will fall, but anyone within this house will be spared." I was surprised by the confidence in my voice. "The gods are shadows of the great Power that underlies all. Perhaps this invisible god is really god."

"Astarte is the Lady of Victory," Jerusha stated. "The priests say that Astarte will save Jericho."

"Do the priests accept Esther's offerings? No. They scorn her as harlot even though she serves Astarte as we do." My arguments were irrefutable. "Do not the Ammonites, Midianites and Moabites worship Astarte as well? Did the gods of Ammon or Midian save them?"

Both my friends stared at me. Doubt and confusion, as well as suspicion, registered on each face. I stood silent waiting for a response. If the women did not believe me, then my life was forfeit. The sisters looked at each other.

"God of the Hebrew who I have confessed." In my heart a prayer began. "Let Jerusha and Esther see that you are their only hope for safety."

Finally Esther spoke, "I can see that you do believe that this god of the Hebrews is greater than Astarte. You are right; the priests no longer want our offerings despite our loyal service. If this god and the spies do not betray your trust, I too will believe."

I accepted the hand she held out. Convulsively the woman grasped my fingers as if it was a lifeline.

Jerusha added her pledge, "One god is like another. Astarte has never blessed me. I have not known you to be wrong in judging a man. I too will trust your spies and their god."

The next day brought confirmation of the merchant's story. Joshua, leader of the Children of Israel, was indeed camped with the forces north of Gilgal. He had ordered every man to be circumcised.

Awe and amazement were equally mixed in the comments whispered from woman to woman around the well and in the market.

"Their god is a fool to ask such a sacrifice."

"Can it be true that all the soldiers have been circumcised?"

"What faith it must take for grown men to agree to the act."

"Gabeath Haaraloth is the new name of the place."

"A hill of foreskins has been created," joked Jerusha. She easily translated the unfamiliar name for her sister. "What do you think of your fine soldiers now, Rahab? Our army will fall on them while in pain and wipe them from the face of the earth."

Surprisingly, neither the fighting men from Gilgal and the hill communities nor the troops from Jericho moved against Joshua's army. The leaders and priests concentrated on the Feast of Astarte. The holy union took place as every year. Promises of safety and protection from the gods were greeted with cheers. Still the army of Jericho remained within the walls.

"Why doesn't the chief of Jericho attack?" On every street corner the question was debated.

"Astarte has promised to give us victory," Esther insisted with pathetic hopefulness.

"Fear of the god of the Israelites holds them back," I told my friend.

"I cannot stand the suspense." There were tears in the woman's eyes.

"We will be safe." Even the reminder did not ease her fear.

We had no customers. The gates of Jericho were closed. No strangers or travelers were allowed within the walls as a defense against spies from the Hebrew camp.

It was odd to sit quietly in the evening with no men to enter-

tain and ply with wine or beer. I did not mind that the profits
were affected. Even Esther seemed to relax when nothing happened. At night I stared out the window. Between my fingers I
held the scarlet belt left by Salma.

"God of the Hebrews, you are indeed mighty." My whisper to
the night was a plea. "You strike terror in the hearts of the leaders and gods of Canaan. Move swiftly to free me."

One tear trickled down my cheek and I sighed almost impatiently. It was hard waiting for this strange, nameless god to act.
Yet somehow I knew that something would happen soon.

Another day and night passed. Rumors were rampant that
battle was imminent. From my window I could see the empty
valley between Jericho and the hills. It was clear that the talk of
approaching war was false. The armies of Joshua were not surrounding the city. They were nowhere in sight. So it was with
astonishment that I awakened to the heavy sound of tramping
feet. At first I could not identify the noise. I sat up on my pallet,
rubbing sleep from my eyes. The steady marching did not come
from within Jericho but from outside the walls. The realization
sent me scrambling to the window.

"They are here." Jerusha joined me. Her voice was tinged
with excitement. "Your Israelites are in front of Jericho!"

I pushed open the lattice and caught my breath. Rank after
rank of silent armed men paraded past. Spear points glinted in
the morning light. The only sound from the troops was the thud
of feet on sand and the rustle of leather shields against leather
breastplates on broad chests. It was awe inspiring.

Esther crept up beside us. Her plump fingers gripped the
edge of the window in terror.

"Will they attack?" the quivering whisper betrayed the
woman's terror.

"I do not know." A shrug and shake of the head was the only
response I could make.

By mid-morning the army had marched back to Gilgal. Only
then did we move from our window. Curious about the reaction
in the city to the unusual events I dressed rapidly. At the well
there was near panic. Women who had hidden inside all morn-

ing now clustered together as much for courage as to draw the needed water.

"The armies of Israel—did you see them?"

"There are so many armed soldiers!"

"Why did we not shoot arrows at them?"

"They were so strangely silent."

"It was terrifying!"

"Did you see the golden ark of their god that is carried ahead of the troops?"

"If their god fights we are doomed!"

Even the men of the city were stunned by the display. In small groups they gathered near the Temple. I was unnoticed in the shadow of the alley. The priests stood on the steps.

"Astarte, Lady of Victory, will save us." Still the servants of the goddess insisted on the supremacy of the stone figure in the center of the Temple.

"We have been faithful, unlike the people of Ammon and Moab." The High Priest tried to offer courage. "The Feast of Astarte and her union with Baal were not interrupted by this threat. Our gods will protect us for we honor them."

"Even the chief of Gilgal has fallen away," shouted one of the city elders. "Our northern approaches are unprotected because of his treachery."

"May Astarte strike down the one who gives our enemy haven." The proclamation loudly came from several priests.

A cheer greeted the curse.

"Great is Astarte! Honor to the Queen of Heaven! Praise to Astarte and her consort!" Several priests took up a chant that was repeated by the crowd.

I slipped away and wandered home. The streets were oddly silent. Everyone, it seemed, was at the Temple or hiding inside. Jerusha and Esther were not in the house.

When they returned, Esther reported, "The priests sacrificed a dozen goats and a bull with mounds of wheat to influence the goddess."

"The crowds were impressed by the flames and smell of

incense." Jerusha smiled as though remembering the event. "It was very exciting."

"Yes, everyone fell prostrate when the flames leapt up after the priests invoked Astarte. Then trumpets sounded from within the Temple."

Jerusha added, "All the men were reassured by the words of the High Priest when he called the flames an omen. 'See how our mighty goddess will scorch the heels of the invaders.' I have never heard such cheering."

I absently agreed with the comments. "I am sure it was grand."

"Do you still doubt that Astarte will protect Jericho?" Esther challenged. "The city has beggared herself with offerings. Surely the gods will listen."

"You know as well as I that the priests can create illusion for the faithful. Yet how much of it is real?" I did not directly answer my friend.

I could offer no reassurance. In my heart I was sure that Astarte would not descend riding on a winged lion to help the men of Jericho withstand Joshua's army, despite the priestly protestations. I recalled my father's insistence that the city was well fortified and protected by the ramparts of sharp stones and the outer wall.

"Their god opened a path through the waters from Egypt, provided food for the multitude in the desert and dried up the Jordan. What good are walls of stone against such a god?" I mused to myself, unaware that I spoke aloud until Esther gasped.

"Then you do think we are doomed!" Her anguished sob made me turn.

Jerusha hurried to her sister. An angry look was directed toward me. I took a step toward my friends. They drew back.

"We are safe in this house. That is the promise of the spies." The reminder did not ease the palpable fear in the room.

Esther continued to sob. Her doubts had returned. I could see that she had no faith in either the goddess she once served or the unknown god of the invaders that I tried to explain. The woman turned away when I reached out to offer consolation.

With a sneer, Jerusha asked, "Do you really believe that the spies will honor a promise made to a prostitute sworn to a foreign god?"

The accusation hurt. I wanted to scream a denial; instead I answered softly, "The men swore by their god. Yes, I believe they will spare all in this house."

"You are a naïve and foolish girl." The woman tossed the words over her shoulder as she led Esther from the room.

There was no friendly conversation that night. We ate a simple meal of hummus and flat bread in near silence. Jerusha only put out one piece of bread for each of us.

"We do not know how long this siege will last," she pointed out to her sister. "We must conserve our food and money for as long as possible."

I was left alone with the empty platters when my companions sought their pallets. With a sigh I carried them down the stairs to stack with the other dishes. The women appeared to be asleep when I returned to our upper room.

Rest was far from me. I stood at the window looking out across the moonlit landscape. A partial moon illuminated the deserted network of roads converging on Jericho. Astarte seemed distant and unmoved by the cares of the world. Beyond the highway, fields were covered with what looked like soft fur in the night. Day would show the hint of green in the awakening fields. Below my window, the deeply gouged, treacherous rock-strewn buttresses were meant to entrap invaders so that arrows could be shot into them from the walls. The hills, not so far away, stood as shadowed sentinels over Jericho. It did seem that the city was impregnable and that the armies of Israel would be trapped between city and mountains.

I thought of the multitude within the walls of Jericho who prayed and believed that, in the union with Baal, Astarte promised protection from the nearby enemies. Surely the chief of the city had already sent word to his allies among the hills for aid. My hand sought the red cord. I gripped the talisman tightly. The promise from the young Hebrew, Salma, was the hope I clung to.

"Surely the God of the Hebrew did not bring them this far to desert the army now," I told myself as the moon slowly slid behind the hill leaving all in darkness. "I will continue to trust in this god whose power seems greater than anything I have seen from Astarte. Perhaps in the camp of Israel I could become someone else besides Rahab the Harlot. I could be a refugee, a woman without a past."

Comforted by dreams of a new life, I finally fell asleep at the window. My head was pillowed by my arms and the red strand remained clenched in my fist. Morning chill, trumpets and the thud of marching feet awakened me only a short time later. Startled awake, I looked out at the procession of the Children of Israel.

First in the parade, marched trumpeters blowing instruments of ram's horn. Others blew the more familiar bronze trumpets also used in Jericho to announce an official or summon worshippers to the Temple. Fanfare after fanfare sounded until the air vibrated. I felt my heart thrill at the display. Myriads of armed men were led by a gilded box. It was the ark of the God of Israel borne by linen-clad priests. This was followed by more trumpeters. A great procession of soldiers fell in behind the symbol of the presence of their god. One circuit of Jericho was made. Again the army marched north after the show of force, which took all morning to complete. Rank after rank filed past my window and around the city. I tried to pick out the men who came as spies. From the distance all the faces looked alike.

Jerusha and Esther joined me at the window but they did not speak a word to me.

"I do not want to watch." The older sister buried her face in Jerusha's shoulder.

"Then come downstairs." My friend added a scornful aside, "Rahab can watch for her saviors. Let her believe that a red belt would be recognized by destroying warriors."

It was lonely at the window. My own faith in the unknown god trembled. I desired companionship from my friends. It would have been easy to seek the women out and tell them that I had repented of my betrayal of Astarte. They were nowhere in sight when I came down the stairs after the Hebrew forces marched out of sight. I decided to walk to the market.

Although it was nearing midday, men, women and merchants were just emerging from their homes to engage in the daily commerce now that the threat had marched back to Gilgal.

"What kind of game is this?" I heard the question blurted in a familiar voice when I passed a group of men.

Curious about the answer, I turned to look at my father and his companions. It was easy to see why he confronted the men. The lengthy fringe on their garments easily identified them as important officials.

"Hamash, the chief has counseled patience," the taller man responded.

"We do not know the intention of this display." His associate tried to speak placating words.

"Not know the intention!" My father was livid. "Does your master think the armies of Israel are out for a stroll? We cower like frightened pups behind our walls while this Joshua parades past with thousands of armed men. A few arrows into the pack would create a panic in that rabble."

One of the counselors lowered his voice. I could hardly hear the reply. "Hamash, we must wait for support from our allies. Even you can see that we are outnumbered."

I saw my father narrow his eyes. He looked from face to face.

"Just where is this help to come from?" The man's voice dripped sarcasm. "Gilgal has shown she will not raise a finger. Moab and Ammon are defeated. What forces can Bethel or Ai muster?"

"If attack came from the hills and our walls at the same time, we could rout the Hebrews. They are only sons of slaves. What do such men know of war?" the elder statesman insisted.

When my father shook his head, I noticed with a slight shock that his hair and beard were entirely gray. He wore them neatly crimped and oiled, but I realized that he was becoming an old man.

"Our defenses will keep the invaders out. That is why there has been no attack," added the other official.

"Believe what you will." With a shake of his head, Hamash turned away. "Tell the chief that I counsel showering the next procession with arrows and stones. If they stand firm, we will know their mettle."

I watched the man stalk away. Although I had not seen him recently I suddenly felt sorrow that my father would die when the Children of Israel triumphed as I knew they would. Deep in thought I purchased a small bundle of carrots and a measure of wheat. Already prices had edged up. I barely noticed as I pondered my dilemma.

"He is my father; I should do what I can to save him," my heart whispered.

From my mind came an argument, "Hamash disavowed you since you chose service to Astarte over marriage. He has not come to see you since your mother was laid in her tomb."

"I must try to save his life. The man cherished me. He was proud when I became the Daughter of Astarte." The affection of my childhood begged to be heard.

"The man could report you as a conspirator." Reason attempted to be heard.

I was distracted when I set about preparing the evening meal. My mind circled around and around the issue like a dog with a bone.

"Where is your mind?" Jerusha's sharp question reminded me I was not alone.

"What?" Startled, I turned my head.

"You are going to add too much salt to the beans." My friend pointed to the jar in my hand.

"Oh . . . I . . . uh . . . I was thinking." Confused, I stared at the container.

It did indeed hold salt, but the spoon was much too large.

"I am glad you saw that." My laugh sounded flat. "There is no telling what taste sensation I might have created."

As soon as the meal was finished and the platters stacked in their places, I wandered up to the roof. A strong wind from the hills swept across the plain. It caused me to shiver when I heard the sound howling in the cracks along the walls.

"Why must all die?" The question was asked of the wind and the gathering clouds that obscured Astarte on her journey.

I knew the answer. It was the same in all holy wars. In the name of Astarte the armies of Canaan had burned and ravaged other cities not more than a couple of generations earlier. My mother told me how the sons of Jacob had destroyed Shechem in the northern mountains in order to protect their sister's honor. Now the descendents of those men threatened the gates of Jericho.

"Is death and destruction really all that the gods want?" I wondered aloud to the darkness, not really expecting an answer.

I remained on the rooftop until the evening chill drove me inside. Esther and her sister already slept. They were not troubled by thoughts of the gods. Even the encroaching army did not seem to affect their slumber. Feeling very alone, I rolled into my blankets and soon drifted into a restless sleep troubled with dreams of blood and fire.

❦ 8 ❧

FOR A THIRD MORNING, dawn brought trumpets and marching feet to awaken me. Today, women with tambourines danced among the musicians. It seemed almost mocking. Esther refused to leave the house. Jerusha walked with me to the well after the army marched back northward. My friend was silent. I did not try to interrupt her thoughts; there were too many questions in my own mind. Along the streets the speculation was about the strange actions of the invaders.

"See how little the sons of slaves fear us. Their women march with the army."

"What manner of woman would dance before soldiers in that way?"

"It must be true that the Hebrew women have no shame."

"What incantation were they chanting?"

"Praise to their god. That is what my Embaal said."

"They dare not attack, says my father. Jericho is too strong."

"There are many men in that army."

"Have you seen them?"

"All of them are strong and well muscled."

I had to smile slightly at the sigh of pleasure that accompanied the last comment. Then I remembered that those strong muscles would be used to destroy all of Jericho. Tears clogged my throat at the thought that all these gossiping women would die in the eventual attack.

I could barely speak when my companion nudged me and whispered, "It sounds as if the daughter of Lamash, our *gal,* has her eye on some of the soldiers. Best watch out for your spy or her pretty innocence will snare him."

"You are a fool." My voice was hoarse in grief.

"Rahab, I did not mean anything." The young woman peered at me, startled by my unexpected response.

"Don't you understand?" I choked out a response. "No one here will survive when the armies of Israel enter the city."

Shaking my head and unable to explain my sorrow, I pushed past Jerusha and rushed away. I rounded a corner and ran blindly into my father.

"Watch your step, woman." The gruff tone showed he did not recognize me.

The man barely slowed his rapid progress down the street. The light cloak he wore swirled behind like wings. I could see the broad fringe decorating the garment. He was almost to the corner before I made my decision.

"My father." Two words stopped the abrupt departure.

Slowly Hamash turned. Eyes narrowed and mouth thinned as the man stared at me. The silence stretched out between us. I did not think my father was going to speak. My eyes lowered to study the fine leather sandals planted firmly in the dusty street. The feet moved and I knew that I was rejected.

"I have no daughter. The child of my heart chose to remain a harlot rather than to return to my home after her mother died."

Repudiation was in the haughty way my father turned away. I gasped a breath against the pain his words inflicted.

"Not even a daughter who might be able to save your life?" In that moment, I risked voicing an offer I prayed I would not regret.

My words stopped Hamash. The man swiveled to face me again. From his position near the corner I saw the gray head tilt and brown eyes narrow. My father took a step toward me. We were alone in the street; still the man glanced around before stepping closer. A rough hand gripped my arm.

"What do you know, girl? How can one like you save my life?" The questions were low and intense.

My arm hurt where hard fingers dug into the flesh. Proudly I lifted my chin and refused to cry, even though the pain in my heart was greater than the bruising of my arm.

"I meant nothing." I tugged, trying to free myself.

My father tightened his hold. "You will tell me why you said you could save my life."

"My house is in the wall." The answer I gave was a half truth. Already I regretted the impulsive offer. "If the army of Israel breaks in you could escape while the fighting is in the streets."

"Is that what you harlots plan?" A sneer appeared at the idea. Gray eyebrows met in frowning consideration. "You might be right. It could work, but I do not hide behind women's skirts, especially those of known harlots."

With the final scornful comment, Hamash shoved me away. I stumbled and only kept myself from falling by a hand against the stone wall of the nearest house. I felt the rough texture scrape my skin. My heart broke as I watched my father stride away, contempt in each swing of his cloak. Sagging against the wall, I rubbed my throbbing arm. After a moment I forced myself to walk toward home. It took all my pride not to allow the tears to fall until I reached the refuge of my door.

Inside the sanctuary of the inn, I sank to the floor. When I began to cry it was in great gasping sobs. Esther hurried to my side in sympathy when she heard my wails.

"What happened?" Her startled glance noticed my bleeding hand and the already visible bruises on my arm.

"I saw my father." The answer was low and spoken through the tears that I could not stop.

My friend clucked in distress. Forgotten was the argument of just days earlier. She hurried to bring water to wash my hand. A cool cloth was gently tied around the bruises. Jerusha arrived a moment later. The full water jar she carried was almost dropped as the woman hurried to my side.

"He did this to you?" An outraged frown appeared on her pretty face.

"I wanted to offer him sanctuary." With more tears I confessed my rash suggestion to both women.

"Was that safe?" Esther immediately became concerned.

"He spurned me and called me a . . . ha . . . ha . . . har . . ." I could not finish the word.

Eventually I was able to stop sobbing.

Jerusha offered consolation, "Do not worry, we are safe here. Our loyalty to the goddess will not be questioned."

I hoped the woman was right. If Hamash told the officials of Jericho, then an investigation would begin. All day I worried that soldiers might arrive. I sat staring at the door in fearful anticipation. Nothing happened.

My friends gently urged me to bed after Astarte rose to begin her nightly journey. I lay for a long time wishing I knew what god to believe in. Finally, exhaustion lulled me to sleep. I did not awaken until the trumpets of Israel heralded the dawn with another procession. I spent the day inside. No longer did I desire to hear the fantastic rumors and speculation in the city. Even less did I want to meet my father or any other priest or official of the city.

Jerusha brought word after her trip to the market. "The chief has called a grand council to meet tomorrow. The priests and most important men of Jericho will be there. All night sacrifices are to be offered at the Temple. People still believe that Astarte will strike the enemy, perhaps with fire."

"No doubt Lamash has heard the rumor that he is secretly allied with Joshua." Esther twisted her mouth in derision. "The man is too foolish to have made such a plan. He will listen to those as rash as he is. Every man is this city believes we are safe behind the walls."

"No one can stand against the army of the Living God." I made the assertion in a monotone. More and more the coming massacre weighed on my heart. "Jericho will fall. Not one person will be spared. Only those within this house will be saved."

"The priests are calling for an attack on the camp of Joshua. 'Let us march against Gilgal and utterly annihilate these slaves.' I heard the High Priest speaking to Lamash this morning." Jerusha quoted the overheard words in an attempt to console me.

A shudder rippled through me.

Esther spoke aloud my thoughts, "The gods cannot desire such action."

"It is a sacrifice pleasing to the gods." Again my friend repeated words heard at the Temple.

"Any god that demands such sacrifice is . . ." my voice failed. I almost ran from the room.

On my bed I sobbed and pleaded with the gods to spare Jericho. I knew in my heart it was a vain hope. No longer did I have any faith that Astarte would sweep from the heavens on her lion to defend the city. There was only silence as the moon rose. I hid my face from the mocking light of the goddess.

It was clear that my hope was only in the God of Israel. Still I was tormented by the knowledge that all in Jericho would die when the city fell to the invaders. In agony I gasped out questions that were almost a prayer.

"God of the Hebrews, must you cause such vengeance on this city? Can you not spare the women and children?"

I stayed in my room all the next day. Smoke from ceaseless sacrifices at the Temple hung over the city like a pall. It seeped through even the closed lattice of our home. The only time I rose was to watch the Children of Israel parade past. It was not the fierce march of an army. Except for the orderly ranks of spears and the polished leather breastplates, the people resembled priests in procession. The seven trumpeters escorting the great golden box of their god made the only sound. When they blew the horns every man raised his spear or sword, but they made no shout.

"Why don't they *do* something?" Jerusha joined me at my vigil.

Esther too came to stand beside us. She shivered. "The men are too quiet. It is almost as though they were performing a ritual."

In surprise I looked at my friend.

"Perhaps they are." In sudden clarity I understood. "The people of Israel are preparing for attack in this way."

"Maybe they seek their god's favor by carrying that gold box around Jericho," guessed Jerusha.

"I have heard that the God of Israel is not represented by a statue or even contained in that box," her sister whispered in awe. "Some of the southern traders insist that the Hebrew claim that their god is everywhere and has no form."

"All gods have form," argued the younger woman. "How else would we know what to worship?"

"Have you never considered that giving the gods a body brings holy things down to human size? Do you not wonder why a god needs to be represented by a statue?" I pondered, half to myself, as the procession marched north toward Gilgal yet again. Now I vaguely understood what my mother tried to explain fifteen years earlier. "If a god is god, how can we represent the god in wood or stone?"

"To give us all something to focus on," snapped my friend in answer.

I shrugged and made no further comment. Another argument with my companions was not something I wanted to enter into. I was relieved when Esther changed the subject.

"What do you think the council will decide?" The woman turned from the window to flop down on cushions nearby.

Jerusha shrugged. "Who knows? They will talk all day. Every man will have a different solution. In the end, nothing will happen."

It seemed that she was right. There was no massing of the troops in the street. Briefly I feared that my father would expose what he believed to be my escape plan. When night came without the dreaded knock, I relaxed.

It was the next day, not long after the Children of Israel marched past again, that a knock sounded on our door. Fearfully we gathered. Jerusha opened the door. A heavily cloaked figure stood in the street.

"Let me in," a muffled voice commanded.

"Sir, we are closed," Jerusha replied. I saw her hand tighten as she prepared to close the door.

"Wait." Something about the figure made me narrow my eyes. "Let him in."

The cloaked man roughly brushed past the sisters.

"Close the door." Even now this person expected obedience. He was not disappointed. Esther latched the door before facing our visitor. I stepped forward to confront my father.

"What do you want, Hamash?" My voice was cold.

Jerusha and Esther moved closer to each other in surprise and fear.

"You know me then, girl?" Without trying to deny his identity, my father brushed the hood back from his head and shrugged out of the bulky layers of robes used in his disguise.

I nodded, waiting with clenched hands for an explanation. Unable to stand still, the man began to stride back and forth across the room.

"The council is filled with fools." The statement was angry. Scorn dripped from his tone as he added, "They agree with our chief that we can wait out the threat. 'The sons of slaves will see that we are not intimidated. Our walls are secure. Soon they will march away and never return.' They are all fools."

"You do not agree?" I spoke because my father seemed to be awaiting a response. The man paused in his pacing to look at me.

"I encouraged Lamash to rain flaming arrows into their midst to create confusion. Then a charge from the city by our finest soldiers would rout this rabble entirely."

The man took a turn around the room, coming to a stop only inches from me. In the brown eyes I saw not only rage and frustration, but a hint of fear.

Harshly the condemnation was repeated, "They are fools. Over and over I heard the excuse, 'The armies of Israel march with their god.' Only cowards or fools would fear men such as the Hebrew rabble. Sons of slaves cannot learn to fight in one generation."

I had to press my lips together so he did not see the wry smile that threatened to mock my father's vehemence.

"Have you seen them?" Jerusha bravely ventured to ask. "There are many well-armed men in the daily procession."

"I have heard of their numbers and armor," the man scornfully sneered. "Untried youth, most of them."

"What of Ammon and Moab?" I had to bring up the defeated nations.

"Weak and poorly defended villages." With a gesture my

father dismissed two of Jericho's staunchest allies.

"Why are you here?" Returning to the original question, I repeated, "What do you want, Hamash?"

"You reminded me that this house is built into the wall with access to outside of Jericho. Without a doubt the Hebrew will attack eventually. I seek a safe way out."

"You would abandon your family and this city to the sword while you scramble for safety?" It was my turn to sneer. My father's rejection had left my heart hard and cold.

"I will bring my wife and young son here," he shrugged. "Your brothers too, if they want to join us."

Jerusha and Esther gasped at the audacity of the man. Before I could think of anything to say, my father turned to look around the room.

"Show me the windows out of this house." Gripping my wrist Hamash moved toward the stairs. I had no choice but to follow.

Peering into each room, the man investigated every part of the house. Crossing to one window, my father leaned out to gaze north and south. He looked down and nodded in satisfaction.

"This is good. We will return after dark. I must say, for a harlot, you have done well." The phrases were clipped and precise.

Gathering the many robes, my father added to his size. He drew the hood tightly around his face before opening the door just enough to glance up and down the street. Except for a yellow mongrel prowling for scraps and a couple of young children playing at the corner, the street was bare. In a moment the man was gone. Quickly he rounded the corner and disappeared.

"What are we to do?" Esther was near panic.

"Hamash does not know about the spies." I tried to reassure my friends. "He only wants a place to escape from Jericho when the attack happens."

"How long will they live here? We cannot afford to feed many more mouths." Jerusha was outspoken in her disapproval.

"He will not risk leaving until there is fighting so he can escape under cover of the confusion." My guess was hesitant and a little apologetic.

The answer did not reassure my companion. For the remainder of the day, while we made preparations for my family, she wore a frown. I almost regretted the impulse that led me to approach my father in the street. Only when I looked at the scarlet rope in my window did I relax. There was hope to save the lives of my father and brothers if they were within the house when the Children of Israel attacked. My hand stroked the talisman and I remembered the honest eyes of the man called Salma.

I reassured myself by repeating the last words of the spy, "Your life and the lives of your family are sacred to God."

There was no sleep that night. Throughout the long hours members of my family slipped through the door from the dark street until the house was bursting. Although barely civil, my siblings were glad of an escape plan. My sisters-in-law tried to avoid touching the walls and spread their own blankets over the beds before lying children on the pallets.

Hamash and his new wife occupied the finest bedroom. She avoided my smile of welcome. My father hustled her up the stairs with my baby half brother in her arms.

I looked after the couple with deep sorrow. My choice to serve the goddess had brought me nothing but separation from my family. They believed me to be a harlot, as did all in Jericho. I thought of the times Balak used my body and sadly acknowledged that I had bartered my reputation for the illusion of independence. The only thing I gained was repudiation. The realization drove me to the rooftop to seek solace in the silence. The late-rising goddess seemed to mock my grief, peering at me through scattered spring clouds.

Daylight brought a sixth morning of silently marching troops. Except for the trumpets, not a sound came from the men. My father stared at the endless ranks with narrowed eyes.

"There are a lot of soldiers," Jonadab stated, a little nervously.

Newly married, the thirty-one-year-old held his wife tight at his side. I was reminded of his low words the evening before, when he arrived.

"Debora, you must stay by me. These women are not fit for your innocence."

The girl was barely nubile. I knew my youngest brother had lost his first wife and the beloved son I besot the goddess for so long ago. They succumbed to a fever while I was serving in the Temple. Marriage to this child was his hope for an heir.

"Untried and young." Hamash sneered at the procession and recalled me from my thoughts. "A few well-aimed arrows would destroy those smug looks. I would aim for those musicians. How can anyone stand such a sound?"

Off to the north marched the sons of Israel. My father demanded food. My sisters-in-law hurried to prepare a meal for the men and children. Jerusha and Esther escaped to the well and market. I was left to deal with whining children and rude brothers.

"I do not know why Father has brought us to such a house," Perez snarled at me. "That we should even darken these doors is a credit to our obedience to Hamash. Tirzah should not have to risk bearing my son in such surroundings."

Hamul spoke words of truth that were better left unsaid, for I saw the woman pale. "Better to bear the child in the house of a harlot than have her belly slit by a sword."

I bit my tongue to keep from snapping the answer that sprang to my lips. There was no sense upsetting the expectant mother who waddled slowly and painfully between the fire and her husband. Her distended belly was evidence of the imminent arrival of an eighth child. The three youngest sons clung to their mother's skirts. A trio of older nephews imitated their father in his disdain of my presence. Even the oldest, Hamash, the first-born, seemed to forget our playtime at the inn when he was a toddler. The boy was five when I left home. My only niece, Rebekka, born not long after I went to the Temple, stayed close to her mother. I saw her watching me with a mixture of curiosity and awe.

Hamul continued his contemptuous comments, "Our father has a plan. We do not need to acknowledge this woman. Her kind will be game for the troops when Jericho triumphs."

I turned away to avoid a confrontation with my brother. As he was a guest, I would not trespass on the rules of hospitality and lash out in anger. The man took a chunk of bread from the platter his wife held without looking at Adah. I remembered the years of play with the young woman in the courtyard of the Inn of Hamash. Our shared dreams were dust now. She was wed to my brother with his shifty eyes and sly ways instead of the rich, handsome merchant of our childhood imaginings. I was Rahab, harlot of Jericho, scorned by my own family unless I could be of some use. When I moved near my former friend, she hurried to her husband. It hurt deeply that my one-time friend pretended I was invisible.

Only pride born of anger prevented me from fleeing to the rooftop for refuge from the antagonism of my brothers and their wives. It did not surprise me that my father's wife expressed her contempt of the lodgings. The young woman who replaced my mother was kin to the *gal*. Lamash was her uncle, and I was sure my father had been quite delighted to receive permission to wed the girl. The infant she bore him was further cause for rejoicing. Her complaint trailed down the stairs from the room they shared.

"Hamash, we would be just as safe in the palace. My father is dead, but Lamash remembers me fondly. Can we go to the palace? I do not want to stay here."

"Wife, we remain here until we learn what the council and *gal* will do to defeat this rabble." It was a stern reply and silenced my stepmother.

With head bowed I moved about the daily tasks of sweeping the dirt floor and shaking crumbs from the breadbaskets into the street for birds and stray dogs. With so many people in the small house my work hardly seemed to matter. Everything I straightened was almost immediately out of place again.

Jerusha was bursting with news when she returned. My friend signaled me to follow her up the stairs.

"You will never guess what I heard." Suppressed excitement tinged the voice.

"Tell me." Too tired for guessing games I snapped the reply.

"Tomorrow the *gal* will announce plans to attack the camp of Israel. The allies from the hills are massing for an attack in three days." My friend was almost breathless with eagerness.

"How do you know?" Such news did not seem something that would be discussed in the streets.

Shrugging and trying to look innocent, the woman smiled slyly, "I happened to hear a conversation."

My look must have shown disbelief because Jerusha giggled and acknowledged, "One of the councilors has a . . . um . . . certain tastes that can be catered to."

I did not want to pry further into my friend's methods. Instead I pondered the news.

"Why three days?" The timing seemed odd.

Bursting to share her news, Jerusha quoted from her informant. "Well, 'Everyone knows that the Hebrew will not budge from their camp tomorrow. It is the seventh day and their holy day. They are forbidden to travel. That gives us time to bring our allies into Jericho and set up ambushes from the hills. The following day, our armies will observe the sons of slaves and plan an effective attack. There will be great dedication services and sacrifices all night. On the third day we will destroy the interlopers.' That is what I was told."

My heart sank. "I guess Lamash has come up with a plan."

I had heard of the Sabbath law. It was one of the more surprising tenets of this strange one god. A day given over to rest and worship was unheard of but very appealing. However it could spell doom for the invasion. I wished there was a way to send word to the man I pinned such hopes on.

The crash of shattering pottery and Esther's voice raised in anger interrupted our conversation and my worried thoughts. Jerusha and I raced down the stairs. In the middle of the floor lay the largest water jar in the house. From the pieces water flooded the floor, soaking into the dirt and drenching the bottoms of cushions.

"Foolish, clumsy girl," raged Esther. "Now we will not have water until tomorrow."

My niece clung to her mother and wailed. All my sisters-in-law ranged themselves behind Tirzah. Everyone talked at once while trying to comfort mother and child. My nephews whooped in delight and began to splash in the mud forming in the puddles. The men gathered to look at the devastation.

"Stop sniveling," Hamash ordered to his granddaughter. To Esther he commanded, "Go to the well again."

"We cannot . . ." began my friend.

"Do not argue with me, harlot." My father's face was becoming an alarming shade of purple at her refusal.

"During this siege we may only draw water from sunrise until the sun is high. Even then only one jar per household is allowed. It is now past midday." I spoke loud enough to be heard over the turmoil. Then I started to establish order again. "We will have no water except what can be saved from the larger pieces of the broken pot. Adah and Debora, you will find smaller jars on the shelf. We must salvage as much as we can. Boys, you must stop splashing or all the water will be full of mud and you will have nothing to drink. Esther, I am sure that Rebekka did not mean to break the jar. Accidents happen. We will make the best of the situation."

The women hurried to find containers for the water.

"The men will have first use of the water," stated my father, tramping past me to the stairs.

"We will share equally." My reply was calm and firm.

Without fear I met the man's angry look with lifted chin. I was surprised when Hamash sneered, shrugged and continued to the upper level followed by his sons.

"Women should never be allowed to have independence; it goes to their heads," I heard him tell my brothers. "See how these harlots believe that they can order our lives."

After a deep breath to calm my nerves I turned to assist the women. My stand against Hamash appeared to have resulted in a grudging admiration. Tirzah even smiled at me in a tired way when I brought her a cup of water. She sat with my niece cuddled against her. The child was no longer sobbing now that the broken jar was cleared away. Even the floor was beginning to look less like mud since Adah swept dry dirt into the puddles. My former playmate offered a timid smile across the room. My smile was warm and accepted her unspoken apology.

The rest of the day was uneventful. After the evening meal, I

carefully banked the fire before following my houseguests to bed.
Long practice made it a mindless job to arrange the ash and wood
so that in the morning the flame could be blown to life. Tired feet
plodded up the stairs to my pallet. Esther and Jerusha had
already begun preparations for bed.

"It was the start of the Hebrew holy day at sundown." I
voiced the thought that had come to me as I latched the door and
climbed the stairs.

The comment was greeted with silence. Esther continued to
comb her hair, and Jerusha shrugged while applying beauty
lotion to her face.

"I wonder if Hamash is right in thinking we will see no
troops tomorrow. That will give the allies of Jericho time to
assemble," I mused as I stood at the window. Unconsciously my
fingers twined in the scarlet rope still hanging there.

"We will see," Jerusha stated. "Screaming children and sour-
faced kin may not bother you, but I have had my fill of both."

"I just hope this ends soon," her sister agreed. "It makes me
angry to see how Rahab is treated by her family."

When the older woman came to slip her hand around my
waist, I was touched. The gesture of support and friendship
erased the weeks of silent rancor that existed in the house.

"It is true, Rahab does not deserve to be blamed," Jerusha
joined us.

Together we stared out across the early spring landscape for
a silent minute. I wondered what my friends were thinking. My
gaze traveled up the nearby mountains. It looked as if more shepherd fires than usual dotted the outcroppings. I wondered if the
allies of Jericho were even now in the hills preparing to rush
down and slaughter the armies of Joshua. I turned to my bed in
an attempt to shut out the picture my imagination painted. Even
on my pallet the images remained. I saw the army of Israel
trapped between city and mountains with the blood of their
young men spilled on the earth.

"God of the Children of Israel." My heart cried out in fear.
"Defend your people. Do not let Salma and the young men be
slaughtered by treachery."

I lay awake for a long time wishing I had some way to warn the spies. Eventually I slept, only to rouse with the first rooster. Jerusha and Esther still slept. The sky was barely gray with the coming dawn. I wished my window faced north so I could see if the daily march would happen. Looking down I wondered if armed men were secreted amid the protective ditches and bulwarks surrounding Jericho. Nothing seemed to move in the shadows. The leaders of the city were so sure that the Hebrew would remain in their camp this holy day; it seemed that no precautions were taken.

The sky turned from gray to blue. Rays of the rising sun lit up the mountains across the valley. It was a serene scene with the light green of the new plants breaking through the soil in the terraced fields along the hillsides to the west. Danger lurked somewhere beyond my sight, I was sure.

"No parade yet?" yawned Jerusha as she awakened.

"It is barely light," grumbled Esther drowsily. "What are you doing up? If the Hebrew come, they come. I want as much sleep as I can get before facing your family."

With that the woman pulled the blanket over her head.

"Perhaps my father was right," I stated as the sun flooded the road with morning light.

No trample of feet or cloud of dust heralded a marching army. Instead the wail of a hungry child sounded. Soon a childish altercation was heard followed by tears. The day had begun.

Perez ordered, "Tirzah, see to your sons!"

From his wife, a sharp reprimand to the children brought momentary silence. In another room voices were raised in argument as my father and his wife awakened. I turned from my vigil. Hastily I pulled a comb through the thick waves of my hair. Hamash would be calling for food soon. A quick glance in the bronze mirror showed me that, even in the serviceable and old brown gown, I was a dramatic-looking woman. From my flame-colored hair, which I could no longer believe signified the favor of Astarte, to the carefully, if rapidly, painted eyes, lips and cheeks, I had to admit that I looked the part of the harlot everyone believed me to be. With a deep breath, I straightened my

shoulders and prepared to face the day. Serving in the Temple had
seemed my destiny. The life as the one known as the Harlot of
Jericho was not what I hoped for myself. There was no time for
repining; already my father shouted his demands.

Barely had I stirred the fire to life when I heard them.
Unmistakably, the notes of the trumpets of Israel sounded.
Dropping a piece of wood into the brazier I hurried back to my
room. Hamash was right behind me. He brushed me aside to look
out the window. I crowded close to the man in order to see. His
interest in the approaching troops was obvious when he did not
draw back from my touch.

"The council was wrong." His sneer ignored the fact that
only yesterday my father agreed with the leadership of Jericho.

The procession appeared the same as every other day of the
past six. Men walked in formation carrying swords, javelins or
spears. There were the white-robed priests escorting the shining
golden ark at the head of the army. Oiled and polished leather
and bronze gleamed in the sun. Over the sound of thousands of
marching feet rang the ceaseless trumpeting from instruments of
metal and ram's horn.

My eyes moved past the parading men to the hills. I could
detect no movement. Leaning out of the window slightly, I
peered up at the walls of Jericho. It did not look as if there were
any more guards than usual on patrol. It appeared that the *gal*
neither planned nor expected an attack.

The last man in the army of Israel passed beneath my view.
Strangely the trumpets did not seem to be growing distant as on
every other day. Instead the sound was coming closer. The
entourage marched into view a second time.

Hamash cursed, "By Baal's beard, what are the sons of slaves
doing? Is this a trick?"

The man leaned out the window to stare at the line of soldiers again passing in review. When the army made a third circuit, my brothers joined our father.

Rudely I was thrust away from the window. "Out of the way,
woman."

"Father what does this mean?" I heard the sound of panic in Hamul's voice.

"It is a tactic to intimidate," stated Perez authoritatively. "The endless circling makes them appear more numerous."

"They are a great army," Jonadab pointed out. "The last man has barely passed before the first man comes into view again."

I caught my breath and barely dared let the sudden thought enter my head. The Children of Israel were surrounding Jericho. They planned to attack this morning. When they completely encircled the city, each man would be in position. A shiver ran through my body as if the cold hand of someone from the Great Under had touched me. As the trumpets grew louder for the fifth pass beneath my window, I hurried to find Jerusha and Esther. They were in the kitchen stirring dough for the day's bread. None of my sisters-in-law were present.

"Leave that." My intense tone made the women frown even as they followed my beckoning finger.

We were alone in the street. Not even a soldier patrolled past. Everyone was inside watching the unusual actions of the Hebrew army or hiding in terror.

"The attack will come today."

Neither friend questioned my confident words, although Esther began to sob.

"Do not be afraid." I shook the woman gently by the shoulders. "We will be safe in this house. You must quietly gather your things so when Salma comes, we are ready."

Jerusha softly asked the question I wanted to avoid, "Will you tell your father now?"

"I suppose I must," I sighed as the words came from my lips.

"We will stand with you," my friend offered.

"Thank you, but I must face Hamash alone." Although grateful for the support, I explained, "You do not need to be involved in what he may see as treason."

Dread gripped me as I forced myself to mount the stairs. There was not much time. The trumpets drew close in a sixth circuit of the city. I ignored my nephews playing on the steps. With sticks the boys were pretending to defend Jericho. Too soon the reality would come.

"Father . . . Hamash, I must speak to you." In the doorway I paused.

"What do you want, woman?" Angry at my interruption, four men turned from watching the Hebrew army.

"The army of Joshua is preparing to attack." The statement brought a familiar sneer to my father's face.

"So you are an expert on military matters now?" challenged Perez, before Hamash could speak.

"What can a woman like you know of such things?" Hamul angrily stepped toward me.

"Perhaps she entertains officers," suggested my youngest brother with a leer.

The words fell like blows. For a moment I regretted my desire to offer refuge. Then I heard Tirzah's tired voice calling to one of her sons.

"For the sake of your wives and children, listen to me. Set aside your hatred of me and the path you believe I chose." I held out a hand in supplication as I looked from my siblings to my father.

In that moment I realized that I still loved the man and needed his approval. It was the reason I opened my doors to my family. For a second I let the love fill me. Before I could speak to express it, Hamash spoke.

"Woman, what are you trying to say? What do you know of this attack?" Narrowed eyes pinned me in place.

"You will not die in the attack if you remain here in this house." Even as I spoke, I hoped vainly that no one would ask for an explanation.

"How can you promise that?" Even more suspicious my father stepped toward me. "Are you a spy for that rabble?"

"I told you she slept with the officers," jeered Jonadab triumphantly.

"You are all fools." Anger came to my rescue before I burst into tears. "You waste time judging me. Better spend it preparing to save your families. If you still believe you can climb out that window in the turmoil of the battle, I will not stop you. What I know is that all those in this house will be safe. The Hebrews have sworn by their god to spare all within these walls."

The trumpeting increased in volume as the priests drew near again.

"How many times the army will circle Jericho I do not know." My voice was raised over the blasts of music. "This is the seventh time around. You probably have very little time to make a decision."

Silent after I made my statement, I looked from face to face. Disbelief, anger and scorn were seen in my brothers' expressions. Only on the face of my father was a considering frown.

Softly, I began to plead for the women. "Perez, think of Tirzah and your unborn child. How could she escape through the window?"

The man looked at the opening. I hoped he was thinking about the distance to the ground and the rough terrain between wall and road.

"Jonadab, think of Debora. If you die, what will be her fate? Adah too would have to face the invaders alone."

My words seemed to reach the men, for I saw a shudder ripple through my youngest brother. Without further conversation my three siblings hurried from the room to join their families.

"Hamash, my father, I am sorry that I am a disappointment to you. My independence has caused you shame. I sought to bring honor by serving the goddess even here." There was not time for long explanations of my motivation of years earlier. "I can offer you the chance to live even though all of Jericho will fall. You may call me treacherous and a harlot, but I do not desire your blood on my hands. The Hebrews are led by the Living God. They will triumph over the army of Jericho."

A low snarl was the reply, "It is because the council is led by fools."

"If you choose to risk escape by the window, now is your chance." Looking past my father, I saw that the marching had stopped.

The troops now faced the walls of the city. A long blast from the trumpets echoed between walls and hills. What happened next made my scalp tingle and my heart pound. From thousands of throats came a shout. It did not sound as much like a war cry as an exultation of praise.

"Alleluia, El Elohim Israel!"

Again the words came through the window, "Alleluia, El Elohim Israel!"

For a third time the shout was repeated, "Alleluia, El Elohim Israel!"

Then came the shriek of swords drawn and clatter of spears raised. The army charged straight forward from all four sides of Jericho.

"Astarte, defend us! Send your armies against this horde!" Belatedly my father sought his god. The man rushed from the room.

"Salome." I heard him call my stepmother.

Her piercing cry tore through me, "We will be slain or worse! This house is a trap!"

I found myself alone in the room. There seemed to be very little resistance from the walls of the city. Only a few arrows rained down on the attackers. As the army charged forward, the Hebrew soldiers uncovered ladders secreted in the scrub beside the protective ditches around Jericho. There was barely time to wonder when they were hidden before the sons of Israel were scaling the walls. I turned from the window to seek my family and friends. The creaking of the giant hinges on the gate echoed down the deserted street.

"They are in the city." I breathed the words in astonishment at the ease of conquest. "Truly the God of Israel is mighty."

The reply from my window was startling, "Blessed be the Name of the Lord."

I spun around to see Salma's grinning face framed in the opening.

"We have come," the young man stated, swinging into the room followed by Jamal and three other armed men.

The space seemed too small. I held my breath when Salma stepped close to me. I looked up and leaned toward the man.

"Are you alone?" His question brought me back to sanity.

I shook my head as much in response as to clear away the girlish desire for a kiss.

With an effort I found my voice to explain. "No, my family is here and my two friends. My father and brothers are not . . . may not . . . they thought . . ." The words stumbled to a stop and I started again, "I have just explained to my father that all in this house will be spared. I do not know if they believe or not."

Salma nodded at my explanation. "We will soon see." The order to his companions spoke volumes, "Be ready for anything."

"There are women and children, too," I added hastily, as the men moved toward the door with swords drawn.

"Where are they?" It was Jamal who asked.

"Everyone is in the rooms on the second floor or in the main room." I heard a nervous quaver in my voice.

"We will get them," a broad-shouldered young man volunteered. It was as much a threat as a promise.

"Yes, Levi, you and Joash go with Jamal and Eli," Salma ordered.

My heart pounded when the men turned to hurry down the stairs. I heard masculine curses and women's sobs but no clash of swords.

Salma touched my shoulder. "Gather your things. We must leave before the city is set ablaze."

"No!" I could not stop my cry of horror. "What of all the people?"

"It is the will of the Living God. All Jericho is a sacrifice to the One Lord." Implacably the young man stated the order. "Would not your armies have burned our camp tomorrow?"

Amazement at this knowledge of the council's plan silenced me. I picked up my small bundle and led the way down to the main room. My brothers stood protectively in front of their wives and children. Perez's older boys stood beside him. Hamash and Salome stood near the door. My infant stepbrother wailed in fear. Jamal barred their exit with one hand on his sword hilt.

Salma spoke before I could think of anything to say. "We come in the name of the God of Israel to offer you safe passage

out of Jericho. Because your sister feared the One God and hid us
from the soldiers, all in this house are safe from the swords of the
armies of El Elohim Israel."

I felt the tension in the room. Muffled sobs were heard from
Tirzah and Adah, although they tried to silence the sound with
their veils. Hostile looks were directed at me from my brothers.

"How can we trust you?" Perez shifted his attention to Salma.
"You are nothing but the sons of escaped slaves. What do you
know of honor?"

I heard movement as hands shifted to swords, and from
Jamal came a growl of anger.

"Perez," my father spoke heavily, "you do poorly to insult
these men. What choice do we have but to obey? The Hebrews
have taken the city. Unless you want to die, we must do as we are
told."

"Well spoken," Salma chuckled softly. The young man
seemed to find the encounter entertaining. I heard suppressed
laughter even in the ironic question he asked. "Will you come
with us to the safety of our camp or die in this city?"

Sullenly, Perez, Hamul and Jonadab dropped their daggers to
the floor.

"Come then. Jamal and Levi, you lead the way." With a nod
of satisfaction, the Hebrew spy gave instructions. "Everyone
must stay close together behind our guides. Joash, you and Eli
will march beside our group. I will bring up the rear."

Salma's orders were swiftly followed. In only a few moments
we were assembled in the street. Hamash drew his cloak over his
head so none could recognize him. Salome followed suit, as did
my brothers. Jerusha and Esther clung to my hands like children
as we hurried down the street. My heart was rent by the death I
saw as we rapidly walked the short distance to the city gates.
Men, women and children lay where they fell in futile efforts to
escape from the invaders. There was no ransacking of homes, just
death everywhere.

The red turbans worn by our guards were obviously a sign to
the other soldiers for they saluted and let us pass at the gate. I

smelled smoke as we made our way along the highway toward Gilgal.

"You are burning the greatest city in Canaan," Hamash accused.

My father stopped. We all looked back. Smoke rose from the center of Jericho.

"It is the palace and Temple," sobbed Salome, easily identifying the location of the black cloud.

"All Jericho is ablaze," Jerusha gasped only a moment later.

What had been a thin black column thickened as the fire spread. In a few minutes we could see flames above the walls.

"Alleluia, El Elohim Israel," Salma spoke in an awed voice. "Our God has given the victory. To the Living One belong the spoils."

The men of Israel were now marching from the burning city. Even from the distance I could see that they formed into columns behind the ark and priests. At the familiar sound of the ram's horn and trumpets, the army began to march along the highway.

"Come," Jamal ordered, "you must be in the encampment before the soldiers return."

He set a brisk pace for the remainder of the journey. Trumpet calls and drifting smoke pursued us. The size of the encampment near Gilgal astonished me. It spread from the city walls to the main road from the north. I had a brief glimpse of many tents. Cooking fires were visible in front of each family's home. Women and children moved among the structures.

"Here are your tents." Salma led us to a group of three pole and hide structures slightly apart from the main camp.

I expected my father to argue. He seemed oddly subdued. Silently the man entered one of the shelters. Salome followed. Her lovely face was blotched from the tears shed all the way from Jericho.

My brothers, too, were silent. The trio ushered their wives toward the next tent. Even the children sensed the strangeness and followed their mother quietly. The flap fell into place with a sense of closing out the fearsome world. Esther and Jerusha took their small bundles and disappeared into the third tent.

Salma gave a brief order. "See that two more tents are erected." Turning to Perez, the Hebrew offered assurance, "You will each have your own home."

Levi and Jamal hurried away. I was not sure if my brothers heard Salma. They stared white-faced at the ruin of the city that had been our home. Pity filled my heart. I took a step toward Perez. Coldly the man stared through me before entering the tent to join his family.

"You have brought this disaster on us." The accusation came from Hamul before he followed his brother. "You turned the goddess against her city with your welcome of the spies."

Jonadab did not even look at me as he too disappeared into the shelter.

I stood alone with Salma. A wave of embarrassment flooded me. I wished the Hebrew spy had not been a witness to my rejection. With an effort I swallowed the choking tears that threatened.

"Thank you for saving the lives of my family." I covered my heart and bowed to the soldier of Israel.

"Life for life, it is fitting." The man seemed withdrawn and distant, not at all like the grinning friend at my window such a short time earlier. The frown he directed at the retreating backs of my siblings softened when his blue eyes turned back to me.

Trumpet blasts announced the arrival of the ark and army. There was no time for any more conversation. Jamal and Levi returned to set up two more tents for my family. I saw the women of Israel gathering to await news of injuries and deaths. There were few casualties, I knew. Five miles away the smoke and flames were still visible as Jericho, with its sad burden of dead, became a sacrificial fire to a god I feared and yet felt strangely drawn toward.

Salma and his companions hurried away to greet the triumphant returning hosts. I watched the spy until he was lost in the crowd, then I slowly turned and entered the tent.

৵ 9 ৵

IT APPEARED THAT WE were mostly forgotten in the celebration that followed. The entire camp gathered to greet the conquerors. Husbands, sons and brothers were welcomed back with joyful relief. From our tent, I watched the community gather in the late afternoon. At the sound of a single ram's horn blast everyone moved toward the center of the camp. A large man with a flowing brown beard that showed the beginnings of gray stood between two priests. His height and breadth of shoulders made his companions appear small. This had to be Joshua, leader of the invaders. The trio waited in front of a curtained enclosure. I guessed this was the tabernacle that housed the ark. Various guests at the inn had described the place of worship. It was larger than I expected. The curtains billowed in a slight spring breeze but not enough for me to see into the holy area. An altar of bronze stood just inside the entrance. At this a tall thin priest presided. He was wearing a breastplate of jewels. Sunlight struck the gems so that they sparkled and flashed. The turban on the man's head was fastened with some ornament. I could tell that it was also made of gold and jewels by the way the sun glinted from the object. Flames and smoke rose from the altar. I held my breath wondering what was going to happen.

The imposing man stepped toward the congregation. "Men of Israel." His voice carried across the encampment to where I stood transfixed. "The Living God has given us a mighty victory this day. Let us praise the name of the Lord."

"Alleluia, El Elohim Israel!" The shout rose from every throat.

I recognized the words from the morning. Again and again the cry resounded until I was sure that the words could be heard from the Jordan to the hills.

I suddenly realized that a cloud had enveloped the tabernacle. I was never sure if it was from the incense on the altar or a manifestation of the god the people called on. My mother had told of how the presence of the God of Moses was manifest in a fiery cloud that the people followed. The High Priest, for so the wearer of the ephod of jewels must be, held up his hands.

Men and women fell silent. I stared at the central figure. Although his graying beard spoke of many years, the erect body and commanding appearance proclaimed a general with much strength and vigor. This was the man chosen as successor to Moses. I wondered if the staff in Joshua's hand was the one used in Egypt to call forth the judgment on the land. My thoughts rapidly reviewed the life of Moses, famous even in Jericho for his career. He was born a slave, raised a prince, exiled as murderer only to return in the power of the strange One God to perform miracles and force Pharaoh to free the Hebrew slaves.

Now this Joshua, who had been the revered leader's lieutenant throughout the forty years of wilderness travel, was the chief of the people. The apparently aimless wandering in Sinai had forged a mighty nation from a group of fearful and disparate families. I caught my breath in amazement at the fortune that brought me into contact with the man and people singled out by such a god.

The priest was speaking. "God has truly given Jericho into our hands. We have obeyed the word of our God and kept nothing for ourselves. The city and her inhabitants are a sacrifice to the Holy One of Jacob our father. Only the silver and gold have been set aside for the tabernacle of the Living God."

"Alleluia, El Elohim Israel." As though on signal, the chant rose again.

At a slight movement of Joshua's staff, the roar ceased. The High Priest looked around at the assemblage.

"Bring forward the offerings to the God of Sinai."

My head was dizzy from all the names applied to the god of

this people. The One who had no statue or form seemed to have a great many names. I hoped I could ask Salma to explain it. Then I wondered if the man would ever come near me again. He had heard my own family repudiate me.

"Will I be an outcast in this camp?" I was barely aware that I voiced the thought aloud.

I felt Esther slip her plump hand into mine. The older woman's gesture sought comfort even as her presence eased my sudden loneliness.

"We are here." Her hand squeezed mine with reassurance.

"What is happening?" Jerusha joined us in staring toward the ceremony.

In a low tone I responded, "The High Priest has just called for the offerings."

"More sacrifices?" Esther tightened her grip on my hand.

"I do not know." My eyes were fixed on Joshua and the priests.

"By tribes bring forward the gifts for the treasury." The order came from the thin priest.

A short man in a turban spoke while several young men emptied sacks of treasure. "From the tribe of Reuben, gold from the palace of Jericho."

I heard a gasp from the nearby tent and glanced in that direction. Salome stared aghast at the pile of gold ornaments and dishes piled near the sanctuary. Pity for my father's wife almost made me start in her direction. Movement in the camp forestalled me.

"The tribe of Simeon brings fine woven goods from the looms of Canaan." The next family chief stepped forward and spoke as bolts of fine cloth were produced.

The weaving of Jericho was famous from Egypt to the Euphrates. The finely wrought linen with gold threads was worn in kings' palaces. Now it would grace the tabernacle of the conquerors.

"Judah offers bronze from the wealth of Jericho." Shields and arm ornaments were piled high.

"Asher has brought iron to the God of Israel." The speaker was a tall man who waved expansively at the offering of swords and spears that joined the mound of tribute.

Still the tribes came forward. Platters and statues and coins of gold and bronze from all corners of the city were piled near the curtained sanctuary.

"Thieves," Hamash grumbled. "Murderers and thieves are all this rabble is."

Salome looked up when my father moved to stand beside her. He stared at the gathered people and booty near the tabernacle. Gray eyebrows drew together in a frown and the man pinched his lips together in anger.

"Do not all warriors bring home plunder?" I felt compelled to defend the men of Israel.

My father did not hear me. Turning back to the tent, he vanished behind the door of hide followed by my stepmother.

Jerusha answered my question after a moment. "The victor does plunder the defeated. I have never before heard of everything being given to a god. Usually, each man is allowed to keep what he has taken. It is the pay for his serving in the army."

"They left nothing of value within the walls. The army has been well paid," agreed her sister.

"Yet they offer it all freely to this strange god who has no statue and many names," I marveled. "Astarte herself does not have as many titles as this god."

"It is a wondrous thing," agreed Esther. "These men freely give all that they took from Jericho."

"Look!" Jerusha cried out. A shaking hand pointed to the object being carried forward between two men. "It is the silver and lapis basin from the Temple of Astarte. The Water of Awakening the Goddess is held in it."

"No longer," I whispered as a chill swept over me.

"What will happen when one god faces the other?" Esther's fingers bit into my arm in her fear.

"Surely Astarte is defeated." Jerusha could barely voice the words as the huge bowl was tilted onto one side of the pile of booty without any dramatic action from the goddess.

The procession of offerings ceased after the pair of soldiers stepped back from the final humiliation of the city and her gods.

"Blessed be the God of Israel," proclaimed the High Priest.

Joshua raised the staff over his head. From the entire camp came the familiar acclamation, "Alleluia, El Elohim Israel!"

For the first time the general spoke, "The God who brought from Egypt a diverse people has given us this victory. Truly to God belongs this treasure of Jericho!"

The man turned to face the altar. He raised his hands shoulder high and extended the palms toward the incense-covered place. There was submission and majesty in the figure.

"Behold, we your people have kept nothing back." A gesture with one hand indicated the booty as though the One addressed could see. "God of Israel, bless our entry into this land promised to Abraham so long ago. You, Lord God, affirmed the vow to his son, Isaac. Jacob, our father, saw this day on his deathbed. In our midst are the bones of Joseph to be buried at Shechem, the town given by Jacob to his most favored son. Go before us, Lord of Hosts, we pray, and give us continued victory."

I was astonished when the leader fell facedown before the altar. All the people prostrated themselves. The wave of kneeling figures looked like a field of wheat falling before the reapers.

"The One Living God has heard your prayer," intoned the High Priest.

He alone remained upright. I saw his hand move, and incense billowed from the altar across the congregation.

"Arise to serve the Holy One. Your offering is acceptable to the God of Sinai. You have offered all the plunder to our God; therefore the God of Abraham, Isaac and Jacob has given the victory!"

Joshua stood and faced the people. Men scrambled to their feet followed by wives and children.

"Behold, God has stricken Jericho." The leader pointed his staff toward the smoldering ruin. "Cursed before the Lord is the man that rebuilds the city. At the cost of his firstborn son shall he lay the foundation. The life of his youngest son will be forfeit at its gates."

"Rahab, we can never go home." Esther suddenly began to sob.

As cheerfully as I could, I assured my friend, "This will be our home now."

"But this is a city of tents. I am afraid. There are no walls to keep danger out." Esther wrapped her arms around her body as if chilled.

In that moment she looked very old and tired. Her sister hurried to slip a supporting arm around the woman. I held out a hand to offer comfort. With a slow shake of her head Esther refused my aid.

"We will learn their ways. We must learn their ways. No one will dare to rebuild Jericho." The curse rang in my ears. "Our fate is bound up with this nation."

"I cannot." The sob was pitiful. "The gods have dealt treacherously with me. Again I am left homeless."

Angrily, Jerusha turned on me. "Why did you make such a deal with the spies? We are truly homeless."

"Would you rather be dead?" I asked, somewhat taken aback by the unexpected assault even though I knew it was motivated by fear of the unknown.

"It would be better than to be outcasts of this people." The sisters drew closer together. "What will we be to them but harlots and defiled unbelievers?"

"We have been given a second chance. Maybe we will find husbands here." I heard my voice pleading for patience and understanding.

Jerusha's lips curled in derision. Venom poured out. "You are a naïve girl. Your dreams of a life with Salma are doomed. If he ever thinks of you again it will be because of the livelihood you chose. You may have fooled yourself all these years with your myth of service to the goddess. However, you cannot deny that you paid Balak with your body. No man of this people will want to wed you. You are Rahab the Harlot in their eyes. Never will you leave that behind."

Satisfied with my silence, both women entered the tent. I stood numb. My mind cringed from the truth in the angry words. Blindly I stumbled away from the small grouping of tents that held my family. I tripped on a small pile of rocks and crashed to my knees. It was too much trouble to stand. From my crouched position I could watch family groups moving away from the tabernacle. Wives clung to husbands in gratitude for the safe return. Children darted between the adults, happy that they could now scream and play after the solemnity of the ceremony. I felt very alone. There was no sound from my father's tent or the three tents that housed my brothers and their families.

"God of Israel." I used the term most often heard. A cry of despair was whispered into the silence that surrounded me. "Who am I? Why did you spare me?"

Not even a breath of wind answered my heartfelt cry. I knew that Jerusha was right. No man of Israel would consider any of us as a bride. We were outsiders and would never be welcomed into any of the tribes. Even the god I placed such hope in mocked my plea.

Night fell before I sought my blankets. At last it was too cold to remain outside. The spring breezes that rose in the evening chilled my body even as the deserted silence chilled my soul. Jerusha and Esther appeared to be asleep. I curled up desolate and alone on a pallet of blankets someone had taken time to arrange for our comfort. The thought drifted through my mind as I slid into sleep.

My dreams were troubled. I woke before dawn sobbing. The images seemed etched on my eyelids. I could not close my eyes without seeing the dead in the streets of Jericho. What awakened me was seeing Jerusha and Esther among the slaughtered masses. The ground was red with their mingled blood. A child stood wailing beside them, the only survivor. That little girl was me, an orphan alone in the devastated city.

I sat shivering in the wool blankets too tormented to try and sleep again. Like the child in my dream, I was bereft of family and friends. A feeling of terrible desolation settled over me. More alone than the day my mother died, my sorrow was too deep for tears.

Eventually the rising sun lit the tent walls. I forced myself from the bed. Gathering up a heavy outer cloak and veil I covered my body from red hair to bare feet before stepping outside. Gleaming almost white in the early sunlight, the tents of the sprawling encampment gradually came to life. Women issued forth with water jars. Others stirred fires to life and began to prepare a meal. Men emerged to stretch and scratch. They gathered in small groups to talk. Children in short tunics ran from tent to tent. Older girls helped their mothers. It was a comfortable scene.

Several women with water jars began making their way to the stream nearby. I could not hear the conversation but it was obvious that they were exchanging happy greetings. Glancing around, I saw that our water jar was empty.

"I should get water." The observation was spoken aloud.

Immediately I shook my head in denial. Why should I be the one to face the gossiping of yet another crowd of women? My friends had not stirred. Looking from the empty pottery to the chattering women of the camp I took a breath. After a little more hesitation, I squared my shoulders, picked up the empty jar and intercepted the line moving toward the water.

The easy conversation ceased at my appearance. Suspicious looks were directed my way. Bravado born of years of ignoring gossip and sarcasm came to my aid. I lifted my chin and forced an unconcerned smile.

In Semitic, the language of all in the area, I spoke, "Thank you for welcoming us into your camp. We are most grateful for your hospitality."

Ignoring the hostile looks and frowns, I walked on. Dipping the water jar into the cool stream, I let the water wash over my shaking hands. Behind me, whispers erupted.

"It is the harlot from Jericho."

"Does she plan to steal our men?"

"There are two others, you know."

"What is her name?"

"Rahab is the one with the red hair who hid our spies."

"I hear that her father has not spoken to her in years."

"Is her family here too?"

"I suppose Salma and Jamal had to honor their vow."

"Makes you wonder what sort of payment she offered for her life."

Cheeks burning, I lifted the full jar to my shoulder. Head

high, I marched back through the women. They fell silent and separated to let me pass. The murmurs followed me. My past was not buried in the ashes of Jericho. Jerusha was right.

Hamash stood watching me approach. The hands on his hips and deep frown filled me with foreboding.

"Girl, you have made us all outcasts and refugees. What am I to do with no way to make a living? Nomads do not need an innkeeper. Your actions allowed this rabble to overrun Jericho. Look at her, the queen of cities, now a smoldering heap."

Following the man's pointing finger, I saw that smoke still drifted from the wreckage.

Jonadab joined us. "Are we to continue to live in tents? It is not civilized to live like this. I barely slept and I am certain that there are insects in the blankets."

I knew my brother exaggerated. Snores had issued from all four tents before I sought my bed the night before. Now I stood silent before the criticism.

"This woman gave no thought to the future when she insisted we accompany her." The lie by Hamash hurt. "It would have been better to flee to the hills and meet the reinforcements from Ai and Bethel."

There was no answer that would be acceptable to my family. Lowering my head, I plodded to my own tent. I set the water jar down. Silently I stirred the fire. Taking a measure of barley from a convenient basket, I stirred it with water over the blaze until a thick gruel formed. My siblings continued to harangue me. I had to tightly grit my teeth together against an angry response. All the women and children gathered to watch me work.

Eventually I broke my silence to speak four words, "Your breakfast is ready."

"Is that all we are to eat?" whined Debora.

Even if they did not consider the meal fit for their palates, the group managed to gobble down the entire potful. The men ate while squatting in front of our father's tent. My friends joined the other women near Perez's new home. In solitary silence I ate my breakfast.

I noticed that Tirzah seemed uncomfortable. She shifted slightly and winced. With one hand the woman rubbed her lower back and gasped softly a couple of times.

Her request after a few more minutes was greeted by near panic. "Debora, I need a midwife."

"It cannot be time," Adah gasped. "What can we do? Mora, the midwife is surely dead in the ruins of Jericho."

"I must have a midwife." This time the words were followed by a sudden intake of breath.

"There will be midwives in the camp of the Hebrews." I doubted that anyone heard my suggestion.

The men seemed to realize what was beginning. Perez received encouraging thumps on the arm and back from his brothers before all the men entered the tent furthest away from the impending delivery.

Salome hurried to join my sisters-in-law clustering around Tirzah. I doubted that their exclamations and pats on the arm were helpful. The woman was carefully helped inside Perez's tent. Alone, I stared from the tent to the nearby camp. A small sigh slipped out. My sister-in-law cried out as another labor pain came. I knew what had to be done.

Heart pounding in dread of more scornful looks, I set off toward a group of Hebrew women cleaning cooking pots at the edge of the encampment. The children playing nearby gave me hope that someone would answer my query. Obviously this group had recently needed the services of a midwife.

Conversation stilled when I drew close. Mostly curious, the young women stared at me.

"What do you want?" A plump figure stood up to confront me.

"I . . . we . . . my sister-in-law needs a midwife." My hand indicated the tents I had just left.

When the only response was the laughter of the children at play, I pleaded, "Please, Tirzah is in labor. Is there a midwife among you who will come?"

Uncertain looks were exchanged.

The plump spokeswoman slyly asked, "Are you not skilled in the bringing of children into the world?"

"No, I . . ." The implication of her words rendered me speechless. She was not asking about my child-birthing abilities as much as my supposed livelihood.

I tried one final plea. "Tirzah is wife of my brother. This is her eighth child. There is no time to waste."

A slender woman with waves of brown hair framing her face joined the group.

"Come, I am Sarai, wife of Caleb," she introduced herself. "Let us go to your sister-in-law. Miriam, run for Elizabeth. Tell her to come quickly."

Without further words, she shamed the women into action.

"I will bring blankets, Sarai," offered one woman who still carried her own infant in the cloth sling formed by her veil.

"Can we help?" Other voices were now raised to offer assistance.

"Thank you, we will be fine." Ignoring all the suddenly eager offers, the woman smiled and led me back to our refugee tents.

Tirzah was still begging for a midwife between the contractions that gripped her more frequently now. Adah and Debora clung together, sobbing each time the woman cried out. Esther soothingly stroked one hand, while Jerusha tried to arrange the blankets. Each time the pain gripped her, Tirzah threw off the covering. The younger children tried to reach their mother, although Salome was managing to prevent them from grabbing her.

Sarai immediately took charge. None too gently she shook Debora by the arm.

"Take these children outside and entertain them," she ordered.

Wide-eyed, the woman obeyed, followed by Adah.

"Go with your aunts." The children sensed authority and hurried outside.

In a soothing voice, the Hebrew addressed Tirzah. "Now, how are you doing?"

"Are you the midwife?" Hopeful eyes looked up at the newcomer.

"Elizabeth is coming." The assurance calmed the frightened woman.

"Rahab says this is your eighth child." Still softly and gently,

Sarai started a conversation to distract the woman.

Tirzah had no chance to reply for another contraction rippled through her body. I had never been near a woman in labor and felt my palms grow sweaty.

"Heat water and warm a blanket for the baby." The next order was directed at Jerusha.

"I do not want that traitorous harlot here when my baby is born." For the first time Tirzah noticed my presence.

Surprised at the vehemence our visitor looked startled.

"Rahab is the one who sought out a midwife." The explanation made no difference.

"Leave, my child shall not see a harlot's face when he is born." Still the woman pointed to the entrance.

"I will go." My sister-in-law was becoming almost hysterical. It was easier to comply.

Outside the tent it was more peaceful. Adah and Debora played with the children as far from the tent as possible. Jerusha bent over the fire. From my father's tent came the murmur of men's voices and an occasional guffaw. An older woman hurried from the main camp. She was accompanied by several of the young mothers I met only a few minutes earlier. Satisfied that Tirzah would have the assistance she needed with the birthing, I walked away from the activity.

My feet took me in the direction of the stream where I drew water only a short time earlier. I sat down on a convenient rock. Behind me lay the camp of the Children of Israel at Gilgal. Still vaguely smoldering, the ruin of proud Jericho lay desolate. My mind replayed our flight through the streets and out the gate. Tears fell. I wept for my neighbors dead in the streets.

My heart cried for pity as I looked toward the ravaged city. The whisper was a desperate whisper for understanding. "I saved the lives of my family, why do they hate me?"

No one heard my despair. The soothing murmur of the water over the rocks did slowly ease the hurt and loneliness in my soul. Sarai found me when the sun was beginning to descend.

"Tirzah is delivered of a fine son." Her words held a touch of pride.

I did not even lift my head. My eyes remained fixed on the twig I trailed in the water.

"Rahab?" A note of concern entered the woman's voice.

"My brother will be pleased." My tone was bitter and harsh from the emptiness in my heart.

Sarai was silent for so long I assumed she had slipped away. I let tears of self-pity roll unchecked down my cheeks. The shadows lengthened slightly, reaching out to embrace me.

"I know the pain of being rejected by a father." The softly spoken statement came as a surprise.

The Hebrew woman slipped an arm around my shoulder as she joined me on the rock. Ashamed of my tears, I averted my face.

"Rahab of Jericho, the God of Israel has given me a family in place of the father who disowned me at birth." I listened to the low-voiced consolation. "I believe you too will find a home in our tents."

Now I turned to look at the woman beside me. My mouth twisted in a grimace. In an angry movement I threw the twig into the current and started to stand. Looking down at my companion I let all the hurt and fear boil out.

"Like my family, your Children of Israel judge me a harlot. Any defense I would make is useless. I am thought unfit for any other life. The choice I made will haunt me forever. I was a fool to expect anything else. Like Astarte, your God is unforgiving."

Gracefully, my companion rose. Before I could move, the woman caught my hands.

"Rahab, if the God of Israel was unforgiving, this people would not have survived." The words were earnest and the expression in the dark eyes was compassionate. "God has shown me that you are special. You alone of all Jericho believed that our God would accomplish the defeat of that city. Many, even here in this camp, doubted Joshua's orders and murmured against the command to silently march around the walls. You stand here alive because of your faith."

"Better to have perished in the flames of Jericho than bear the hatred and scorn of all who see me." Bitterly I tried to jerk my hands free.

Sarai tightened her hold firmly, "Rahab, hear me. I was on my way to seek you out this morning."

"Why?" Suspicion made me hesitate to believe the strange statement.

The answer was even more confusing, "You cannot remain in tents outside the camp."

Uncertain how to respond, I tilted my head and asked again, "Why?"

Sarai smiled almost tenderly, "You shall be an honored member of the community."

Memory of the whispers earlier in the day brought a new sneer to my lips. "Honored . . . what harlot is ever honored?"

"You are no longer a harlot," the woman severely reprimanded me. "We both know that you never were a harlot. Your service was to the god of your people."

"I will always be a harlot in other's eyes." Shamefaced, I lowered my head.

"God does not see anything except a woman seeking a new life." The insight from this near stranger frightened me.

"How do you know?" Wide-eyed, I gasped the question. I did not know how anyone could understand so much about my secret hopes and barely articulated dreams.

"Rahab, all who seek the True God desire a new life. It is not always easy to find your place, I know. For a long time after I learned of my father's repudiation, I doubted my worth even when all in the camp assured me of their love. The woman who took me in and called herself my mother was Miriam, sister to Moses, our great leader. Even she did not understand the ways of the Holy One. She had to be struck with leprosy before she accepted herself and her role in the community."

"Leprosy!" The name of the dreadful disease made me shudder.

Lepers were beaten from Jericho with special staves kept for that purpose. Anyone even suspected of being so cursed was better off slipping away before it became public knowledge.

"She was healed by the hand of the Living One." Sarai smiled in understanding at my reaction. "The hand of God is not short-

ened. You too can find a new life in the camp of Israel. You will
live in my tent until you find a husband."

I felt my face turn red at the thought of the one man I desired
for a husband. What this woman offered was too remarkable to
be believed.

To divert my thoughts, I brought up a stumbling block, "My
family."

"Your brothers and father may move into the camp if they
desire. Joshua came to welcome them today. I do not think they
will be happy with our life," she shrugged, "but it is their decision."

"Jerusha and Esther?" Even though my friends repudiated
me, I did not want to forsake them.

For the first time, the Hebrew woman refused to meet my
eyes.

"If they are not welcome, I cannot be welcome." Loyal words
spilled out even as I feared they would ruin my own hopes for
this promised new life.

"Rahab, it is not what you think." Sarai linked her arm
through mine.

We started to walk back toward the tents. I moved stiffly and
remained silent waiting for an explanation.

My companion cleared her throat twice before speaking,
"Tirzah has asked Esther to be the nurse for her children. She has
agreed to remain with your sister-in-law."

A lump formed in my throat. I tightened my lips and barely
breathed the name of my other friend. "Jerusha?"

"Will be Salome's maid."

At my sharp gasp, we stopped. Sarai held out her arms.

"I am so sorry," she murmured.

The words sounded sincere. I wanted to believe the near
stranger at my side. Anger welled up inside me overcoming the
grief at the desertion of both women. Breaking free from the comforting arms, I stormed the rest of the distance to the five tents at
the edge of the camp. Jerusha was bent over the fire again. This
time a savory smell of lentils floated up.

"How could you? We were friends. You have abandoned me. May the gods judge you."

My raging startled the woman. She raised her head defiantly.

"Take back your curse." Narrowed eyes glared back at me. "I have done what I could to ensure my security."

"How soon will you occupy my father's bed?" My accusing words were out before I thought. As soon as I spoke I knew I was wrong. It was too late to take back the charge.

The response was swift. Jerusha lifted her hand. The sound of the slap to my cheek seemed to echo in my head.

"I will serve Salome, not Hamash. Her beauty will be enhanced by my skills. It will not fade away like your mother's."

I caught my breath against the painful memories the words raised. My friend walked away from me toward my father's tent. I stood shaking with rage and sorrow. Esther peered from Tirzah's tent. She drew back when I glanced at her. With a moan I sank to my knees.

"May the gods grant me vindication." In the rapidly falling darkness I wept for all that I had lost.

Sarai found me still kneeling near the fire. Like a child I let the older woman pull me to my feet and lead me to her tent. Without a word she brought me warm goat milk with herbs mixed in. Grateful for the care, I drank the draught. The sleep that came was dreamless.

I did not stir from my sanctuary all the following day or the next. In solitude I licked my wounds like an injured animal. Sarai seemed to understand. She brought me food which I absently nibbled. My appetite was gone. All I felt was a drained emptiness and deep misery.

On the third morning, Sarai brought me the morning meal of flat bread with goat cheese. I listened halfheartedly to the news she brought.

"Hamash and Jonadab leave for Ataroth in the north today. I am told that your brother has vineyards and a house there. Perez and his family have decided to cast their lot with us. Your brother Hamul has not made a decision."

"He will go with my father," I prophesied.

The statement seemed to loosen the grip of my grief. If my family was moving on, I must also face my new life. It took courage even to sit just inside the tent flap watching the busy camp through the slit. I saw Caleb, Sarai's husband, pull her into his arms for a quick kiss.

"Hamul of Jericho has set out after his father. It is good." The announcement was no surprise.

"They would never have been content in our tents," the young woman agreed.

"How is your guest?" Genuine interest was apparent.

"Rahab is grieving." I saw a pucker of concern on the round face. "When she is ready, she will come out."

"I am not complaining, wife." Again the man stooped for a kiss. "I enjoy sharing my bed with you."

A low chuckle and playful swat was the swift reaction. Caleb caught the hand aimed at his chin and kissed the palm. The intimate gesture was more than I could stand. Cheeks flaming, I slid back from my post. Although I knew little about my host, I felt embarrassed to have observed such a private moment. Later the Hebrew woman entered the tent with a gourd of stew and piece of fresh bread.

"You are feeling better." The observation came after a brief glance at me.

I had combed and braided my hair. No longer were there tear streaks on my face. The pillows and blankets were piled neatly rather than in tumbled disarray from my restless days and troubled dreams.

Hurriedly I stammered out an explanation, "Sarai, it is time to accept my new life. I cannot remain a recluse. You should not be driven from your tent."

"I am so glad you are feeling better. My prayers have been heard." The woman set down the food to embrace me. A slight rose colored her cheeks as she continued, "The tent is yours until you are wed. I do not regret sharing Caleb's bed."

"Rahab, will you eat with us beside the fire?" The offer was made with outstretched hand.

Shyly I nodded and followed my new friend into the early

evening. I knew we were very dissimilar, but it seemed that this Hebrew woman wanted to be my friend.

Our appearance could not have been more different. Sarai was a short, brown sparrow of a woman. I guessed that she was several years older although her hair was still dark. Despite a life in the desert sun, her skin was smooth. She knew no other life than tents and wandering. Manna was a regular part of her diet until recently. Despite her confession near the river, love and serenity were worn like a mantle born of never knowing fear or want.

On the other hand, I was city born and raised. My height made it difficult for me to be inconspicuous even in the more modest dress of a Hebrew woman. I no longer wore the snake armlets of a servant of the goddess. The gold, copper and silver chains that had weighted my slender neck were also laid aside. Gone also were the kohl-brightened eyes, rouged cheeks and lips. I used the makeup as a kind of a mask and almost missed the concealment.

The spring air smelled sweet as the breeze brushed across the blossoming fruit trees surrounding nearby Gilgal. Contentment gathered me in an embrace as I inhaled the fragrance.

A deep voice greeted me, "Welcome, Rahab of Jericho." Caleb smiled from his seat opposite the fire. "May the God of Israel bless you for your faith."

The couple set out to make me feel at ease with stories of the trek in the desert.

"I was born while the Children of Israel wandered near Sinai," Sarai explained. "Caleb was my champion from my birth. When he asked me to be his bride, I could not believe that I was so blessed."

"Wife, you will make our guest believe that I am more than a man." The laugh that accompanied the complaint told me that he was actually pleased.

"You have your moments." With an answering giggle, the young woman gave me a glimpse of the love between the pair when she patted her husband's hand.

For just a moment I felt like an interloper.

"Then there is the rest of the time." Sarai turned to me with a smile. "You do not know how fortunate you are to not have a husband who leaves his tunic crumpled under the blankets and complains when the hummus is not seasoned correctly."

"I am chastised." Caleb nodded to his wife as he stood up. "Now I must leave this fire to meet with Joshua. God give blessing to you this night."

When the man was out of sight, Sarai turned to cleaning the platters and preparing for the night. Easily she banked the fire for the morning.

"May the God of Israel bless you." The prayer was repeated when we parted for the night.

"Blessings on you, Sarai." My response felt sincere.

I did not think I could sleep, but before I knew it the dawn was breaking.

❧ 10 ❧

THE MORNING SUN SEEMED to embrace me when I lifted the tent flap.

"Come and eat. Joshua has asked to meet you." Sarai smiled happily.

"I cannot." Startled and more than a little frightened, I shook my head.

"Of course you can." Tilting her head my friend nodded encouragement.

The idea that the great general wanted to talk to me was terrifying. My mind tried to find a reason for such an interview.

"Why would he want to meet me?" I sought an answer from the calm woman.

"Our leader wants to make you feel welcome. It is a great honor." Even the response did not ease my fear.

After a meal of flat bread and cheese that I could barely swallow, Caleb escorted me to meet Joshua. I clutched Sarai's hand as we drew close to the gray-bearded leader. Shorter than I expected from my glimpse of the general with the priests, he was still a tall and imposing figure. Broad shoulders built to wield a sword and wear armor seemed almost too large in the nomad's robe.

"Joshua." Caleb interrupted the conversation with two young men who appeared to be arguing in an impassioned way for some course of action.

"We will march at the Lord's command." A stern rebuke was the final answer to the pair.

Still unconvinced, the taller of the men would have continued to argue. Joshua turned to face his lieutenant.

"Caleb"—a smile changed the planes of the face as he addressed us—"and Sarai."

I shrank behind the woman certain that my welcome would be short-lived.

"Joshua, here is Rahab of Jericho." Sarai abandoned me when Caleb took my arm to gently draw me from behind his wife.

"It will be alright," she whispered, pushing me forward.

Head down, I waited for condemnation or scorn. Instead, strong hands took hold of mine.

"Welcome, Rahab of Jericho." Sincerity rang in the deep voice. "You are honored for your bravery and faith. I am pleased that you will make your home with the Children of Israel."

The kind words were unexpected. I lifted my head. Even though I was tall for a woman, I had to look up at the warrior. There was gentleness in the brown eyes looking at me. He seemed to accept me just as I was. My knees grew weak and I felt my hands start to shake.

"I . . . I . . . thank you," It was all I could do to stammer a short sentence in reply.

Sarai slipped an arm around my shoulders in support. Somehow the small woman understood my feelings.

"Sarai will help you learn about the Living God of Israel. Indeed you will see that the Lord bears this people as an eagle her young. Just as El Elohim Israel gave Jericho into our hands, so shall all Canaan fall before the army of the Lord. Blessed be the Name of the Lord!"

"Amen," Caleb and Sarai both responded.

I forgot my fear in awe at the ecstatic utterances from the warrior. In Jericho such prophecy was left to the priests who required drug-induced trances before they could give oracles. I stared at the man standing in worship with arms raised to the sky. The faith of the leader was obvious. When he lowered his hands they rested on my shoulders.

"Rahab of Jericho, you are welcome in this camp." The man smiled as he repeated his salutation. "May the Living God of Abraham, Isaac and Jacob bless and keep you."

I felt something like serenity flow into my body when Joshua spoke. Even when the leader turned away to talk with Caleb, I stood still. The warmth of the leader's welcome and approval continued to wash over me. At last I took a deep breath and turned to Sarai.

"Joshua is a holy man as well as a mighty general." I made the statement with complete confidence.

"His blessing comes from God," agreed the woman with a hug.

"Yes," I nodded.

With a last look at the two men now deep in conversation, Sarai took my hand. Together we crossed the distance to the tents.

"It is the day to wash," the woman told me when we came to the fire.

I accepted the pile of tunics and other garments from my friend. The smell of smoke clung to the clothing to remind me of the devastation of the only home I knew. Nervously I followed the Hebrew woman through the camp toward the river. The chatter of many voices could be heard before we saw anyone. All along the banks of the stream small clusters of women and girls pounded their clothing on rocks and rinsed them in the water.

"Sarai, you have come."

"Here is a spot."

"The water is deeper here."

"I have saved you a place."

All around friends vied for the woman's presence. I was glad that no one seemed to notice me. I held the pile of laundry close to my chest with my head lowered. The veil Sarai thoughtfully provided covered my flame-colored hair. I hoped I could remain anonymous.

"Here, Rahab, this looks like a good spot." Although she spoke softly, my identity was no longer a secret.

Up and down the stream my name was repeated.

"Rahab, who is that?"

"The harlot from Jericho is named Rahab."

"How did a harlot come to be with Sarai?"

"Doesn't she know what that woman is?"

I felt my face redden and pulled the veil close to cover my shame. The pile of laundry I carried fell to the ground. Seeming to be oblivious to the whispers, Sarai picked up the tunics I dropped. By one arm she dragged me to the water.

"Joshua is pleased that you are among us." It seemed an odd topic for discussion.

"He was very kind." I sighed at the memory of the touch and words.

"What was it he said?" The woman seemed to be musing to herself.

I stared in astonishment. The words were imprinted on my heart forever.

"Oh, yes." She smiled triumphantly and winked at me as she quoted, "'Welcome, Rahab of Jericho. You are honored for your bravery and faith. I am pleased that you will make your home with the Children of Israel.'"

Then I understood. My friend had subtly informed the avidly listening women of Joshua's acceptance of my presence. A surprised ripple ran up and down the stream bank. Sarai scrubbed the clothing and asked how washing was done in Jericho. She seemed oblivious to the excitement her words generated.

"We used troughs and had to pour the water ourselves. It is a great luxury to allow the river to rinse the clothes," I admitted.

The cold water stung my wrists as I rinsed each garment and wrung out the water. Then each piece was spread on bushes or the warm rocks nearby.

"In the desert we would beat our robes against the rocks to clean off some of the sand. It was always wonderful to find a running stream where we could soak our tired feet," Sarai explained. "If we camped at an oasis, we would draw water enough to clean at least our tunics. Whenever we found a running stream near our camp there was a festival of washing. It is indeed a luxury to have the time to thoroughly clean everything from loincloths to blankets."

Almost shyly I opened the subject, "I have heard some stories of the years in the wilderness. Is it true that when snakes attacked you all were saved by a bronze serpent?"

Small teeth flashed in a grin and the woman chuckled, "It was not quite that simple."

The smile was replaced by a serious expression. My friend stared at the tunic in her hand. For a moment she studied the water she was wringing out of the clothing.

With a frown the woman finally spoke, "Some of the people complained. I think they were afraid."

"Afraid of what? Did not your God go with you?" I found it hard to understand how anyone could doubt the power of the god who did such wonders.

Gazing across the plain, the woman was silent. She smoothed the garment in her hand as she recalled, "From my earliest memory the Lord God led us with a pillar of cloud during the day. At night the pillar glowed with an inner fire. Yes, our God was with us. Still, when it was time to face the forces of Edom . . ."

We were interrupted by the arrival of Esther with my nieces and nephews. Somewhat hesitantly the group approached. My friend carried the clothing on her head as all the women of Jericho did. There were new whispers about the lack of a veil and questions about the identity of the newcomers.

"Welcome, Esther of Jericho," Sarai spoke clearly. "Set your burden here and join us. Rahab tells me that this is a different way of washing clothing than you are used to."

"Yes," the woman nodded with a sidelong glance at me.

"Here is a veil to keep the sun off your face. We have learned to care for our complexion in the bright desert sun. The cloth is also good for keeping dust out of your eyes when the wind blows." The wife of Joshua's lieutenant gently helped the woman of Jericho.

"How is Tirzah?" I felt uncomfortable with the silence and the listening ears while Esther arranged the head covering.

"She and the child are well. The gods have been kind." For the first time Esther looked at me.

"Or the One God is gracious," Sarai provided a gentle reminder.

"Yes, of course, the One God of Israel has blessed us," Esther hastily corrected herself.

"It will take time to be comfortable with a single deity." My defense was rapid.

"I know." Understanding was in the Hebrew woman's tone.

She squeezed my wet hand with her soapy one. "You will learn. Even among us there are doubters. That is why the snakes came."

When Sarai resumed her story, I leaned toward her to listen. The children drifted away to play with the other boys and girls nearby. Esther scrubbed diligently. My former friend seemed to be listening but I was not sure.

"Aaron, brother of Moses died. We mourned for a full moon cycle. His son became the High Priest, but Eleazar lacked the authority of his father. Then the chief of Arad took some of the congregation captive in a raid. I guess he thought us an easy target."

"We heard that the city and tribe of Arad was destroyed," Esther inserted.

"Well, we could not allow our people to remain slaves," Sarai responded. "The men of Israel made a vow. Joshua led them against Arad."

She stopped and gathered her thoughts with a deep breath. "The slaughter was great. The battlefield is called Hormah now."

"That means 'destruction'," I translated softly.

"Yes, there were only a few women and children spared. They fled in the night to Beersheba. Our army returned to Mount Hor."

"Why didn't you continue into Canaan then?" I could not stop the question.

"That is why there was grumbling," admitted Sarai. "The instigators whispered that Moses was leading us back into the desert when we could have already entered the Promised Land. They raised the complaints of years earlier. 'There is no food or water in this wilderness. You have brought us out of Egypt to die in the desert.'"

I stared in astonishment at the woman. She smiled when I stammered, "B . . . b . . . but I thought you were given special food."

"When has the truth ever stopped complaints and rebellion?" Esther surprised me with her insight.

"That is true," Sarai nodded. "The discontent spread. I missed my foster mother, Miriam. She had a gift for peacemaking. Perhaps she could have forestalled the punishment."

Esther stopped her work and leaned toward Sarai. My own hands stilled when the woman spoke solemnly.

"In the midst of the confrontation with Moses, men began to cry out in fear and agony. A nest of vipers must have been disturbed by the shouting and stamping. There were dozens of the snakes among the feet. The loudest of the combatants were on a small hill facing Moses. They were struck first. Everyone fled from the snakes. There was pandemonium." The woman grimly smiled at the memory.

"It must have been awful!" I gasped with a shudder.

"Surely the gods were angry," Esther whispered in awe. "The rebellious are brought to justice by Nehushtan."

"The God of Israel brought judgment," I corrected my friend. "Is that not so?"

The Hebrew woman nodded, "The vipers were sent by the Living God as punishment for the disobedience of the people. Many died. That is why Moses beat a serpent of bronze. 'The Lord God says look on the bronze serpent and you will live.' That was the promise of Moses. Those who believed survived."

For a moment Sarai was silent, staring at the running water.

"We buried many young men and even women and children there. Those of us who were not bitten mourned our companions. There are some who call the bronze figure Nehushtan, as you said Esther." A gentle smile accompanied the admission. "They say that the snakes were God's vengeance among us."

Eagerly my friend nodded. "Yes that must be so, for Nehushtan is both life and death."

"What you have known and worshiped is only a shadow of the True and Only God," Sarai tried to explain. "You will learn of El Elohim Israel as you live among us."

I busied myself with folding the garments now dry from lying on the hot stones and hanging on the bushes. This strange God of the Children of Israel was complex. In the Temple of Jericho stood statues representing the gods, but this One God was all life and more. El Elohim Israel was among the people and gave them victory after victory. Yet, this God demanded unflagging obedience. I wondered if I could ever measure up to such a deity.

Sarai and Esther hurried away when a fight broke out among the older children. My nephews stood against a group of mud-slinging Hebrew boys. I sighed, wondering if it was possible for my family to be accepted by the conquerors. With a heavy heart I plodded back to Sarai's tent with my bundle of clean clothing. Eventually the woman returned.

"All is well," she assured me. "Boys are usually able to work out their own problems."

Although relieved by the woman's optimism, I found myself worrying about the reaction Perez would have to his son's recitation of their fight. Fear that he would do something foolish kept me awake most of the night. Troubled dreams left me heavy-eyed in the morning. Sarai did not notice. She was already busy when I lifted the tent flap and stepped out into the dawn.

"Today is preparation for the Sabbath," I was informed. "Every seventh day is ordained by the One God for rest and worship. No work is done. We must prepare food for today and for tomorrow."

The day flew by as I followed the woman's instructions. Not only did the meal have to be made ready but all over the camp a frenzy of straightening tent poles, shaking blankets and rugs with fluffing of pillows created a softly settling cloud of dust in the late afternoon. Each family disappeared into their tent to emerge as the sun set. We all made our way to the Tabernacle.

Caleb and Sarai urged me to come when I hung back, "Come with us."

In a whisper I voiced my fear to Sarai, "I am a stranger, an alien. Your God may strike me dead."

"God has accepted you for your faith," Caleb asserted heartily. "Joshua himself has said so."

"Do not be afraid." My friend drew me close to her side.

There was no time for further discussion. Reluctantly I let myself be led by the hand through the camp to join the rest of the congregation. The High Priest stepped forward and cast incense on the altar. Smoke billowed up.

I recognized the exclamation spoken by the man, "Amen, Alleluia, El Elohim Israel."

All around the people repeated the words with enthusiasm.

"Our father went to Egypt a few in number. God raised us from bondage a mighty nation," Eleazar proclaimed.

"Alleluia, El Elohim Israel!" was the shouted response.

"Blessed be the God of Abraham, Isaac and Jacob who has brought us to the land promised to our father Israel." With exaltation the priest continued. "The way to our homeland is open. None can stand before the might of the Living God."

"Amen, Alleluia, El Elohim Israel." Again the cheer sounded.

"The last Sabbath was sanctification of the army to God in battle. Victory over Jericho has been given by the Holy One. This Sabbath is dedication of our lives to the service of the Holy God who will lead us in conquest!"

All around me rang out the chant, "Amen, Alleluia, El Elohim Israel."

Prayers for strength and victory followed. Blessings were pronounced over the people and warriors. I found myself caught up in the fervor of the nation. Their God had led them from bondage to this place. Nothing would stop the advance and settlement of the Children of Israel in the Land of Canaan. I prayed that their God would accept me. My heart yearned to be part of the devotion I felt around me. My voice joined with the rest.

"Amen, Alleluia, El Elohim Israel!"

Sarai squeezed my hand when she heard my response.

With a last prayer the people were dismissed. "Go in peace. The God of Moses is our bulwark, our cloud, our defender."

"Amen, Alleluia, El Elohim Israel!" Again and again the words rang out in the darkness.

The only light came from the flames on the altar consuming the last of the incense to leave a lingering cloud over the camp. Through this each family returned to their tent.

Beside every fire, the same scene played out. Women set out food already prepared. Meat kept warm in a pit next to the fire was served with fresh bread from the morning and new vegetables. Instead of cleaning the platters, Sarai covered them with a cloth.

"We will clean up after the Sabbath is over," she explained. "Sleep well, Rahab of Jericho."

I waited beside the banked fire until every person in the encampment was in their tent. There was much to think about. The God of the Hebrew was powerful, yet the people were not terrified of the deity. The priests of Astarte invoked the wrath of the goddess and intimidated everyone in Jericho with threats. How could this people continue to test their God? I thought of the tales I heard from travelers. They spoke of special food and water springing from stones in the desert. The story of the vipers in the camp chilled me until I remembered Sarai telling of the bronze serpent that healed those who believed.

"What kind of God are you to provide healing even as you punish?" Into the darkness I breathed the question. "Astarte requires endless propitiation. The goddess does not do the wonders I have heard of nor does she answer prayer. It seems that you are a god who offers succor even in the midst of the pain. Truly you must be great, El Elohim Israel."

The silence was reassuring even though no answer came. I slipped into the tent and under my blankets still pondering the faith of these former slaves and the God who they worshipped.

"El Elohim Israel." I murmured the name of the god into the night until sleep claimed me.

Morning light through the tent flap awakened me. The camp was not the usually bustling hive of activity. Each family stayed near their tent until the sun was high. Then we all converged on the Tabernacle.

Eleazar led many prayers. Then Joshua stood up with Caleb and the other captains.

"Blessed be our God who gives us victory. The Lord promised the Land of Canaan to Abraham and his seed forever. By the mighty hand of the Living God the waters were parted for us, but the Egyptian hosts drowned. With loving care the Lord of All led us forty years in the wilderness. We ate food from the hand of God until we crossed the Jordan. Now at the command of our God we go forward in holy conquest. The cities will fall before us

as fell the walls of Jericho. The Living God casts down our enemies before us."

A cheer echoed off the hills behind Gilgal. Across the crowd
I glimpsed my brother in front of his tent. At the mention of
Jericho he drew back behind the flap.

Joshua waited for the shouts to die down.

"The Lord has shown me that we will march against Ai. The
people depend on the mountains to protect them. We trust in the
Lord our God."

"Alleluia, El Elohim Israel!" The familiar cry burst from
thousands of throats.

"Gird on your swords, O Israel!" Eleazar stepped forward to
stand beside the general. "Our God has given you the victory!"

A resounding response of cheers and stamping signaled the
willingness of the men. Silence from the women was not noticed
in the enthusiasm.

"At first light we will set out. Three hundred men will be
chosen from each tribe. Only a small force is needed. Ai is not a
powerful city," Joshua assured the congregation. "The God of
Abraham, Isaac and Jacob, the God of Moses will be our victory!"

"Amen, Alleluia, El Elohim Israel!" Again the chant echoed.

I overheard some grumbling as Sarai and I walked across the
camp to our tents.

"Can only three thousand men take the city?"

"It is not fair that only a few share in the glory."

"The captains will choose their favorites."

"We will get none of the spoils."

My friend was very quiet. I knew she feared for Caleb. When
he finally returned from a strategy meeting she ran to him.

An impassioned plea burst from her lips, "My husband, say
you will not go up against Ai. My heart warns me that this is
folly."

The man softly kissed her forehead before replying, "Beloved,
the men who scouted the town say it is small and poorly fortified. Only a small force will march against the city. I am to stay
in camp. Joshua wants my advice about other matters."

Sarai ignored the disappointment in her husband's voice.

"I am glad that you will not fight this time." Tears stood in the woman's dark eyes.

Caleb gathered his wife into his arms. "My wife, my love, do not weep. The Lord will give us the victory."

I looked away while the man comforted my friend. Despite his disappointment, Caleb was an entertaining host. We ate the remains of the meat and vegetables as the Sabbath ended with the sundown.

"You should have heard the excuses from the men. Every one has a reason why they must be part of the raiding party." With a chuckle the man shared some stories. "Joash of Judah swears that he has taken an oath to God to fight in every battle. We all know that his oath is to Eve. He promised her a gown from every town. Then old Hezikiah begged to go along. Sadly he is so feeble that he can only drag the sword behind him."

"The reason Hezikiah wants to be part of the group is to be away from Leah. Her nagging would drive any man to war." Sarai leaned close to me to confide the motive.

After more tales that had us smiling at the pretexts of the warriors, Caleb belched his satisfaction of the meal and disappeared into the tent he shared with Sarai.

I was awake to see the soldiers march west in the morning. The army looked grand with banners flying in the breeze as they tramped past Gilgal toward the pass.

Three days later it was a disheartened and defeated troop that returned to camp. Bloodstained, dusty and exhausted, the grand army stumbled into camp with a report of defeat. They bore the bodies of three dozen fallen comrades. At the sound of wailing, Sarai rushed from the fire.

We were kept busy bandaging wounds all day. Wives and mothers keened over their fallen men. The thirty-six soldiers lay in the center of the camp. Joshua was devastated. He went from family to family offering condolences. The man's face was gray with grief.

"We were not in formation when the men of Ai attacked."

"They came from the city, a mighty army."

"Arrows and spears poured down like rain from the heights."

"Men were killed as we advanced."

"There was no choice but to retreat."

When the leader finally made his way to where the wounded lay, we had already heard the sad tale of surprising resistance.

"God was not with us." One young captain gripped Joshua by the arm. "El Elohim Israel has deserted us."

"We have sinned," Joshua stated. "I must pray. We must all pray that the Living God will show us our error."

Striding across camp the general knelt and then prostrated himself before the Tabernacle. Caleb, Eleazar and the tribal elders joined him in obeisance.

"Why, Lord God?" the heartbroken cry was heard throughout the camp. "Why did you bring us into this land? Will you now destroy us?"

The petitions continued until late afternoon. As the sun approached the hills, Joshua stood up.

"Assemble, O Israel." The order rippled through the camp. A call from the ram's horn summoned everyone who could walk.

No longer the confident people of the Sabbath, a subdued congregation gathered to hear their leader.

"Thus says the Lord, the Mighty One who goes before us. 'Sanctify yourselves. There are those among you who withheld spoils from Jericho. All of the booty of that city is holy to the Living God.' We dare not stand before the Lord." Joshua seemed to look at each person. "In the morning each tribe will be tested until the perpetrator is found. That man and all he has will be burned outside the camp."

In silence the congregation dispersed. I was astonished and appalled at the order until I remembered how the priests of Astarte had stoned one of their own for daring to touch the foot of the lapis-studded statue of the goddess.

"It was an accident," the poor man had cried in desperation. "I tripped."

"Better to fall on your face than profane the most holy Queen of Heaven." The ringing judgment had seemed right to me as the Daughter of Astarte.

Then I was a child, awed by the grandeur of the Temple, the statues and the power of the priests. Now, as a woman, the punishment seemed extreme. I was saddened that the God I almost trusted also demanded such a penalty.

I was glad that Sarai did not speak as we worked together preparing the evening meal. Her eyes kept straying to Caleb who paced restlessly. He seemed to be waiting for someone. The Hebrew captain was finally met by a man that I recognized even in the moonlight. It was Salma. Together the men moved to the fire. My heart beat faster at his approach. Intent on their conversation neither soldier noticed us.

Sarai placed the platter in front of Caleb then drew me into my tent. Her tension was evident in the way she braided her hair again and again. We both strained to hear the conversation.

"You reported a small town, easily defeated." The accusation sounded angry.

Salma's reply was equally heated, "Both Ai and Bethel are small. The towns are poorly protected even though they straddle the pass to the north and to the west. They have low walls and few soldiers. The wall at Ai is a crumbling ruin already. A child could walk over it."

"Why, then, were we defeated?" Caleb spoke slowly.

"Jesse led the troops straight up the road allowing the defenders deadly access." I heard scorn in the response. "A frontal uphill assault is destined for failure."

"What would you suggest?" Caleb spoke around a mouthful of food.

"There are ravines through which an army can get between Ai and Bethel. It is like this." Without looking we knew Salma was drawing in the sand. "Our entire force could lie in wait here while a small contingent draws the men from both towns. Then the ambush would be complete."

"Hmmm," the older man seemed to be weighing the idea. "Then we would be uphill and the men of the towns would be caught between our forces."

"Defeat would be total." With enthusiasm the spy agreed.

"I will speak to Joshua. He will appreciate a plan." Approval was evident in the tone. "You have done well. God will yet give us a victory."

"Thank you for hearing me out." The younger man sounded more relaxed.

In silence the men completed the meal. I heard the rustle of garments when they rose. Cautiously I peeked around the corner of the tent flap.

"Salma, you are of great service to your people." Caleb slapped his comrade on the back.

The spy did not respond. He glanced around as if seeking something. I ordered myself to not dream of the young man and prepared to turn back to Sarai.

"Is Rahab of Jericho still here?" I almost missed the question as I let the flap slip out of my hand.

Caleb chuckled at the shy inquiry. "Yes. When we return victorious you should come to visit."

"I . . . um . . . yes . . . um . . . sir." Stammering with embarrassment the man hurried away.

Sarai slipped past me to stand by her husband. I knew she too had heard the last exchange but I was grateful that she said nothing. My heart was too excited for sleep. It was my turn to absently braid my hair and dream of the handsome young man long after the remaining bread was wrapped in the basket for the morning and my friend slept beside her husband. When I did finally sleep, I dreamt of Salma's smiling face at my window in Jericho.

⚬ 11 ⚬

I WAS AWAKENED BY Sarai tugging my arm. Slowly I opened my
eyes. It was hard to leave the dream where Salma embraced me
and called me beloved.

"Hurry, we must go to the Tabernacle." The order was sharp
when I slowly yawned and stretched.

"Oh, the test." The defeat and rationale of the previous day
resurfaced.

Dread erased the lingering memory of the dream. I scrambled
from my pallet. It was the work of a moment to slip a gown over
my tunic and toss a veil over my hair. Caleb was nowhere in sight
as I followed my friend across the camp. When we drew close to
the Tabernacle I saw that he was already with Joshua, Eleazar and
the elders. The leaders looked very stern. Their set faces made
me shudder with fear as we drew close to the holy enclosure.

"We are commanded to love the One God and to have no
other idols," the High Priest spoke. "By withholding a portion of
the spoils of Jericho, one of you has set up an idol in place of the
God of Abraham, Isaac and Jacob. The Lord has turned from
Israel. Only by rooting out the transgressor can we be made holy
before our God again."

"Have mercy," groaned someone in the crowd.

The plea was taken up all around, "Have mercy, oh God, have
mercy."

Eleazar raised his hands for silence. "Our God is merciful as
well as holy. The Holy One will not blot out the nation, only the
one who disobeyed. This man has set himself against his com-

mander and against the Living God. Such treason is redeemable only by death."

I felt as much as heard the sigh of agreement that moved through the congregation.

"Let the man who has done this thing step forward." An order came from the general.

No one moved except to look expectantly around.

"The Living God will tell us who is at fault," Eleazar warned the men and women.

Still no one moved.

"Let the tribe of Reuben come forward." With a resigned sigh the High Priest began the examination.

A section of the congregation moved out to stand before the ark and leaders. I did not know what to expect. Nothing happened.

"You may return," the priest waved the men away.

"Simeon, step up," Joshua spoke.

Another line of men stood before the priest only to be waved back.

"Levi?" The general looked at Eleazar. I wondered why he hesitated.

"We too will stand before the judgment of God," the High Priest nodded.

The array of priests and their families was impressive. Many wore the white turbans of their office.

"It is not from Levi that this sin comes," Joshua announced.

Men returned to their place in the congregation. The general stood silent. A stern look searched the crowd. We all stood motionless. Even the children sensed the seriousness of the occasion and clung to their mothers.

When the silence seemed almost unbearable the man spoke, "The tribe of Judah."

I saw Salma among the men and held my breath.

"Hold," Eleazar spoke when Joshua would have motioned the tribe back. "Let the head of each household come forward."

Again Salma stepped up. His head was held high although I could see that his jaw flexed when he clenched his teeth. I was sure he had nothing to hide. Standing before the altar, the High Priest scanned the face of each man. When he moved it was to stop in front of an old man.

"Zabdi, let each man of your house step forward."

"Not Zabdi," I heard shocked murmurs all around. "Poor old man, how dare his sons shame him again?"

With lowered heads two dozen men stood before Joshua.

"Achan, son of Carmi." The leader spoke one name clearly.

Every other man stepped back a pace leaving one young man alone. Joshua placed his hands on the broad shoulders of the warrior.

"My son." Almost tenderly the general spoke. "To El Elohim Israel belong the spoils. Tell me what you have done."

I thought the man would refuse for he raised his chin in a gesture of defiance and sneered. He moved as if to throw off the restraining hands.

"Do not hide it from me." A stern note crept into Joshua's voice and the grip tightened on the accused.

Achan looked at Eleazar, the crowd, the elders. His mouth opened and closed. The silence grew. A baby cried and was quickly hushed. From Gilgal could be heard the sounds of a town at its business. With a final panicked look around, the young man fell prostrate. The confession he sobbed out was hard to understand.

"My Lord Joshua, it is true. I have kept booty from Jericho. Hidden under the dirt in my tent are two hundred shekels of silver wrapped in a cloak and leather to keep out the moisture."

A gasp greeted the admission. Rising to his knees, Achan spoke again.

"I entered a wealthy house. The family had fled from us. Much fine clothing and piles of gold and silver pieces were added to the spoils. I saw to it that they were added to the wagons and only kept what fell to the ground." The voice was proud and defiant. "When I saw the fine embroidered mantle from Shinar I coveted it. It was easy to slip it inside my tunic. Under the breastplate no one would know that I carried a secret bundle. I knew that Mara would love the cloth. My wife deserved a gift from the battle. She let me go with many tears. I could not return empty handed."

The silence was heavy. Joshua gave a nod. Two men ran to Achan's tent. In a short time they were back. The leather packet was handed to Joshua. He unfolded the covering. Rippling silk tumbled toward the ground. Achan reached out and caught the material. Even now his desire was apparent as he caressed the evidence of his guilt. As the garment unrolled, a bar of gold and shower of silver coins tumbled to the ground as well. I heard the intake of breath around me.

Eleazar frowned. "Because you have sinned by holding back these things that should be offered to God your life is forfeit."

Strangely the young man no longer seemed repentant. He stood up and scoffed, "You think that my death will appease your One God? Am I alone in my guilt? Are there not others who looted the spoils of Jericho?"

"Bring all that is of the household of Achan." The priest made no response to the challenge.

I caught my breath when a woman was shoved from the crowd to stand beside her husband. Four children clung to their mother. The boys tried to imitate their father with bravado while the girls hid against the woman's legs. A dozen armed men surrounded the family. Among them was Salma. The handsome face was stern and white above his mustache. I could not tell what emotion the man felt. My own heart was troubled by the appearance of the children.

With Eleazar leading the way, we all followed the condemned man and his family. I was unwillingly drawn along with the movement of the crowd. Beyond the camp was a hill. At the top of the hill we overlooked a peaceful valley. A few men were just completing a pen for the sheep, oxen and a couple of donkeys that were milling in the hastily erected enclosure. Before the contingent reached the valley floor, the animals lay dead beside a fire. The tent and few belongings of the family were piled nearby to be added to the flames.

Eleazar marched implacably forward. The guards urged the man and his family down the path. Mara began to sob hysterically.

"I never wanted the mantle," we heard her accuse Achan. "You forced me to keep it."

"Woman, do not lie. I remember your words as I left for the battle. 'Bring me something a fine lady would wear.' It was your fault that I kept the garment."

Everyone heard the harsh response and saw the slap he administered to his wife.

"I never meant it." Pitifully, the woman appealed to the soldiers with outstretched hands.

There was no response from the guards. Salma's face was set in grim lines. He looked away from the sobbing children. Achan and his family were herded into the fenced area with his animals and other possessions.

Joshua spoke. His voice was filled with sorrow. "Achan, son of Carmi ben Zabdi of the tribe of Judah, you stand before the congregation guilty by your own words. Why did you bring trouble on the Children of Israel and your own family? Truly you are named Achan, which means trouble. This place must now be known as Achor, the Valley of Trouble."

Eleazar raised his hands, "Blessed be the God of our Fathers. Faithful is the Name of the Lord. The Holy One spares not those who sin in order to preserve a holy heritage forever."

A loud "Amen" echoed against the hillsides. I saw Achan flinch.

"Achan of the house of Judah, you have confessed your guilt. All Israel stands in judgment upon you. Death is the punishment decreed for touching holy things with unclean hands. Therefore the tribe of Judah must cleanse this evil from our midst."

Only then did I understand that the dozen soldiers were all of the same tribe. As one man they stepped back three paces. Each man stooped and picked up a heavy stone. On some unseen signal the rocks flew true to strike Achan, his wife and children down. Then every man of Israel rained down stones until the family was buried. The acrid smell of burning leather and animal flesh curled up from the valley as fire consumed the possessions of the condemned man.

"It is done." Joshua's hoarse voice was heard calling a halt to the rain of stones. "Return to your tents."

I was relieved. Even young children had begun to pelt the cairn with more rocks. The congregation drew back from the edge of the valley. A few last stones rattled onto the mounds that were once human figures.

"The Lord will lead us in victory now that the abomination has been cleansed from the midst of the camp." Eleazar seemed almost fanatical when he led the cry of "Alleluia, El Elohim Israel."

I was glad to leave the scene. The smoke made me choke. Sorrow over the wasted life overwhelmed me. In my mind I could still hear the pitiful cries of the children.

Perez accosted me when I returned to the camp. "Did the people really execute that man for taking a mantle and some coins?"

"It was not the theft," I struggled to explain. "Achan kept back what was to be offered only to God. All the spoils of Jericho were dedicated to the God of Israel."

My brother shuddered. "A harsh god."

"Are not the priests of Astarte just as harsh? I have seen a man stoned for touching the foot of a statue." My defense surprised me as much as Perez. "Can Astarte do what the One God has done? Would the priests of the goddess welcome an outsider into their ceremonies as we have been included? Truly this God is greater than Astarte or any of the gods of Jericho."

"Perhaps," the man mused. "Perhaps what you say has merit but we all know that you are easily swayed by religious pretension. Like our mother you seek to explain the holy. It is not for you to understand."

Before I could bristle with resentment, my brother added, "Esther and Tirzah would like to see you. The ways of this people are strange to my wife."

Staring after the man as he walked away I wondered if he was offering reconciliation. I remembered, too well, Tirzah's harsh words at the birth of my newest nephew. Glancing around, I saw that each family was making preparations for the evening in a subdued fashion. The trial and execution of Achan had taken the entire day. With much to think about I wended my way to Sarai's side. She too was silent as we sliced vegetables and boiled hummus.

After the meal I watched as my friend sought comfort from the events of the day by snuggling into Caleb's arms. I wished I could blot out the terrified expression on the face of the convicted mother when the dozen soldiers released their deadly barrage. Even worse was the image of the bloodied bodies before the rocks hid them from sight. Too restless to sleep, I wandered toward the stream.

"God of this people." I talked to the unseen and unknown deity as I walked. "I want to understand how you can condone such savagery in the name of obedience."

I did not see anyone until my foot snapped a twig. A crouching figure beside the water sprang erect with a dagger in his hand. Startled by the sudden appearance, I cried out and stumbled backward to trip on my own feet. As I fell to the ground, I cowered in fear. Terrified, I covered my head with my arms and waited for the blow.

"Rahab?" My name was a question.

The voice was familiar. Cautiously I raised my head to look into Salma's eyes. The young man crouched in front of me. I saw concern in the pucker between the blue eyes.

"Are you alright? I did not mean to frighten you. I thought I was alone." Babbling questions and explanations, Salma reached out to me.

"Y . . . yes." The touch of strong hands on my shoulders made me quiver.

Gently I found myself lifted to my feet.

"I . . . I was . . . not . . . looking. I was thinking." It was my turn to stammer.

"You were there today." His statement brought a nod and shudder.

Almost as though trying to convince himself, the young man looked away and said, "Achan had to die."

"I know." The two words were all I could say.

The man drew me to a seat on a nearby flat rock. I did not

want to talk about death. Instead I yearned for the comfort of this man's arms.

"Achan sinned against Israel and against God." Still, Salma rationalized. "His wife was equally guilty."

I had nothing to add but I wished I could ease the obvious torment that mirrored mine. The next words were so low I nearly missed hearing them.

"The children . . . they haunt me. What evil could they have done?"

"Salma." His name was all I could say.

The man turned and buried his face in my neck like a boy. It felt natural to caress the head and stroke the heaving back. We sat together for a long time. I sought for some words of comfort.

"God of Salma, ease your faithful servant's grief." Prayer seemed the natural response. "Your law ordered the punishment meted out today."

A breeze from the mountains made me shiver. I wished I had brought a shawl. Salma raised his head. He seemed calmer.

"Rahab, you are cold. How foolish I have been to let you become chilled while I moaned like an infant."

Rapidly the man wrapped us both in his cloak.

"It was only the breeze," I insisted, although I did not resist being pulled close to the well-muscled side.

"You are an amazing woman." The tone was tender.

I swallowed the longing in my throat and moved my head in denial against the soft wool of his tunic.

"Do not deny it." I heard a smile even if I could not see his face.

The moonlight struck the river but did not reach into the shadows where we sat. Again I shook my head.

"My family believes that I am the harlot of Jericho who betrayed her people." I could not stop the bitter statement.

"They are wrong," Salma confidently argued. "The Rahab I know is the brave, proud woman who sacrificed herself in service of her beliefs. The Rahab I know is a faithful woman who trusted in the Living God even before you came to know the Holy One. You have seen the Children of Israel at our worst, yet you remain. That is not the action of a treacherous person."

My heart soaked in the affirming words even though tears stung my eyes.

A denial started, "I am not . . ."

Salma stopped my words by gently pressing his lips to mine. I forgot everything in the enjoyment of the kiss. It was so different from Balak who took satisfaction without any tenderness. When the man lifted his head I felt bereft and sighed.

"Have you never been kissed?" The amazement in the question brought hot blood to my cheeks.

I was glad that night hid my blush. Trying to draw away, I mumbled, "Not really."

"I am glad." With a happy chuckle Salma reclaimed my mouth. Too soon the man drew away and stood up. "Rahab, I am a man of flesh. I honor you too much to continue."

I backed away, half afraid I had offended the man. My hands pressed tight against the pounding of my heart. I heard the deep breath my love took and watched him rake a hand through his hair.

"Salma?" Hesitantly I spoke his name.

"Now is not the time or place to discuss our future. You must return to your tent." As if afraid to trust himself, the man kept his hands behind his back. "When the armies return from Ai we can talk."

I held out one hand. "Salma." I needed to be reassured that he was not angry.

"Rahab." The stern tone and hands on my shoulders stopped me. "I will come to you when we return. Then we can talk."

With that dismissal the soldier strode away up the river. I watched him go, unsure whether to cry for joy or sorrow. The wool cloak I still wore smelled of the man, and I wrapped it around my body.

"Bring Salma back safely," I whispered into the night, hoping that the God of Israel was listening.

⤳ 12 ⤶

I UNDERSTOOD THE REASON for Salma's abrupt departure in the morning. Sarai packed a leather pouch with food. Caleb kissed his wife on the cheek and accepted the bundle. With a nod in my direction, the man turned away. He walked across the camp. It seemed odd. Every other morning the embrace was sustained and amorous.

"The army will pray today and sleep before the ark this night to be sanctified for the war. They will abstain from women for three days before entering battle against Ai," my friend explained with a smile at my quizzical expression. "It is a sacrifice our men undertake before any important battle. The vigil before God makes them strong and dedicated.

The woman's wry smile and sigh led me to ask, "Do you believe that is true?"

"I miss my husband. My arms are empty at night." A blush colored her cheeks. The woman rapidly changed the subject.

Her fingers brushed the fringe on the cloak I wore.

"You have a new mantle to keep you warm." The knowing smile caused my face to turn as red as my hair.

"I . . . he . . . yes . . . no." I could not form a coherent sentence that would explain Salma's garment around my shoulders.

Like a mother, Sarai drew me against her side. "I think it is a blessing when a man finds a woman desirable. I would rejoice to see you a bride."

Speechless, I could only stare at my friend. Her smile assured me that the words were not mocking.

I repeated my excuse, "I am not worthy." It was my defense against any future disappointment.

"Let Salma be the one to decide your worth," counseled the woman.

There was no further teasing when the Hebrew turned to her morning tasks. After folding the cloak carefully onto my pallet, I joined her.

Two days later the army marched out of camp. Past Jericho and up the pass toward Ai they streamed. It was a larger group of soldiers than the first assault. I was sure that the small city would fall to the forces of Israel.

Cheers and shouts of "Alleluia, El Elohim Israel" rang from the army to be answered by the congregation.

All the women fell silent as the last of the men disappeared from sight past the ruins of Jericho.

"God give them victory." All around I heard the prayers.

My heart repeated the plea, "Please bring Salma home safely, and Caleb."

The men who remained in the camp gathered before the Tabernacle. I heard loud prayers addressed to the cloud of sweet-smelling smoke covering the altar. The worshippers included the elderly and injured with a meager handful of the valiant fighting men who were our defense. I thought I glimpsed Perez among the men but could not be sure. When there was no longer even a hint of the diminishing dust, I turned back toward my own home. Across the camp, I saw Esther standing in front of my brother's tent. I remembered the odd request the man made. Taking a deep breath, I changed direction to move toward the woman.

It was easy to cross the partially deserted camp. Children and dogs played here and there. Women bent to the daily work of cooking and weaving. Several nodded to me as I passed. I was nearly to Perez's tent when I realized that the ripple of whispers was absent. The thought that I was no longer a subject of gossip and speculation took my breath away for a moment. Barely able to believe it, I paused and glanced back. My presence did not dis-

turb the rhythm of the morning. It made my step lighter as I
approached Esther. She warily watched me approach.

"What do you want?" The question was more fearful than
hostile.

"I came to see you and Tirzah and the baby." Belatedly I
remembered I should have found a gift for my nephew.

"I will ask my mistress." Coldly formal, the woman turned to
enter the tent.

From nervous habit my fingers closed around the amulet at
my throat. Long ago my mother gave it to me.

"This will protect you against evil," she told me each year on
my birthday when the pouch was strung on a longer cord.

The little figure inside was of lapis. I wore the talisman more
from habit than from any belief in the power residing there. Now
I slipped the cord over my head. It seemed a fitting gift for my
nephew. Perhaps he would be reminded of the grandmother he
would never know. Her spirit might even keep the boy safe as he
grew older.

Esther reappeared. "Come in." She seemed almost surprised
that I was to be invited inside the tent.

It felt awkward to cross the dirt floor. So much had happened
since I fled from her angry words. My sister-in-law sat rocking
her infant on a low stool. We looked at each other. I did not see
my nephews. Rebekka peered from behind her mother. After a
moment I crouched down in front of my sister-in-law.

Finding my voice I held out my hand. "I have a gift for my
nephew." Nestled there was the pouch. "This amulet has kept me
safe since I was a baby. It was a gift from my mother."

Opening the little leather bag, I let the tiny blue figure roll
out into my palm. Memories of my mother holding the talisman
and praying for me on each birthday flooded over me. Choking
back tears, I dropped the sacred object back into the soft leather
bag. Tying the top closed I held out the gift.

"I know my mother would be pleased that her grandson will
now wear this." I laid the gift on Tirzah's lap when she made no
movement. I felt as if my mother was nearby, approving of my
action.

My sister-in-law sat silent. I could not see her expression for she sat with head lowered over the child. I wished I dared ask to hold the baby but he slept content. When no one spoke I rose from my crouching position.

"May the God of Abraham, Isaac and Jacob who protects this people also bless and keep you and yours."

I did not know if either woman heard my softly spoken prayer as I turned to leave. With head lowered I covered the few steps to the opening. My hand reached for the tent flap.

"Rahab." I looked back when Tirzah spoke my name. "Thank you. It will mean a great deal to Perez that his son is protected by this talisman."

With an incline of my head, I acknowledged the thanks. Lifting the hide I felt the increasingly familiar empty pain in my heart. All I wanted to do was find a secluded spot to nurse my loneliness. There was to be no reconciliation. I wished I had not risked coming.

"Wait." The order was accompanied by a rustle of movement.

I paused. My hand clenched tight where I gripped the edge of the opening. The woman was behind me.

"Rahab, we should talk." Her voice was respectful and sounded almost humble.

It was my turn to be silent.

"I believed what Hamash said about you." I could hear embarrassment in the tone. It was easy to see that the admission was not easy. "He said, 'Rahab is a harlot and sells her body for money. She shames her family without regard for them.' Others repeated the claim."

"Yes." As much as it hurt, I had to agree with what Tirzah said.

The next statement took me completely by surprise.

"I think people lied."

The leather flap dropped from my limp hand. In amazement I faced my sister-in-law. The dim light within the tent showed her holding out both hands to me. The tears in her eyes were mirrored in mine.

"Esther has told me how you served the Temple and how the

priests supported the inn. You hated the situation with Balak. I know now that you did not offer anything but food and lodging to travelers. I might have been forced to similar extremes when my father died. Your brother accepted me without a dowry. I could have ended up in a worse situation than you without his protection." In a rush Tirzah poured out her plea for understanding. "Forgive me for judging you."

The confession surprised me. I took the offered hands as tears spilled down my cheeks.

"My sister." Sobbing, we embraced.

I heard Esther sniff in sympathy. She stood beside the nursing stool holding the baby. A broad smile split her face even as tears streamed down her cheeks.

Tears spent, I allowed Tirzah to draw me to a seat. She reclaimed her sleeping son and laid him in my arms. It was the first baby I had held since I left my father's house. A wave of longing for a child of my own took me by surprise.

"He is perfect." I gathered the small body close to my heart and bent to kiss the soft curls that covered the tiny head.

"Perez has named him Joshua, after the man who leads this people." At the simple announcement I lifted my head in amazement.

"It is a good name." My attention returned to the baby I held.

The name meaning "God saves" was indeed perfect for this child born so soon after our flight from Jericho. Still I was astonished that my brother would have chosen to honor the leader of the armies of Israel by giving the same name to his son.

The baby squirmed and whimpered. I rocked back and forth until he quieted.

"The man has been good to us," Tirzah explained even though I did not ask. "He came personally to invite us to live with the Hebrews. I could not travel and Perez agreed to the offer. Now my husband seeks to learn about this new god. The gods of Jericho are enough for me. I do not want to follow any god who causes such destruction."

In my sister-in-law's adamant words, I heard a challenge.

"Any army would have despoiled Jericho," I reminded both

the women and myself. "The wonder of this God of Israel is that the defenses melted before the soldiers. Not only that, all the spoils were given to God, not kept for each man."

"The punishment for failure to comply was enough to deter anyone," Esther commented with a frown.

"I know that it seems harsh to stone the man and burn his possessions, including his family." A sigh born of my own remembered sorrow was in the answer. When neither woman replied I added, "We have seen the same punishment meted out. Esther, do you remember what the priests of Astarte did to Poltar? All he did was touch the feet of the statue in the Temple when he tripped."

"Ooh." The drawn-out, thoughtful sound came from Esther who exclaimed, "I had forgotten! That punishment was stoning, too. I can hear the priestess screaming 'Poltar defiled the Great Lady. He must be stoned.' Then they dragged him from the room despite his pleas."

The woman was silent for a moment before adding, "What is holy is to be protected."

I had to shake my head, "I do not understand why. If the gods are truly powerful then they should need no protection."

My words brought a confused pucker to my friend's face. She was still considering my statement when Tirzah spoke.

"Then this god of the Children of Israel is no different than Baal and Astarte?"

My reply was a question as well. "Has Astarte done the things this God has?"

"What things?" The woman's confusion reminded me that she never heard the stories of the mighty deeds. My mother recited many of the tales to me. Esther, Jerusha and I had listened to the traders tell further wonders while we sought information for the Temple and leaders of Jericho to use against the invaders.

Esther spoke before I could. "We have heard of springs of water in the desert and flocks of quail to eat. There is talk of the earth opening and snakes among those who doubted."

"A generation ago, the God of this people performed mighty miracles against the gods of Egypt until Pharaoh freed the nation from slavery." I expounded briefly, "My mother told me stories as she heard them from her father at the shrine of Bethel."

A wail from the baby interrupted our conversation. As one we turned to the boy. Esther picked up the child and gave him to his mother. My niece shook a rattle made from a dried gourd. Happy now that he was the center of attention, the crying stopped. The baby reached out for the enticing toy. I smiled at my nephew and wished again that I might someday hold a child of my own.

"It is time for me to return to my tent." After a moment of watching mother and child, I stood up to leave.

"You must tell me more," Tirzah stated. "If we are to live among these Hebrew, I will need to understand their ways. Can you come again?"

"If you want me to." Her smile and nod were all the encouragement I needed. "I can bring Sarai to tell of the mighty deeds of the Living God."

"Yes, we will learn together the ways of this nation." Another nod of agreement warmed my empty heart.

Overwhelmed by love, I bent to hug the woman and kiss my nephew. He sought his mother's breast as I turned to leave. Esther followed.

"Are you angry with me for deserting you to serve Tirzah?" Almost pleading, my friend begged understanding. "She needed someone to help her. Having a new baby in such strange circumstances is difficult. You are so strong, I knew you would survive."

"I was hurt." Soberly, I admitted the truth. "Everyone seemed to have turned against me. Tirzah ordered me from her sight. Jerusha went with Hamash, and you joined Tirzah. I felt bereft. My family and the gods all seemed to have deserted me."

The apology came as the woman turned her face away. "I am sorry."

"Wait." Detaining Esther with a hand on her arm, I continued, "I am not angry any longer. How can I be when the God of Israel has given me new friends and restored you and Tirzah to me? I rejoice in my nephew."

"You talk as if you believe in the god of this people." Awe was in the tone. "You spoke of this god even in Jericho. I am not sure if I could ever turn my back on Astarte. Rahab, you have always seen our relationship to the gods differently even than the priests in the Temple. I do not understand."

"Maybe I do want to believe." I considered my answer as I looked around the busy camp. "It is because of the God of Abraham, Isaac and Jacob that I am here. I could be happy with this people. Is that not reason enough to believe in a god? What have the gods of Jericho done for us? Even your offering was rejected during the siege."

The nod was slow. "That is true. Perhaps there is truth in the claims of the women. They say there is only one God and he resides with this people."

"I am willing to let go of the old gods." With a little surprise I heard my proclamation. "We will be judged by our actions from now on, not by the past in Jericho. Who can say that the god of this people will not offer blessings?"

The older woman smiled at my sudden enthusiasm although her eyes remained sad and skeptical.

"We will see," was all she said.

After a hug to reaffirm our friendship, I hurried away to help Sarai with the evening preparations. We did not speak. I was lost in thoughts of my conversation with Tirzah and Esther. Sarai missed Caleb, I was sure, but I did not know how to comfort my friend.

The days crawled by filled with the humdrum tasks of washing, baking and weaving. Priests and the elderly men spent their days in prayer for the army. Speculation flooded through the camp after two days. Opinions were divided.

"Last time our men returned on the second day."

"They ran from the men of Ai in defeat."

"I am sure that my Jacob is searching the defeated towns for a gown for me."

"What if all the men lie dead?"

"Such a thing could not happen to the Army of the Living Lord."

"It takes time to defeat a town."

"God will give a great victory to Joshua."

We all gathered on the Sabbath for fervent prayers. A week had passed since the men gathered in preparation before the Tabernacle. Now it was the women, young shepherds and white-bearded camp guardians who listened to the priests.

"Lord God of Abraham, Isaac and Jacob, you led this people from bondage in Egypt, give to Joshua the victory. Bring your armies back in safety. God of Moses, your arm is not shortened. Your hand is stretched out still!"

"Amen, Alleluia, El Elohim Israel." Our response was bold.

I felt oddly comforted by the recitation of the priests. Sight of Perez in the crowd reminded me to speak to Sarai as we dispersed.

"My sister-in-law gave birth the day we came to this camp." My reminder diverted the woman from her frowning contemplation of the empty mountain road beyond Gilgal.

"That has been three Sabbaths. Time has slipped by quickly!" With astonishment my companion looked at me. "At the next Sabbath we must offer the sacrifice for a woman's cleansing. Then Tirzah will be able to join in the life of the camp."

Momentarily I forgot the reason I mentioned the woman. I was surprised into silence thinking about all that happened in less than a moon turning.

"Has the baby been named?" My friend did not seem to notice my lack of response.

"They want to call the boy Joshua in honor of the welcome received from your leader," I reported.

"I have been forgetful of my duties." Scolding herself, Sarai turned toward Perez's tent. "Joshua is a good man. I am sure he will want to be present for the circumcision and naming. That should have been done when the child was a week old. Now we must await the army's return."

I expressed the hope we all clung to, "The men will be back soon."

"Yes, God is faithful." Sarai paused in her haste to smile at me. "Caleb and Salma will return after the Sabbath."

The serenity and warm hand in mine reassured my heart.

I wondered where my friend found such faith and wished it were mine.

"Let us go to your family." The woman slipped her hand through my arm.

I saw Esther look up with a pleased smile as we approached.

"My mistress will be honored at your visit." Her formal welcome seemed out of place.

Sarai opened her mouth to protest. Before she could speak, Esther ushered us into the tent with an elaborate introduction.

"Sarai, wife of Caleb, lieutenant to Joshua, has come with Rahab of Jericho, blessed by the gods, to see you my mistress."

I had to smile at the formality of the words. Tirzah sat spinning while the baby dozed on skins nearby. Again my heart yearned for a child of my own. The tiny figure was so perfect and peaceful.

"You are welcome and we are honored." My sister-in-law greeted us with a formal bow. It was as though we were some important foreign visitors.

Sarai smiled and shook her head, "We are equals. We are women together. There should be no formality between us. Rahab is of your family and I am her friend."

Astonished at the reversal of importance, I stared with mouth slightly open. Like Esther and Tirzah I thought the wife of Joshua's aide much more important than a refugee from Jericho. The woman beside me calmly smiled. A twinkle in her eyes only reinforced the seriousness of her words.

"Let us forget that we are of a different heritage. Are not the ways of women the same in the camp of Israel or the city of Jericho? We bear the burden of tending, waiting and loving the men and children in our lives."

"You are wise, Sarai the Hebrew." Tirzah placed her spinning whorl on the ground. Gracefully the young woman rose with hands outstretched in a cordial welcome. "I would like to learn more of the ways of your people."

"And you will." Hands browned in the sun grasped hands that until recently had rarely been outside.

We four women spent the rest of the day talking of husbands,

children and the differences between life in Jericho and as a
nomad. Tirzah was amazed by the food eaten in the wilderness.

"Manna is small and round. It is sweet as honey yet firm
enough to grind or boil. I learned to cook with manna. It has
been a challenge to use real flour," Sarai confessed with a smile.

The Hebrew woman was equally surprised when Esther and
I insisted, "We had meat in the market every week, year round.
At the Feast of Astarte the *gal* provided meat and grain even for
the poorest in Jericho."

When talk turned to family life, I felt out of place. Even
Esther seemed to know more about children and husbands than
I did.

"Malachi was not bad." My friend defended the man I had
never heard her talk of before. "It was only when he was drunk
that he became enraged. When sober, my husband was the gen-
tlest man alive. He never meant any of the things he did after a
night of drinking with his friends. He was killed in a drunken
fight in the street. I mourn the man he might have been."

Tears rolled down Sarai's cheeks at the grief still audible
through the monotone recitation. My own eyes were damp. We
all gathered around the woman who sat staring into her memories. With an effort Esther raised her head.

"When he died, I was destitute. It was Rahab who freed me
from what would have been a life of drudgery. Although I was
once called the Daughter of Astarte, I could not again serve in the
Temple except as slave. My duties consisted of cleaning the floors
and rooms and pots. At our inn, we had a type of freedom even
with the control Balak maintained over our lives and property."

Again my friend fell silent. I reached out a hand in comfort.
Gripping my fingers tightly, Esther looked up at Sarai.

"We did what we had to do, especially Rahab." Esther
defended me with a hint of defiance. "A woman without a husband has no rights in Jericho. Balak gave us legitimacy."

"We are also under the control of our husband or father.
However, a widow or orphan is treated with honor and cared for
by the congregation. The nearest kinsman must accept responsibility for a woman. If no one is found, then any can speak on her

behalf. My father rejected me at birth," the woman admitted with a grim face. "Caleb stepped forward before witnesses to save my life. Barely of an age to sprout a beard, he stood firm for me. I was raised by Miriam, sister of our leader Moses."

The softening of Sarai's face told of the love she experienced in her childhood. Looking into the past the woman mused aloud.

"I once thought Caleb would not marry me. During the time I was growing up, the man took a concubine. Maacah was a dark foreigner from Haran. When she conceived I was jealous even though I was only a child. The man is proud of his sons but it is his daughter that he adores. Achsah is a beauty and will make some man very happy. My husband keeps her safe from the men of this camp. The girl lives with a family of the tribe of Reuben near Mt. Nebo, beyond the Jordan. Caleb swears that only someone who has proven himself in battle is good enough for his prize."

My friend paused. I had seen how Caleb loved his wife and could not imagine him with anyone else. The revelation that he had a family elsewhere was hard to believe.

When the silence stretched out, Tirzah leaned forward, interested in the romance. "What happened? How did Caleb come to marry you?"

Sarai came back from her memories with a radiant smile. "I should not have worried. Caleb approached Miriam when I was barely old enough to be betrothed. My husband played both the part of the kinsman to redeem me from my father's rejection and the suitor when I was of an age. We have been happy together. I have accepted his children as my own. Their mother died a season before Moses the Prophet was taken by God."

There was much she did not say and I guessed that her own childlessness was a sorrow the Hebrew woman did not easily share.

"Oh, how wonderful," Esther sighed at the lovely story.

Tirzah looked down at her hands. "It must be a blessing to know your husband does love you. Perez spoke to my father when I was declared to be of a marriageable age. He kept to the contract even when my father died and we learned that there was nothing for a dowry. The debt collectors took all we had, even my own mother's dowry. Perez cared for her until her death a year after our second son was born. I know he says he cares for me but sometimes I wonder if it is my fertility that he admires."

Little Joshua began to fuss. Talk turned to babies and children. I felt the now familiar longing to hold a child in my arms as I watched Tirzah coo to her son. As the sun set, Sarai and I walked toward our tent.

"You are quiet," the woman commented.

"Will I ever know the joy of a baby in my arms or the comfort of a man's love?" The question was blurted out before I thought.

Sarai looked at me sympathetically. We stood before the tent she shared with Caleb. My small tent was a step away.

"Rahab of Jericho, I cannot tell what the Living God has in store for you." Claiming my hands the woman spoke seriously, "Know this, the God of Miriam, my mother and Leah the Faithful is the God who has brought you to this place. They were not abandoned, nor will you be."

When I did not reply the grip on my fingers tightened. "Wait for the Lord to act. If God can open the womb of the barren, so too can the Holy One bring you the love you desire."

Humbled by the faith so evident in the words, I nodded slightly, "Thank you."

"God does not fail," Sarai concluded with a final squeeze of my hands. "You will learn."

I watched the woman enter her tent before slipping inside my own.

"God of Sarai, help me to trust you as she does." For the first time I really wanted to believe that the One God was someone who could comfort me.

Something like contentment settled over me in the darkness. I slept soundly.

ᴇ 13 ᴈ

STILL THE ARMY DID not return. Not even stragglers arrived. The priests prostrated themselves constantly before the Tabernacle. Incense clouds rose to God. Speculation ran between optimism and fearful despair.

"The men are defeated!"

"Our army must be pursuing the enemy."

"God has abandoned us."

"The Lord is enlarging our territory."

Sarai maintained a calm demeanor and went about her daily tasks.

"The Living One has not deserted us," she asserted. "Joshua and the men are offering prayers of praise at some shrine.

The Sabbath was two days away when a boy from the flocks on the mountain ran into camp.

"They are coming!"

His panted announcement raced from lip to lip. Nahum, son of Eleazar, strode toward the boy. Everyone held their breath to hear the report.

"I saw the banners above the dust," the boy told the priest.

"Could you see the men?" Not a sound was heard. We all strained to hear the reply.

"No." The child's face fell as he admitted, "They are still in the pass. But I heard the trumpets and saw the banners."

Still the priest questioned the youngster, "You are sure that the pennants are of the army of the Lord?"

"I saw the lion of Judah rampant on the lead banner." The boy thrust out his chin with conviction. "You will see."

"Yes, we will see." Almost absently, the priest nodded to the messenger.

"The men are coming!"

"My Aaron is returning!"

"Your father will be here soon!"

Joyfully each woman began to prepare for the return. The priests and soldiers appeared less positive. In a group they murmured together. I overheard the concerns.

"What if this is a trick by our enemies?"

"We must prepare a defense."

"Better to die now than learn God has abandoned us."

I shook my head at the obvious doubt and followed Sarai. She took the shepherd by the hand. The offer of water and one of her renowned fruit tarts was greeted with a grin and nod.

Crouching in front of the messenger, Sarai sought information. "How far away is the army of the Lord?"

The boy replied around a mouthful of food, "They are just descending the pass toward Gilgal."

"Mid-afternoon," the woman calculated half aloud. "The men will be here by mid-afternoon."

My friend pursed her lips in thought, nodding slowly before holding out the platter again. "Take another so you will not be hungry as you return to your flocks."

Not unwilling, the boy picked the largest treat on the tray before ambling away. Delicious odors of cooking and baking started to drift over the camp. It seemed that each woman was planning a feast in honor of the returning heroes.

Sarai became businesslike, "Rahab, there will be wounded. Even a victorious army sustains some loss."

"Then you think this is Joshua and the army of Israel?" I needed reassurance.

"Of course," came the reply, without hesitation. "There would be no reason for an enemy to pretend. We are weakly defended here. An army could sweep over us without trickery."

Only then did I consider our situation. Shepherd boys with the flocks scattered on the hills enjoying the spring grass were too young and distant to offer aid. The priests, though many, were armed only with staves. Joshua had left a contingent of soldiers in the camp, but they were the older men and those recovering from injuries sustained in Jericho or the first assault on Ai. Gilgal, our ally, was small and might not respond if we were attacked.

"Pray God that this is our army returning," I whispered.

"It is." Sarai was unconcerned and radiant.

We had barely finished gathering baskets of bandages and set water to heat on the fire when we heard the ram's horns from beyond Gilgal. The tones echoed between the city walls and the mountains.

An answering blast from the priests startled me. I slopped water from the pan I held. Eagerly all the women clustered together. At Nahum's instruction, the meager troop of camp defenders faced the road. I was surprised but delighted to see Perez in the line. My brother had always scorned those who chose a soldier's life.

"Nothing more than vicious killers with a desire to enrich themselves with the spoils," had been his assessment, even of the well-trained, armed men of Jericho. Now it appeared he aligned himself with the defenders of the camp of the Hebrews.

When the approaching force rounded the wall of Gilgal it was obvious that Joshua and the army of Israel had returned. The array of defenders broke into cheers of welcome and charged forward to meet their comrades.

"Alleluia, El Elohim Israel!" The well-known cheer sounded from the ranks.

We women and children responded joyfully. Soon there was chaos as men greeted their families. Sarai was right. There were wounded to care for. Some were helped by friends. A few were so badly injured that they had to be carried to the tent set aside for that purpose.

Sarai and I worked with other women skilled in the healing arts. Herbs to ease pain were brewed into tea. Injuries were washed and bandaged. Those with festering wounds were taken to a separate tent. There the priest would decide on treatment. For some the dead flesh could be removed with a red hot knife.

Their screams cut into the air. A few would be treated with herbs to draw out the poison.

Sadly for several there could be no cure. Fever would claim them as the deadly infection spread. These poor men were carried to the third tent. Here those deemed unclean and incurable awaited death. Families gathered outside to mourn. They did not dare enter and risk being considered unclean as well. Only a designated priest and the women who cared for the dead were allowed to enter the tightly closed space.

Women arrived to seek their husbands and sons among the wounded. Many of our patients were hysterically or stoically claimed. Reunited families returned to their tents as night fell. Only the most severely injured remained in the tent. A wife or mother sat at their side to care for them.

Some men did not return at all. I heard the keening start as one by one the widows learned the truth. I remembered what Sarai told us only a week earlier and prayed that each of the women would find a kinsman or other protector among the congregation.

Sarai and I finally left the tent. I knew my tunic was beyond cleansing. It bore the stains of the blood from many a man and boy. However, there were men who would live to settle in Canaan due to our ministrations.

"Let us go to the river and wash." I agreed to my friend's suggestion with a tired nod.

Too exhausted to speak, we plodded to our tent for clean clothing and then to the river. The setting moon did not cast much light. I was glad to strip off my soiled garment. Shivering in the chill water, Sarai and I washed swiftly. We donned the clean tunics and wrapped a heavy cloak around our bodies. Silent still, we hurried back to seek our beds. I envied Sarai, knowing she would be snuggled close to Caleb while I lay alone on my pallet. I had not seen Salma and dreaded hearing that he was among the fallen. My comfort was in wrapping myself in the man's cloak as I had every night since we spoke beside the river.

Day came too soon. Yawning, I emerged into the dawn to

begin another day. Nearby Caleb whispered something to his wife and followed it with a kiss to her cheek. My parents had never been demonstrative. I could not remember ever seeing such a tender gesture from Hamash. Longing brought a lump to my throat and tears to my eyes. I turned to stir the fire.

"May the Lord bless you this morning, Rahab." Caleb's hearty greeting was unexpected. "The Living God has given us a great victory. All will share in the bounty and spoil."

When I looked at the man, I realized he was holding out a length of finely woven cloth. Hesitantly, I touched the pale blue wool. It was as soft as a child's skin and beautiful.

"It is yours," Sarai insisted when I did not reach for the gift. "I told Caleb you needed cloth for new gowns."

"This is too lovely for me," I stammered in horror. "Queens wear such cloth. It should be yours."

"No, this is for you." The woman took the cloth and draped it around my body. "How well the color sets off your hair. Do you agree, my husband?"

My face flamed with embarrassment when Caleb slowly smiled. "I know at least one young man who will agree."

"I . . . he . . . there is . . ." I could form no rebuttal.

"It is perfect!" Sarai insisted while carefully refolding the material. "We will make you a lovely gown."

It seemed impolite to argue further. I allowed my friend to place the bundle in my tent. The feel of the soft wool lingered on my skin. I dreamed of a gown that would make Salma find me irresistible.

Immediately after the morning meal, the entire congregation massed before the Tabernacle. Eleazar wore festive garments, including the jeweled breastplate of his office. I had seen the ephod from a distance when we arrived in the Hebrew camp as Jericho burned. Now seen in the sunlight it was even more fabulous. Twelve jewels formed a square on the front of the breastplate. The buckles at the shoulder reflected back the light from their highly polished surfaces.

"Each tribe is represented when the High Priest wears the

ephod," Sarai whispered when I gasped in awe at the splendor of
the breastplate and other accoutrements. "The Name of God is
inscribed on the brooch within the turban."

"Here oh Israel, the Lord our God, the Lord is One." The
opening acclamation announced the start of the ceremony.

As one the congregation responded, "The Lord our God, the
Lord is One! Amen, Alleluia, El Elohim Israel!"

"People, chosen by the One Living God of our fathers, the
God of Abraham, Isaac and Jacob," the man spoke from beside
the altar. His voice came through the cloud of incense that billowed upward. "Again the Lord has given us a mighty victory.
The city of Ai has fallen. It is a ruin. Bethel, where Jacob rested
on his journey to Haran and the place he returned to as the leader
of a great family, is also ours. The armies of the God of Moses
have traveled as far north as Shechem. That is the place where
our father Jacob first settled with his wives and sons when
returning to this his homeland. There the armies of the Living
God renewed their covenant with the Holy One. This will be
done each year in remembrance that the God of Abraham, Isaac
and Jacob has fulfilled all that was promised to our fathers. All of
Canaan lies before us. The True God renewed the promise to
Moses in Egypt and again at Sinai. We will enter the land promised to Abraham and his descendants. The land is rich and flowing with milk and honey. There are vines and fig trees. Fields and
pastures await our herds. Each man will sit before his own home
and under his own vine."

The priest waxed eloquent in his ecstasy. Throughout the
crowd I heard "Alleluia" spoken or shouted.

"Joshua, son of Nun, blessed by God as successor to Moses
the Prophet." Now the High Priest turned to the leader with a
command, "Step forward."

I held my breath, wondering what would happen next.
Bareheaded, the general knelt before Eleazar.

"At Mount Hor you were given the staff of Moses to lead this
nation into the Promised Land. I now anoint you, for God has
affirmed your leadership in the victories against the inhabitants
of this our homeland. May the Lord strengthen your hand

against our enemies until they are all as Jericho and Ai.'"

Oil was poured over the man's head. It ran down into his beard.

The words were clear. "I am the servant of the Lord. May the Living God use me to fulfill the promise made to Abraham, Isaac and Jacob."

The obvious humility was a surprise. The generals I remembered in Jericho were all haughty and arrogant in their office.

Again the priest called out a name, "Caleb son of Zephunneh."

Sarai grabbed my hand. She was not expecting this. Head bowed, the man stepped forward to kneel beside Joshua.

"To you, Caleb, faithful son of the tribe of Judah, is given the honor of leading the settlement of the nation in the land promised to your fathers. May the Holy One grant you wisdom and courage in this task. As Moses promised, you will settle in Hebron when all the tribes find rest."

Oil was poured over the younger man's head. My friend clung to my hand and sobbed. I was not sure if it was joy or sorrow that brought the wrenching sobs that were muffled against my shoulder. I barely heard the names of other leaders who were called out and anointed for special service. Then I heard a name I recognized.

"Salma of Judah and Jamal of Asher." My head jerked up to watch.

The young men strode forward. Salma kept his eyes fixed on the priest and altar. I held my breath and felt myself quiver when the priest spoke.

"You have spied out the land and brought a good report. By your guidance the army of Israel finds their way. To you is the commission to determine the location of cities of refuge for each tribe as decreed by Moses. May God use your knowledge of the land to make wise choices. You will lead a representative from each tribe throughout the land so the people will have a place to flee for sanctuary against their accusers."

I was not sure what Salma was being asked to do. My heart pounded joyfully to see the broad shoulders unharmed by the

battle. His oil-soaked hair glistened in the sun. I wanted to run
to the man and smooth the oil from his face. I bit my lip against
the fire of desire that raced through me. Dimly I heard Eleazar
conclude the ceremony with a prayer. All around rose the
response from men, women and even children.

"Alleluia, El Elohim Israel!"

The newly anointed leaders rose from their knees. Family
members rushed forward to envelope the men in congratulations. Sarai left my side. Caleb caught his wife in a tight embrace.
I took a step toward the young man where he stood beside his fel-
low spy. My heart lodged in my throat when a slender young
woman with a toddler embraced both Salma and Jamal. Tears
blurred my vision for a moment.

My mother's instructions came clearly to my mind, "Do not
let anyone see your pain."

With the ease of years of practice, I drew pride around me.
Lifting my chin and smiling with a serenity I was far from feeling, I turned and walked toward the tent that held the injured
men. There were bandages to be changed and clean water to be
brought.

My presence was greeted with relief. Wives and mothers took
the opportunity to stretch their legs and prepare fresh food for
their injured heroes.

Briefly I answered questions about the ceremony.

"Joshua was anointed as leader over Israel, and Caleb will be
his lieutenant. Together they will lead the nation into the
Promised Land."

"God is merciful," whispered one old woman. "My son is
returned to me. We will enter the land together."

I smiled in sympathy as I watched the woman sob with joy.
She knelt beside the young man and bowed over his face with a
kiss. The son stroked his mother's hair with the uninjured hand.
I moved on.

"Eleazar poured oil over each man's head," I explained when
pressed for more details.

"It must have been a holy moment," sighed a young warrior
barely old enough to bear arms.

My nod was apathetic. The joy of the event was dimmed by my memory of Salma swinging the small child into the air.

"Your wound looks healthy." It was easier to change the subject as I washed and rebandaged the sword cut in the young man's leg.

Each patient was visited in turn. The activity kept my hands busy. Many questions prevented me from dwelling on the sight of the young woman who so happily greeted Salma. Eventually I had no more excuses to linger in the tent. Every injury was tended. The sun was descending in the west and would soon disappear behind the mountains. Even with the torches and fires around the camp the night was dark. For a long time I stood just outside the tent watching the shadows lengthen.

"If there is a God who cares, give me courage," I prayed when I started toward the fire before Caleb's tent.

"Where did you disappear to?" Sarai's question was not unexpected. The woman looked up from the pot she was stirring.

"I went to tend the injured. There was no one who needed me." The carefully rehearsed words sounded like a complaint when spoken aloud.

"You were missed," asserted my friend. She leaned forward to try and see my face in the firelight.

"This was a celebration for the Children of Israel." My argument was met with a firm shake of the woman's head.

"You are one of us now," she insisted.

"I am very tired." Not wanting to argue I cut the conversation short.

The excuse was true. Weariness suddenly seeped into my bones. All I wanted was to be alone in my blankets.

Sarai became solicitous. "You should eat. I am sure you have not eaten since this morning. After working so hard, you need to eat."

"No." I moved my head in denial. "I wish to rest."

Before my friend could form more arguments, I slipped inside my tent. Alone in the blackness, I dropped my veil on the floor and collapsed onto the pillows. Finally I could let the pain of my loneliness wash over me.

Emptiness was an old friend. Innumerable times I hid from the taunts of my brothers and from the scorn of Jericho. Behind the mask of serene confidence, I lived in constant fear that someone would see behind the façade and discover that Rahab was only a frightened little girl.

Now the rest of my life appeared to stretch out before me, a travesty of the acceptable norm. Neither wife nor widow nor harlot, I would forever be on the outskirts. Not a slave, yet never truly free, I would remain a companion to Sarai and never know the joy of a family. My past weighed me down and I knew despair. Dull sorrow filled me while I neatly folded the cloak. I knew I had no right to find comfort in the warmth of the garment. Still my hand lingered on the folds. My lips felt again the tender kiss that I thought promised fulfillment of my dreams. Then I forced myself to place the bundle across the tent from my pallet.

Sleep did not give me rest and I rose heavy-eyed to greet another Sabbath. Silence hung heavy between Sarai and me. I gnawed the flat bread spread with cheese. The food was tasteless in my mouth. Because it was the Sabbath, no fresh baking could be done. I felt guilty that I was not thankful for the meal. My skin felt taut and swollen from the tears in the night.

"I will tend the injured." Keeping my veil pulled forward, I did not look directly at my friend.

The woman tried to stop me. "You should rest. All yesterday you worked alone in that tent."

Easily I eluded the outstretched hand. Forcing a cheerful note into my voice, I insisted, "No, I am of use there. You should be with your husband this day. Surely it is not forbidden for me, as an outsider, to tend the injured on this holy day."

I walked away before bitter jealousy could slip in. By striding swiftly and keeping my head lowered I was able to reach the tent without anyone stopping me. I paused to take a deep breath, summon a smile and focus my mind before lifting the tent flap.

"Rahab, we are glad you came." The greeting from several mouths soothed the loneliness.

With a nod, I began to check each wound.

"You have a gentle touch. Not like some of the women," an old soldier whispered. "Do not tell my wife, but her hands are rough and make the pain worse."

"You will soon be well and not need your bandages changed," I assured him.

"Do you really think so?" behind me, his wife voiced the question.

"Yes, see how the flesh is closing the wound. Soon you will be in your own tent." I found myself smiling when the old woman crouched beside her husband.

"Praise the Living God." The sigh was a prayer.

I marveled anew at the faith so obvious in the couple as well as others of the camp. Even after the loss of life and wounding of many, the people still thanked their God. My own knowledge of religion was different. The priests of Astarte would have sought to propitiate the goddess for each lost life. Not for the first time I wondered if it was greed on the part of the priests rather than the gods who demanded such extravagant offerings.

All day long, I worked among the wounded. By keeping busy I was able to almost forget the other women happily enjoying the day with husbands and families. Within the tent with the injured men, I found a strange sense of peace. The prayers uttered within the hide walls as the light dimmed at the end of the day were of praise not petition. I stood listening to the words that made the close of day sacred to the Holy One.

"Blessed are you, Lord God of the Universe. You ordain one day in seven for rest. In six days you created the heavens and all creation. On the seventh day you rested for it was good."

"Blessed be the God of Abraham, Isaac and Jacob." The response was repeated again and again.

A great longing rose in me to be part of a community that believed so fervently in their god. I once had such faith in Astarte. That was gone and now the God of the Hebrews seemed to mock my dreams as well. When I looked toward the hills I could almost believe that whatever gods existed were responding to the praise. Rays of light shot up behind the peaks and the entire sky was a radiant orange and red banner. Drawn outside by the beauty, I absently lifted my veil to cover my head. In the distance I saw a grove of trees near Gilgal. From the tight grouping I knew that it was dedicated to Astarte.

Chatter from the camp faded as I walked toward the shadowed hillside. My heart longed for peace. I hoped that I might find it amid the groves that beckoned. Perhaps a visit to the sacred place of the goddess would help me find an answer to the nagging question of which god was truly to be worshipped. The way was further than I expected and darkness fell quickly. Confused, disoriented and a little frightened, I stopped. My destination was lost in the night. There was no moon to light the way now that the sun had set. I knew it was a sign that Astarte had truly failed me.

Gilgal was a huge looming bulk ahead but I knew the gates would be shut. Looking back toward the camp, the fires appeared far away. Somewhere in the city a dog barked and was answered by a Hebrew hound from the encampment. Both sounded distant. An owl hooted, a signal that he was setting out for an evening of hunting.

I stood irresolute on the path. No longer did I want to seek the groves of Astarte. Fear of animals in the night kept me from moving back toward the camp. A rustling in the bushes made me gasp and look around. The hand on my arm startled a scream from my throat.

"Rahab, do not be afraid." The familiar voice sought to calm my fear even as the man tightened his hold to prevent my flight.

Fright combined with the strangeness of the night and the tender touch caused me to burst into tears. Strong arms gathered me against a broad chest.

Soothing words were spoken into my hair, "Hush, it is alright. You are safe now."

I clung to my rescuer, knowing that I ought to step back, but the soft words and gentle pats were too comforting. Eventually I stopped sobbing.

"There, there." Salma still rocked me in his arms.

His voice continued to caress me. Memory of the young

woman and child from the day before finally helped me draw back. Still the man held me loosely in his embrace.

"We should return to camp. Sarai will be worried about you." I could not see the man's expression when he spoke.

Swallowing a lump of guilty disappointment, I nodded. The strong arm remained around my shoulder. With the gentle guidance we walked toward the encampment. No words passed between us. My throat was clogged with unshed tears. I knew that despite his care, the man beside me could never offer me love.

When the light from the torches surrounding the camp made the road easier to see, Salma slipped his hand from my shoulder although he retained my hand. I wanted to believe that the young man was reluctant to release me. Still I expected him to let me go my way while he returned to his own family now that we were within the camp.

"I will see you safely to Caleb's tents," the man announced when I glanced up to say good-bye.

I was grateful for the veil that shielded my face from both curious stares and from my guide. By a gentle hand on my elbow Salma guided me across the camp to Sarai.

Half scolding, the words tumbled out, "Where have you been? The sun is long set. You were not with the injured. We have been worried. Are you hurt?"

Salma gave a calm explanation, "Rahab is safe. She wandered from camp along the highway. It is not a safe place to be alone, even for a man."

"She is here now." My friend sprang to my defense against the censure in the soldier's tone.

"Yes." A softer note crept in as the man addressed me. "I hope you will not wander alone again. It would be safer to walk with, um, someone."

I glanced up at the suddenly hesitant ending. Tender eyes full of concern were looking at me. I wanted to believe that Salma was going to offer himself as escort. Then the memory of the mother and child intruded.

"I will not walk outside the camp again." The low hoarse

tone barely sounded like my own. I hoped no one noticed that my voice was clogged with suppressed tears.

With the promise made, I slipped into my tent, grateful for the darkness and silence. I hoped no one would follow but not many minutes passed before Sarai pushed aside the flap. She carried a lamp and bowl of soup. The woman placed the lamp on the stand in the center of the tent before crossing to my side.

"Come, sit up and have something to eat. You must be exhausted and hungry. I know you worked all day," the woman coaxed. "The men and families are grateful but you must take time to eat."

I wanted to insist that I had eaten a meal but my stomach growled in anticipation of food. The soup smelled delicious. Gratefully I took the full gourd from my friend. We sat together on my pallet while I sipped the hot liquid heated over the rekindled fire. The restrictions on cooking ended with the sunset as the Sabbath ended.

"Anna and Seliah have both told me how gently you changed bandages. Deliliah and her daughter-in-law cannot stop praising your care of Irah. They credit you with saving his life." Sarai was full of pride. "Even sharp-tongued old Rebekkah speaks of how you made Elam laugh in spite of his pain."

The words were a balm to my spirit. Listening to the repeated comments, I felt needed.

"The women are kind." I mumbled around a bite of carrot.

"More than kind," Sarai clasped her hands in excitement. "You have a gift."

Shaking my head in denial, I looked away. "What do you see when you look at me?"

Sarai's eyebrows drew together in confusion at my intense question. Still she tried to respond.

"I see a lovely young woman with hair the color of fire. I see a kind and generous heart. I see a woman with more courage than I would ever have. I see a friend who left all she knew to save an ungrateful family."

The woman would have continued, but I held up a hand.

"You do not know me." Looking away from Sarai, I focused

on the lamp. "I am Rahab, scorned by kin and acquaintance alike. I will never have a husband or child, for all who see me know my past."

"Rahab." For the second time that night, my name was spoken with tenderness. "Dear Rahab, a new life is before you."

Stiffly I resisted when my friend tried to gather me into her arms. She contented herself with rubbing my back as a mother would a troubled child.

"Hush now. The Rahab I know is a brave and faith-filled woman. God has not abandoned you." Gradually the soothing motion of the gentle hand eased my torment.

I ignored the nonsense Sarai continued to murmur until I fell into an exhausted sleep. In the morning I lingered in the tent. Never before had I allowed anyone to see the depths of my despair. Half fearful that Sarai would disdain me, I finally lifted the tent flap and stepped into the day.

"Good morning." My friend looked up with a smile.

From the kettle she spooned warm goat's milk into a mug. Grateful that she said nothing about my collapse of the night before, I accepted the offering. The warm liquid felt comforting in my stomach. I was even able to respond to the friendly smile that came with the piece of bread the woman held out.

"Today Tirzah is welcomed into the congregation. Her time of confinement is ended." Sarai was eager to share the news. "It was announced yesterday during the evening service. You were too busy with the injured. I had no chance to tell you last night."

Partly relieved that my outburst of the night was so easily forgiven, I felt a twinge of hurt that my sister-in-law was to be accepted into the life of the camp. It did not last. Sarai's excitement was genuine and contagious. I found myself caught up in the anticipation.

"After a woman bears a son, she is unclean for thirty days," the Hebrew woman explained. "Then she is reintroduced to the congregation. An offering of two doves is expected. As her sponsor you will provide them."

With a flourish, a small cage was produced. Inside sat two small birds.

In amazement I stammered the question, "I . . . I . . . am . . . her . . . sponsor?"

"Of course." It was simple to my friend. "You are the nearest female kin. If you do not want to . . ." Sarai let the comment hang.

"No . . . it is not that . . ." I hated to remind this generous woman of the one problem I saw.

"Well?" An eyebrow cocked inquiringly while she waited.

"Should not the sponsor be one of you? One of the Children of Israel, I mean." Spoken out loud, the concern loomed large.

"Your trustworthy action has shown that you have faith in the God of Abraham, Isaac and Jacob. Today you too will be made a member of the congregation." Sarai could barely contain her delight at my astonishment.

I opened my mouth to protest that I was unsuitable. The woman forestalled me with further news.

"Joshua himself insisted that you be part of the celebration. He is acting as sponsor for Perez."

My mouth fell open. That the great leader wanted me to become a member of the tribe was almost more astonishing than the fact that my brother had agreed to the physical demands made on a man in order to be included in the culture.

"Here." My friend had yet another surprise. "Put this on for your special day."

My eyes opened in astonishment at the garment she handed me. I recognized it as soft cotton from Egypt. The pale green color must have been dyed by an expert for it was all of one hue instead of various shades. Only the wealthiest women in Jericho possessed such gowns. As the Daughter of Astarte I wore thin draperies but they did not flow as smoothly as the dress Sarai held out. Hamash's young bride had worn fine linen on her wedding day, but the material was not as soft as what I held.

"Miriam gave it to me for my wedding." A tender smile crossed the woman's face at her memory. "Now you shall wear it to become one of the Daughters of Israel. It is perfect for the occasion."

"It is fit for a bride," I demurred. "Not for such as me."

Almost brusquely my friend insisted, "Nonsense, it is my gift for your most blessed day. It will give me joy for you to wear this gown."

I nodded in submission. The gift was obviously important to Sarai. Together we entered my tent. My serviceable, brown home-spun was tossed onto the bed. After bathing with water warmed by the fire, the woman smoothed sweet oil on my body and then dropped the lovely gown over my head. My hair was quickly braided.

"You are beautiful." Sarai nodded happily as she admired her handiwork. "Come and see."

Taking my hand the woman dragged me back into the sun-light.

"Wait." Sandaled feet barely seemed to touch the ground as my friend hurried to her tent and emerged with a bronze mirror.

I did not recognize the reflection gazing back at me from the small rectangle of polished metal. The slim green gown and crown of braided red hair brought color to my cheeks. It was how girlish dreams had pictured my wedding day. Sarai gently laid the matching veil over my head. A rush of tears blurred the image. Impulsively, I hugged the Hebrew woman.

In choked tones I thanked my friend, "I may never be truly a bride, but you have made me look like one."

"You are lovely." The broad smile was filled with agreement. "Come, we must get Tirzah and your brother."

The entire camp, it seemed, was aware of the event.

"Blessings on you, Rahab," Several times I heard the greeting.

Tirzah, too, looked lovely, if nervous. Somewhere she had acquired a new gown and veil. My sister-in-law held baby Joshua. Perez stood beside his wife. Oil glistened in his hair and beard. My nephews stood around their parents. Rebekka wore pretty ribbons in her hair in honor of the special day. Caleb waited with my family.

"You look beautiful," Esther whispered to me as we followed Caleb and his wife toward the Tabernacle. "I think you are love-lier now than the day you were the Bride of Baal."

I had no chance to reply although the color rose to my face

at the memory of that long ago day. Caleb indicated where we were to stand before taking his place beside Joshua. I wondered if Salma was present but did not dare turn around to look. It would hurt too much to see the man with his wife.

"People of Israel." Eleazar stepped forward.

The whispering stopped. The silence felt as if everyone was holding their breath in anticipation.

"We are gathered here this morning for a ceremony that happens only rarely. Into our midst have come strangers. We will welcome them as members and friends this day. Because each one has indicated a willingness to accept the God of Abraham, Isaac and Jacob as the True and Living God, we accept them as members of the congregation."

My heart began to beat rapidly. I remembered that my destination of the evening before was the grove dedicated to Astarte. Even though I knew that the goddess had no power, I felt guilty for my action. If the priest knew, I would be cast out. Sarai put her hand over my nervously twisting fingers to calm my anxiety.

The old man droned on, reciting the mighty deeds of his God. I only heard a few words of the history. My mind was too busy trying to decide if I really did believe in the God of the people gathered nearby. Then I heard my name.

"Rahab of Jericho has proven herself a handmaid of the Living God," Eleazar intoned.

I wanted to cry out that I was not worthy for I had served the gods of Canaan. Shame colored my face crimson, but I was not given the chance to respond.

The priest continued to proclaim. "When Joshua sent spies to the city to find a weakness, it was Rahab alone who knew that the God of Abraham, Isaac and Jacob was with them. She hid Salma and Jamal from the swords of the chief of Jericho. Rahab is among us now. There are many who can attest to her healing ways."

The murmur of assent brought a blush to my cheeks.

"Step forward, Rahab of Jericho." Suddenly the man turned to me and held out his hand.

I looked helplessly at Sarai. Her broad smile and encouraging nod, along with a gentle push, set me walking toward the High Priest. My eyes focused on the bronze altar beside the man. The smoke of incense curled toward me as if in invitation from the One God. I knelt in awe, barely noticing that Caleb stepped forward with a young goat in his arms.

"Do you believe that the God of Abraham, Isaac and Jacob is the only True God?"

The question I dreaded came. Without conscious thought my response was low. "Yes."

It seemed the natural response to the One I realized I did trust and believe in. Smoke swirled around me offering an embrace from the Living Lord. Peace entered my heart.

A second question was addressed to me, "Will you obey the Law of Israel as given by Moses the Prophet of God, our Deliverer?"

"Yes." Again, I responded as if in a dream.

The scent of the incense filled my nostrils. I felt lifted beyond myself when the priest placed his hands on my head.

"Rahab of Jericho, we welcome you into the congregation of Israel. By sparing the blood of the sons of Israel, you are bought into the household of God. Caleb of Judah has agreed to act the part of kinsman to pay the price of your freedom. Let the blood of this goat be a sign of your birth as a Daughter of Israel and remove all stain of your past." In the sacrifice of the young animal held by Caleb, my old life was acknowledged and exorcised. "From now on you will be known as Rahab the Faithful, Healer of the Warriors of the Lord."

A sudden rush of tears blinded me. I felt weak and unsteady. Like a child learning to walk, I staggered slightly when Caleb and Joshua helped me to my feet. With their support I walked toward Sarai. Distantly I heard cheers from the crowd. Then Sarai was holding me. My sobs gradually eased. It was almost as if I was washing away my old self. The feeling of being embraced by God lingered throughout the morning as Perez and his family were also welcomed into the congregation. In amazement I watched my brother and his sons emerge from a small tent near the Tabernacle, followed by Joshua and one of the younger priests.

The sobs of the little boys and the strained expression on my brother's face told me what had transpired.

Eleazar gestured for the family to come forward.

"Perez, son of Hamash of Jericho, brother of Rahab the Faithful, you have remained with us. The faith of Rahab spared your entire family from the sword of the Lord at Jericho. Perez, you have undergone circumcision as a sign of your willingness to begin anew. By this act of obedience to the covenant given to Abraham for all generations, Perez, you are adopted as a Son of Israel."

The man swayed slightly as he stood before the priest then dropped to his knees. My nephews imitated their father. A lump came to my throat and I was surprised to find myself missing Hamash, Jonadab and Hamul. A brief prayer slipped through my mind for my family. I wondered where they were and hoped that they would find peace and happiness.

"No longer will you be known as Perez son of Hamash, but Perez bar Joshua for Joshua will act as your father in the faith of Israel." The announcement from Eleazar recalled me to the ceremony.

Joshua strode forward to hold a lamb over my brother's head.

"Do you accept this man as your son?" Eleazar spoke clearly.

"Yes," the leader affirmed. "Perez is now my son in the Lord and my brother in the congregation."

One of Eleazar's sons took the lamb. In a swift motion the sacrifice was accomplished. The High Priest sprinkled both men and then the boys with some of the blood.

"By the life of this lamb, you are severed from the old ways," the priest solemnly stated. "See that you do not turn back for the Lord our God is a jealous God."

Cheers rang out when Joshua helped Perez to his feet. The men faced the crowd. With his sons beside him, my brother made his way back to where Tirzah and Esther waited.

"We have yet one more joyful ceremony." Eleazar was in his element. "A son was born to Perez bar Joshua when he arrived among us. It is time and past for the infant to be made a Son of the Promise. Offering will be made for his mother's purification."

Sarai took Tirzah by the hand. A gesture of her head indicated I was to follow. Holding the cage with the doves for the offering, I followed the two women.

Perez took his son from my sister-in-law. Again he entered the tent with Joshua and the young priest. The baby's wail made Tirzah shudder. A moment later the men emerged and the priest lifted the boy high for all to see.

"Behold Joshua bar Perez bar Joshua. Welcome the newest of the Sons of Israel. He is an inheritor of the promises of our God," proclaimed Eleazar proudly, almost as if he was the father himself.

Cheers again rang out. Then the old man turned to where Sarai and I stood with Tirzah.

"Tirzah, Daughter of Israel as wife of Perez bar Joshua, you have born a son. The time of purification is complete under the law of Moses, Prophet and Deliverer."

The old man held out his hand. At a whispered word and nudge from Sarai, I handed the birds to the priest.

"As offering and in thanksgiving for this life, we present to you, Lord God, Creator of the Universe, this brace of doves as you have commanded."

With a rapid movement, both birds lay dead on the altar. A drop of blood was touched to the woman's forehead and hands.

"You are cleansed from the blood of birth. May the Living God bless you to bear more sons." The solemn words left me with tingling with a wonder I had not felt since I listened to my mother tell of the renaming of Jacob at Bethel. Even amid the sacrifices and ceremonies of the Temple I had not known such awe.

I felt sanctified when "Amen" sounded from thousands of throats. It seemed as if the entire camp was rejoicing for my family.

Perez looked overwhelmed when, after Eleazar pronounced a blessing, men surged forward to congratulate him on his new status. Tirzah too was surrounded by women eager to see the baby. Sarai saw me backing away from the crowd.

"You must stay and let everyone welcome you," she urged.

Wryly, I gestured toward my brother and sister-in-law. "I cannot compete with a man-child and a merchant."

My friend would not let me leave. Despite my misgivings, I too was surrounded by smiling faces.

"Welcome, Rahab."

"My brother owes his life to you."

"Can you show me how to braid my hair into a crown?"

"I wish my hair was as lovely as yours."

"How brave you were to save our spies."

Now that the leaders of Israel showed their approval, I was surprised at my popularity. The only thing lacking was an embrace from a young man with eyes the color of a summer sky. I did not see him anywhere in the crowd despite my surreptitious glances around. Neither Salma nor Jamal seemed to be present. It was late morning before we made our way back to our tents. The men sat down to a covenant feast of bread, mutton and wine to welcome Perez into the congregation.

"You see," Sarai told me as we sat close to our fire after a much smaller meal was consumed. "Your past has been erased. Before you lies a new life."

"Thank you." Emotion choked my words.

I could not think of anything else to say to my first friend in Israel. The woman seemed to understand for I found myself embraced almost fiercely.

It seemed a part of the new beginning spoken of by Eleazar. A feeling of peace still held me. Even the memory of a smile from the young woman who I believed to be Salma's wife did not disturb me. Briefly I wondered again where the man was.

❧ 14 ❧

LIFE TOOK ON A routine. Until all were healed, I spent time with the injured men each morning. Sarai and I shared the daily tasks of baking and cleaning. It became common to wash clothes in the river and carry jars of water from the newly dug well between Gilgal and the camp. I did not see Salma and assumed he was busy with his family. I set aside the dream that I had briefly dared to consider.

Not long after the ceremony that made my family members of the congregation, whispers raced through the camp. Ragged and travel-stained emissaries had arrived. We were all curious about the visitors.

"Look at their filthy clothing."

"They must have come a long way."

"The poor donkeys look exhausted."

"I heard that they only have stale bread left."

"I will eat with Joshua and these messengers this night," Caleb announced in the late afternoon.

"Who are they?" Sarai asked the question we all wanted to know.

"These men come from far away," the man explained. "They have heard of the mighty deeds of the God of Israel and seek peace."

"Where are they from?" I thought I recognized the style of turban but could not remember what locale it was from.

"They claim to be from beyond the mountains." Caleb shrugged. He was more interested in the second part of the news. "These visitors bring word that the nations of the coast have formed an alliance. We will have to fight a coalition."

"Did the men name a town?" Sarai was as curious as me.

A bit brusquely, her husband replied, "We have more important concerns than the exact name of a distant town. News of our enemies is worth more than silver."

"Then the men will go in peace?" Trying a different approach my friend still sought information.

"Yes, Joshua has sworn that we will not attack their town." The man turned to leave. "We have made a treaty and will ratify it at the covenant meal this night."

Sarai watched her husband hurry back to the council.

"I think those men are not telling the whole truth." With a puzzled expression I added, "The way they tie their turban is familiar. I wish I could recall what town uses that fashion."

I was still mulling the problem when I fell asleep. Caleb had not returned from the meeting. Across the camp a blazing fire could be seen. The elders and leaders of Israel met with the strangers. My last waking thought was to try and remember where I had seen such a style of turban.

The visitors departed in the early morning. Many salaams of thanks and protestations of loyalty were offered. Fresh clothing and sacks of food were provided. I was still staring after the departing men when Caleb spoke.

"Joshua believes we have made a wise alliance," the man stated.

I had not seen him arrive and turned in time to see him kiss Sarai. Without lingering for food, Caleb yawned before he entered his tent to sleep. My friend looked after her husband with a slight smile on her lips. She was always happiest when the man was nearby. In a moment she turned to join me in grinding wheat for bread. We chatted about the few warriors still recovering from their injuries as we prepared the Sabbath food for the next day.

It was two days before I had a chance to visit my brother's tent. Everyone stayed close to their own homes on the Sabbath. When I arrived, Tirzah was sitting outside with her spinning while my nephew lay in her lap. Nearby Rebekka was carefully carding a pile of wool. Her serious expression reminded me of my own early efforts at women's work.

Esther bustled around with the rest of the children at her feet. She struggled to straighten the tunic on my father's namesake. The boy brushed off Esther's hand and hurried back to his games. My friend looked up when Tirzah greeted me.

"Did you see the men from Gibeon in the camp?" The woman chuckled. "I do not know how they got so dusty coming such a short way."

"Gibeon, of course!" My exclamation startled both women. "I have not been able to remember who wears turbans like that. It *is* Gibeon. The men did lie!"

"What do you mean?" Esther asked the question.

"The visitors said that they came from a far land. They sought a treaty ensuring safety against attack." I was growing increasingly angry.

Tirzah tilted her head at my answer. At first my sister-in-law looked confused and then the humor of the situation struck the woman from Jericho.

"So the great Joshua has been made a fool of," Tirzah giggled. "Perhaps the God of Israel should look at a map."

"Yes," agreed Esther with a grin. "Gibeon is barely a three-day journey over the mountain pass. That is hardly a far country."

"The God of Israel will not be mocked." Of that I was sure. "Someone must tell Joshua of the guile of those men."

"You would not dare . . ." My sister-in-law stared at me aghast that I would consider interfering with the decisions of the leaders.

I shook my head. "No, the man would not listen to me. Still, he must be told."

"I am sure they will learn the truth soon enough." Esther still smiled slightly at the thought that the great leader had been tricked.

Tirzah changed the subject. "Esther, take the baby. I must see to our meal."

Readily my friend accepted the baby. He yawned up at us both when I bent close to look at my newest nephew. I found the warm bundle in my arms when a scream of pain from another child sent both Esther and Tirzah running.

"Will I ever hold my own baby?" The question was asked of the drowsy infant.

Brown eyes blinked in response. My lips brushed the curls just visible above the baby's swaddling wrap. Unbidden, the image of a baby with blue eyes came to mind. I shook my head to erase the dream. Rocking from side to side, I was gratified to watch the eyelids close.

"You can put him down there," his mother directed when she returned. Her nod was to a blanket-filled basket nearby.

The woman held my niece in her arms. A scraped knee explained the sobs. Esther had young Hamash by the collar.

"You shall never push down your sister or younger brothers again." The scolding continued. "A son of Perez should not be a bully. You must set a good example."

That the boy did not appreciate the lecture was obvious from the thrust-out lip and averted face.

"I must go." After gently depositing the baby on his blankets, I turned away from the family crisis.

"Sarai." Eager to share my news, I sought out the woman. "The men who came to Joshua and the elders were not from that far away."

"How do you know?" One eyebrow raised as my friend looked up from the loom set up between our tents.

"By their turbans," I explained triumphantly. "I knew I had seen that style!"

Sarai was interested. "Where are they from?"

"The men came from Gibeon. It is not too far away. The town is only three day's journey over the mountain." My revelation was spoken with an exultant toss of my head.

The woman's mouth formed an "Oh" of comprehension. Her busy hands stilled on the yarn of her loom.

"Joshua should be told." I made the suggestion when no further response was forthcoming.

"Yes." The reply was somewhat abstracted. "I will tell Caleb. The elders will be very angry at being tricked."

I nodded in agreement. There seemed nothing more to say. We finished our evening tasks and prepared food in near silence. All through the meal I waited for Sarai to speak. Finally I could contain myself no longer.

"Caleb, those men who came were not from a far-off country." I blurted out the words despite the man's astonished expression and Sarai's warning head shake.

"How do you know that?" The man forgot his manners and looked me in the eyes.

Chagrined by the frown on Sarai's face, I lost my courage.

"I saw . . . that is . . . the turbans . . . um . . . are . . . Gibeonite." My voice got lower and lower, as did my head.

"Gibeon! Are you sure?" I heard building anger in the voice and drew back.

Still, I nodded and spoke one word, "Yes."

"Rahab is right." Unexpected support came from behind me.

Caleb looked past my shoulder.

"Salma, you have returned from scouting out the cities of refuge." Gone was the rage in joyful welcome.

Caleb sprang to his feet. The two men met in brief embrace. I scrambled to my feet and drew my veil over my face. Longing surged through me. Resolutely I forced myself to remember the young woman joyfully embracing her husband.

"Rahab is right." Salma returned to the topic. "The emissaries came from Gibeon, not far away. Jamal and I encountered them at Bethel. They were celebrating their trick and did not recognize us as Hebrew."

"You do not look very Hebrew," admitted Caleb with a slap on his friend's back. "Clean-shaven and wearing the garments of a northern wine merchant's slave, you would have fooled me if not for your voice."

I risked a glance at the new arrival. Without his beard, Salma looked younger. The tunic covering only one shoulder, the slave earring and oiled hair did give the man the appearance of a wealthy man's slave. He looked like he came perhaps from Haran. I was amazed even as I remembered the first time we met. Then he did not look Hebrew either, but Moabite. It had been the curious accent that roused suspicions.

"The trio from Gibeon was drunk and voluble." The spy was speaking. "They could not wait to impress the foreign merchant and his servant with their craftiness. I thought Jamal might speak out, but for once he acted calmly and probed for the truth."

"What is the truth?" Caleb took the cups of beer from Sarai.

One was offered to Salma as he motioned the newcomer to the fire. A plate of vegetables and bread with cheese was gladly accepted. My friend drew me into the tent. From there we could listen unobserved as once before.

"As Rahab said, the men are from Gibeon," Salma explained while savoring a mouthful of bread. "This is good. You are blessed by God in your wife, Caleb."

"How far is Gibeon?" His host returned to the topic of the visitors.

"It is twice as far as Ai. Maybe three or four days march for an army. It is over the mountains to the western hills before you begin the descent to the Plains of Sharon."

"Why would the elders of Gibeon have taken such measures?" Caleb asked the question that puzzled me.

Salma chuckled, "That is the best part."

"How can you laugh?" The older man sounded irritated.

"Because God has indeed given all Canaan into our hands," explained the spy. "Leaders in all the cities fear us. The news of the defeat of Jericho and Ai has spread throughout the land. Jamal and I barely had to spread any rumors."

"How does that affect the actions of the men of Gibeon?" Still, Joshua's lieutenant sought an answer.

I held my breath.

"They fear being annihilated as well and used deceit to form an alliance." The young man was more serious now. "That much the emissaries admitted to the merchant and his slave. They explained the great care they took to find the oldest clothing and wineskins. The scraggliest donkeys in the area were purchased. Bread was baked until dry and hard. Then they set out for this camp."

Salma paused. I heard the sound of liquid being poured and guessed that Caleb was refilling the cups from the skin beside the tent.

"The ruse seems to have worked." A grim note entered the

conversation. "The elders must have believed that the trio traveled a long way."

Caleb ground his teeth. "Yes." The reply was like a growl. "We never questioned their story."

"And why would you?" Salma was quick to absolve his friend. "I saw the donkeys and heard the explanation of all the preparations. I doubt that Jamal or I could have created a more perfect disguise. The one mistake was in the tying of their turbans. As Rahab recognized, that is the style of Gibeon."

"Joshua must be told," Caleb spoke decisively.

"Yes," his companion sighed. "I had hoped to spend time with . . ."

"The safety of the people must be our priority," the older man interrupted.

I heard another sigh and movement as both men stood. Longing rushed through my veins. I wished it was me that Salma missed. The two men strode away. Sarai led the way to the fire.

"You were right." Soberly, the woman began gathering the remnants of the meal. There was little left. Salma had been hungry. "I wonder what Joshua will do."

"Who is Salma's wife?" My mind was still on the young man.

My friend looked at me. The firelight caught the astonishment on her face.

"Salma has no wife." Her voice implied that such an idea was inconceivable. "Why would you think he was wed?"

"I saw . . . when . . . Joshua . . . the army . . . the victory . . . the ceremony." In short gasps I stammered an incoherent reply. My mind was spinning from the information.

Still Sarai looked confused. Drawing a breath, I released it slowly to steady myself.

"A young woman with a baby rushed to Salma when the commissioning was done." My voice was very low and my face flushed. I bent close to the flames pretending to stir the last of the hummus. The heat in my cheeks was not from the fire.

"Oh." Now Sarai was smiling. "I understand."

My friend moved to my side. The spoon was removed from

my grip. Sarai led me to the stool recently vacated by the young man we were discussing.

"Salma is unwed." The statement confused me even more. "He has always claimed that his duty is to God and the safety of the congregation.

I returned to my question, "But the woman?"

"That is Elisaba. She is wife to Jamal and sister to Salma."

At my indrawn breath of comprehension, Sarai drew me close to her side.

"The baby is the pride of both men. His name is Judah." My friend continued to explain, "Now that he is starting to toddle, Elisaba will be kept busy. It is time you met. Tomorrow I will introduce you."

Embarrassment and relief competed for dominance in my mind. I was glad that darkness hid the bright color in my face.

"Why has Salma never married?" I had to learn the answer.

"I think he has never found a woman who intrigues him." The woman paused before drawing back slightly and looking at me with a smile. "That may be changing."

Unsure if I could trust what my friend seemed to be implying, I did not reply. My hands became busy plaiting the fringe on my veil in nervous excitement. In my heart a hopeful rhythm began to pound.

"You and Elisaba must meet," Sarai repeated. "We will go to her tent tomorrow."

I spent part of the night arguing with myself. My heart insisted on hoping that my friend was hinting that Salma liked me. The rational part of my mind insisted on reminding me that the man had shown very little interest in me except the one evening when we were alone near the river. When I did finally sleep my dreams were of children toddling toward me. They all had Salma's blue eyes.

Sarai practically dragged me to meet the young woman after the men adjourned to discuss the Gibeon matter. Suddenly shy, I was not sure I wanted to meet the man's sister. She warmly welcomed me. Almost immediately I felt comfortable with Elisaba.

"It is not that we have not tried to help Salma find a wife." His sister brought up the subject after we had sampled the special goat's milk cheese the woman was known for. It was delicious, with an almost sweet taste.

Sarai contributed an opinion, "Everyone agrees that it is the duty of every young man to marry and raise sons for Israel."

"My brother does not dispute that," sighed the sister. "It is just that he cannot find a woman that he feels is right for him. I fear the man wants a paragon like the wives of Abraham, Isaac and Jacob."

Just in time the young mother caught her son by the collar of his tunic. His toddling steps had taken him too close to the fire. She deposited the boy a safe distance away.

"Salma made this," Elisaba mentioned, as she produced a carved horse for the child to play with.

"He loves little Judah and would make a fine father. The man is just stubborn." Sarai grimaced.

"I pray that God will send my brother a bride," Elisaba sighed. "None of the girls interest him, though."

The two women continued to discuss the young man and his shortcomings. I shifted on my stool slightly to play with the boy. Happy for the attention, Judah showed me his horse. Soon I was on my knees building a fence with sticks and stones. It was great fun and reminded me of my childhood before I went to the Temple. The child laughed as we played together.

Entirely engrossed in our game, I only noticed the newcomer when Judah scrambled up, shouting, "Unc Sala! Unc Sala!"

"Judah!" The child was lifted up and tossed into the air.

I froze in place. The horse was clutched in one fist. My hands were filthy from playing in the sand. Probably my face was smudged and I knew my dress was dusty. All I wanted to do was vanish into some convenient burrow but none was available.

"Come, see." Back on the ground, my playmate caught his uncle's hand and pulled him over to our game.

The man crouched beside the boy. I felt my face redden. All that Sarai and Elisaba had discussed ran through my mind. I was not the multitalented, serene beauty they envisioned for Salma. Instead I knew myself to be an outspoken, red-haired exile with an unforgettable past.

Judah did not notice my motionless silence. He was too busy pointing out our construction to his uncle.

"Shalom, Rahab." The everyday greeting did nothing to still the pounding of my heart.

I nodded but could not form a single word in response. Rather than look up I kept my hands busy rearranging the sticks that formed the little fence.

"It is kind of you to play with my nephew," the man continued when I did not speak.

"He is a sweet child." My voice was barely audible.

"Unc, look." I was grateful for the interruption when Judah took the horse from my hand. He began to show his uncle how to play the game.

"I should go. I am sure Sarai will want to leave." Sitting back on my heels and dusting my hands together, I prepared to stand up.

"No!" the child caught my hand. "Play!"

I saw the flash of teeth as Salma grinned.

"My nephew wants you to stay," the man stated. "So do I."

The last words were spoken for my ears only. I felt a blush rising again. To hide my confusion, I bent close to the little boy. It seemed safer to focus on Judah than his uncle. Already I was too aware of the tanned hands in the sand near mine.

Only a short time later Elisaba called her son, "Judah, come here. It is time to clean up."

The toddler stuck out his lower lip. A storm threatened.

"We will play another time," Salma told the boy. "I will carve more horses and we can all have one to play with."

My face turned red again at the suggestion that I was included. No one noticed because the man swung the boy into the air again.

"Look who is coming. It is your Abba." The man distracted the child by pointing out his father.

Game forgotten, Judah scampered to the man. Jamal scooped

his son up. From a seat on his shoulder the child rode triumphantly to the fire. Childish giggles made us all smile. Happy
to be forgotten, I stood up and tried ineffectually to clean my
gown and hands.

"Will you stay and eat?" Elisaba asked her brother.

"I will walk with Rahab and Sarai back to Caleb's tents," was
the reply.

Another wave of color rushed to my face when everyone
looked at me.

"Thank you for entertaining Judah." His young mother gave
me a quick hug. "You must come again so we can visit."

"I . . . oh . . . yes." Her unexpected invitation left me stammering.

"Elisaba is kind to invite me back," I voiced my thoughts to
my companions after we started across the camp.

"My sister wants to know you better. You are Rahab the
Faithful. There is no other more worthy or braver in the camp."
Intentionally the man stressed each syllable.

Swallowing hard, I dropped my gaze. We stood silent. Then
I slipped from Salma's grasp and ran the rest of the way to my
tent. Sarai called to me but I ignored her. I was not sure I dared
believe the admiration deep in the blue eyes of the spy. Inside the
tent I gathered Salma's cloak close and buried my face in the
folds.

"Rahab?" Sarai called through the hide walls.

"I am fine." My voice was muffled by the garment I held
tight.

I heard the murmur of voices but no words. She was talking
to Salma, I was sure.

"God of Salma and Sarai," I wept in despair. "Why did you
save my life? God of Abraham, Isaac and Jacob, does Salma care
for me? Better to have died in Jericho than live if all I will ever
have is unfulfilled dreams."

For a long time I rocked back and forth remembering the
look in his eyes. I let myself imagine what it would be like to be
the bride of Salma bar Nashon.

"If he does love me, then I will know that the past is forgotten." I dared bargain with the Living Lord. "I will be a good wife even if I am not Hebrew born."

Near dawn, I slept. In my dreams someone held me and told me that I was loved. There was no face, only loving arms and a voice more tender than my mother's.

Heavy-eyed, I greeted the morning. Sarai looked up from the kettle.

"Rahab are you well?" Her concerned expression was almost too much. I summoned anger to cover my emotion.

"My feelings are not your concern." I regretted the tone and words as soon as they left my lips.

The woman looked surprised.

Contrite, I mumbled through sudden tears, "I am sorry. It is not you. I slept poorly."

"It must be very hard to learn all our ways." My friend was at my side. "I would not have half the courage you do."

Shaking my head I tried to explain. "It is not that."

"Come, you will feel better after you eat."

I was urged toward the fire. Unresisting, I moved. It was easier than arguing. Meekly I nibbled at the food placed in my hand. It had no taste to me, but I chewed and forced myself to swallow the bread and cheese until my hunger was assuaged.

Changing the subject Sarai pointed toward the Tabernacle. "The men leave today to punish Gibeon."

Looking up, I saw the men of the congregation gathered. Even across the camp the angry response was audible.

"They are not pleased with being tricked," the wife of Joshua's lieutenant pointed out grimly. "Joshua will have a hard time keeping them from spilling blood. It is fortunate that Salma will be the guide. He can keep the army away from cities."

"Salma is going?" My face flooded with color. "He might . . . he said . . . I . . . what if . . ."

Sarai understood my fearful stammering. "God willing there will be no fighting. Caleb says that the mere appearance of the army of Israel will reduce the men of Gibeon to groveling slaves. Salma will return safely."

Coming to my side the woman took my cheeks between her

hands. I tried to avert my face but could only lower my eyes.

"Salma does not see you as a foreigner," my friend firmly spoke.

Ready to argue, I opened my mouth. "But . . ."

"Anyone who calls you such things should be beaten. You should be ashamed to think that of yourself." The woman championed and scolded in a single breath.

"But . . ." Again I tried to interrupt.

"Joshua himself calls you Rahab the Faithful. Your past was burned in that city." A gesture to the southwest indicated Jericho. "God preserved your life for a purpose. Eleazar himself signified that you are accepted as one of the inheritors of the promises of the Holy One. The God of Abraham, Isaac and Jacob does not judge as people judge. Who would have thought that a liar and cheat would become the father of these tribes? Jacob tricked his brother and his father-in-law. Would men have used a spoiled brat and prison slave to save the world from famine? The Almighty raised Joseph from Pharaoh's prison to second in command in Egypt. Did Moses know why he was spared the swords of Egypt when he fled as a murderer? Yet the True and Living One changed him from prince to prophet and from murderer to leader."

The woman paused in her litany to take my hands.

"Rahab, the past is over." With soft persuasive words my friend tried to convince me. "It is forgotten by all except you. Let go of the past and let yourself blossom as God promises. Salma is coming to love you. Will you trust God and accept the honest love of that man?"

"I want to."

When the woman stopped talking I realized that tears were running down my cheeks. My heart ached to believe her words. With the edge of her veil, Sarai wiped my tears away.

"You will see that I am right," my friend confidently spoke.

I forced myself to stop crying. A moment later, voices approached. Sarai turned to greet her husband. The men were approaching our fire. I wished I could slip into my tent when I saw the man's companion.

"We leave when the sun is high," Caleb announced. "How long will it take to reach Gibeon?"

"We will arrive in three days at a steady march," Salma replied.

"Then we can be at the gates at sunrise on the third day?" The lieutenant was still planning strategy.

"Without a doubt," agreed the younger man.

"My wife, have you prepared a pack?" With only the briefest of kisses, Caleb addressed my friend.

"I was just finishing." The woman hurried to her task.

My heart thudded painfully when Salma did not address me. With a brief nod to Sarai the young man hurried away.

"I must bid my sister good-bye." His words were a brief explanation.

"You need fresh water." Grabbing the water basket from beside the tent, I almost ran from the camp.

At the river I let the cold water flow over my wrists as tears ran down my face. My hopes and dreams of the night before vanished into the water.

"You are foolish to think that Salma will find love with you," I scolded my heart.

"He is busy this morning." Stubbornly I found excuses for the man.

Back and forth I argued until I heard the trumpets and cheers when the army marched out toward Gibeon. The shadows lengthened before I summoned my pride.

"You are Rahab, a name that means proud. Your mother dreamt great things for you. Your grandfather served the God of Jacob at Bethel." Clenching my hands tightly, I made a covenant with myself. "The gods of Jericho are dead. Even if the God of Abraham, Isaac and Jacob does not hear a foreigner, pride must be my shield."

After the camp was in complete darkness and silence I returned to my tent. Tears dampened my pillow but in the morning I gathered my dignity and smiled serenely on the world. Head high, I hid my loneliness from all. It was easier when I found things to do that kept me busy. Folding bandages and blankets in preparation for the return of our men filled one morning. I sat at the loom beside my tent and began weaving blankets against the winter chill that would be arriving, even though the summer was upon us.

"You have your son to tend," I told Elisaba when she and Sarai offered to help. "This is something I can do since I do not have the duties of wife and mother."

Sarai asked no questions after I coldly informed my friend, "The way of wife is not one I will follow. Men are too capricious and interested in war. I have chosen the path of service. Leave me to my work."

Each night I told myself I needed nothing more. "I am content. What need do I have for the burden of a family?" Deep inside, I knew I lied.

The army of Israel had been gone three days. Already some of the women were looking hopefully toward the west. I sat beside Sarai watching the sunset that signaled the beginning of the Sabbath.

"Our men will not return until at least after the next Sabbath," Sarai told me as we sat idle.

"They will barely have arrived at Gibeon," I agreed.

"Do you know anything about the city?" Worry was evident in the way my friend folded and refolded the garment in her lap.

"I do not know much," I had to admit. "They cultivate rich grapevines in the hills above the valley. The wine is some of the best in Canaan. Every year the chief of Gibeon met with the priests of Astarte. They purchased many skins of it for use in the Temple and to sell. No one was allowed to buy Gibeon wine except from the priests. They were able to gain a good profit from the sales."

Sarai looked astonished. "That is awful."

"The wealthy of Jericho found it convenient," I shrugged. "The rest of us used wine pressed locally. It is perhaps not as clear, but has a good taste. Wine merchants from Gilgal always attempted to underbid the traders from Gibeon, but the priests insisted on purchasing from over the mountains."

"So Gibeon is a rich community seeking to preserve a way of

life," mused my companion. "They are not warriors."

"No, I have never heard that Gibeon even has any armed men. Their walls and water system have always been protection enough. It is said that they could withstand a long siege. The patronage of the priests of Astarte protected their traders even from the antagonism of their rival wine merchants in Gilgal. You are right, the people are peaceful and wealthy." My words were a reassurance to me as well as Sarai.

"Thank you for telling me." The woman leaned over to take my hand. "Caleb and Salma will return safely."

"I am glad for you." I tried to sound uninterested, but knew I failed when my friend tightened her grip.

"Rahab, I wish you would confide in me. You are not happy. Salma tried to find you before the army left." Her words scraped at the raw wound of my emotions.

"I was here, but he went to his sister." My angry whisper gave the woman her clue.

"Oh, Rahab." Sarai caught my hand when I pulled free. Her voice caught somewhere between tears and laughter at my passion. "You are jealous."

"No!" I denied, vigorously shaking my head.

"My dear, Salma is a man." Sarai seemed to think that explained everything. When I frowned, she added, "He has no idea how to fall in love. The man does not know how to respond to the one who has captured his heart."

"No." I continued to shake my head in denial of my dreams.

"You will see." The confidence in my friend's voice spurred me to response.

"I am not Hebrew. I know nothing of his God. Salma could not, should not . . ." My tongue became tangled as I tried to explain.

"Have I not told you that the Holy One, like the wind, acts as God wills? By casting your lot with us, you accepted the protection and guidance of the God of Abraham, Isaac and Jacob."

"We shall see." Unconvinced, I turned to stare away from camp. The pass beyond Gilgal was empty. Softly I repeated, "When the men return, we will see."

It seemed I was right about Salma. The army returned five
days later. Triumphantly the men strode into camp. Caleb hurried to kiss Sarai, but I only caught a fleeting glimpse of Salma
with Jamal and Elisaba. An assembly was called in the morning.

"Praise the God of Moses," Joshua announced. "The riches of
Gibeon are ours. There was no battle. The people of the city are
forever in our service. The way lies open to the coastal cities and
to the south."

"Amen, Alleluia, El Elohim Israel!" The shout rose again and
again until Joshua had to hold up his hand.

"There are still battles to be fought to gain all the land promised to Abraham." His caution was barely heard.

The rejoicing could not be contained. Instruments appeared
as if by magic. Tambourines and pipes, drums and stringed harps
all joined in a glad cacophony. One of the young women began
to dance. She drew more and more women into her celebration
until I too was caught up into the circle. Then the men began to
stamp and clap. They formed their own circle surrounding the
women. Around and around the two sets of dancers capered. I
was surprised to find myself enjoying the experience. Laughing,
clapping and whirling, I felt more alive than I had in years. On
some unseen signal the music stopped. Panting and laughing I
found myself face to face with Salma.

All the encouraging words Sarai had said raced through my
mind. Vaguely I was aware that other men and girls were forming couples. Still the Hebrew spy and I stared at each other.

"Salma."

"Rahab."

We spoke simultaneously. It seemed to break the tension.
The man smiled. His teeth gleamed through the newly growing
beard. I was tempted to reach out and touch the hairs to see if
they were soft or coarse.

"We have to talk." Salma did not wait for an answer.

I found my hand in the strong, calloused grip of the warrior.
Together we walked to the river. Finding the same rock where we
met once before, Salma spread his cloak over the stone before I
sat down.

Without preamble, the man addressed me. There was real distress in his voice. "Why have you hidden from me?"

"Why have you avoided me?" Equally hurt, I responded with my own question.

"I did not . . ." The denial was swift but I interrupted almost angrily.

"You never even looked at me before you left for Gibeon. Instead you hurried to your sister." I had to look away while accusing the man.

With his confused eyes staring at me tenderly, my complaint seemed trivial. All I wanted to do was kiss the pucker between the unusual blue eyes.

"But I came back after Elisaba gave me the pack of food for the march." In trying to explain, the deep voice became pleading.

"You did not greet me when you returned." Low-voiced, I knew I sounded petty.

"Rahab." Ever so gently one hand cupped my chin and turned my head. His lips were very close. I watched them move, mesmerized by desire. "I am sorry I hurt you. There was much to do. I had to report to Joshua."

The apology was so unexpected that I burst into tears.

"Do not cry, my love." Appalled by my response, Salma tried to soothe me by drawing me close and stroking my hair.

"I am sorry." Through sobs I begged for understanding. "No one ever cared for me before."

"Rahab, my love, I will take care of you, if you will let me." Into my hair the man whispered his promise. "I honor your bravery and beauty. You are like no other woman I have ever known."

I was not sure if the words were a declaration of love, but I accepted the man's embrace. When his lips met mine, I offered no resistance.

"We will be wed." Lost in the joy of my lover's embrace I barely heeded the statement.

"Yes, beloved." My response was murmured, as I tried to press close to the man.

Gently Salma removed my arms from his neck.

"We must wait." The huskiness of the man's voice betrayed

his desire as did the deep kiss he pressed on my lips.

"There is much to do in preparation." Again he raised his head to take a ragged breath.

With a great effort the Hebrew spy stepped back.

"Salma." I held out my hand.

"Rahab, we will do what is right." The man overrode my protestations. "Come, we must return to Sarai."

Reluctantly, I stood up, shivering a little in the late afternoon shadows. The sun had almost set. Seeing me rub my arms against the chill, Salma wrapped his cloak around me. I was reminded of the other time I wore the man's outer garment. It served as a blanket at night. The warm folds reminded me of the owner and brought me pleasant dreams.

With one hand around my waist we walked back to Caleb's tents. Sarai knew the news before a word was spoken.

"I am glad." Her dark eyes gleamed with delight. "Caleb will be pleased."

The woman refrained from an extravagant display of joy. She contented herself with giving me a hug and smiling at my companion.

"I must tell Elisaba," he explained. With a grand flip the cloak settled over Salma's shoulders.

My heart beat with contentment as I watched the man walk away.

"I am glad," Sarai repeated with a fond smile when I looked back at the woman.

We did not linger in conversation. I wanted to be alone to revel in my joy and soon entered my tent. The soft cloak I wrapped around my body reminded me of the embrace of my love. My dreams were untroubled until sunlight awakened me through a crack in the hide.

Word spread through the camp rapidly. By morning, when I walked with Sarai to draw water, the congratulations rang from every side.

"Rahab, may God bless you."

"The Lord make you fruitful."

"How lucky you are."

Elisaba sought me out. "Rahab, I see by your glowing face that it is true! My brother has found a bride!"

The young woman embraced me while balancing Judah on her hip. The child recognized me.

"Ra-ab." Little arms were held out to me.

Gratefully, Elisaba allowed me to take her son. He was heavier than my nephew and smelled of the dirt he had been playing in. Smiling at the child I hugged him close.

"He has grown so quickly," his mother marveled to Sarai. "It seems only yesterday when I held a tiny infant. Now he can almost talk clearly."

"What is this I hear?" Tirzah's excited question caught my ear.

I turned to see my sister-in-law pushing through the women. Esther trailed behind carrying my nephew.

"Are you really marrying a Hebrew?" I was not sure if my brother's wife was glad or appalled.

"Yes," I admitted, feeling heat in my cheeks.

My red face was observed, I knew by the giggles from some nearby girls not yet of marriageable age.

"I am so glad." Her next words assured me that the woman was ecstatic. "This is wonderful news."

"May the gods be kind to you." Esther spoke low as she hugged me.

My soft response astonished me even as I spoke, "It is in the God of Israel where I find my comfort."

Judah reached out to touch the baby in her arms. I drew back as the older boy reached for the curly hair on the infant. We all laughed. It broke the uncomfortable pause caused by my unexpected words.

Later I pondered my confession while watching the water pour from the bucket into my water jar. Sarai and Elisaba chatted with other women nearby.

"Truly the gods of Jericho have no power." My thoughts were suddenly clear. "The God that has brought forth this nation from the grip of Egypt is a true God. Only such a God could have given me the chance for a new life. I have found the freedom I sought."

I was deep in my thoughts until we parted halfway across the camp.

"It is good that Salma has chosen you for his bride." Elisaba removed Judah from my arms. "We will talk soon."

Caleb and Salma were talking seriously when we returned with the water jars balanced on our shoulders. A basket of herbs and vegetables hung from my hand. Sarai carried a plucked chicken for the evening meal.

"My husband, what is it?" My friend immediately sensed tension.

Across the fire, Salma stared at me as though memorizing every feature. I felt my face flush and barely heard Caleb reply.

"The chiefs of the southern tribes have formed a coalition. They have surrounded Gibeon in siege. We must march against these Amorite leaders, for Gibeon is now our ally."

"No!" I heard myself cry out.

The water jar tilted dangerously when I set it down to run to Salma. Only a swift movement from Caleb saved the pottery.

"Will you go too?" My hands gripped Salma's tunic in fear.

"I must." His response was implacable. "How could I stay behind while my brothers fight?"

Looking up, I saw the jaw set firmly, although desire in the deep pools of blue spoke of other things.

Choking back tears and stifling the words of recrimination, I burrowed close to the young man. Sarai and Caleb held one another. My friend looked worried but calm. I envied her faith. After a moment both men drew back. With a kiss each soldier released the woman he loved. Sarai and I held hands as we watched the two men walk across the camp to join the rest of the troops in vigil beside the Tabernacle.

"It is not what I hoped for." His parting whisper was for my ears only. "God will give us the victory and peace will follow. Then we will be together."

I hoped that Salma was right. It did not ease the emptiness I felt watching him march away with the morning sun glinting on the spear points as it rose. Once again, the women stood together bravely waving farewell to husbands, brothers and sons. The camp seemed too quiet without the men, although each woman bravely returned to her duties.

"Why must men fight?" My question was addressed to Elisaba and Sarai as we sat spinning outside Jamal's tent.

The whorl rotated almost hypnotically and the soft wool yarn spun out smoothly into the baskets at our feet.

"The Lord will give the army of Israel victory," stated Caleb's wife.

"At what price?" I was ashamed of the anger in my voice.

Elisaba dropped her spinning whorl to slip an arm around my shoulders. She was younger, but her words gave comfort.

"Rahab, it is hard to wait. Even after all this time, I lie awake when Jamal is gone. It is then that I pray to the God of Abraham, Isaac and Jacob and remember how God blessed their wives with fortitude."

I looked into the younger woman's eyes. She had seen the armies of Israel march away many times and return. Her husband had traveled deep into enemy territory and been protected by the God she trusted. Deeply moved I embraced my newfound friend.

"They will return." Sarai wrapped her arms around us both.

"How can you be certain?" My question was low.

"The God who brought us from Egypt will not abandon us now." The statement was made with such conviction that I almost believed the words. "The armies of Israel will triumph. We will dwell in the land in peace."

I wanted to believe the promise spoken by my friend.

My fears eased as Caleb's wife continued, "Elisaba, has not the Living God brought Jamal safely home each time he has gone out as a spy?"

"Yes," the young woman nodded and sniffed. Using her veil to dab her eyes, she added, "You are right, Sarai, God even used Rahab to protect him."

A quick hug accompanied the words.

Sarai addressed me. "Rahab, we are blessed to have you among us. You are a reminder of the loving presence of God to all people."

I was not sure I understood what was meant but nodded anyway. The concern and sympathy from both women comforted me. Each night I prayed for the safety of all three men and felt that God was with me.

In the days and weeks that followed Sarai had to reassure many of the women in the camp. Word came of victory at Gibeon and pursuit by Israel of the chiefs of the south. Then we heard nothing. The heat of summer was settling into the Jordan valley when the armies returned. They were triumphant. The ram's horns, drums and trumpets all sounded in glad hymns as the men marched into camp. Eagerly each woman scanned the lines of troops for the one beloved face. My own eyes sought for Salma's figure among the lines. He did not appear to be present.

When the dismissal order was given, men sought wives and mothers. Caleb swung Sarai around. I averted my face from their joyful reunion to look again at the dispersing troops. I was taken completely by surprise when Salma caught me from behind and drew me into his arms while I stood alone in the midst of so much joy.

"You are here!" I could not help the relief in my voice.

The man chuckled, "Of course I am. How could I not return to my Rahab?"

Drawing back slightly I tried to assess whether the man had any injuries. His bloodstained tunic betrayed a wound. Rapidly I unwrapped the bandage on Salma's upper arm, exposing a deep sword cut.

The Hebrew spy tried to shrug off my exclamation of distress, "It is nothing. I foolishly let down my guard at the end of the fight."

"Let me clean the wound and put herbs on it." The first signs of an infection in the injury chilled my blood.

Only when the gash was freshly bandaged could I relax into Salma's arms.

"Let me tell you how much I missed you," the man whispered against my lips. "We must be wed soon."

I offered no argument. We sat together long after Sarai and Caleb entered their tent. The fire burned low as we planned our life together.

~ 15 ~

JOSHUA AND ELEAZAR CALLED the congregation together at dawn. The *shofar* dragged me from dreams of a life where I held a son while Salma proudly looked on. Somewhat slowly I dragged myself from the tent. Men and women assembled before the Tabernacle. Joshua stood beside Eleazar. The fire on the altar blazed bright in the early morning light.

"Hear the mighty works of our God," the general proclaimed. "The land of the south lies open to our settlement. The chieftains of the south are no more. The country is rich for planting and grazing."

"Amen, Alleluia, El Elohim Israel!" My voice joined in the cheer.

All the elders of Israel stood arrayed behind their leader. Salma stood beside Nashon, his father. The old man insisted on representing the tribe of Judah even though he was so old and crippled he could barely stand. The patriarch leaned heavily on his son and feebly raised his cane at the cheer. My heart went out to my beloved who looked tenderly at the once strong stone-smith. Salma had never known Egypt but his father bore scars from the taskmaster's whips.

There were only a few in the camp who could remember Egypt. Nearly all that generation died in the wilderness before the nation reached the Jordan. Those who did have memories of the Black Land were children when Moses led the people from the Land of Kings. Nashon was one of the small number of adults who had served under Pharaoh.

I had not met the man. Elisaba took care of her father even

though he lived in his own tent. Pride kept the old man from accepting a home with Jamal. I wondered if the patriarch would want to live with Salma after our marriage.

Joshua's voice interrupted my musing.

"The Lord fights for Israel," he began.

"Amen, Alleluia, El Elohim Israel," interrupted the priests.

With his hands Joshua signaled for quiet. When the cheers subsided, the man continued.

"Listen and hear what God has done for this people. The army came to Gibeon and the chiefs of the south fled before us. The day was not long enough to complete the victory, so the Mighty Lord of Hosts caused the sun to stand still at Gibeon and the moon over the Valley of Aijalon. The God of our Fathers threw down great stones that killed more men than our swords."

"Amen, Alleluia, El Elohim Israel!" Our cry rang out again.

I felt my breath coming in great gasps. Never had such a thing been heard of. My slowly forming faith was affirmed. I could not doubt that the God of Israel was greater than Baal and Astarte. The priests of Jericho told the people that Baal ruled the sun and Astarte the moon but they never claimed that the gods had stopped their circuit of the day to fight for the faithful. The God of the Israel had shown power over even the sun and moon.

"Woe is me," I whispered, suddenly feeling a great gulf between me and the chosen people of this God. "I am less than a worm before such might. I am not worthy to be counted among this people."

Sarai caught my arm when I turned to flee. Her quick ears heard my mumbled, fear-filled awe.

"No one who believes is cast out of the presence of God." The woman spoke into my ear for all around us were shouts of praise and rejoicing. "The God of Abraham, Isaac and Jacob has accepted you for you have believed."

"How can you be sure?" I shook my head in denial.

It was too much to believe that any servant of the goddess would be allowed to stand before the True God of all. Everything I had believed was false. My only hope was in the memory of the way my mother insisted that all the gods of Jericho were simply shadows of the same greater power. The God of Abraham, Isaac and Jacob was that Holy One.

"You have a new life. Is that not proof?" Exasperated, my friend gave me a shake.

Ashamed but not totally convinced, I stood still. My head was bowed. I did not dare look up when Joshua began to speak again.

"We pursued the armies of the south. The chiefs hid in the cave at Makkedah. It became their tomb." The statement was stark and the picture he painted was bleak. "After the warriors of Israel defeated their enemies, the chiefs of Hebron, Jarmuth, Lachish and Eglon were brought from the cave. At our feet they groveled in a show of obeisance. 'Will you serve Judah, Benjamin, Simeon and Dan?' The question was asked of each man."

I raised my head and held my breath in anticipation. It was beyond imagining that the proud chiefs of Canaan would bow to Joshua. I remembered the men from my childhood. Full of their own importance, they angered Hamash even though he served them with apparent humility. Stories of their proud defiance even toward the *gal* of Jericho were well known in the city. On the one occasion that the chief of Hebron stopped at the Inn of Astarte his demands and insolence were beyond bearing. It was the only time Jerusha became angry at a guest. I could still see her raise the pitcher high and smash it to the floor in exasperation.

The leader looked around at the congregation. Every eye was fixed on Joshua. We all waited for him to continue. His gaze traveled to the faithful lieutenants at his side.

Almost sadly the man announced, "Not one of the chiefs was willing to become a slave to Israel. We hung them on trees and buried them in the cave of Makkedah, which they chose for their own. Now the armies of Israel have completely subjugated the land from Gibeon to the Negev in the south and from the Land of the Philistines to the Jordan."

"Amen, Alleluia, El Elohim Israel!" The people would not be silenced.

Again and again the cheer rang out. Finally Joshua was able to quiet the ecstasy.

"The land will be given to Judah, Benjamin, Simeon and Dan

for their settlements. They will not go in until their brethren also find a homeland. The Lord will open the way to the rest of the Promised Land, as has been done from Jericho to the Negev. We must obey the will of the Lord. Sanctify yourselves for we will offer sacrifices to the Lord in the morning."

With that promise the congregation was allowed to disperse. I was humbled and silent all day. My mind was busy pondering the events recited by the general. That evening Salma walked with me to our favorite rock near the river.

"Great and mighty is our God," my lover spoke with awe.

"Yes," I nestled in the man's arms. "Your God drives out the gods of Canaan before you and subdues kings."

"More importantly, the True and Living One has created for me a lovely bride." I felt tender lips against my forehead.

Tilting my head, I offered my mouth for a long kiss.

"My Rahab." We were both panting when Salma lifted his head. "Let us be wed soon."

I was more than willing and nodded against the broad chest. Beneath my cheek I could feel the rapid beating of my lover's heart.

"If God gives us rest from our enemies, we can be married at the new year after the crops are gathered in. It is a good time to be wed." Passionate lips claimed mine again. I stirred in the security of the strong arms and he added, "If that is what you want, my love."

"Yes, that is a good time." Again I moved my head against the man's chest in assent. "I will begin my life as your wife at the beginning of the year when all the old is cast aside."

Privately I wished we did not have to wait so long.

"I will speak to Eleazar." The eager promise was sealed with another kiss.

Joshua and Eleazar agreed to a shortened betrothal time because of the imminent settlement of the country. The ceremony was short and solemn. In the green gown from Sarai I felt shy and beautiful. A letter of agreement was sealed by Nashon before Eleazar. The old man peered nearsightedly at me before he made his mark in the wax. I stood at Salma's side while he recited

promises to care for me all his life. Then Caleb sealed the contract with his signet.

"Here I release the claim of kinsman to Salma bar Nashon.
All care of Rahab the Faithful is now in your hands." The husband of my friend smiled at us both.

"Only death can separate us now," Salma whispered with a
gentle kiss. "Betrothal vows are as binding as the marriage feast
itself."

After the ceremony that bound me to Salma I walked beside
the man to the feast prepared by Sarai. I rejoiced and barely heard
the renewed whispers. It was easy to lift my chin and pretend not
to hear the words that swirled like the leaves in our wake as we
returned to the tent of Caleb after the ceremony.

"Is that the foreigner that was a harlot?"

"That was a false rumor."

"Remember how she tended our injured men?"

"Do you recall how Joshua welcomed her to the camp?"

"She is called Rahab the Faithful for saving our spies in
Jericho."

"Of course, that is how she met Salma."

"Even if they do not know my past, people will find something to gossip about," I confided to Sarai with a wry smile.
"After all, I am still a stranger to some."

"You must not mind those girls," Sarai patted my arm. "They
have never seen such a lovely betrothal. Salma is fortunate
indeed in his bride."

"Yes, I have found a gem for my wife," agreed the bearded
man coming to stand beside us. His hand caught my clenched
fist. He brought the fingers to his lips. "Beautiful Rahab, I can
hardly wait for you to be my wife."

"I am not worthy." The old doubts resurfaced briefly.

"You are a heroine and we are proud to welcome you into our
hearts," insisted the married woman with a smile.

"Pray that the Living God sends peace. In only three moon
turnings we will be wed." The Hebrew spy held me close when
we reached the familiar fireside.

"I will pray for peace," I promised, offering my lips for a kiss.

It seemed that God heard our prayers. The summer days passed with no word of any threat. Joshua and the elders seemed content to let the men and women enjoy the peace instead of pushing for conquest toward the north. The fields around Gilgal grew green with thick stands of wheat and barley. On the not so distant hills, plump lambs seemed to grow bigger each day. Even though the river's flow lessened, as it did every year, there was still plenty of water for the entire encampment.

We were busy with the harvest and with it preparations for my wedding. Cutting, threshing and storing the grain grown near Gilgal kept everyone in the camp busy from sunrise to sunset.

The grapevines on the terraced hills near Gilgal were ripe. Children spent the daylight hours gathering the fruit. We joined the women of the city in pressing the plump purple globes until the juice ran into tubs. It was a time of celebration. I counted the passing of the days impatiently and watched the moon wax and wane and wax full again. The next full moon would signal the day I would become bride to Salma.

Sarai, Tirzah, Esther and Elisaba were almost more excited that I was about the approaching nuptials. Each woman seemed intent on ensuring that my wedding chest was well supplied. Blankets, rugs and pillows, as well as pottery and carved platters, jars and utensils, were steadily filling the leather trunk Caleb thoughtfully provided.

"I am not going to ever be able to use all this bounty." Again and again I protested.

"Blankets are a necessity," Sarai argued. "You do not know how cold winters may be in the hill country where you will settle."

Esther seemed to be convinced that I would be feeding a great multitude. Every time she came to my tent, it was with another wood platter or pottery jar. The skill with which she painted them astonished me.

"My friend, you should keep these for yourself. They are too lovely to be used." My remonstrations fell on deaf ears.

"Rahab, I will have no need of such furnishings. You will be the wife of an important man in Israel. These small tokens of my affection will be an honor to his hand."

With tears in my eyes, I hugged the older woman. She seemed content in her role as my sister-in-law's handmaid. I wondered if she longed for a husband and children or if the memory of her own marriage so many years ago still haunted her.

Pillows embroidered in lovely designs came from Elisaba's needle. The patterns were lovely despite the fact that they did not represent living things like the Canaanite designs I was familiar with.

"God forbids the representation of any animal or plant lest it become an idol." She offered the explanation even though I did not ask.

"You are so creative." I held up one of her gifts to admire the colors.

"Tirzah, how can you make the wool so soft?" My question was asked in amazement when the woman presented me with a gown of wool so finely woven it felt like silk from the east.

I remembered the lovely material Esther and Jerusha bought before the siege of Jericho. That cloth was given to the gods in futile intercession. It was not as soft and smooth as the gift from my sister-in-law.

"My husband's sister deserves the best," was her reply, although the woman flushed with pleasure at the compliment.

"Try it on." Sarai dragged me into her tent where the bronze mirror stood.

Almost hesitantly I slipped the garment over my head. The soft material draped my body and the creamy color brightened the shade of my red hair without making it gaudy.

In unison the trio of women clapped their hands. "You will be a lovely bride."

I stared at my reflection. Where had the hurt and frightened Rahab the harlot gone? Who was this confident woman staring at me?

"It is perfect," Elisaba sighed happily. "Salma will be delighted."

Color rose in my cheeks.

"Do you think so?" Uncertainty returned and I looked at my companions for reassurance.

"My brother loves you." The confident assertion was made without hesitation.

Sarai too nodded, "Be happy. Salma adores you."

Almost before I was ready, the moon grew full for the harvest festival. I was sure that no bride could possibly be as nervous as I was when the time arrived. Just like in Jericho, each bride had a retinue of bridesmaids. The groom had comrades who would carry the bridal litter. I knew that Jamal and Caleb were among those chosen to accompany Salma.

Sarai, Elisaba, Tirzah and Esther attended me. A ritual bath was followed with the application of a sweet-smelling oil to my skin.

"A bride is holy on this day," Sarai explained. "The water washes away your childhood and past. The oil is a sweet offering to the Lord."

My friends had more surprises for me.

"Caleb wants you to have this necklace." Sarai held a chain made of finely beaten gold. Many pendants of gold and some brilliant gems hung from the metal links. "My husband honors your presence among us and the joy you bring to Salma."

"Jamal too has a gift for the bride," Elisaba smiled. "This jeweled bracelet from Ai is for the loveliest of brides."

Tears gathered at the unexpected thoughtfulness, even as I admired the broad gold band inset with jewels.

"For your ears." Esther hugged me tightly before attaching a pair of earrings that I recognized as her favorite. One hand reached up to feel the golden loops.

"I do not know what to say." Almost overcome with emotion I shook my head and looked from smiling face to smiling face.

"Say nothing," advised Sarai. Her own brown eyes sparkled with the hint of tears.

The beautiful gown made by Tirzah was slipped over my head. I stroked the soft cloth. The texture was comforting with a reminder of the love my sister-in-law wove into the fabric.

"May your marriage be blessed by the gods," the woman softly spoke. She still sometimes forgot that all in the camp worshipped the One God.

Heedless of the crumpling of my gown, I hugged the woman when she kissed my cheek.

"I am so glad you have become my friend."

It was true. In Jericho I would never have come to know my sister-in-law. By the hand of the Living God we were friends.

I was not surprised when henna was painted on my palms. From time before time every bride wore the red dye on her hands until the work of everyday life erased the symbol of a newlywed. With soft strokes Elisaba applied the symbolic color.

I was reminded of the day eight years earlier during my initiation as the Daughter of Astarte. Then it was the priestess who painted the holy snake symbol on my hands and arms. Unlike the brides in Jericho and Canaan, there was no design drawn to represent Astarte. The crimson shade covered my entire palm.

"May the Living God grant that you and my brother find joy in one another." My young friend smiled as if there was no doubt of the outcome of her prayer.

Esther draped the bridal veil over my head. It covered me to the knees. Through the sheer weaving, the women appeared to move through a mist. When Tirzah settled the dowry crown on my head I was startled by the weight. I tried to free one hand from the material to feel the bangles hanging around my face.

"Your brother has provided a dowry." The explanation was even more surprising. "You will never know want."

"The man has given you a dowry for a queen," Elisaba spoke in a low, awed tone.

The generous gift brought tears to my eyes. Perez had changed since the fall of Jericho and his initiation into the congregation of Israel. That my brother honored me in this tangible way caused my heart to rejoice.

"Now you are ready." After a final tug to adjust the long veil, Sarai stepped back.

"Beauty and grace personified," nodded Tirzah.

"Salma is a lucky man," smiled his sister. I saw her dab at her eyes with the edge of the festive veil she wore.

Esther too tried to surreptitiously dry her eyes when she turned to face the tent entrance.

"Here come the groomsmen!" Cymbals and cheers announced the approach even without my friend's comment.

"We seek Rahab the Faithful as bride for Salma bar Nashon!"

The chorused request brought a brief chill of panic to my soul.

There was no time to hesitate. Sarai and Elisaba led me from the tent to the waiting litter. Enthroned behind the curtains I could see nothing of the procession through the camp. All I could do was hang onto the edge while Salma's friends wove here and there, announcing and inviting all to attend the nuptials. I could tell from the sound that more musicians had joined the procession. Eventually the swaying stopped, the curtains opened and Salma himself lifted me out. My hand trembled in his and I heard a reassuring whisper.

"My Rahab, do not be afraid, I am here."

The man's tender understanding wrapped me in a cozy cocoon. The words spoken by Eleazar were a blur. He recited the story of the first man and woman. The names were different but I recognized the Garden setting from the Canaanite stories of my childhood.

"You are flesh of my flesh and bone of my bone." Salma repeated Adam's words with such conviction that tears again sprang to my eyes.

"Therefore, a man shall leave his father and mother, be joined to his wife and the two will be one," intoned the priest. "Salma bar Nashon, the Lord God has provided for you a mate. Honor this woman as you do your own self."

"Blessed be the Living God of Israel," responded the man at my side.

"Rahab of Jericho, Faithful of the Lord, from henceforth you will be known as Rahab, wife of Salma. God has provided for you a strong tower and defense. May the Holy One make you fruitful with sons for Israel."

"Blessed be the God of my husband." My response was barely audible.

"The Lord has made you one flesh, go in peace." With the blessing we were wed.

Salma swung me into the litter. Amid shouts of congratulation I was carried to my husband's tent. The feast that waited was provided by the wives and mothers of the groomsmen as well as my friends. Baskets of breads and fruits vied with platters of meat

and vegetables for space on the blankets. Children ran happily
nearby. When they thought no one was watching, sticky fingers
snatched a sugared date or other sweet morsel from the many
trays.

Cushions were placed in front of the tent. Salma lifted me
from the litter. With ease he carried me the short distance to our
places. Clapping hands joined with the tambourine, cymbal and
pipes to make a merry cacophony. I found myself laughing and
clapping too.

Jamal brought a jar of wine and poured a cup for his broth-
er-in-law. "May the God of Israel bless you with flocks and sons
like our father Jacob."

Caleb also raised a cup in benediction. "May your sons be a
joy to the tribe of Judah and a blessing to the nation."

Nashon himself tottered over to offer a blessing, "May the
Lord bless your union with the same joy my own Judith gave me.
My son, I see that you have at last found a woman who will make
you a happy husband."

"My father." Salma rose to grip the old man's hand. "It is a joy
to hear your blessing. The Holy One has indeed blessed me with
the finest of brides."

With a smile I watched father and son embrace. A round of
clapping acknowledged the patriarch. My husband led his father
to the place of honor at his side.

I grew dizzy from the shower of blessings poured on us by
the men present. If all the prayers were answered, I would be in
constant childbirth. I was too happy to care. Boldly I leaned my
head against Salma's shoulder. A strong arm encircled me and I
felt safe. All day the feasting continued, intermixed with dancing.

As the sun was setting, Jamal called out, "Let the bride and
groom join in the dance."

I was glad because I longed to whirl and spin with the other
women. Two circles formed. The women circled to the right. In
the outer circle men circled left. Faster and faster beat the music.
The dance progressed until each man claimed his mate. Salma
lifted me high. I saw his broad grin even though my veil still
made everything appear hazy.

More wine was served and new platters of food appeared when the sun disappeared behind the mountains. The gathered well-wishers showed no signs of departing. Sarai and Elisaba led me into Salma's tent. Esther and Tirzah were already waiting to help me prepare for the bridal night. Suddenly all my fears returned.

"What if Salma despises me?" With hands crossed over my breasts, I looked from woman to woman.

"Who could despise such beauty?" Sarai did not pause in combing the length of my flaming hair until it was a wavy curtain around my shoulders.

"Salma will desire you," Tirzah added almost enviously.

Esther tugged the tunic for night into place and whispered in my ear, "Rahab, my friend, forget Balak and all that has gone before. This is your bridal night. Praise the gods who have given you a man who loves you."

I drew a deep breath at her words. They held both advice and blessing.

"Thank you," was the only reply I could make.

The four women arranged pillows and blankets around me until they were satisfied that I looked beguiling. Two oil lamps were left burning.

"May the God of Israel bring you joy and many sons." Sarai kissed me on the forehead. "You are like the sister I never had."

Then I was alone. Nervously I twisted a strand of hair around my finger. I tried to smooth it back into place only to start tangling it again as a fresh wave of apprehension swept over me. I wondered how long I would be left alone while the festivities continued. No position seemed comfortable. Even with all the pillows around me, I could not relax but sat stiffly erect on the pallet of soft skins and blankets.

Salma did not delay. The tent flap lifted soon after my friends left, and my husband entered. Behind him, cheers from the men competed with the musicians.

"My Rahab." The awe in my husband's voice stilled my fears.

Crossing the short distance, the man knelt beside the pallet. He took my face between his hands. Our lips met in a kiss full of promise. Hours later, I lay beside my husband watching the gray sky turn to pink where dawn peeked between the hide panels of the tent. The night had been filled with Salma. His gentle love made me forget the past. My heart treasured the words of adoration spoken throughout the hours of lovemaking interspersed with dozing in each others' arms. I rolled on my side to stare at my beloved. The man was watching me. Color rushed to my face at the expression in the blue eyes.

"My wife, my Rahab, you are lovely in the morning light." His deep voice stirred my heart.

Unresisting, I nestled into the man's arms. My fingers strayed across the broad chest.

"Beloved tormentor." Chuckling, Salma caught my hands to still their wandering.

He kissed the fingertips and then my lips. Soon we were lost in the joy of our love.

The wedding week passed in the same way. Isolated from the busy life of the camp, we lived only to love. My husband told me about the town where we would eventually settle.

"Bethlehem has been special to the Children of Israel for generations. Rachel, wife of Jacob, is buried nearby. There is much rich grazing and many fields of wheat and barley. It is a peaceful and sheltered town in the hills. We will be happy there."

"When will we go?" It sounded wonderful to be amid the cooler hills and inside a house with walls again.

Serious now, Salma rested on his elbow. He looked down at me and brushed a strand of red hair off my forehead. I sensed the man was preparing to ease my disappointment.

"Only after all the tribes have a portion in the land can any of us settle in our homes. That is only fair." Still my husband twisted the strand of hair he held and watched my face.

"Yes." I slowly nodded. I could not suppress the small sigh that escaped. "It could be so long."

"The God of Israel will not delay." Optimistic words sought to allay my sadness. "We will be in Bethlehem before the winter."

I hoped my husband was right.

✑ 16 ✑

THE WEDDING WEEK ENDED and life resumed a new routine. Sarai and Elisaba rejoiced in my new status. Tirzah and Esther often joined us as we spun yarn or worked on the looms. Tirzah's son, Joshua, was accepted by Elisaba's child as a playmate even though my nephew was barely crawling. My niece was always with her mother. She no longer seemed to fear me. The girl sometimes tried to spin the yarn but her hands were not yet large enough to spin the whorl properly.

"You will be able to do more than just card the wool soon," Tirzah consoled Rebekka before turning back to her own work.

Joshua sat at her feet. He was just learning to crawl but still usually found it easier to wave his hands and point to what he wanted.

"I am not sure Judah understands that Joshua will not always be so easily contained," smiled Elisaba as her son handed a toy to his small friend.

The baby pounded the block on the ground with glee. When he tossed it away, Judah patiently brought it back until he became involved in his own game.

"May I play with Judah?" Rebekka turned to Elisaba.

"If your mother says you may," agreed the young mother.

My sister-in-law readily gave consent, "It is alright if you want to play with Joshua and Judah."

The girl loved playing mother to the two babies and eagerly left the yarn to carry Joshua over to where Judah was building a tower of wooden blocks carved by his uncle. We all laughed when the baby crawled to the blocks and took the lowest one.

The tower fell. Judah howled in rage and frustration. Joshua cried in fear when one of the little wooden cubes hit his head. Tirzah scooped up her son to soothe his fears.

"You can build it again," I promised the distraught child, joining him on the ground. "I will help you."

Mollified by my promise, the boy dragged me to his toys. Together we rebuilt the structure while Tirzah nursed her son. Rebekka watched for a couple of minutes before dropping down in the dust to join us.

I felt my heart expand with longing for a child of my own. When my monthly flow failed to come, I barely dared hope. Not wanting to raise false hopes, I did not share my secret with anyone. Even Salma would not be told until I was certain.

The days were shortening toward the coldest and shortest day of the year when we heard the news that brought fear to the camp.

"The chiefs of the north have made an alliance against Israel," Joshua announced to the congregation when we gathered for the Sabbath rituals. "We must go up against them. God will give them into our hand like Jericho and Ai. The land will be ours from Tyre to the Negev. Blessed be the God of Abraham, Isaac and Jacob who gives us the victory!"

"Amen, Alleluia, El Elohim Israel!" The familiar cry rang out in response.

Salma held me tight that night.

"I will return, my Rahab." Over and over the man repeated the assurance.

Desperately, I clung to my husband. "How can I bear to let you go? You will be in danger."

"Jamal and I will go ahead and spy out the land." With his explanations the man tried to ease my fears. "Who would attack a pair of innocent traders from across the Jordan? God will keep us safe. I will return before you can really miss me."

"I already miss you." I burrowed close to my husband.

Tenderly the man kissed my hair. He tried to soothe my fears. Our lovemaking was tempestuous. Exhausted by emotion I slept. When I awoke in the dawn, Salma had already left. Nashon found me sobbing beside the fire when he slowly emerged from his tent. The old man was bent over the two carved branches he used as canes. With surprising speed my father-in-law was at my side.

"They will return." The patriarch easily guessed the reason for my tears.

"How can you be sure?" With a keening cry, I buried my face in my hands.

"I trust that God will keep my son safe as always." I barely heard the reply through my sobs.

"How can you trust this unseen God?" Almost angrily I faced the old man, who started toward his leather seat beside the fire. "The priests of Jericho said to trust Astarte, but the city fell. My mother told me to trust my father and where is he? Balak told us to trust him. Yet he took all the promised profit."

Ashamed of my outburst I turned to hide my face in my veil. I had not meant to allow anyone to know of my doubts.

"The Holy God is not like that." A gentle hand touched my shoulder. The old man had come to my side. "We Hebrews, of all people, have reason to question the trustworthiness of the God of Jacob. We labored under Pharaoh four hundred years. There was terrible oppression and death. The Lord did not seem to hear. Many were the questions shouted to the heavens by desperate men and women. Yet, the Living One is faithful. Here we are preparing to possess the land promised generations ago to Abraham."

I drew in a shuddering breath and tried to stop sobbing. The man was trying to comfort me. "I know that the God of Abraham, Isaac and Jacob has done great things. Even for me," I admitted slowly. "I knew that your God would conquer Jericho. My family was rescued from the destruction and I have seen the armies of Israel move forward in victory. I only want to find love and peace with my husband."

When I looked up, I saw tenderness in the bearded face. He rocked slightly to keep his balance.

"My father, you must sit." I suddenly realized the old man was standing.

One wrinkled hand still patted my shoulder. With the other he steadied himself on a single cane. Carefully I helped Nashon to his stool. When I crouched beside the man he rested both hands on my shoulders.

"The Holy One will answer your questions." My father-in-law seemed to empathize with my uncertainty. No one except my mother ever had understood my need for answers about holy things.

"I would not dare to distrust your God. There is no other god who has done such wonders. It would be folly to question the Holy One." Appalled by the suggestion, I gasped.

A low chuckle surprised me. I raised my head. There was a smile beneath the watery and wise eyes. The color was so similar to the ones I loved that I felt my heart lurch.

"If the God of Abraham, Isaac and Jacob did not turn away from four hundred years of angry questions, the Lord will not turn away from you, Rahab." The old man patted my cheek tenderly. "Do not be afraid, my daughter."

The loving name on the lips of my father-in-law surprised me. My eyes opened wide and I looked at the old man.

Again the promise was repeated, "Do not be afraid. The Lord will not turn away from you."

"Yes, my father." Only half believing the assurance I tried to smile.

A moment later I scrambled to my feet to prepare a meal for the patient man. Throughout the day I pondered his assertion that it was alright to question the God of Israel. Later, alone in the tent that seemed so empty without my husband, I cried out to God.

"How can I trust you? You try to rob me of all I hold dear. Where were you when my mother died? Were you sleeping when Balak took what he wanted?" Anger built of years of silence poured out toward the silent God of my husband. "Did you hear the mocking words of the women of Jericho who named me harlot? My own father rejected me once he was safe from the downfall of the city."

In my rage, I pounded the pillows until I was exhausted. I lay on my pallet, no longer sobbing aloud. Dimly I remembered just such agony from my childhood. My puppy had disappeared. Astarte did not seem to hear my frantic plea to bring him back again. None of my brothers understood my grief. I fled to the farthest corner of the orchard to cry. My mother found me. Without words she rocked and held my sobbing body.

Finally she spoke after I stopped weeping, "My child, grief comes and only the gods know why. I have had sorrow in my life and you will in yours. Even in the midst of the deepest pain, if you release your despair you will find peace. My father said that it is the God of Jacob that he has served in Bethel that offers this calm. I do not know or understand. What I can promise is that there is a power that does bring solace. Dearest Rahab, my prayer is that you will find that peace in your life as well."

I was astonished to feel that same love enfolding me in a tent in the midst of the camp of Israel. The consolation my mother spoke of reached out and embraced me. Only then, in my heart, did I feel an answer. It was as if someone spoke.

"Rahab, I was there each time in the darkness of your despair."

I felt a peace settle over me like a blanket.

"You were there?" Awed, I spoke aloud.

"My child, I wept with your grief and stood beside you when you were afraid."

Suddenly I did understand, if only in that moment, that there was indeed only One God. I recognized that throughout my life, I had indeed been upheld by someone beyond what I was taught to believe in.

"I did not know your name but I have known your power and touch." I fell to my knees in wonder. "My mother told me of the God of Jacob. She wondered if the God her father served was the True One. When Jamal and Salma came to Jericho I recognized that they served you. Truly all my life you have been beside me. Yet how can you love someone like me?"

An often-quoted saying sprang to my mind unbidden, "This day have I begotten you."

In the darkness of my tent the words took on a new mean-

ing. I understood that the God of the Hebrews accepted me as if
I was a child. For a long time I knelt in the darkness. The anger
and fear drained away. Peace settled over me. I slept deeply, no
longer afraid to face the future.

My newfound faith and confidence were tested in the next
few weeks. Sabbath followed Sabbath. The army that marched
north did not return. Word of fierce battles trickled back to the
anxious women waiting near Gilgal.

"Our men will be defeated."

"The alliance in the north is too strong."

"Would that we had never come to this place."

I surprised myself by responding to the fears around me.

"Daughters of Israel, the God of Abraham, Isaac and Jacob
will not fail us now. Do you not know that the Holy One will continue to sustain this entire people? Have you already forgotten
the fiery pillar of cloud in the wilderness by which the presence
of your Lord was visible? Have you ever known hunger?"

I looked around at the faces of women busy at their weekly
washing. Some hostile, a few curious and many interested looks
greeted my voice.

"No, the Living God has provided for you, even to food in the
wilderness." I answered my own questions. "The power of El
Elohim Israel has proven greater than the chiefs of Jericho. I saw
the greatest soldiers in Canaan fall before the shout of the armies
of the Living God. The coalition of the southern chiefs was not
able to withstand the will of the Holy One. The arm of the Lord
is not shortened. God will bring about the freedom that was
promised to your forefathers."

Sarai stared at me in amazement. Elisaba stood with openmouthed astonishment at my defense.

"You have changed," my friend mentioned in wonder that
evening. We three women sat together by the evening fire with
Nashon nearby.

"A moon turning ago I thought you were in despair," added
my sister-in-law. "Now you are the champion of God."

"I have learned that there is only one God who has sustained
me all my life." Color crept into my face at the assertion. With

one hand I pointed to the myriad tents stretching from the stream to the mountain. "If the one God can love me, surely he will not fail so great a people."

The women followed my gesture. Around each small fire a family gathered. Like us they waited for husbands and fathers to return. Nashon caught my eye and smiled. I returned the smile with a nod. The old man nearly always joined us for the evening meal now. He seemed to enjoy the company of his daughters-in-law.

"The God of Sinai brought the congregation here for a purpose. The Living God of the entire world wants us to share word of the love the Holy One has for all. This love is shown in all mighty deeds done for you. To the Children of Israel is given the honor of showing the way. My grandfather maintained the sacrifices of Jacob at Bethel until he died. He taught my mother of your patriarch Jacob, who was renamed Israel before the altar at Bethel. She tried to teach me that there is only one god and that the multitudes of gods worshipped in Jericho were simply shadows." There was no doubt in my heart any longer. I leaned forward to speak urgently. "That True God led you from Egypt and gives you this homeland."

I took a deep breath that was almost a sigh of submission. The words had poured from my heart. A little nervous after my confession I looked at the group near the fire.

Sarai was nodding with a small smile on her lips, "Just so would Miriam have spoken. God has chosen you to encourage the people."

Elisaba stared at me. Her brown eyes were wide. After a moment she whispered, "You will bring blessing to my brother and this people."

Old Nashon intoned what sounded like a prophecy, "The wife of my son is a blessing."

I shook my head even as I knew that I had no choice except to speak the words that came to my lips. Over the next weeks there were many opportunities to remind the women of their God. Two more moon turnings passed before the armies of Israel returned triumphant. The Shortest Day passed without any great

fire lighting as was done in Jericho. There was no need to call
Baal back from the farthest reaches, for the One God controlled
the sun and moon.

Our flocks had grazed far up the mountain during the summer months. When the colder days arrived the animals were
driven lower and lower following the last patches of grass. From
the heights the shepherd boys could see as far as the ford of the
Jordan at Adam to the north. They took turns acting as sentries
from the cliffs. Young Ezra brought first word of the returning
army just as they had after the victory at Ai.

The boy ran into camp one afternoon shouting for the priest,
"Eleazar! Eleazar!"

At the sound of his voice each woman looked at her neighbor. We were busy with the washing. Now that the weather was
cooler it was not done weekly, but only when the sun warmed the
air. Startled questions raced up and down the length of the
stream.

"What could it be?"

"Have the flocks been attacked?"

"Why would Ezra be in camp at this time?"

With varying degrees of concern and anticipation we hurried
toward the camp. From tents within the camp the older women
gathered as well.

"Eleazar." Panting from his run, the messenger stood before
the priest.

"My son, what is it?" A frown drew the gray eyebrows
together. "Why have you disturbed the camp in this way?"

Still gasping for air, Ezra did not quail before the old man.
"To the north . . . our army . . . returns."

"Are you certain?" Wrinkled hands gripped small shoulders.
Eleazar bent close.

"The sun shines on spear points at Adam," the boy explained
more coherently.

All around the women held their breath.

"How do you know it is our army?" The priest asked the
question. I was reminded of his same doubt in the spring.

"We saw no chariots," responded the shepherd.

"Praise the God of Israel," someone called out.

"We will offer sacrifices and pray that this is the army of Israel safely returning," countered the priest.

Turning toward the Tabernacle the old man signaled for his sons to prepare the altar. As the sun set, smoke from incense mixed with the odor of the sacrificed lamb burning on the altar. Throughout the night the priests kept vigil, alternately chanting prayers and prostrating themselves before the altar.

"They look like the priests of Baal, except that they do not slash their skin with knives," commented Esther. "Perhaps as you say, Rahab, all gods are one."

Without hesitation I replied, "There is only One God. All prayer that is honest ascends to the throne of the Most High."

"Yet all priests employ the same actions whether they call on Astarte or the God of Israel," commented the woman. After a thoughtful pause she added, "However, I have not seen the priests of Israel use the secret arts of the Queen of Heaven."

Like my friend, I remembered the secret passages and mirrors used to create the illusions through which Astarte seemed to respond to the worshippers in Jericho. In the open space of the camp there were not any hidden and secret ways.

"There is no need for trickery when worshipping the Living God," was my answer. "The priests of Israel do not need to fool the congregation. The God of Abraham, Isaac and Jacob alone does miracles."

"Perhaps," was the only answer from Esther.

With a wave the woman walked away to my brother's tents. The scent of the incense and sacrifices mingled with the smell of our evening meals. A cloud hung over the camp and I was reminded of the stories about the pillar of fiery cloud that led the Children of Israel in the desert. I watched the priests for a short time longer before entering my tent.

Morning brought a messenger from the north. Tired from his night long run, Jeremiah bar Ethan trotted into camp at dawn. Almost before everyone was awake the news had spread from one end of camp to the other.

"It is the army of Israel returning!"

"Great victories are won!"

"Our men are on their way home!"

Esther and I spent the day preparing bandages and ointments for any injured soldiers. We did not return to our conversation of the previous night. Still the priests offered prayers. Now the words were of thanksgiving, not petition.

"There will be some wounded," my friend pointed out.

We met at mid-morning near the newly erected tent being prepared for those with injuries. Neither of us voiced the fear that among the dead or injured would be my husband or my brother. I refused to even think of such a thing. Sarai joined us in our work. We were silent, each with our own prayers for the safe return of the men we loved.

Afternoon shadows crept across the camp before we heard the ram's horns and trumpets approaching. Eleazar stood at the altar but his eyes looked north as did everyone in the camp. Children darted in and out of the gathering, barely noticed by each wife and mother straining for a glimpse of her man.

I found myself twisting my veil around my hands until it was tight. Then I shook it loose only to repeat the process.

My heart beat a fervent prayer, "God of my husband, if you truly love me, bring Salma safe to me."

Briefly I caressed my belly with its still secret burden. Then my hands resumed their nervous twisting and untwisting of the material.

Proudly the men marched into camp. The welcoming cheer from our throats was answered by the soldiers.

"Amen, Alleluia, El Elohim Israel!"

Then, as always, it was chaos as the army dispersed. Women ran to their husbands. Mothers sought sons in the ranks. Afraid to hope, I took a halting step forward then stopped. My eyes searched the crowd for the one face I desired. Then I saw the man striding through the congregation. Salma was looking right and left. Joy freed my feet and I rushed forward.

"My Rahab." I found myself in his strong arms. Our lips met and I forgot the lonely nights.

"Salma, my husband, are you safe?" Only after a very long

time did I draw back to run my eyes over the man, searching for any injury.

"I am not hurt." Catching my chin in a gentle grasp, my beloved drew me to him again.

Fingers rough from using the sword caressed my cheeks and throat, sending waves of desire through me. Much later, we lay in each others' arms. For one more night I kept my secret in order to enjoy the embrace of my love.

In the morning Joshua called all Israel together before the Tabernacle.

"Amen, Alleluia, El Elohim Israel!" The leader opened the meeting with the familiar words. "The God of Abraham, Isaac and Jacob has opened to his people the Land of Promise. From Mizpah to the Negev, Canaan is ours."

The roar of joy was deafening.

"Before the power of the Almighty, the chiefs of the north have fallen. No longer will the Hittites, Amorites, Canaanites, Periezites, Hivites or Jebusites control the land given to Abraham and his descendants. We will go in to possess our homeland. Each man will sit under his own vine. Your children will play about your doors."

"Amen, Alleluia, El Elohim Israel!" Three times the praise rang out.

I clasped my hands together as I thought of the son of Salma playing in front of a real house. It would not be a few rooms in a city wall, I was sure. Lost in my dreams, I barely listened while Joshua droned on about the defeat of each city and chieftain. I did not care about the divisions of the land that were announced. Caleb's name caught my attention.

"Caleb, son of Jephunneh, to you is the inheritance called the city of Arba, known as Hebron. With a mighty hand, you have driven out the Anakin who were giants in the land. Therefore, the city will be an inheritance for you and yours forever, just as was promised by Moses before we came to the Jordan."

"The Lord is gracious." Caleb saluted his general and bowed toward the Tabernacle.

I smiled at Sarai a few feet away. With glowing eyes my friend watched her husband proudly. Her dreams were of a family, too. We had shared our hopes in the long weeks of waiting for the army to return. Caleb would bring his daughter and sons from across the Jordan. I wondered if a young man would be found for Achsah who would meet her father's standards.

"I hope you will be nearby." The woman moved close to whisper to me.

"Yes," I nodded. It would be difficult to live in a new place where I knew no one.

I tried to remember if I knew how far Hebron was from Bethlehem as the ceremony dragged on and on. After a few minutes I had to admit that I had no idea. I resumed my dreams of the house I would keep for Salma and our son. When the day ended, we dispersed. Caleb and Sarai walked beside my husband to our tent.

"We will dwell in Bethlehem," Salma announced as the men squatted beside the fire. "There is rich grazing for my flocks and safety in the hills."

"A wise choice." Caleb nodded his approval.

"I will build a fine house for my bride. My sons will not know war." The man moved close to me and laid a hand protectively on my shoulder.

A wave of love swept over me and I rested a cheek on my husband's hand for a brief moment. When the men began to discuss the campaign just passed, Sarai and I prepared a simple meal that was eaten almost absently when talk turned to the approaching settlement in and around the cities of Canaan.

"The One God has given us a great victory," exalted Caleb.

"We must strive to remain faithful," cautioned my husband. "What is given so freely must be honored."

"You are right, my friend. We must not forget that it is by the hand of the Holy One that we have a homeland," agreed his friend. "The Children of Israel will be a great people for the God of Abraham, Isaac and Jacob is with us. My hands itch to stick a spade into the soil of my land near Hebron. I am sure you want to begin to build your flocks at Bethlehem as well."

The men began to plan their prosperity. Sarai helped me

clean the platters and then after an impatient frown at her husband she walked the short distance to her own tent. The conversation no longer interested me. I slipped into the hide structure that had become my home.

I wrapped myself in the blankets to wait for Salma. Outside the waning moon cast shadows. Still Caleb and my husband talked. The younger man sought advice from the older. Impatient, I played with the fringe on a pillow and thought of the words I would say to make my beloved the happiest of men. Finally, the rustle of leather signaled his entrance.

"My love, I thought you would be asleep." Real amazement was in the words.

"I waited for you." Now that the man stood before me, I felt shy.

"You are too beautiful to be alone." Rapidly throwing off his robe and tunic my husband drew me close under the blankets.

Only as we lay side by side, sated and glowing did I remember my plan.

"Husband." My hand crept across the broad chest and I raised myself slightly on one elbow.

"Mmm." His response was drowsy.

"Salma, listen." I tugged the side of his beard until the man looked at me.

Moistening dry lips I found it hard to make my announcement, "I . . . do you . . . we . . ."

Slightly concerned by my stammering, Salma frowned and sat up. "Love, tell me what is troubling you."

"It is not a problem," I hedged, glancing away. With a deep breath I looked back at my husband and blurted out the surprise. "I am with child."

I watched his mouth open and close several times as the words sunk in.

"I . . . you . . . we . . . Rahab . . . how? . . ." It was time for the man to stammer.

Blue eyes traveled down my still slim figure and up to my face. In the dim light, I felt myself flush.

"Are you sure?" Finding his voice, the man pulled me against his chest. "I have only just returned."

"Have you forgotten our marriage week?" Half teasing and half hurt I pouted.

"And you kept this secret until now?" With kisses I was tumbled onto the pillows.

"You *have* only just returned." I forgot my reproach when the man claimed my mouth.

"A son." Raising his head, my husband rested a broad hand on my belly.

"As God wills; the baby could be a girl." I could not help but smile as I reminded the man, although I too prayed to bear a boy child.

"Will you leave me now?" Very low I asked the question whose answer I feared.

"Why would I?" In confusion the man frowned down at me.

"Is it not the law?" Barely audible I made a reply.

The frown deepened. Stubbornly, Salma lifted his chin. "A man must not have relations with a pregnant woman, but I will sleep beside my wife."

"My love, your God has blessed me." Tears began to slip down my cheeks in relief.

"Beloved, you are a rich jewel among women." Tenderly, with kisses and caresses, Salma showed me his adoration until we fell asleep.

⌒ 17 ⌒

THE MAN'S PRIDE KNEW no bounds. As soon as Nashon emerged from his tent, my husband bowed to his father.

With barely suppressed eagerness the son shared his news, "You will be a grandfather soon after we settle in Bethlehem."

Nashon nodded and motioned me to come forward.

"Rahab, you will bear a son who will be a pillar in Israel." As I knelt beside the old man he took my face in his dry hands. "The Holy One is gracious."

"Yes, my father." I turned my face to kiss the palm of the old man's hand.

As soon as the meal was over, Salma insisted that we share the news with Caleb and Sarai. Both men hurried away to tell Jamal after the excited exclamations died down.

"Salma is delighted." My friend smiled. "I had wondered. Your appetite changed and you have the new habit of stroking your belly."

"I did not know anyone noticed." To hide my blush I looked down at my traitorous hands.

"No, it is wonderful news." Sarai took my hands in hers. "I hoped I was right."

Esther embraced me when she heard the news. "Rahab, it appears you are right in trusting the God of this people. It is time that you received blessing and not curses from the gods. We have both prospered since leaving Jericho. My mistress is good and gentle. You have a husband who loves you as you deserve."

The sincere joy from my friend brought tears to my eyes. We clung together until my nephew's whimpers recalled the woman to her duties. She turned to pick up the boy who reached out arms to me.

"I have longed for a baby." Bending over the child in my arms, I brushed the soft hair with my lips.

"And you will have a son born of love." The confident words were reassuring.

As the news raced through the camp, Elisaba and Jamal were among those who congratulated Salma.

"My brother, may your wife be a fruitful vine and bear you many sons," exclaimed the older spy, while my sister-in-law hugged me.

"A baby will complete your joy," she prophesied.

Nearly every woman in the camp had advice for me. Many of the suggestions seemed somewhat superstitious, but I smiled and nodded at each suggestion.

"Walk straight and the child will be a boy."

"Eat the fruit of the pear so the child will be strong."

"Avoid forked trees lest you have hard labor."

Only my own brother remained aloof. Tirzah stayed away too. Even Salma's delight in my barely rounding figure did not entirely displace the sorrow at the renewed avoidance by my own family.

"Why does Perez shun me?" One morning I confronted Esther as we filled our water jars. "After the Passover, at the next full moon, we will each disperse to the homes prepared by the Holy God. I wish I could have peace with my brother. Surely it cannot be that he holds the fall of Jericho against me."

"My friend, it is not for me to tell you what is in my master's mind." Esther spoke low. The woman paused as if considering. Then she blurted out her suspicion. "I fear that he believes you played the harlot again and that this child is not of the seed of your husband."

Rage replaced grief in an instant. Eyes blazing, I rose to my feet. My breath came in short gasps and I looked toward the camp. From the edge of the water, I could not see my brother's tent.

Through gritted teeth I hissed the question. "How dare he judge me so?"

Concerned by my reaction, Esther grabbed my arm when I started away.

"Remember your baby," she urged, tugging me to a stop. "Anger may harm him."

It was the one thing that could halt my enraged charge to confront my brother. I sank down on the ground and began to sob.

"He has no right." Over and over I repeated the statement.

Sarai and Elisaba hurried to my side. They must have seen me confront Esther. Together they got me to my tent. All I could do was shake my head in response to the questions my friends asked. I felt sick at the thought that my own brother still believed me a harlot. A tea of soothing herbs helped me sleep. Esther must have confessed the reason for my distress. When I awakened Salma sat by my side. His frown cleared when I opened my eyes.

"My love, are you alright?" Distress was visible in the worried blue eyes and comfort came from his kiss.

"Yes, I . . ." Memory of the scene at the river halted my words. I took a shuddering breath and breathed the name. "Perez . . ."

"Your brother is here. He would like to apologize for causing you pain." Even though he smiled, something in the grimness of my husband's tone told me that the men had already spoken.

A little hesitantly I agreed, "Very well."

Salma helped me sit up and placed pillows at my back. Picking up the carved wooden comb Sarai had given me, he gently drew the teeth through my tousled hair.

"My son will have no reason to be ashamed of his mother. Rahab, my beloved, is the most beautiful woman in the camp of Israel. I am fortunate that the God of my fathers has blessed me with her." With each stroke of the comb the man expressed his love.

"My husband." Turning suddenly I threw myself into his arms overwhelmed by the affection. "Your God has blessed me with your love, even though I am an unworthy foreigner."

Taking me by the shoulders, Salma looked into my eyes and reminded me, "You are no longer a foreigner. You are a Daughter of Israel."

A kiss sealed the words. Then my husband rose and drew me to my feet. I draped a veil over the smoothly combed red hair. Hand in hand we walked into the afternoon. Perez stood, head bowed, beyond the fire. Tirzah essayed a slight smile when I glanced at her. My nephews and niece stood arrayed beside their parents. They stood surprisingly still. Tension hung in the air. Beyond my family, I could see men and women pretending to go about their afternoon business, although everyone's attention was fixed on the drama in front of Salma bar Nashon's tent.

"My sister." The humble tone astonished me.

Never had I heard such a beseeching note from my proud brother. It was hard for the man to continue. Several times he opened his mouth only to close it again.

"Perez, son of Hamash the Canaanite, what do you say to your sister? Rahab is my wife, called Faithful by the God of Israel." At last Salma's stern words fell into the silence.

"My sister," Perez began again. He looked at me and took a step forward. "It is known that you have left the old ways of life along with service to the gods of Jericho. I envy you. I have always envied you. There was a faith in you that none of us understood. You and Mother did not seem to fear the gods. I do not think you were afraid of anything. Even as a child, you did not fear our father when he raged about the demands of officials and priests. Jonadab, Hamul and I quailed in the face of his anger. You smiled up at the man and he melted and gave you what you wanted. We all hated you for that power over our father."

The man looked past me toward the destruction that had been Jericho. For a moment he seemed lost in thought. I almost spoke but then my brother turned to me. His face looked haggard and old.

"You innocently believed that your prayer caused the dog to attack Elon and gave a child to Penninah. Then the priests of Astarte accepted you into their midst. None of us knew you still served Astarte even when you left the Temple. No one knew that you had the trust of the priestess to bring news of the invaders. We believed the rumors in the city. You sought to serve the gods even in the face of the lies about your life. It was worse that the inn you ran was successful. I was jealous that my sister seemed to effortlessly achieve what I worked so hard to get. Our father is not an easy man to satisfy."

"My brother." I wanted to absolve the man. He did not seem to hear my voice.

"Never have I seen such courage as it took to hide the spies of Israel. I suppose you saw in them the faith that our mother spoke of. You desired to find the True One that she was so certain existed. I see now that all your life has been a search for what is truly holy. Now you have found the One God our mother spoke of in the midst of this people."

The man paused and looked down. Before I could speak, Perez continued. It seemed that he could not stop the flow of words.

"My sister, you are honored by this people and accept their ways. I still seek answers. The gods of my childhood have forsaken me, but I fear to let them go fully. I allowed my jealousy to poison my thoughts of you. Tirzah tried to tell me that you never were a harlot, but it was the only explanation I wanted to believe. Rahab, forgive me. Can you teach me to have faith and bravery like yours?"

When my brother fell to his knees at my feet, I stared openmouthed. My hand reached out to touch the dark curls now streaked with gray strands. For the first time I realized that the man was no longer young.

"Perez, I never knew you were jealous. I thought you hated me for my independence. Our father did not understand my need to find answers. He sent me to the Temple for his own reputation." Tears choked my voice. "I am only a woman who has been seeking to find freedom, love and peace. How can I teach you anything?"

Real respect was in the reply. "Rahab, it is right that you are called Faithful. Even though we shunned you, you sought us out and saved all our lives. It is more than I would have done. Show me how to have such faith as to believe that good can come in the midst of evil."

"That is something you will have to learn for yourself from the Holy and Living God." I took my brother's cheeks between my hands. Looking down into the brown eyes I saw the same yearning I had long felt. Gently I tried to explain, "The One God of all seeks only to love each of us. I have not found it easy to accept that love. For a long time I raged at the gods. Neither Astarte nor the God of Israel seemed to hear my cries. Then, in the middle of my despair and loneliness I found that the Holy One has always been with me. I no longer fear my past. The God of Abraham, Isaac and Jacob has given me redemption and a new life. My husband is living proof of the great love of this God. Within my body grows the promise of a new generation to carry the message of that love to the world."

As I finished my declaration of faith, I turned toward Salma. The tears that stood in his eyes surprised me.

"My love." Two words were all he could say.

I was drawn close to the man. Perez remained kneeling.

"My brother, you only need to look around you to see what the Living God has done for you. From your confession of jealousy we have reconciliation. See how from the ashes of Jericho you and yours have a new life and freedom to choose how to live it." I held out a hand in plea to the man. "The God of this people will honor your desire if you let go of your pride. Let the Holy One love you."

At first I did not think the Canaanite would respond. Then slowly he stood up.

"How can you forgive me?" Even then the man almost could not accept my hand.

"You are my brother." My answer was simple.

My brother swallowed convulsively before reaching to grasp my hand as if it were a lifeline.

"My sister." Then Perez was in my arms.

I held out my hand to Tirzah and the children. Slowly they came forward until the woman embraced me. I was not ashamed of the tears streaming down my face. They mingled with Tirzah's. Even my brother's cheeks were damp. All my nephews crowded close. For the first time in my life, I felt at peace with my brother. Rebekka shyly came forward to cling to my hand.

"It is good." Salma seemed to speak a benediction as he rested his hands on my shoulders.

"My brother." Perez saluted my husband with a humble salaam.

"Rahab is in your care. She could not have a better champion."

"I wish that my father could learn of the God who gives new life." As we stood together I voiced my thought.

"Hamash, Jonadab and Hamul are all well," Salma interjected. "I saw them in Ataroth. The vineyards of Jonadab were not destroyed. The promise to Rahab the Faithful is on her family even there. Who knows, perhaps they will learn of the God of Abraham, Isaac and Jacob among the sons of Ephraim who will settle there."

I was glad to hear of my family but there was not time to ask more questions. Tirzah drew me aside to ask about my pregnancy. Too soon, my brother and his family crossed the camp to their own tent. That night I lay beside Salma. In the dark his hand held mine.

"What did you say to my brother?" Curiosity I tried to suppress bubbled out.

The man chuckled softly. "My beloved wife, I spoke as a man speaks to an equal."

"No," I whispered back, "that would not have brought my brother here to meekly seek reconciliation."

"But my words did just that, my wife," Salma insisted with a kiss on my forehead. "Rest now. The mother of my son will need her strength."

I never learned what passed between the two men. Neither Salma nor Perez spoke of it again. My brother treated me with kindness, and Tirzah was able to rejoin our group of women for the Passover preparations.

Much baking and chopping and preparation was needed for the yearly festival in memory of the freedom God promised. This year the feast was in celebration of the fulfilling of the conquest of the Land of Promise.

The seven-day remembrance of the freedom won for the Children of Israel by the Living God affected me deeply. The recitations of the marvels in Egypt and in the wilderness served to deepen the flowering faith in the God whose power I had seen and whose love I experienced.

"Blessed are you Lord God of the Universe." Without hesitation I repeated the prayer of dedication, adding in my heart, "You are my God."

The week of holy celebration passed. The meal that was the culmination of the week was joyful. Perez with Tirzah and his family joined us for the lamb and other foods of remembrance. Sarai and Caleb along with Jamal, Elisaba and Judah completed the group. There was much laughter. As the symbolic meal was consumed I felt my heart expand with love for each person present.

I sought to share my feelings.

"The God of Israel did not forget the promises made to Abraham," I marveled. "Through all the generations the Holy One remembered. When the time was right, the Living Lord acted."

Assent came from Caleb, "It is true."

"Before you left Egypt, you were divided as tribes. God formed you into a mighty and united people capable of inhabiting this land."

Looking around at my Hebrew friends, I spread my hands to indicate the vastness of the territory available to the Children of Israel.

"Rahab, what you say is true." Salma drew me close to his side. "My father speaks of the slave pits of Egypt. I remember the long years in the desert. Both were hard to bear."

"Yet, like my life in Jericho, the experiences are part of who you are." I had to share the sudden insight. "The Living God used what seemed evil and transformed it into freedom. Before I knew what I sought, that same God found me. Now I am the most blessed of women. You, my husband, and this child of our love are proof of the love of the God of Abraham, Isaac and Jacob to all people. I was a foreigner, yet the Holy One found me faithful and accepted me. It must be true that all people are one to El Elohim Israel."

Now that I had shared my perceptions I leaned against the man. I felt a tender kiss.

"My wife, you never cease to amaze me." The whisper was spoken for my ears only.

Across the fire, I saw Perez studying me.

"My sister," the man paused, "do you really think that your

life in Jericho was part of what God planned for you?"

"The One God uses all our experiences to form us, just as a potter kneads the imperfections into the clay until all are smooth." The answer slid from my lips without much thought.

My brother was silent. It was obvious that the idea was foreign to him.

I spoke not only to Perez as I mused, "I once thought it odd that the God who has no name has so many names. Astarte has abundant titles, but I thought that the unseen God would have only one name. Now I begin to understand that El Shaddai, Elohim, Adonai, Sinai are all just attributes and parts of the One who can never be fully known or seen."

"Even the great Moses saw only the back of the Lord," Nashon suddenly inserted from his stool.

"Such glory is too much for me to comprehend." With a smile at the old man who was a dear friend, I added, "I am content to trust the one who has taken me from Jericho and given me new life as a Daughter of Israel and wife of the mighty Salma."

Turning in my husband's arms, I buried my face in his tunic overcome by love. The man held me, rocking slightly, unsure how to respond to my sudden emotion.

"My love, you are my beloved Rahab," he crooned into my hair. "You are the only woman I ever cared for."

"I am not sad." Although the sparkling teardrops in my eyes gave lie to my words, I insisted, "It is for joy that I weep. I have been so blessed."

I felt rather than saw Salma shake his head slightly before he lowered his lips to mine.

"Rahab, you give me much to consider," Perez told me, while Tirzah gathered the children who were already beginning to doze from the surfeit of food.

The man and his family walked away. Soon Jamal and Elisaba carried Judah away to his bed. Caleb and Sarai lingered only a moment longer before bidding us good night and entering their tent. Salma and I sat together for a long time. I felt secure in the arms of the man and the love from God that I could not ever explain.

ᚱᚠ 18 ᚷᚠ

SOON AFTER THE PASSOVER, preparations began in earnest for settlement. Groups of men from each tribe had scouted out the areas allotted. The head of each household met with the scouts, Joshua, Eleazar and the elders to decide where their new home would be. Among the women speculation ran high.

"I told Mattan to get rich land."

"What I want is a real house."

"Eli says we will live near Madon, a rich city."

"What if we do not like where we settle?"

"My son may grow up to be the chief of a city."

I did not join the conversation. All I knew was that Salma had said we would settle in a place called Bethlehem. I knew it was in the hills south of the city of the Jebusites. Everyone in Canaan knew of the huge threshing floor the citizens owned. Much of the grain sold in the area was beaten out there. The place called Bethlehem I had not heard of.

"It is a good place but not a huge city. The name means House of Bread. Wheat and barley grow in the fields. Sheep can graze on the hillsides," my husband assured me.

"Will the people be friendly?" A little bit of fear remained.

"How can they not love my beautiful bride?" The man hedged as he placed a kiss on my forehead.

"But we are taking their homes." I sought assurance.

"No, love, we will live among those who have decided to remain. Any who reside in Bethlehem will learn the ways of our God. It is their choice."

"A hard decision," I whispered, turning my face away.

In my mind, I remembered the proud men and women of Jericho who would never have relinquished worship of Astarte for the God of Israel.

"You will see, everything is taken care of," insisted my husband. "Among the hill people exists the memory of Jacob and his sons. Rachel's grave is at Bethlehem. It is not like Libnah and Eglon toward the coast. There the Philistine influence is strong. They have the poles and groves of Astarte although they call her Asharoth. Baal has altars in that area as well. Bethlehem is not like that. You have told me of your grandfather at Bethel keeping the sacrifice ordered by Jacob. Bethlehem has always provided the bread for that yearly remembrance of the patriarch."

The explanation eased my fears although I still felt pity for the people who had no choice but to accept the presence of foreign settlers. Even if they wanted to, I was sure that many were too poor to find another home.

At the next full moon some of the settlers departed. Laden donkeys plodded beside herds of sheep and goats. Women and children set out, some joyfully and some with trepidation. The men were armed as a guard against bandits. It was hard to bid farewell to the families I had come to know. Each time a new group departed, the camp seemed quieter.

Sorrow came when Nashon died quietly in his sleep. Even though he was old and weary, I mourned for the man who I had come to love. Salma and Jamal buried the patriarch in the tomb with my mother outside of Jericho.

"He did not get to settle in the Promised Land," Elisaba sobbed. "It is not fair."

"My sister, Nashon was happy to have seen the land. He knew that his children and grandchildren will inherit a homeland." I put my arms around the young woman to offer what comfort I could. "Your father saw the fulfillment of the promise made by the Living God to Abraham, Isaac and Jacob."

My friend wept for her father. "His grave is in a strange land."

"Nashon will rest safe with my mother." It was the only reassurance I could give. "She too knew of the power of the One God although she never knew the name of that god."

When the tomb was sealed again, we returned to the camp. Soon I had a private sorrow to deal with. My brother was in the next group of settlers to leave. Tirzah and Esther visited often as they began preparing to leave the camp for a new home. Perez agreed to settle in Bethel. He had become friends with Elidad, elder of the tribe of Benjamin. I wondered if the decision was affected by the knowledge that Jericho herself was part of the land given to this smallest of the tribes. His own reason was different.

"Perhaps among those who knew our grandfather, I can discover the God you have found," my brother admitted when the family came to bid me farewell.

"I will pray that the God of Jacob will visit you and give you peace." In all sincerity I did hope he would find the comfort I knew in the Living God.

The little caravan moved away to the west, up the pass past Gilgal until it was lost to sight. In perhaps a week they would arrive at the city. When my family departed an emptiness settled over me that was only eased when Salma held me that night.

"Will my brother be happy?" I asked the man who stroked my hair.

"It is a choice he must make."

His wise words did not answer my question. With that I had to be content. I never knew if my prayers were answered.

Then came the day that Salma announced, "We will be leaving for Bethlehem when we have packed our tents."

Even though I wanted to begin my own life in a real house, I found tears springing to my eyes at the thought of leaving behind the now familiar camp and especially Sarai. We wept together as she helped me pack. My rounding belly made it difficult for me to bend over the leather trunks.

I learned that a man named Elimelech was to be our neighbor in Bethlehem. He was related somehow to Nashon. I knew little of him in the camp at Gilgal. Still, I did not like the man with his haughty ways and claims of greatness.

His wife was named Naomi. Everyone felt sorry for the woman who had the burden of making certain her husband's food was prepared to his exacting tastes as well as the care of their two sons. Like their father, the two boys were demanding. Although ten and thirteen, they refused to take responsibility for their own lives. On the journey we all heard their complaints and whining.

"The boys are aptly named," Sarai told me when I informed her of our traveling companions. "Mahlon was a sickly boy and Chilion a whiner."

After the Sabbath we gathered before the Tabernacle, ready to set out. Somewhere Salma found a donkey for me to ride. After Eleazar said appropriate prayers, Sarai and Caleb walked with us part way up the road to Gilgal. Our route would take us up into the hills to Gibeah and then south past Jerusalem to Bethlehem.

"All the land we will travel through is allotted to the tribe of Benjamin," Salma told the group. "Until we pass to the south of Jerusalem, we will be under the protection of Elidad."

His explanation was greeted with nods by our traveling companions.

"With luck we will make the journey before the next Sabbath," my husband informed our friends when we parted. "The Lord watch between us until we meet again."

"May the Lord, who came to us in Egypt and at Sinai, be with you, my friend." Sarai held me close on the morning of our departure.

Caleb added his prayer, "God of Abraham, Isaac and Jacob look graciously on this family and all who travel to Bethlehem. Protect them with your power and bring them in safety to the land promised to our fathers forever."

The woman hugged me one last time and whispered what seemed almost like a prophecy, "Do not be afraid, Rahab. The child of your womb will be a blessing to you and to Salma and to all who know him. Your son will be a pillar of strength to the nation."

From the first turn in the road above Gilgal, I looked back. My friends were small now in the distance. I knew that I would not see Sarai again.

I sent a whispered prayer to the woman who from the first

looked beyond my past and found good within my lost soul, "May the Living Lord bless you, my dearest friend."

The day was long. The rocking of the donkey sometimes made me feel queasy even though I was past the time when women were usually ill with the new life beginning. When the feeling swept over me, I begged Salma to let me walk for a little while. Step by step we moved up the hill road.

During the day I had a chance to observe Elimelech and his family.

"I am sure that Mahlon would be stronger if his parents made him work," I muttered to myself watching his mother cater to every need each step of the way.

Certainly, if he wanted to, it looked as if the youngster was capable of caring for himself. He simply seemed too lazy to do so. The only time I saw him exert his bulk was in the quest for food.

Chilion, on the other hand, dogged Naomi's footsteps with complaints and petitions.

"I am hot."

"This tunic is scratchy."

"I want a melon."

On more than one occasion, I had to restrain myself from slapping the boy for the whining dependence on his mother. I once found myself walking beside the woman. Chilion was always nearby.

"Mother, must I carry this pack?" The nasal whine grated on my ears.

"For now," his mother answered, in a tired voice.

"Mahlon is not carrying anything," protested the boy.

"Your brother is not feeling well," stated the woman, glancing back at her elder son. Indeed the young man was sweating already, even though the morning was still cool.

The constant complaints, even when we stopped in the heat of the day, caused Elimelech's brother to speak harshly.

"Your sons are hindering our march. Everyone needs to help. It is time for Mahlon and Chilion to watch the herd so the other boys can rest. It does not take much skill to watch resting herds."

Grudgingly, the man nodded and the two boys were sent to

keep the flocks from straying. I was resting in the shade that Salma rigged from a blanket when we all heard a commotion from the animals.

"Is it a wolf among the flocks?"

"Are bandits attacking?"

All the men grabbed swords and set off at a run. The women gathered together fearfully. I tried to see what was happening, but the dust of the milling animals obscured my view. Eventually the herds settled again and the men returned. Ahead of them shuffled the two boys.

Naomi rushed forward. "My sons, are you harmed? Did a wild beast frighten you?"

"Step back, woman," Elimelech's brother growled. "My nephews have brought shame to this house. In their foolishness they have cost half a day's travel and two strong ewes and their lambs. They will walk at the end of the caravan and carry wood for us all as punishment."

Naomi opened her mouth. I was not sure if she planned to protest. Elimelech spoke first.

"What have my sons done to deserve such a penalty?" I was not surprised at the rage in his voice. "It is your fault, my brother, for setting inexperienced boys to watch the herds."

"Even the youngest child knows better than to throw stones to hurt and frighten the animals." Salma stepped forward as the men appeared ready to fight. "The sentence is just. I say this as the one who bears the loss. Let it be."

Elimelech subsided with a frown. The sun was moving downward, signaling the end of the day. It was true; we had lost half a day's travel. We ate with little appetite that evening. It was a subdued pair who trudged behind our march in the morning. Chilion sported a bruise on his cheek and Mahlon rubbed his arm, which also showed bruising. I wondered if Elimelech had beaten the boys for causing embarrassment. Naomi walked dejected and silent with us. Regularly she glanced back at her sons.

I tried to ease the concern. "It will not hurt them to bear the dust and carry wood."

"Wait until your child comes," she hissed. "Then you will understand that a mother must be a protection for her child against all dangers. Men do not understand how delicate a child is."

I left the woman to her worries. No one was surprised to see that by the end of the day she was trudging beside her sons in the dust. Her shoulders carried the packs. I even heard an attempt at enthusiasm.

"We are almost at the camp. Look there is plenty of wood here. You will barely have to bend over to gather it."

My heart ached with pity for this mother so bound up in her sons that she could not even allow them to bear a fair punishment alone.

In the morning, we turned south from the remains of Ai.

"Two days travel along the hills and we come to Jerusalem." The announcement brought nods and murmurs of pleasure.

Salma entertained us with a brief history of the city we would see. It helped distract us from the family of Elimelech. They sat apart because the man was still angry with his brother and Salma.

"The priest, Melchizedek from Salem, gave homage to Abraham our father after he defeated the allies of the chiefs of Shinar and rescued Lot. Therefore the city is holy to the sons of Jacob as well. You will see the threshing floor used since that time when we start the descent toward Jerusalem," my husband explained. "Most of the grain in the surrounding areas is brought to the city and beaten there. The Jebusites hold a great feast that is celebrated every harvest at Jerusalem. In order to maintain the traditions of the One God, we will use the threshing floor in Bethlehem and not participate in such rites. The chief of Jerusalem has been defeated by the armies of the Living God. We have allowed the people to remain in their homes provided they are willing to worship the God of Abraham, Isaac and Jacob. It will take time for them to forget the old ways, however."

I would have liked to hear more about the story, but the stars in the sky signaled that we should seek our beds in order to be ready to travel with the coming day.

It was not so easy when we turned south. Our road led through the mountains and travel was slower. Through the hills and up the valley we plodded. Tired feet longed to reach the destination. I was surprised by the size of Jerusalem as we descended toward it on the third day. The sun was high and lit the massive threshing floor that dominated the valley. It was easy to see how great festivities could be held on the broad, flat area.

"I advise you to visit the markets in Jerusalem for supplies you may need. Bethlehem is a small town." Salma gathered the caravan around him outside the gates. "We will remain here tonight and complete our journey in the morning."

After a guard was set, my husband accompanied me into the city. The merchants in Jerusalem looked much like those of Jericho. Each vendor sought to attract attention by shouting the value of his wares and the bargains offered. I purchased extra wheat for bread and some fresh vegetables as well as a grinding stone.

"I do not have anything to prepare the grain for bread," I explained. "At the camp, I shared Sarai's stone."

"Get whatever you need," urged Salma with a fond smile. "I would not have my lovely wife lacking."

"I do not need much. Sarai and Tirzah have been so generous in giving me things." I shook my head when the merchant tried to interest me in a pottery bowl set.

"We will take it." The decision was from Salma. He also added a fine wool blanket to my purchases. "The nights will be cool in the hill country and I would not have you chilled."

With our purchases we returned to our small camp. Other members of our group also added new items to their packs.

"Tomorrow you will sleep in Bethlehem." Salma kissed my forehead. "Are you very tired, my love?"

"A little," I admitted. "My back aches, but I can hardly wait to see our new home.

"You will be pleased," my husband promised.

"If I am with you, I am content." Sleepily I snuggled into the curve of the man's arm and fell asleep.

It was with great anticipation that we set out toward the south in the early morning light.

The sun was high in the sky when Salma pointed, "There is

Bethlehem. You can see the grave of Rachel there."

I was more interested in the appearance of my new home. Nestled against the hills was a squat town of mud houses. Others looked as if they were carved out of the hills themselves. However, we came to a stop in front of the cairn. Our way was barred by a man wearing the turban that identified him as the elder of the town.

~ 19 ~

SALMA SPOKE TO THE old man standing in the center of the road, "We come in peace."

"I recognize you, Salma bar Nashon. We have been expecting your arrival." The raspy voice was not unfriendly, although there was not an expansive welcome in the tone either. With a gesture toward the pile of stones he added, "May the God of Rachel, well-loved wife of Jacob who we remember, help us to be as neighbors and not as enemies."

"We come in peace to settle among you, not to displace you. All who reverence the Lord of all Creation are welcome." My husband offered a salaam and held out his hands empty of weapons as evidence of our intentions.

"The people of Bethlehem honor the faith of Jacob bar Isaac, the one you call Israel," asserted the elder. "Bring your wives and little ones. A feast has been prepared for the travelers."

"May the God of Israel bless you for this hospitality." Salma made the sweeping salaam in acknowledgement.

With the formalities over, the old man stepped aside. Salma gestured for our caravan to move forward. I was not surprised when the old man fell into step beside my husband. With his escort we moved toward the village. Some curious onlookers watched our approach. I tried to determine if the looks were antagonistic or friendly. The people appeared indifferent, as if new arrivals were an everyday occurrence. Catching the eye of a woman in the doorway, I offered a smile. Stolidly, she stared at me. After we passed most of the inhabitants followed our caravan.

A short time later we were in the middle of the town. Food

of all descriptions was laid out. The smell of roasted mutton competed with herbs, boiled turnips and onions. The sweet odor of honeyed cakes was complimented by the tangy scent of citrus. I realized that I was hungry. Naomi's sons and the other children were already wandering around peering at the dishes.

The chief stood in the center of the gathering. "People of Bethlehem, this day we welcome into our midst the sons of Israel. The God of Abraham, Isaac and Jacob promised this land to those who believe. Behold the fulfillment of the covenant in our lifetime. Surely we will find blessing with our new neighbors.

A halfhearted cheer greeted the speech by the old man.

"The God of our Fathers has been gracious to us," responded Salma on behalf of the Children of Israel. "We come in peace, as brothers, not as enemies or conquerors. May the Living God bless you in proportion to your hospitality."

The Hebrew men offered their own praise, "Amen, Alleluia, El Elohim Israel."

Another cheer echoed from the hills when our new neighbors repeated the words. The elder of Bethlehem picked up a loaf of bread and jar of wine. He offered the gifts to Salma.

"Then come, eat of our bread and drink of our wine. May the blessing of the One God be with us all."

The old man's words were a signal for everyone to begin the celebration. Wine flowed freely. The inhabitants tried to outdo one another in serving us although some of the smiles were strained. It was not hard to see that many in the town still doubted our motives.

"Here is mutton with herbs."

"Try these roasted onions."

"My date cake is renowned."

"This wine is made from grapes grown here."

After a few hesitant advances, the children of Bethlehem and our youngsters began a game of tag around and between the adults. Busy mothers smiled to see the interaction. I was glad that among the youngsters there was a chance to forget that we came from different heritages.

The sun reached the zenith and began to descend. Shadows

grew long and still we were feted by the residents of our new home. I found a seat under a tree to rest my back and legs. Salma found me there.

"My wife, are you ill?"

I met his concern with a smile.

"No, my love, only a little tired." I admitted my weakness with a yawn I could not suppress.

"It is time I took you to our home." After a decisive nod, the man patted my shoulder and hurried away.

My husband returned a short time later with the chief of Bethlehem. A short, plump woman scurried behind him. I had to smile because they reminded me of a pair of sparrows, both so plump and brown and bustling.

"My dear child," the woman lisped. When she came closer I noticed she lacked front teeth. "You must rest. Come with me. Your home is ready."

Salma helped me to my feet. His arm was a welcome support. I only realized how exhausted I was when we began to walk down the street. At the end, a mud-brick fence enclosed an estate set against the hillside of Bethlehem.

The old man bowed as he pushed open the gate. His wife bustled through.

"Come, come." She waved me in. "All is ready. Here is your house, my dear."

"Salma, is all this yours?" I stared in amazement at the house and buildings.

"It is ours." My husband guided me into the courtyard. "Our sons will have plenty of room to play."

Mouth agape, I looked from the house to the stables.

"Are you pleased?" When I did not speak, the man bent close to ask.

"Only the richest lords and priests in Jericho live in such splendor with a house and stables and courtyard." The tears that began to flow embarrassed me. Futilely I dabbed at them with my veil. "Even my father's inn yard was smaller. I do not deserve such grandeur."

"Do not cry, my love." Soothingly, the man tried to comfort

me. "Jericho is gone. This is your new life."

"Come and see the house and furnishings." The old woman spoke up in an effort to distract me.

Sniffling and mopping my eyes, I allowed myself to be drawn inside. Wool rugs covered the dirt floor and blankets hung in the doorways. Cushions and low stools provided places to sit. Beyond, a stairway led to the upper levels where I assumed bedrooms were located.

"This is Hagar. She will help you." A slender girl was indicated by the elder of Bethlehem.

The young woman bowed her head to the floor.

She offered homage, "My mistress, my master."

"Your mistress is tired." Salma gave the order. "Help her to her room to rest."

The girl scrambled to her feet. Keeping her head lowered the servant scurried toward the stairs.

"We will see the remainder of the house when you have rested." My husband kissed me and gave a slight shove to propel me after my guide.

"Yes." Too overwhelmed to argue, I followed the girl to the upper level.

In the room where curtains hung at the windows, Hagar helped me remove my veil and dusty outer garment. Clothed only in my tunic, I lay down on the mat. Soft pillows welcomed my head.

"Does my mistress need anything more?" The question came softly.

"No, I . . . that is all." I watched the figure slip past the curtain over the doorway.

Alone, the tears fell faster. They were formed of joy, exhaustion and not a little insecurity. Old fears and uncertainty flooded back to my tired mind. Sleep claimed me before I could sort out the confusion.

In my dreams, Hamash stood over me. My father was angry.

"How dare you prosper? You have left me with nothing. Enjoy this now, for it will not last. The gods will not be mocked."

When the dream figure raised a fist to strike me I cried out, "No . . . sorry . . . please." My exclamations brought Salma.

"Beloved, I am here. It is a dream."

Kisses awakened me. Still in the horror of my nightmare, I clung to the man.

"It is over." Rubbing my back gently until I stopped shaking, my husband repeated the words.

At last I took a shuddering breath and looked up at the man I loved.

"Why do you love me?" The question slipped out.

"You are the only woman who ever captured my heart. My Rahab, ever since I saw you at the window in Jericho I prayed that God would be gracious. The Holy One has blessed me with you."

Salma's assurances, punctuated by kisses, eventually convinced me. The man held me for the remainder of the night.

"How is all this yours?" I asked my husband later, after he showed me the entire house.

"Rahab, the people of Bethlehem have given us this house in gratitude for not destroying their town." A deprecating shrug came with the explanation. "Samson has an even grander home. He will be chief of the city because of his age. As Nashon's son, the duty could have fallen to me, but he is better equipped for such duties. I would rather have time for my wife and son than deal with civic issues."

"The God of Israel has given me so many blessings." Thankful tears trickled down my cheeks.

In the morning I explored my home. When I exclaimed over the beauty and neatness, the serving girl preened. After I allowed her to comb my hair, she was devoted.

"My mistress has the loveliest hair," the girl enthused. "I will be the envy of all in Bethlehem for you are gracious as well as beautiful."

Hagar proved to be a great help. I learned the ways of the markets at Bethlehem with the servant at my side.

"Do not buy from Mumud. His prices are too high. Samuel has better vegetables at an honest price," the girl warned.

Soon every woman in the town had conflicting advice for my pregnancy.

"It is clear that the child will be a boy. See how she carries the weight."

"My sister had twins and she was no bigger than you."

"You must soak your feet in oat water to relieve the swelling."

"Hepzibah, everyone knows that barley water is better."

My past was no longer an issue. No one in the town knew that I was not a Hebrew. Those who traveled with us from Gilgal had their own lives to live as we all settled into the new homes. Salma rejoiced in my blossoming body.

"Rahab, see how strongly our son kicks." With his hand on my belly the man marveled at the vigorous activity of the unborn baby. "Our child will be the first son of Israel born in Bethlehem. He will be great and the first of many."

Naomi surprised me one afternoon in the late summer by appearing at the gate one afternoon as I rested in the shade near the door. The time was approaching for my delivery and I found it tiring to do much work.

"I brought you this for your baby in thanks for your kindness to me on the road." Almost shyly the woman handed me a soft wool blanket.

"Naomi, this is lovely." I held the gift to my cheek. "It is so soft. I will need it when the baby is born as the days will be getting colder by then."

"Elimelech does not like it here." I was surprised by the sudden confession. "It is true that some of the children have made fun of Mahlon and Chilion, but most people are kind."

The woman paused as if hesitant to continue. When I waited patiently, she gave a sad smile.

"Elimelech says that the land is poor and that we will starve."

My response was amazed. "I have never seen such green hills. Even the hills near Gilgal did not grow grapevines as sturdy as those here."

My visitor shrugged. "My husband expected that he would not have to work. His vision of the promised land had milk and honey dripping from the trees."

"The God of Abraham, Isaac and Jacob has given to us all that we need." I tried to keep scorn out of my voice.

Naomi winced slightly at the tone and replied with a lift of her chin, "We believe what we want. I must go. My husband will be wanting his meal."

"Thank you for the lovely blanket." Levering myself up, I held out my arms. "Your thoughtfulness is very kind. Naomi, may the God of Israel bring you comfort."

After a moment's hesitation, the woman threw herself into my arms. "I wish we could be friends," she whispered before hurrying away.

Later I told Salma, for the woman's confession troubled me, as did her parting whisper that seemed to speak of great loneliness.

Although he sighed, my husband did not seem surprised. "There are several who think we should have enslaved the people and become lords over those who built this town. Not everyone wants to work for the richness God has provided."

I was appalled. "The God of this nation is a God of freedom. How can anyone doubt that? Your God brought you from Pharaoh's scourge to be a free people. The Living Lord has brought me to freedom from my past!"

"My wife, what you say is true." Salma drew me close. "Not everyone is as wise as you."

With kisses I allowed myself to be consoled. Still I fretted about those who did not seem to have the faith necessary to accept the blessings I saw so freely offered. Even when other things claimed my attention, I returned often to ponder the ungratefulness of the few malcontents. The ingratitude seemed out of place in a people of faith.

My body grew larger as the days started to shorten. One night I felt the first pangs of birth. They deepened in intensity.

"Salma, you must send for the midwife." As dawn was breaking, I sent the man away.

Dinah, the aged midwife of Bethlehem, and her daughter arrived quickly.

"How long have you had labor?" The question was abrupt as the young woman examined me.

"Since the moon setting," I panted as another contraction struck.

"You will have a child before the sun is high," promised the old midwife.

I was drenched in sweat by the time the baby was born. His cry was music to my ears, as was her announcement.

"You have a son, a healthy boy!"

The child was given to me. With the help of both women, I gave him suck. I barely cared that the midwives continued to tend me. I was lost in awe at the infant in my arms.

Finally satisfied with my comfort, Dinah summoned Salma. "You may come in. You have a fine son."

Awed and shy Salma almost tiptoed to my side. Crouching beside my pallet, the man kissed me.

"My love, are you well?" I was touched that the first question was for my welfare.

"I am fine. See, we have a son." Drawing back the swaddling bands I held up the baby.

"A son." Softly the words were repeated." We will name him Boaz, for he will be a pillar of Israel."

"Boaz bar Salma of Bethlehem," I nodded. "It is a good name."

A servant was sent south to Hebron to inform Caleb and Sarai of the news. He brought back word that our friends were settled and doing well. Sometimes I wished that God had chosen Bethlehem for my friends instead of the distant city. I missed Sarai. She sent back a leather bag. Inside was ointment for the baby's tender skin and perfumed oil for me.

"How kind," I whispered, overcome at my friend's thoughtful gesture.

"A fine gift indeed." Salma sniffed the aroma. "This is only available from traders out of the Black Land. The secret of the scents are kept close within certain families in Egypt.

"I will treasure it all the more." Carefully I replaced the stopper in the bottle, resolving to use the precious gift sparingly.

"This ointment will be good if Boaz develops a rash or has an injury." The second jar went on a shelf and I gathered the whimpering baby into my arms.

"You may use it soon. On the eighth day my son will become a Child of Israel," Salma reminded me proudly as I nursed the baby.

"So soon?" I drew my son closer as if in protection.

"It is the law," the man shrugged. "Since Abraham, all the sons of Israel bear the mark of the covenant on their body."

"He is so small." Like generations of mothers before, I dreaded the pain to my baby.

Salma rested a broad, gentle hand on my shoulder, "It will be swift and he will not remember."

I turned my cheek to rest it against my husband's hand. "The Law of God must be fulfilled."

It was still hard to allow Salma to take the baby and present him before the elders.

Samson spoke the ceremonial words and with the flint knife cut away the foreskin in one rapid movement. The resulting wail made me cringe.

"It is harder on us," Naomi consoled me where we stood with the other women of Bethlehem. "The baby will be fine."

Wrapped loosely and inexpertly in the blanket, Boaz was given back to me. There were more prayers before a cup of wine was shared by the men to celebrate the newest son of the promise.

"There, there my son." Crooning words of comfort, I applied some of the soothing ointment before swaddling my son.

Soon the child was content at my breast. Even after he slept, I held the boy. The small plump body was a gift that filled me with joy.

"Thank you, God of my husband, for this son. May he indeed grow to be a pillar for you. I, the outsider and stranger brought into your family, dedicate myself to your service. You redeemed me from destruction to bear this child. Blessed are you, Lord God."

I felt surrounded by the love of God. It was not the first time I sensed the presence of the Holy One. The contentment wrapped me as if I was held in arms. Salma found me dozing with the baby in my arms.

"My Rahab." The man crouched beside me. His tender touch awakened me.

"I was asleep," I drowsily responded.

"Yes, my love." With a chuckle and kiss, Salma lifted me onto his lap. "You and my son were napping. I am the most blessed of men."

Happy in my husband's embrace, I nestled closer.

"We will have many sons," the man announced.

"Will we?" I teased in pretended sternness.

"God and my wife being willing." There was another chuckle and kiss from Salma. "After three more Sabbaths we will offer the sacrifice for your purification. I long for that day, so that we may be together again."

With my husband's arms around me, I felt safe and unafraid. Later I stared down at the sleeping man.

"Thank you, God of Abraham, Isaac and Jacob for Salma. I do not fear him as Naomi does Elimelech nor must I be subservient like Tirzah. Protect him with your favor." The prayer was whispered as a breath to the unseen God that I knew was nearby.

The time of my purification arrived. It was a joyful celebration even though the days were short and cold. I was glad I could wrap Boaz tightly in the warm woolen blanket from Naomi.

"Soon it will be spring," I told the tiny face just visible in all the covering. "You will see flowers and birds. My son, you will learn to run and play in the fields."

Spring came and planting time. Salma was in the fields all day and sometimes all night. Lambs were born. We celebrated the first Passover in Bethlehem with joy.

"God is gracious to the people," I commented to Salma.

"The Living God is indeed blessing the Children of Israel," the man agreed. He drew me close and added, "I am the most blessed of the sons of the promise, for Rahab of Jericho is my wife."

Together we watched our son crawl across the floor to explore the pile of baskets near the door. I was content.

ᴇ Epilogue ᶟᴀ

"MY MOTHER, I NEVER knew." The young man was almost speech-less when his mother ended her saga.

The old woman looked at her son. "Boaz, you have fulfilled the hopes we had for you. It is time that you found a bride. I am glad that Ruth of Moab has caught your eye."

"Why did Elimelech go to Moab?" Boaz wondered aloud.

"He was a discontented man," the woman responded. "One year the rains did not come and the fields remained barren. A rumor started that the famine was punishment for someone's sin. Your father insisted, 'This is not punishment from God. Bethlehem has plenty of grain stored for this year. No one will starve.' It was not enough for some. 'Do you think you are Joseph doling out our rations? We would rather go to Moab where there is food and land and no talk of God's provision or punishment.' The complaints continued. Then one day Elimelech took the small group of the angry men and their families east. It could not have been an easy trip for the summer heat was upon us. I was sad to see Naomi leave."

"That was foolish," the young man frowned.

Looking into the past, the woman sighed and shook her gray head, "They were hopeful that things would be better in Moab. I remember Naomi telling me her hopes, 'Mahlon and Chilion will find brides.'"

"They did find brides," mused Boaz. "But still Naomi returned a widow and destitute with only a daughter-in-law for company."

The old woman nodded and laid a wrinkled hand on top of her son's darkly tanned one.

"The girl Ruth is gentle and faithful. She will be a good wife to some man." A slight smile creased the lips as the mother glanced at her son.

"I will speak to Samson and the elders tomorrow. They meet at the gate to hear claims. If Samson does not want to act the part of kinsman, I will marry Ruth," Boaz spoke decisively.

"May the Living God of Abraham and Sarah, Isaac and Rebekkah and our father Jacob give you blessing," Rahab prayed, brushing her hand in a fond caress of the bearded cheek.

"Amen," was the man's response.

Throughout the night, Rahab sat by her window. Her mind roamed over her life.

"Lord of the Heavens, you have blessed me and been with me even before I knew you. You kept me safe and blessed me with Salma and my son. Who but you, oh God, can make me alive when I was as dead. May your blessing be on Boaz and his offspring forever."

She felt a warm breeze across her wrinkled cheek. The wind lifted the once red hair in a fond caress. Rahab, known long ago as the Harlot of Jericho, knew that she was loved by the God of Israel. It was enough.